Praise for

FINLAY DONOVAN JUMPS THE GUN

"Fasten your seat belts. . . . Murder most madcap." —*Kirkus Reviews*

"Finlay's strong narrative voice carries the reader. . . . This is good, fast fun."
—*Publishers Weekly*

"Readers who love fast-paced, action-packed mysteries should pick this up."
—*Library Journal*

"Sassy, ludicrous, sexy . . . *Finlay Donovan Jumps the Gun* is another great addition to this marvelous series. If you're a fan of crazy, off-the-wall antics and hysterical comedy; sexy, tension-laden chemistry; and an outstanding who's-the-bad-guy mystery, [this] is for you! Highly recommended to anyone who enjoys highly entertaining mysteries."
—*Mystery & Suspense*

"A spiral staircase of imaginative twists and captivating characters, *Finlay Donovan Jumps the Gun* never disappoints. And Cosimano continues to burnish her bona fides as she runs the gamut from murder to mirth."
—*The Free Lance-Star*

"[Finlay and Vero] fall in and out of trouble at lightning speed as a Russian mobster threatens their lives. It is complicated and a funny romp worth diving into." —*Montecito Journal*

"Bawdy, resourceful, and dependably funny, Cosimano is as in control of this material as Finlay is out of control of her life. Finlay may be writing romantic suspense, but *Finlay Donovan Jumps the Gun* often plays like a comic action thriller." —*Shelf Awareness*

"Countless laugh-out-loud moments. Almost as much fun as watching [Finlay and Vero] get into trouble is the amazing and clever ways they manage to get out of their messes."
—*BOLO Books*

"One of those books where you don't know you're holding your breath until you start laughing out loud." —*The Big Thrill*

"The girl power in this book is fierce and the comedy even fiercer. It's a don't-miss addition to the Finlay Donovan series!" —*BookTrib*

"Heart-thumping moments that also made me laugh. Great for anyone who enjoys suspense paired with funny and smart leading women!"
—*Manhattan Book Review*

"I [was] counting the days until my reunion with the hilarious characters that have made the series the hit that it is. Angela Dawe returning to narrate is very much the icing on this reunion cake." —*Audible Blog*

"BRING IT ON! These books have gotten so incredibly entertaining. . . . I'm very eager to find out what happens next." —*The BiblioSanctum*

"Fresh, heartfelt, and witty, *Finlay Donovan Jumps the Gun* is a twisty page-turner, and its relatable heroine Finlay Donovan is irresistible!"
—Janet Evanovich, #1 *New York Times* bestselling author of the Stephanie Plum series

"This series is magical! The premise is absolutely brilliant; the writing is tight, sharp, hilarious, and heartfelt. I'm in awe of Elle Cosimano. Every book lover in the world should be reading Finlay Donovan."
—Christina Lauren, #1 *New York Times* bestselling author of *Something Wilder*

"It would be next to impossible to find another author who writes stories that are as thrilling as they are hilarious. By now, I love Finlay Donovan so much I would 100 percent hide a dead body for her."
—Jesse Q. Sutanto, author of *Dial A for Aunties*

"*Finlay Donovan Jumps the Gun* is an edge-of-your-seat, fun, fast-paced, laugh-out-loud, sexy, and smart novel. It can't be pinned down to one genre because it spans so many, pulling readers all the way in for an absolutely awesome adventure. Elle Cosimano is a word wizard, and this series gets better with every book."

—Sophie Sullivan, author of *Ten Rules for Faking It*

"Finlay Donovan is back! In *Finlay Donovan Jumps the Gun,* Finlay and her sidekick, Vero, are trying to squirm their way out of the mob's grasp while simultaneously trying to not be indicted for (several) murders. As always, Elle Cosimano puts the two women into impossible situations that create the best kind of escapist fiction. Cosimano's newest Finlay book is laugh-out-loud funny . . . a story of second chances, family, and loyalty. Fact: If you're going to bury a body, you definitely want Finlay Donovan by your side."

—Julie Clark, *New York Times* bestselling author of *The Lies I Tell*

"I've never laughed so much reading books about murder. Elle Cosimano's accidental hit woman, Finlay Donovan, is a darkly hilarious, quick-witted, and surprisingly relatable woman. You'll be amazed at how much fun you have reading this brilliant, funny mystery series from one of the best writers working today."

—Jennifer Hillier, award-winning and *USA Today* bestselling author of *Things We Do in the Dark* and *Little Secrets*

"Finlay Donovan remains the heroine of my heart. Murder and hot men while rocking a messy mom bun, yes, please! Elle Cosimano writes fresh, funny mysteries that are an absolute blast to read."

—Chandler Baker, *New York Times* bestselling author of *Whisper Network*

ALSO BY ELLE COSIMANO

Finlay Donovan Is Killing It
Finlay Donovan Knocks 'Em Dead

YOUNG ADULT NOVELS

Nearly Gone
Holding Smoke
The Suffering Tree
Seasons of the Storm

FINLAY DONOVAN JUMPS THE GUN

ELLE COSIMANO

MINOTAUR
BOOKS
NEW YORK

This is a work of fiction. All of the characters, organizations, and events portrayed in this novel are either products of the author's imagination or are used fictitiously.

Published in the United States by Minotaur Books, an imprint of St. Martin's Publishing Group

www.minotaurbooks.com

The Library of Congress has cataloged the hardcover edition as follows:

Names: Cosimano, Elle, author.
Title: Finlay Donovan jumps the gun / Elle Cosimano.
Description: First Edition. First Canadian Edition. | New York: Minotaur Books, 2023. | Series: The Finlay Donovan Series; 3
Identifiers: LCCN 2022044320 | ISBN 9781250846037 (hardcover) | ISBN 9781250891310 (Canadian edition) | ISBN 9781250846020 (ebook)
Classification: LCC PS3603.O84 F57 2023 | DDC 813/.6—ddc23
LC record available at https://lccn.loc.gov/2022044320

ISBN 978-1-250-84605-1 (trade paperback)

Our books may be purchased in bulk for promotional, educational, or business use. Please contact your local bookseller or the Macmillan Corporate and Premium Sales Department at 1-800-221-7945, extension 5442, or by email at MacmillanSpecialMarkets@macmillan.com.

First Minotaur Books Trade Paperback Edition: 2024

10 9 8 7 6 5 4 3 2 1

For Nicole

FINLAY DONOVAN **JUMPS THE GUN**

CHAPTER 1

The man's voice cracked on the other side of the partition. "I'm going to prison for this, aren't I?"

"You're not going to prison," I assured him through the gap in the door. A small, familiar giggle issued from the other side and the man whimpered. "What's your name?" I asked him, distracting him with small talk as I rummaged in my diaper bag.

"Why do you want to know my name? Are you reporting me to the police?"

"I'm not going to report you. Trust me."

"Trust you!"

"Do you seriously think I want this to end badly?" I listened to his ragged breaths, waiting for an answer.

"Mo . . ." he said tentatively. Another giggle came from behind the partition and the man cried, "Mo! My name is Mo! Dear god, please do something!"

"I need you to stay calm, Mo. Listen to me and do exactly what I tell you."

His voice climbed. "You've done this before?"

"Yes," I assured him, "I have dealt with this before." Just never in the men's room of a Walmart. "Listen to me carefully, Mo. I'm going to bend down very slowly and reach into the stall. Whatever happens, don't move."

Mo started hyperventilating in earnest. "Wait, you're going to *what*? I really don't think that's a good idea. There must be some other way—"

"There is no other way, Mo. Are you going to let me help you or do I need to call someone to unlock the stall door?"

"Don't call anyone!" he begged. "Do whatever it is you're going to do. But please hurry!"

I eased to the floor, cringing as I pressed my palms to the sticky tiles. I didn't want to think about what might be growing in the grout between them as I lowered my head and peeked under the partition at Mo's feet.

His slacks pooled around his ankles and a pair of Argyle socks were drawn high over his calves. My son's light-up Buzz Lightyear sneakers flashed a few feet in front of the man.

"Zach," I pleaded as he babbled and grinned at Mo. "Come out of there, right this minute."

Thirty seconds. In the thirty seconds it had taken me to relieve my bladder, my toddler had managed to slither under the door of my stall and slip out of the women's restroom and into the men's, probably on the heels of some unsuspecting young person who had never been responsible for small children or zoo animals and hadn't had the forethought to stop him.

Zach laughed as I groped under the partition for him. The baggy hem of his overalls slipped from my fingers as he retreated deeper into the stall.

"He's coming closer!" Mo shrieked, his knees clamping together. "No, no! Stay back!"

"You don't have much experience with children, do you?"

"No! Why would you ask that?"

"Just a hunch." I dropped my shoulder under the partition, my arm outstretched. Forgoing two other empty stalls, Mo had chosen the larger accessible toilet, and the commode—and now my child—were in the farthest corner of it. "I can't reach him. He's too far from the door."

"I thought you said you knew how to fix this!"

"I'm working on it. Don't panic."

"Don't panic? Do you have any idea what happens to men who get caught in bathrooms with small children without their pants on? I was just in here minding my own business!"

Zach's giggles fell suddenly, ominously silent. I dug furiously in my diaper bag. Where were the damn Cheerios when you needed them?

"Something's wrong," Mo said through a strained whisper. "The child is holding very still. I think he might be up to something."

I wrinkled my nose. Zach was definitely up to something.

"He's grunting and his face is turning red. I think he's possessed."

"He's not possessed. He's having a bowel movement."

"He's *what*?! That's it! I'm coming out—"

"No! Whatever you do, do *not* stand up!" I buried my arm elbow-deep in my bag. There definitely wasn't time to run out to the cereal aisle. The poor man would probably suffer a heart attack and wind up dead on the floor before I made it back, and the last thing I needed to deal with was one more corpse. Especially one with his pants around his ankles.

New year, new me. I wasn't a criminal or a killer, at least not by my own choice. Harris Mickler, the sleazy accountant who had turned up dead in the back of my minivan three months ago, was not murdered by me, regardless of the fact that his wife, Patricia, had insisted on paying me to kill him. And yet, no matter how many times I explained to Mrs. Mickler that I was not a contract killer, disturbingly similar job offers continued to find me. The list of resolutions I'd adopted two weeks ago had included three very important bullets: no more junk food, no more men, and no more bodies in my minivan. Not necessarily in that order.

Zach finished his business with a delighted squeal, clapping his hands with exclamations of self-praise. He stomped toward Mo with an outstretched hand.

"I don't understand!" Mo screamed. "What does it want from me?!"

I dumped the contents of the diaper bag onto the floor. My police officer sister, who would rather clean up crime scenes than wipe her nephew's backside, had spent the last few weeks attempting to potty train my son despite my insistence that Zach wasn't ready. While my barely-two-year-old now grasped what he was expected to do in the bathroom, Georgia's training strategy had only managed to whet his appetite for bribes. "He wants a reward."

"A reward?! Why would it expect a reward for this?"

I grabbed a plastic baggy of Cheerios and thrust it under the door. Zach turned toward the sound as I shook the cereal inside, his chubby hands chasing the bag as I drew it closer toward me. As soon as my son was within reach, I looped an arm around his waist and dragged him out of the stall.

Mo's hands fell limp at his sides. I plopped Zach down on the floor beside me, wiping my brow as he puzzled over the seal on the snack bag.

"It's safe, Mo. You can come out now." I gathered the diaper creams, packets of wipes, and random mom-survival gear, stuffing them back into my purse. A quick glance under the stall revealed that Mo hadn't moved. "Mo?" I paused, listening for signs of life through the door. "Mo? Are you okay?" *For the love of god, let him be okay.*

"I am far from okay."

I released a held breath. "Do you need me to call for help?"

"I'd rather you just go," he said, "and take the tiny demon with you."

"Fair enough." I plucked the bag carefully from Zach's hands and scooped him up. Holding him over the sink on one raised knee, I washed both of our hands twice, rigorously and with plenty of soap, before returning the bag of snacks to him.

"It was nice meeting you, Mo," I called out.

A stoic grunt issued from the stall. I comforted myself with the fact that at least Mo had survived. It was past noon, twelve days into a brand-new year, and I hadn't broken any of my three resolutions—at least not yet.

CHAPTER 2

After a quick diaper change and several more rounds of handwashing, I hefted Zach into a shopping cart, handed him his threadbare nap blanket and a sippy cup, and pushed him around the store, searching for Vero. I found my children's nanny in the women's clothing department, scrutinizing a generic fleece hoodie, which did not jibe with the brand-name-wearing, hip fashionista I'd grown to know and love. She jumped nearly a foot when I rolled my cart up behind her and tapped her on the shoulder.

"What are you doing?" I asked as she dropped the sweatshirt into her cart. She pushed a pair of oversized sunglasses up the bridge of her nose. I could hardly see them under the low bill of the baseball cap she'd been wearing since we left the house that morning. "You already have a black hoodie." I gestured to the designer logo on the one she was presently wearing. She looked like a cat burglar in yoga pants.

"You can never have too many hoodies." She darted cautious glances around the women's department, giving a heavy dose of side-eye to a sketchy-looking man with a greasy comb-over who was talking to himself as he browsed through a rack of padded bras. He'd either shoplifted a pair of tube socks or he was sporting a boner—I didn't want to think very hard about which. She grimaced as he gave a set of double *D*'s an inquisitive squeeze. "How much longer until the van's ready?"

I checked my phone. "At least another thirty minutes. And we still have an hour before we have to pick up Delia at preschool."

"Let's head over to the accessories department. This guy's freaking me out, and I could use a few extra pairs of shades."

"If you were so worried about being seen in public, we could have taken my minivan to your cousin's garage instead of bringing it here. Ramón probably would have changed the oil for free."

Vero gave a vehement shake of her head. "No way. We're safer here." Her last address of record had been her cousin Ramón's apartment, which, according to Vero, was too close for comfort to his auto repair shop to risk being seen there.

"I don't get it, Vero. All this paranoia doesn't make any sense. You're in debt to a couple of sorority girls in Maryland, so you drop out of school and leave the state, and the second these girls' parents show up at your cousin's door looking for you, you run off to Atlantic City and take a marker from a loan shark? Wouldn't it have been easier to just drive back to Maryland and tell your sorority sisters the truth, that you didn't take their money so you can't give it back?"

"I told them a year ago, and they didn't believe me."

"Then they're not worth the effort you're putting into avoiding them. Are you just planning to wear disguises and stay in the house indefinitely?"

"If a couple of sorority girls managed to track me all the way to my cousin's place because they think I stole their stupid treasury money, how long do you think it will take a professional loan shark to find me after I lost his two hundred grand trying to pay them back?"

"You can't hide forever. The spring semester at the community college starts in two weeks."

"Doesn't matter, because I'm not going."

My cart lurched to a stop. Zach gripped the handlebar and giggled in his seat, spilling juice down his overalls. I used his nap blanket to wipe him up. "Vero, you're only a few credits away from your accounting degree!"

"And smart enough to know that the more I leave the house, the higher the statistical probability people will find me. It's a matter of karma."

"Karma has nothing to do with it. Just because you made a few mistakes doesn't mean you deserve to be miserable. Look." I grabbed her hood as she skulked down the aisle. When her cart stopped, I turned her by the shoulders to face me. "Let's focus on solving one problem at a time. Steven's flying home from Philadelphia tomorrow. We both agreed it's probably safe for him to come back." My ex-husband had been lying low at his sister's house for weeks after several attempts had been made on his life. (Don't ask. It's a long story.) "We have no reason to believe anyone's trying to kill him anymore—"

"Because the universe is clearly punishing me," she said, as if that proved her point.

I rolled my eyes and pressed on. "Steven hasn't seen Delia and Zach in weeks. He'll probably jump at the opportunity if I ask him to take the kids for a few days. Then you and I can drive to Atlantic City and negotiate a deal with this loan shark person."

"Loan sharks don't negotiate, Finn. They break kneecaps and chop off fingers."

"He's a businessman. I'm sure he can be reasoned with."

"Like you've been reasoning with Feliks Zhirov?" I pressed a hand to her mouth, as if simply speaking Feliks's name could conjure the Russian mob boss into the women's sportswear department of a Walmart. I checked the surrounding aisles, making sure we hadn't been overheard, but the old man in the lingerie section behind us was too busy sniffing the panties in the clearance bin to care. "*Feliks* is a businessman," Vero insisted over my protests, "and I don't see you waltzing into *his* office and reasoning with *him*."

"Feliks doesn't have an office," I reminded her in a low voice. "He has a jail cell. And he isn't a businessman, he's a narcissistic sociopath with an army of enforcers who like to slit people's throats. Of course he can't be reasoned with."

"He's also expecting you to stay in town and do a job. So unless you want his goons following us to New Jersey and dumping our bodies in a ditch, I say we stick close to home and start looking for *EasyClean*."

EasyClean was the screen name of the mysterious contract killer who had been cultivating hit jobs through one of Feliks Zhirov's websites, a popular women's forum that had doubled as a front for the Russian mob. When I'd learned my ex-husband was *EasyClean*'s next target, I'd coerced Feliks into shutting the entire website down. *EasyClean* had resorted to blackmailing the mob to compensate for his losses, and Feliks was holding me responsible for it all.

"If we can figure out who *EasyClean* is, maybe your very wealthy Russian friend would consider paying us a reward."

"Feliks is not my friend," I whispered. "He tried to have us both gunned down, in case you've forgotten."

"That was *before EasyClean* started blackmailing him." She stirred the air with a finger. "That whole *enemy of my enemy is my friend* thing makes you and Feliks friends by default. And your mob boss friend has rubles coming out of his piroshki."

"One, I don't want to think about Feliks's piroshki. And two, Feliks doesn't want me to turn *EasyClean* in, he wants me to *kill* him." I'd only laid eyes on *EasyClean* once. It had been dark when he'd climbed out of a very cop-like sedan, holding a gun. I didn't stick around to get a good look once he'd started shooting at me. Even if Vero and I could figure out who *EasyClean* was, I seriously doubted Feliks was going to pay us for half the job. I was already in debt to the man for the price of one very expensive sports car—the Aston Martin I'd "borrowed" from a dealership was now riddled with bullet holes and titled in my name. One misstep with Feliks and he'd make sure a copy of that title made its way to the police.

It wasn't hard to guess which detective Feliks would tip off first. Feliks was disconcertingly curious about the nature of my relationship with Detective Nicholas Anthony. Truth be told, so was I. But no matter how charming Nick was (or how amazing he smelled), there'd been too many skeletons in my closet (or, more literally, in my washing machine, my minivan, and Vero's trunk) to risk letting the detective get any closer to me than he already was.

"If Feliks wants *EasyClean* dead, he'll have to do it himself," I said firmly. Killing a man in cold blood was a line I wasn't willing to cross.

Vero shook her head at her reflection as she tried on a pair of dark sunglasses. "I can't believe you're playing chicken with the Russian mob."

"I'm not playing chicken. I'm putting my foot down. Feliks's trial is in less than a month. He's going to be convicted of murder and shipped off to prison, and this whole nightmare will be over."

"If Feliks goes to prison, he'll have nothing left to lose. You'll be lucky if he doesn't tip off Nick just to spite you. He called again, by the way."

"Who?"

"Detective Hottie."

I studied a rack of scarves, feigning disinterest. "What did you tell him?"

"That you were in the backyard, burying a body— Ow!" She giggled to herself, rubbing the spot where my elbow had jabbed her. "You can't keep avoiding him, Finn. He's been leaving messages on your cell phone since that dinner at your mom's, and you haven't once called him back."

I smacked my forehead. "You must be referring to the dinner Nick attended on crutches because he'd been shot by Feliks's thugs, who—incidentally—had really only been intending to murder the two of us. Yes," I deadpanned, "I can see where that would have been a promising start to a healthy and honest relationship."

"You're forgetting about the part where Nick made googly eyes at you across the ham platter while he thanked you for saving his life. Face it, Finn, he's crazy about you. And you two have great chemistry."

She wasn't wrong, but no amount of chemistry was going to change the fact that I had done some pretty terrible things that Nick could never know about. Still, I couldn't help the flutter in my stomach whenever I heard his voice in my mailbox. Or when I remembered the seductive low rumble of it against my ear the last time we'd spoken, under the mistletoe at my parents' house. "What else did he say?"

"That he still owes you dessert. I'm pretty sure that's code for: he wants to see you naked." She drew a scarf over her head, wrapping it around her face until only the dark lenses of her sunglasses were showing. She waggled her eyebrows at me over the rims. "You saved his life, Finn."

"No more than he saved ours."

"Doesn't mean you can't indulge in something sweet if he's offering." She threw up her hands at my shocked laugh. "I'm just sayin', you know he's only going to keep calling until you answer."

A ringtone started deep in my diaper bag.

We both turned to stare at it. Vero drew her sunglasses down her nose. "Whoa. I think you just manifested dessert."

I took a step back. "I'm on a diet."

She reached into the bag with a roll of her eyes, grabbing my phone before I could stop her. "That resolution of yours is a load of horseshit. This is the age of sex positivity, body positivity, and hashtag MeToo. It's Lizzo's world, Finn; we're all just living in it. Don't let anyone tell you you can't have dessert." Her expression dulled as she read the caller's name. "It's Sylvia," she said, holding the phone out to me.

It may have been the first time I'd ever been relieved to see my agent's name on the screen. I swiped to connect. "Hey, Syl. I'm at Walmart. Can I call you back?"

"No, you can't," she said bluntly. Her accent was always more pronounced when her patience was thin. More Jersey than New York. "We have something very important to discuss. Your editor called. She read your manuscript."

I pushed my cart farther from Vero's as she hovered in my personal space, her head tipped to hear. "What did she say?" I asked.

"She's not paying you."

"What do you mean, she's not paying me?" I slapped Vero's hand as she lunged for my phone. "I turned in a finished manuscript, Sylvia. I've earned the second half of my advance."

"Only if your editor approves it. She wants a revision."

"What kind of revision?"

"She wants more of the cop in the story."

"But I put the cop in the story. There's plenty of the cop in the story." There was far more cop in my story than there probably should have been.

"The cop is hot, but the romance is not, and your publisher's not paying you for fifty shades of boring." I held the phone away from my ear as Sylvia shouted for a taxi. A car door slammed and she barked out an address. "You're holding back on this one, Finlay. The cop and your heroine waste too much time staring longingly at each other's assets. By the second act, they should be sampling the goods."

"She's still mourning the attorney," I argued.

"The attorney disappeared in chapter one. That relationship is over. It's time for your heroine to move on."

"Well maybe she needs a minute to figure out what she wants," I said bitterly. I pinched the bridge of my nose. It had been almost three weeks since I'd broken things off with the younger law student/bartender I'd been seeing, and while breaking up with Julian Baker had felt like the right thing to do, I still ached a little thinking about it.

"Your heroine knows what she wants. She wants the cop. She said as much on page forty-three when she was lying in bed, alone, staring at the ceiling. If you're not going to let her have the cop in the second act, at least let the woman have a sex toy."

Vero gave me an *I told you so* smirk. I turned away from her.

"It doesn't matter what my heroine wants, Syl. She's a criminal. She can't just jump into bed with a cop. She'll risk getting caught."

"That's precisely what I'm talking about. Raise the stakes. Take some risks! You've got the perfect setup for a star-crossed romance. Your assassin has escaped from jail. She's on the run from the one man she shouldn't want but can't deny her feelings for. Meanwhile, the cop is hot on her trail, determined to catch her. Only the longer they play cat and mouse, the more he wants to bring her to bed instead of bringing her to justice."

"Oh, that's good," someone said in the background.

"See?" Sylvia assured me. "Even the taxi driver loves it."

"You put me on speaker?!"

"Yes," Sylvia and her driver said.

"The cop and the assassin should give in to their desires," Sylvia insisted. "They should do it someplace dangerous—"

"On a plane," the driver suggested.

Sylvia answered with a "Meh."

"As it's crashing into shark-infested waters?"

"Better."

"Fine," I snapped. "I'll rework a few scenes."

"While you're at it, rewrite the ending," Sylvia said.

I gripped the phone tighter to keep myself from throwing it. "What's wrong with the ending?"

"Your heroine can't ride off into the sunset with her sidekick. This is a romance novel, not *Thelma and Louise*."

"*Thelma and Louise* won an Academy Award."

"They held hands and drove off a cliff, Finlay." I bit my tongue through her exasperated sigh. "The assassin and the cop are good together. Give your heroine the happy ending she deserves. And do it quickly," she added. "I, for one, would like to get paid."

"Me, too," the driver and Vero said in unison.

"Great. I'll tell your editor you're on board with the changes." Sylvia disconnected before I managed to respond.

I handed my phone to Vero. "Happy?"

She shook her head as she took my cell and dropped it in the diaper bag. "I don't understand your hesitation with the cop."

"Because whenever the cop and the assassin get together, somebody dies."

"Only because you make them."

"Way to rub it in." I checked the time and turned my cart toward the front of the store.

"How hard can it be to write a happy ending? Just pretend your characters are Delia's Barbie dolls. Take off all their clothes and mash their faces together."

"It's not that simple."

"You're absolutely right," she conceded. "The cop should ask for the assassin's consent first. Then, when she soberly, mutually, and enthusiastically agrees, they can jump each other like jackrabbits and you can write a bestseller."

"Any other brilliant revision advice?"

She looked at me sideways as we pushed our carts toward the register. "Maybe this time, try not to kill anybody."

CHAPTER 3

After dinner that night, Vero put the kids in a bath while I cleared the dishes and took the recycling out to the bin beside the garage. Glass smacked against glass as I emptied the contents of my tote. A wine bottle bounced off the lip of the bin and shattered against the ground. I cringed, hoping my elderly neighbor hadn't heard the crash. I glanced across the street at Mrs. Haggerty's house, but the windows in her kitchen were dark and her TV flickered between the drapes in her living room.

I knelt to gather the broken glass, gasping when a hand clamped over my mouth. My shouts were muffled by a thick leather glove as someone yanked me backward into the hedges. I threw my head back into my attacker's face. He yelped, hissing at me in sharp whispers as I kicked out blindly with my heels.

"Ow! What the hell? *Jesus, lady!*"

I sunk my teeth through the fingers of his glove and drove an elbow into his ribs. Ripping myself free of his arms, I stumbled out from the hedges and made a run for the house, triggering the motion-sensing lights by the back door. I turned to get a look at him as light flooded the yard. My attacker reared away, shielding his face against the glare. I jolted to a stop as a familiar pair of cynical gray eyes blinked at me.

"Cam?" I asked between pants.

The teenager bent over his knees, cradling his sore ribs. "Who the hell did you think?" He wiped his bloody nose on his glove, looking insulted as he peeled it off to inspect the damage to his finger. "Did you seriously have to bite me? These hands are worth a lot of money and they aren't insured. You could have permanently maimed me."

"What are you doing here after dark on a school night?" He flinched at my mom voice. If Cam was any other high school student, he'd be at home texting his girlfriend or doing his homework, harassing his grandmother instead of me. Until a few weeks ago, Cam had been a confidential informant for the police, working to keep himself out of juvie, but his talent for hacking hadn't gone unnoticed by Feliks Zhirov. He'd been offered a position on Feliks's payroll, and I had a sinking feeling I knew exactly why Cam was here.

"I came to deliver a message." Cam's hand froze halfway to his pocket. His spine stiffened until it was ramrod straight. Slowly, he lifted his chin, his eyes wide as the broken neck of a wine bottle glimmered against his throat.

A low voice behind him issued a warning. "Keep your hands where I can see them."

"We're cool, man. It's cool." Cam laced his fingers behind his head as the man behind him patted down his pockets. I released a held breath as Vero's childhood friend Javier peered around Cam's shoulder. His raven-black hair was tied back from his face, a few loose strands falling over his forehead as his dark eyes raked over me. "You okay?"

"I'm fine," I said, swatting pine needles from my shirt as Javi pulled a cream-colored envelope from Cam's coat and held it out to me.

"See? I told you," Cam said, angling his head away from the broken bottle, "I only came to deliver a message."

I took the envelope and folded it into my pocket, hoping Javi hadn't noticed the crimson wax seal. "You couldn't have called?" I asked, glaring at Cam. I hadn't seen him since he'd last come to deliver a message from Feliks, and while it hadn't been a welcome surprise then either, at least he'd shown me the courtesy of knocking on my door rather than dragging me into the bushes.

Cam dared a glance over his shoulder at Javi. "Boss told me to make sure I delivered it with the appropriate amount of gravitas, whatever that means."

"I'm pretty sure both Merriam *and* Webster would tell you it doesn't mean abducting an unarmed woman while she's taking out her trash!" At his puzzled look, I muttered, "Never mind."

I rubbed the throbbing lump on the back of my head. "It's okay, Javi. You can let him go. He's just a kid."

"I'm not a kid," Cam argued, jerking against Javi's grip. "I'll be eighteen in a month."

Javi's grin was wry as he held stubbornly to the back of Cam's collar. "Want to use my phone to call the cops? I can babysit him until they get here."

"No!" Cam and I answered in unison.

I cleared my throat. "Thanks, but we're fine," I insisted. "Vero's putting the kids to bed. There's a pot of soup on the stove. Why don't you let yourself in and have something to eat while you wait for her."

Javi gave Cam one last searing look before letting him go. Cam and I waited to speak until Javi's sneakers disappeared around the house.

"I wasn't trying to hurt you," Cam insisted as he prodded his swollen lip. "That's the god's honest truth. I was only trying to get you someplace where no one would see me talking to you. That nosy old lady across the street's always peeking out her window. She gives me the creeps."

Mrs. Haggerty was the community busybody and the self-appointed head of the neighborhood watch, but I was pretty sure she was just bored, lonely, and wanted to feel important. I'd resented her for it after she'd told me (and everyone else on the street) that she'd spotted our real estate agent sneaking out of my house after a midday tryst with my then husband. But in the twenty months since Steven moved out (and our subsequent divorce), I'd come to realize it wasn't always a terrible thing to have someone—even an annoying, opinionated someone—looking out for you. I just had to be cautious about the kinds of things

Mrs. Haggerty saw, since every detail inevitably made it into the notebook she kept on the table beside her front door. An after-dark visit by a leather-clad teenager with a criminal record would definitely raise some eyebrows at a neighborhood watch meeting. Or worse, at the police station downtown.

"You think she heard us?" Cam asked.

"I doubt it." If Vero hadn't heard our scuffle then Mrs. Haggerty certainly hadn't. "Pretty sure her hearing is going. What's the message?" I shivered as I gestured for him to get on with it. I hadn't worn a jacket, and our meeting had left me more shaken than I cared to admit.

"Mr. Z wants to know why you haven't handled *EasyClean* yet. In case you haven't noticed, he doesn't like to be kept waiting, and believe me, I'm not the scariest person he could have sent to remind you."

"I'm already acquainted with his goon squad, but thanks for the concern."

"I was talking about his lawyer." Cam shuddered. "That Rybakov chick is terrifying."

A laugh escaped me despite my foul mood. Ekatarina Rybakov was indeed terrifying. And if I had to choose between Kat showing up on my front porch carrying a message with a wax seal or Cam's clumsy attempt to deliver one with gravitas, the choice was easy.

I tore open Feliks's envelope and held his letter under the security light.

Ms. Donovan,

My patience has limits. You have exactly two weeks.

—Z

"Great," I muttered, mentally counting down the days to Feliks's trial.

"We done? I told my grandma I'd swing by the pharmacy and pick up her meds before they close."

"Yeah, we're done. And, Cam," I said as he turned to go, "next time, just ring the doorbell."

He winced as a smile stretched his swollen lip. "Sure, Ms. Donovan. Sorry about the gravitas and all."

I watched Cam limp across my lawn, his long legs disappearing into the hedge that separated my yard from my neighbor's. On my way inside, I collected the broken glass and tossed it in the bin, waving toward Mrs. Haggerty's house in case she was watching. Javi's white panel van was parked in the street in front of my house, the same one he'd been driving the first time I met him, when he and Ramón had driven to West Virginia to help Vero and I break into a storage shed. Vero had been suspiciously tight-lipped about Javi since. All I knew was that he was Ramón's best friend, he was good at picking locks, and he was the only person who could make Vero angry enough to blush.

When I opened the door to my kitchen, I found him sitting at my table, shoveling into a bowl of leftovers from the pot I'd left cooling on the stove.

"You want me to heat that up for you?" I offered.

He shook his head, his mouth too full to speak. His eyes rolled back, his face a mask of pure ecstasy. "Nah," he managed between bites, "it's perfect."

"I wish I could take credit. Vero made it."

"I know," Javi said through a grin. "It's her mother's recipe. Recognized that smell the second I came in the door. I haven't tasted Vero's mom's cooking in years."

"Years?" I asked, grabbing him a soda from the fridge and setting it in front of him. "Why so long?" Vero's and Ramón's mothers shared an apartment in Maryland. It wasn't far. And from the photos I'd seen in Vero's scrapbook, Javi, Vero, and Ramón had been inseparable growing up.

Javi shrugged. "Vero's mom doesn't like me much. It's easier for

Ramón if I don't tag along." A long lock of his hair fell over one eye as he hunched over his bowl. Vero appeared beside him and snatched it out from under him, sending a splash of broth over the rim and soaking the front of his shirt.

"What do you think you're doing?" she snapped.

He held stubbornly to his spoon as he reached for a napkin. "I *was* eating."

"Does this look like a drive-through to you? You can't just roll up in here 'cause a light's on in my window and expect to be served."

Javi blotted his chest. He stood up slowly as he crumpled his napkin, his damp T-shirt clinging to his skin. "Too bad. It tasted every bit as good as I remembered." His dark eyes roved over her upturned face, lingering on her mouth. "I was tempted to ask for more." His grin was roguish as he licked his spoon.

"Give me that," she said, yanking it away from him, "and get your scrubby ass out of my kitchen."

"You've called my ass a lot of things, Veronica, but scrubby wasn't one of them."

She pointed to the door and began shouting at him in Spanish.

"Vero!" I hollered over her, lowering my voice when I remembered the children were sleeping. "*I* invited Javi in after he gallantly came to my rescue. The least we can do is let him finish his meal."

She tore her eyes from him. "What rescue? What happened?" she asked me.

"I was getting out of my van when I heard the crash," Javi said, taking his spoon from her. "Saw the busted glass on the ground and figured something was up, but by the time I got to the backyard, Finlay had the situation under control."

"I'm fine," I assured her. "It was just Cam, but it was heroic of Javi to step in." Vero's mouth parted around a question. I gave a tight shake of my head. Neither one of us would be foolish enough to discuss the details of Cam's message in front of Javi. I directed a pointed look at the bowl she was holding hostage.

She shoved it toward Javi with a huff. "Doesn't explain what you were doing here in the first place."

"Just doing your cousin a favor." He jutted his chin toward a thick stack of junk mail on the table, mostly clothing catalogs and coupon circulars by the looks of it. "Ramón wanted to bring your mail himself, but he was afraid someone might follow him here. He said some people have been to his apartment looking for you. What's that all about?"

"Nothing," Vero said defensively. "Just some girls from my old sorority. They think I have something that belongs to them. I told them I don't, but they won't let it go. It's not a big deal."

"Your cousin seems to think it is."

"My cousin worries too much."

"Maybe I do, too."

"Really?" she snapped. "Because I don't remember you being there to help me pack when I dropped out of school and moved out." I stood silently in the corner, watching Vero's jaw clench. She picked up the pile of mail without looking at it and tossed it in the trash. "I don't see anything here worth saving. You shouldn't have wasted your time."

Javi rose from the table and put his empty bowl in the sink. His T-shirt rode up as he slipped his jacket over his shoulders. Vero stole a glance at him, her cheeks flushing in response.

"You're probably right. Thanks for the meal anyway. See you around," he said as he showed himself out.

I caught a flash of regret on her face as the door closed behind him. She threw up her hands, muttering to herself as she turned to the sink and washed his bowl. When she was done, she tossed the sponge in the basin.

"So," I said, reaching into the pantry for a bottle of wine, "how long have you been in love with Javi?"

"I am *not* in love with him."

I poured two glasses and slid one over the counter toward her. "Methinks thou doth protest too much."

"Well *me*thinks you read too many romance novels."

"Which makes me an expert on the subject."

"Not according to Sylvia."

I ignored that. "There's obviously history between the two of you."

"One that doesn't need repeating," she said as she sucked down the contents of her glass. "What did Cam want?"

I unfolded the note from my pocket and pushed it across the table toward her. Her eyes went wide as she read the message from Feliks. "What are we going to do?"

"We're going to bed," I said, gulping down the last of my wine. "I'm exhausted. We'll figure it out tomorrow." I carried Feliks's envelope to the stove and held the wax seal over the burner, watching the embossed *Z* melt and blacken. Then I shredded the letter into tiny bits and threw them in the trash.

I paused over the waste bin, sifting aside the scraps I'd just tossed in. A thick, brown envelope had come loose from the pile of junk mail Javi had delivered. Vero's name was written on the front. The absence of a return address piqued my curiosity and I fished it out of the can. I held the envelope under the light, squinting at the postage stamp.

"This was mailed from Atlantic City."

Vero's face sobered as I held it out to her. She took it, wedging a finger inside and tearing the seal. A black poker chip fell into her palm. A photo slipped from the envelope, a grainy image of Vero getting into her car. We both sucked in a breath. The picture had been taken in the drop-off lane at Delia's preschool.

"I never thought I'd say this," Vero said in a small voice, "but maybe the kids should stay with Steven for a while."

It was long past midnight, but neither of us could sleep. Vero and I sat at the kitchen table in our pajamas, an empty bag of Goldfish crackers in front of me and an empty bag of Oreos in front of Vero.

I rubbed my temple. "Exactly how much did you say you owe this loan shark?"

“Two hundred thousand,” Vero said hopelessly, her head resting in the cradle of her hand as she traced dollar signs in the crumbs with her finger.

That was one hundred and ninety thousand more than we had. “At least he doesn’t know where you live.”

“Not yet, anyway.” Vero had been living with me when she’d purchased the Charger in the photo, but she’d registered it under her cousin’s address, hoping her former sorority sisters would be less likely to find her. “Did you call Steven?” she asked.

I nodded. “His flight gets in tomorrow afternoon. He’ll swing by and pick up the kids on his way home from the airport. He agreed to keep them for the week. That should give us a few days to figure out what to do about this Marcus person.”

“Marco,” she corrected me.

“Do you know his last name?”

Vero shook her head. She’d been introduced to the loan shark in the lounge of a hotel and casino called the Royal Flush. Aside from his first name and a physical description of him, we didn’t have much to go on.

“How about a phone number?” I asked.

Another shake of her head. “The bellman at the hotel schedules all of Marco’s meetings for him.”

If we were to drive to Atlantic City and start asking for the loan shark by name, he’d probably find us before we managed to track him down.

My sigh smelled like cheddar-flavored crackers and resignation. “You know there’s only one way to fix this.”

“Kill him?”

“Pay him back!”

“I was afraid you were going to say that.”

“First thing tomorrow, we’ll take your Charger to the car dealership down the street and see how much we can get for it. Then we’ll contact the bellman at the casino, arrange to give Marco what we have, and tell him we need more time to come up with the rest.”

Vero sat bolt upright. "I can't sell my car!"

"You can use my minivan to get back and forth to classes. We can get by on one vehicle for a while."

"Finlay, they're called loan *sharks* for a reason! He's not going to be satisfied with a payment plan. If I pay him twenty percent of what I owe him, he'll still break eighty percent of the bones in my body and charge me interest on the ones he left intact."

"What choice do we have? It's not like we have two hundred thousand just sitting in the bank."

Vero glanced up at me with a sheepish expression. "Not exactly in the bank," she said, gnawing her lip. "Remember when I said I would get rid of the Aston . . . ?"

I gasped. "You and Ramón were supposed to destroy that car!" They were supposed to put it in the giant crusher behind his garage, then bury every last trace of it.

"It's a good thing I didn't!" she argued. "Even with bullet holes, that car is worth more than what I owe. If we strip it, we can get rid of the car *and* make enough to pay off Marco. All we need is someone who knows where to sell the parts."

"You promised your cousin you wouldn't tell anyone about the car." He'd refused to help her sell it, too afraid his business would get implicated in whatever shady dealings the car had been involved in. He'd been adamant that no one—not even his best friend—ever know about the Aston Martin we'd left in his garage.

"Ramón doesn't have to know. If I ask Javi to keep a secret for me, he will. He's done it before." Color rushed to her cheeks, hinting at the kinds of secrets Javi had kept hidden from Ramón. "I'll tell Javi to meet us at the garage tomorrow night after it's closed. I'll show him the car and ask him how much he thinks he can get for the parts."

"What you're asking him to do is probably illegal."

"It's nothing he hasn't done before."

My head felt heavy as I stared at the picture on the table, taken at the crosswalk in front of Delia's school. It felt disturbingly like the kind of veiled threat Feliks would have sent. If Feliks Zhirov wouldn't settle for half a job, why should I assume Marco would settle for twenty percent of the money Vero owed him?

Maybe Vero was right. Like it or not, we were still in possession of Feliks's car. With any luck, we'd be able to sell enough of the Aston to get Marco off her back. And if the car was scattered far and wide, then all that would be left was a piece of paper connecting me to Feliks Zhirov. As soon as Feliks was shipped off to prison, I'd find a way to destroy that, too.

"Okay," I said, rubbing my eyes. "Set up the meeting with Javi."

CHAPTER 4

My sister, Georgia, knocked on my door promptly at eight the next morning. When I opened it, she brushed past me into my kitchen and helped herself to a mug of coffee from the pot.

"It's good to see you, too," I said, passing her the carton of milk from the fridge.

Georgia's shoulder-length hair was pulled back in a fancy twist, her slacks were pressed, and a pair of low heels peeked out from under the hems.

"If I'd known you had something important to do, I wouldn't have asked you to drive Delia to school."

"It's nothing important. Just a normal day," she said, stirring her coffee hard enough to make a few drops swirl over the rim. "Where's Vero?"

"Upstairs in her room."

"Why couldn't she drive Delia this morning?"

"She's . . . not feeling well," I said, fumbling over the lie. Georgia stopped stirring. My sister wasn't necessarily a germaphobe, but she didn't cope well with contagious diseases. Knife injuries, gunshot wounds, and blunt force trauma she could handle at close range. Snot, the runs, and projectile vomiting was enough to send her running for the hills. "Cramps," I added.

The tension left her shoulders and she nodded into her coffee. I'd called my sister the night before, right after I'd called Steven. Vero couldn't take Delia to school in the Charger, and letting her drive my minivan was far too risky. The person who'd taken that picture of Vero could track my license plates here.

I'd considered letting Delia stay home for the day, playing it safe until Steven's flight got in from Philly and he came to pick up the kids, but then I'd had another idea. If the creep who took that photo was waiting at the school and saw Delia get out of my *sister*'s car—a car with a few extra antennas on the roof and a dome light on the dash—maybe he'd have second thoughts about stalking my children's nanny.

"Why couldn't *you* take Delia?" Georgia asked.

"I have a meeting with Sylvia." My sister raised an eyebrow at my snowman-themed pajama bottoms. "It's a Zoom," I said, doubling down on the lie. "Why are you all dressed up?"

"I have a meeting this morning, too. It's not a big deal." Her cheeks were pink and her lips were glossy. She avoided my curious stare, picking a lint fuzz off her sweater. It was a deep hunter green that brought out the flecks of it in her eyes.

"Holy shit, Georgia!" I shoved her shoulder. Coffee sloshed over the rim of her mug and she swore as she mopped a few drops from the toes of her shoes. "You're seeing someone at work!"

"I'm not seeing someone at work."

"At the lab, then?" I racked my brain, struggling to remember the last time I'd been there with Nick. "Is it a tech?"

"No," she said gruffly.

"The M.E.?"

She pulled a face.

"That cute toxicologist?"

"Stop trying to guess. You don't know her."

"I knew it! You are seeing someone! When do I get to meet her?"

Georgia held up a finger. "A, we're not seeing each other. And B, you don't."

"Why don't you invite her over for dinner?" I suggested. "Vero and I will cook."

"Finlay—"

"What are you so afraid of, Georgia? Do you seriously think I'd embarrass you? You wore SWAT gear to Thanksgiving at Mom's. You do a perfectly fine job of embarrassing yourself."

"I said I'm not seeing her, okay?" Georgia's tone had sharpened to a brittle edge. I'd never known my sister to be fragile and the sound of it startled me. She drew a calming breath through her nose as I blinked at her. "I'm just handling something for Nick. He's all tied up with this big project at work, so I offered to help him out. That's all." My sister had always been a horrible liar. She and Nick had been close since they'd attended the police academy together years ago, but the effort she'd put into her hair this morning betrayed her motivations. "Speaking of Nick, why haven't you called him back?"

"Don't change the subject."

"I didn't," she said. "That was a perfectly reasonable segue."

"Tell me about this woman you're interested in."

"Answer my question about Nick."

I gritted my teeth, weighing my need to know more about my sister's sparkly new crush against my determination not to involve her in my love life. "I was going to call him back. I've just been busy." Apparently, I was a shitty liar, too.

"Busy? Or chicken?" I slapped away her hand as she ruffled my hair. "Delia!" she called up the stairs. "Come on, squirt. You're gonna be late for school."

Delia bounded down the steps, nearly tackling my sister into the wall with the full force of an exuberant five-year-old. "Whoa, Dee! Go easy on the knees. Save the takedowns for the bad guys." My sister turned to me and said, "You should probably break the kids of the whole tackle-hug thing before they hurt someone."

"Mmmm . . ." I said through a pinched smile. "Maybe you can come over and work on it with them when you've finished potty training Zach."

"Very funny," she said as she ushered Delia out the door.

"Thanks, Georgia," I called after them, "I owe you one."

"Forget about it. I lost count a long time ago. And for god's sake, call Nick!" she hollered over her shoulder.

"Yeah, call Nick!" Delia parroted as she trotted down the sidewalk to my sister's car. My daughter had been nagging me to call him ever since Christmas, when he'd given her a checkers game and promised to teach her to play. But inviting Nick to my home for a game of strategy felt decidedly risky under the circumstances. He had far too many questions about me, questions I'd narrowly avoided that night. Questions I shouldn't answer. Not now. And if I was smart, I never would.

My ex-husband's F-150 rumbled into the driveway just after lunch, earlier than I'd expected. I rushed downstairs, balancing Zach on my hip, startling Steven when I threw open the door.

"Hey," he said, a little breathless. His face was ruddy with the cold, his shirt slightly rumpled under his open coat, as if he'd just walked off the plane. He ran his hand through his hair and smoothed down his short beard, his blue eyes wide as they took me in. "It's good to see you. You look great."

"Thanks," I said, gesturing for him to come in. "It's good to see you, too." For the first time in a long time, I actually meant it. The last time I'd seen Steven, we'd narrowly escaped an attempt on his life, and though our history over the last two years was marked by countless disappointments and betrayals, the night I saved him from *EasyClean* had been a turning point for us. Now that the threat to him was over, as well as his engagement to Theresa Hall, hopefully we could go back to co-parenting our children like civilized adults.

"Thanks for taking the kids on such short notice," I said over

Zach's squeals. He leaned out of my arms, dropping his juice-stained blanket as he reached for his father. "They've missed you."

Steven scooped up our son, a sheen in his eyes as he pressed a kiss to Zach's cheek. "Oh, man. I missed you guys, too!" He turned to me, his throat a little thick when he asked, "You sure it's okay for them to stay with me . . . you know . . . after everything?"

"No one's going to try to kill you, if that's what you're asking." He didn't look convinced. "Trust me, Steven. It's safe."

An awkward silence stretched between us as Vero shuffled about upstairs, packing the last of the children's pillows and toys and zipping them into their suitcases.

He set Zach down and watched him toddle off. "I'll pick up Delia right after school, and I'll text you pictures every day. You can call us anytime you want. How long can the kids stay?"

I wasn't sure how long it would take to sell the Aston Martin and arrange a meeting with Marco. "Let's start with a week and see how it goes."

"A week? Wow, that's . . ." Steven had never had the kids by himself for more than a weekend. I wasn't sure if it was gratitude or nerves that had rendered him speechless.

"If it's too long, I could ask my mom to—"

"No!" He held up a hand. "Please. Don't call your mom. A week's great."

I had called my mother earlier that morning and explained that Steven would be taking the kids for a while. This time, she hadn't argued, content to avoid any unnecessary confrontations. "If it gets to be too much, you can call me. We'll figure something out."

"We'll be fine. We've handled a lot worse," he reminded me. He scratched the back of his neck, glancing up at me with a nostalgic smile. "We made a good team that night. You were amazing, Finn. I don't know what I would have done if you hadn't shown up when you did." He shook his head as he remembered it. "You know," he said, "I've been doing a lot of thinking—"

"That'd be a first." Vero stomped down the last few steps and dumped two Rollaboards at his feet.

His smile was tight. "It's good to see you, too, Vero."

"How's your head?" she asked dryly.

Steven gritted his teeth as he ran a hand over his crown where Vero had knocked him out with my frying pan the last time they'd seen each other. "You're a real comedian."

"What can I say? You keep giving me such great material to work with. Duct tape is a good look on you, by the way. Very slimming."

A vein swelled in Steven's temple.

I inserted myself between them. "Vero, can you please put the kids' bags in Steven's truck? We should get them on the road. We have a lot of things to handle here," I said pointedly.

Vero smiled sweetly at Steven and hauled the children's suitcases outside.

He seethed as he watched her go. "I can't believe you let her move in with you."

I grabbed Zach as he zipped past my legs toward the door. "The children and I love having her here and she needed a place to stay."

"She should rent her own place."

"She's still in school. She doesn't have enough money for her own place."

He cast another suspicious look toward his truck as I wrangled Zach into his coat. "Finn, there's something I need to tell you. Something I should have told you before, but . . ." I glanced up at him. He winced, bracing for the backlash of whatever he was about to say. "That time you found me in the garage . . . that wasn't the first time I was in the house when you weren't home."

My hands froze around Zach's zipper. "What do you mean?" There were more than a few terrifying things he could have found if he'd been snooping around in here. Not the least concerning was the misguided letter from Patricia Mickler, thanking me for killing her husband.

Steven cleared his throat. "Back in October, I came to talk to you about the custody agreement, but you weren't home, so I let myself in. I grabbed a soda from the pantry. I was going to wait for you, but . . ." He let the rest hang as I stood up slowly. He didn't have to finish. Steven hated drinking anything warm. He put ice in everything, which meant . . .

He'd opened my freezer.

"You had no business being in this house!"

He held out a hand to calm me. "I know, Finn, and I'm sorry. I shouldn't have let myself in. But listen to me," he said, his voice growing urgent as Vero secured the children's car seats into the backseat of his truck. "There was money in the freezer. A lot of money. It was hidden behind the broccoli. I was mad at you at first, because you'd been putting off the bills for so long and you kept telling me you were broke, but then it occurred to me that the money could be hers," he said, thrusting a finger toward the door, "and you wouldn't even know it because you hardly ever cook!"

"The contents of my freezer are none of your business!"

"I am telling you, that girl is hiding something. She's too young to have that kind of money, and no one keeps that much cash in a freezer."

"In case you've forgotten, we've found far worse things in yours!"

Steven blanched. He hadn't known Carl Westover's dismembered corpse was in a freezer in his storage unit when Vero and I had found the body in December, but Carl had been Steven's business partner and Steven's name had been the one on the rental agreement, so as far as I was concerned, he was in no position to judge. "That's not fair," he argued.

"Neither is sneaking around my house and making false assumptions."

"For all you know, you could be living with a criminal!"

A laugh burst out of me. "I promise you, Vero's no more a criminal than I am."

"How can you be sure?" he asked as his truck door slammed.

"Steven," I said, drawing his attention back to me. "Vero will be with me all week. If it will make you feel better, I promise to keep a close eye on her."

"Wait," he said with a confused shake of his head, "she'll be with you?"

"Yes, she *lives* here, Steven. In *my* home. Why do you look so surprised?"

"It's just that you were so eager to let me take the kids, and you and Nick were spending a lot of time together before I left for Philly. I guess I just assumed—"

"I'm not seeing anyone," I said curtly.

"Not even that lawyer kid in the Jeep?"

"Julian's twenty-four. That hardly makes him a kid."

"So you are seeing him?"

"No!" I sputtered. "We broke up. Why am I even explaining myself to you?"

Steven's shoulders sagged. He smoothed back his hair, relief naked on his face. "It's just that I had a lot of time to think while I was gone, about you and Delia and Zach . . . about how we never really tried to fix things between us."

"Fix things?"

"You know, like seeing a marriage counselor."

I laughed at the absurdity of the suggestion. "We didn't see a marriage counselor because you told me you wanted to be married to someone else!"

"I know," he said, his ears reddening with his temper. He took a slow breath and lowered his voice. "I know. And proposing to Theresa was a huge mistake, but now that all of that is behind us, and since you're not dating anybody, maybe there's a chance that we could talk to someone. We owe it to Delia and Zach to clear the air between us and try to make a fresh start, and it'd be a lot easier without a third wheel in the house." He didn't bother to lower his voice as Vero opened the door behind him. "I can sleep in the guest room while we figure things out."

Vero clapped a hand on Steven's shoulder. She shoved Zach's nap blanket in his arms and turned my ex-husband toward the street. "It's definitely time for you to be going," she said, holding the front door wide. "Don't let anything hit you on the way out. You know . . . doors, frying pans, a restraining order."

Steven growled at her. "You'd like that, wouldn't you?"

Her smile was devious. "You have no idea."

The muscles in his face worked as if it was taking all their strength to hold him back. He turned to me. "Where's Zach?"

"Probably hiding." At his puzzled look, I explained, "It's a phase he's going through. Whatever you do, don't let him out of your sight in the men's room." I grabbed a bag of Goldfish crackers from the pantry and dangled it below the dining room table. Zach giggled and crawled out from under it. I caught him as he reached for it with a squeal.

"I'll call you tonight," Steven said, stepping in close to take Zach from my arms. I froze at the cool shock of his lips against my cheek, at their distantly familiar bristle, keenly aware that it had been almost two years since those lips had touched me. I rubbed the strange itch they left behind as I watched him carry our son to his truck.

CHAPTER 5

"What was that whole business with Steven today?" Vero asked me later that night as we climbed into my minivan and drove to Ramón's garage. It was almost eleven thirty, long after the garage closed. We had arranged to meet Javi there at midnight.

"What business?" I asked as I pulled out of the neighborhood.

"Steven kissed you."

"So?"

"And he was about to ask you to go out with him."

"You can't possibly know that."

"He said he had a lot of time to think about you while he was gone."

"He said he'd been thinking about me and the *kids*."

"Finlay," she said as if I was being obtuse. "I hate to say it, but his ex-girlfriend was right. He's definitely still in love with you."

I blew out a heavy sigh. "I know."

"And what?"

"And nothing."

"You're not seriously considering letting him come back?"

"Of course not," I said, gripping the wheel. "Nothing is happening between me and Steven."

"Good."

"It was probably just the holidays making him nostalgic," I reasoned.

"After a week alone with the kids, he'll be begging me to take them back. You know how he is."

"Yes, I do," Vero said. "Which is why I am telling you right now, you need to set some clear boundaries with that man or he'll stomp right over them." She pointed to a curb a block from Ramón's garage. "Pull over there. Javi's not supposed to be here for another twenty minutes. We should make sure Marco's guys aren't scoping the place out first." She withdrew her set of binoculars from her bag and studied the street in front of the garage.

"See anything?"

"Nothing suspicious." She put the binoculars back in her purse. "Let's go," she said, tucking it under her seat and hopping out of the van.

We walked quickly, hunched under our coats with our hoods pulled low, our breath streaming out in thin white clouds. Vero fumbled with a key ring as we approached the high chain-link fence that surrounded her cousin's salvage yard. Chains clanked as Vero slipped a key in the padlock and snapped it open, ushering me through the gate.

The highway hummed in the distance as she closed the latch behind us, leaving the padlock hanging open for Javi.

"Come on," she said, pulling me by my sleeve past the rows of parked cars awaiting repair behind the garage.

"What about the cameras?" I asked. I'd noticed at least two hanging from the eaves of the building.

"Ramón's too cheap to pay for a monitoring service. Javi installed them and I run the software. Ramón doesn't even know how to check the feed."

The shadows thickened as she led us deeper into the salvage yard. Mountains of stacked cars in various stages of disrepair rose up on either side of us, forming a maze of crushed frames and abandoned parts. It all looked so precarious, rows upon rows of Jenga towers that might fall at the slightest provocation.

"This all belongs to your cousin?" The true size of the salvage yard hadn't been visible from the road, or even the back of the garage. A giant crane hovered over the yard like a sentry, its claw-shaped hand silhouetted against the night sky. "What does he do with all these cars?"

"After he tows them here? He breaks them down. Sells the scrap. Whatever's left gets squashed or recycled." Vero paused in front of a rusting metal shed. "Hold this." She handed her flashlight to me as she fiddled with her key ring. She wedged a key into the padlock and drew open the doors. I pointed the flashlight into the opening. The beam bounced off the splintered rear window of the Aston. With the exception of the bullet holes *EasyClean* had fired into it, the car's matte black body hadn't suffered a single scratch.

A car door slammed in the distance. Chains rattled as the gate to the salvage yard clanked open. "That must be Javi. Come on," Vero said, tucking the padlock in her pocket. We started back toward the gate to meet him. His shadow stretched toward us, his shoes crushing softly against the dirt as he crossed the yard.

Vero reached for my elbow, dragging me to an abrupt halt beside her. Her body bristled as he approached us. I froze, too. The man's gait was too stiff, his build far too thick to be Javi's.

"Sorry," Vero called out to the man. "Garage is closed. If you're looking for parts, you'll have to come back in the . . . morning," she finished weakly as he stepped clearly into view. A tire iron dangled from his hand. IKE—presumably his name—was tattooed across three of his massive knuckles. Vero and I took a step back as he lumbered closer. A gold championship belt buckle held up his pants, and two gold teeth glimmered from the middle of his scruffy goatee.

"Jesus," Vero whispered, "he's like a refrigerator with feet."

"Cut the crap. You know why I'm here." Ike's New Jersey accent left little room for doubt. "Marco sent me. Time to pay up."

Vero reached slowly into her pocket for her phone.

"Don't bother trying to call your friend," Ike growled, tapping the tire iron against his palm. "He's in the parking lot, taking a long nap in the back of his van. But I promise, he didn't feel a thing." Vero's fists clenched at Ike's smug grin.

"What a coincidence!" I said, holding her back with one arm and tucking her behind me. "My friend and I were just discussing Marco. See, we don't have all of his money right now, but we do have a plan to get it. We just need a few days to come up with the rest."

"Marco doesn't like to wait."

"I don't see that Marco really has a choice."

"Let me tell you how this is going to go down," Ike snapped, making Vero and I jump. "Either you give me the money you owe Marco and I leave you to go nurse your friend's headache. Or you tell me you don't have the money and the three of us go for a nice long drive so you can explain it to Marco personally."

I stumbled backward into Vero as Ike strode toward us. She peered over my shoulder as the tire iron came within striking distance.

"What's it going to be, Ruiz? Do you have the money, or am I taking you back to New Jersey to meet with . . ." Ike's threat trailed as he stared at something behind us. I glanced over my shoulder to see what had captured his attention. The shed door creaked, swaying on its hinges in the breeze, revealing a glimpse inside.

Ike ambled around us, using the tire iron to nudge the door open wide. "Well, well. What do we have here?" He smiled, a crooked slash of gold teeth. "Marco doesn't normally take his payoffs in trade, but this presents some interesting possibilities."

"I think there's been a small misunderstanding," I said cautiously. "We can't give that car to Marco."

Ike turned toward us as he adjusted his grip on the tire iron. "Who said anything about giving the car to Marco?"

Vero's mouth fell open. The car was worth more than Vero owed and Ike knew it. He could probably sell the car, pay off Marco, and pocket the rest for himself. Or he could just as easily keep the car and tell Marco he never found us. Either way, duping his boss would probably be easier to get away with if Vero and I weren't in the picture.

"Give me the keys," he demanded.

"I don't have them," Vero said. Ike was in front of her in three quick strides. She held up her hands, jutting her chin toward the shed before he could grab her. "They're in the car," she blurted.

He shoved her out of his way. "See? That wasn't so hard now, was it?"

Ike turned and headed for the Aston. Vero tugged my sleeve. She pointed at a loose hubcap beside me. I nodded, reaching for it as she charged after Ike and thrust her foot into his backside, sending him stumbling to one knee. I swung the hubcap hard into the back of his head. The metal reverberated with a gong-like sound, sending a wave of vibration all the way to my teeth.

Ike went still.

Breath held, Vero and I waited for him to teeter and fall over, the way Steven had when she'd hit him with my frying pan. Ike only shook his head. His grip tightened around his tire iron as he pushed himself to his feet with a sneer.

Vero grabbed me by the sleeve as she backpedaled away from him. "Run!" she shouted, taking off at a sprint.

Ike's fingertips grazed the back of my coat as his feet pounded behind me. I risked a glance over my shoulder as I chased Vero between two stacks of crushed cars.

"You're going to pay for that! Give me the goddamn keys!" His tire iron swung with every pump of his bulging arms, his thick waist bouncing with his strides. Vero hooked a sharp right, pulling me behind her. Then an abrupt left, desperate to shake him. I had no idea if we were losing ourselves in the maze of the scrapyard or working our way free of it. Vero's head turned back and forth, frantically searching for something as we rounded the next row. Her gaze paused on the rusted frame of an old clunker mounted on jacks and blocks. A tower of crushed cars was stacked precariously on top of it.

Vero yanked me toward it. "Get under. Hurry!" She dragged me with her to the ground, shimmying under the chassis. I scurried after her as her legs disappeared beneath the frame. Loose gravel dug into my knees as I army-crawled after her. If we could get to the other side of the wall of cars, maybe we could make it back to the gate and find Javi.

A cold hand clamped around my ankle. I yelped, my shirt riding up, the ground scraping like sandpaper over my ribs as Ike yanked me backward by my foot. Vero twisted to see me, the whites of her eyes wide as she groped for my hand. I grasped hers, kicking out wildly with my feet. The toe of my sneaker caught Ike's face. He barked out a swear, clawing at my ankles as I managed to scramble free of him.

Vero scuttled out from under the car, reaching back for me with both hands when she was safely on the other side. "Come on, Finn!" Digging her heels into the ground, she leveraged her weight and pulled. I scrabbled forward a few inches until something snagged the hood of my coat. Vero panted between tugs on my arm. She grunted when I didn't move. "I know what I said about body positivity, but you might want to cut back on the Oreos!"

"That's not funny! Keep pulling! I think he has my coat!"

I kicked out again as Ike wedged his upper body under the car. My shoe connected with something solid.

"Push harder!" Vero shouted as she pulled.

I thrust out with my foot. There was a cracking sound, then a horrible groan. Vero gave one final heave and my hood tore free. She flew backward, landing on her butt in the dirt, her momentum dragging me out from under the car until I was sprawled on the ground beside her. The ominous groan grew louder. We both shrieked at a loud snap, ducking into each other's arms. We shielded our heads as a cloud of dust erupted around us and the ground shook.

Vero and I held each other as a hush fell over the salvage yard. We sat up slowly, waving grit from the air. When it cleared, the gap under the car was gone, the jacks and blocks nowhere in sight. The car's chassis was pressed flat against the ground, the tower of smashed cars still perfectly balanced on top of it.

Vero and I scrambled to our feet, backing a cautious distance away from it. We listened for Ike's angry shouts, but the only sound was the quiet hum of the highway a few miles off.

"You think he's in there?" she asked in a shaky voice. "I mean, he could have gotten out, right?"

I swallowed. "There's only one way to find out."

Vero gave my shoulder a nudge. "Great, let me know how it goes."

"Oh, no," I said, turning her toward the stack of cars. "No way. I was the one who opened the freezer in the storage unit the day we found Carl." And my husband's former business partner had not been in one piece when he'd been put there.

"So?"

"So I touched a severed head, Vero! I think that earns me a pass this time!"

"Well I cleaned *eau de Carl* out of my trunk! Not only that, but *I* was the one who found all those dead dudes with their brains blown out in the field at the sod farm."

"Yeah, well I performed mouth-to-mouth on Harris Mickler's corpse!"

"That doesn't count. He was probably still warm."

"He'd been eating blue cheese olives, Vero!"

She shuddered. "Fine, I'll go. But I'm not going alone." She took my hand, leading us to the end of the row and looping us around, until we were back on the other side of the wall of cars we'd crawled under. Vero slowed, creeping toward the flattened station wagon. A pair of denim-clad legs protruded from under the frame.

Vero toed one of Ike's sneakers, grimacing when he didn't move.

I covered my eyes, peeking through my fingers. "Is he dead?"

"Remember that day we went shopping for snow shovels, and I told you we should get garden shovels instead? I take it back. This is definitely a snow shovel kind of job."

"An interesting choice." The rich purr of the woman's voice came from behind us. Vero jumped back from the dead man's legs. I stiffened as I recognized the familiar trace of the woman's accent.

Ekatarina Rybakov, Feliks Zhirov's star attorney, spared me a cool smile as I slowly turned around. And she hadn't come alone.

CHAPTER 6

The tails of Kat's trench coat fluttered around her black stiletto heels, her dark hair rippling like a curtain in the wind. Two huge men clad in black tactical pants, black beanies, and black leather jackets towered beside her. She folded her arms, her crimson lips quirking as she studied me. "I admit, your methods are effective, Ms. Donovan. Unorthodox," she said, raising an eyebrow at the tower of cars, "but effective."

Cam stood on his toes to peek over Kat's shoulder. His face, which hadn't looked too terrible last night after our tussle in the yard, had bloomed two black eyes since, and a pronounced knot perched on the bridge of his nose. He paled when he spotted Ike.

"This is not what it looks like," I said, moving to block their view of him. "This guy . . . he was—"

"I know who he was," Kat interrupted, studying her nails. "I have been watching him for some time, and I am aware of his interest in your childcare provider."

"Accountant," Vero corrected her.

Kat acknowledged Vero's interjection with a dubious sideways glance before continuing. "Finding *EasyClean* is of the utmost importance to Feliks. He felt this man might be hindering your progress, but it seems my client's concern was unnecessary. He'll be pleased to know you already had the situation under control, and that you may now focus your full attention on the job you agreed to do for him."

"Now wait just a minute!" I said, taking two steps toward her, pausing abruptly when her goons stepped forward, too. "I never agreed to anything."

Kat gestured to Cam. "Cameron mentioned that you've expressed some reluctance to complete the job." I glared at him over her shoulder. He touched the bruised bridge of his nose as he shrank from view. "Which brings us to the reason I am here, Ms. Donovan. Mr. Zhirov sent me to provide you with some incentive." One of Kat's men dropped a fat black duffel bag beside her, withdrawing a brick of cash and laying it in her hand. Kat fanned herself with the thick stack of bills, ignoring Vero's covetous moan. "Feliks instructed me to pay off your nanny's debt to this unfortunate man's employer; however, that problem seems to have resolved itself—for the moment." Kat grimaced at Ike's legs. "Now it seems you have a more pressing issue to deal with, so this is what I propose." Vero made a small noise of protest as Kat dropped the money into the open duffel and her goon zipped it closed. "You will complete your task for my client before the commencement of his trial, and in return," she said, gesturing to her entourage, "Mr. Zhirov's associates will not contact the police to disclose what they witnessed here tonight."

"That's not an offer! That's blackmail!"

Kat gave a careless shrug. "You call it *to-may-to*. I call it *to-mah-to*."

"Well, *I* call it bullshit," Vero interrupted. "Unless your offer includes that stack of cash," she added in a more tractable tone. "Then you can call it whatever you want. What?" she asked at my cutting look. "Those tomatoes were not small!"

"True," Kat admitted. "Two hundred thousand dollars is no negligible sum. But, again, this is no small mess to tidy up." She inclined her chin toward my feet. I glanced down, gasping at the blood trickling from Ike's remains toward my heels. Vero swore, frantically scraping her sneakers against the dirt.

Kat was right. Concealing Harris's murder, and even Carl's, had been as simple as moving a body. But nothing would be easy about moving this one, or cleaning up the mess.

"The answer is simple," Kat said. "Give me your word that you'll handle *EasyClean* before the trial, and Feliks will make sure all of this disappears."

Vero stirred her finger in the air. "And by *all of this*, you mean . . . ?"

"No one will ever know what happened here, unless you fail to meet your end of our bargain."

"There is no bargain," I reminded her.

"And all we have to do is *handle EasyClean*. That's it?" Vero asked.

"Before the trial," Kat clarified.

"When do we get the tomatoes?"

"We're not handling anyone's tomatoes!" I snapped.

"When the job is completed to Mr. Zhirov's satisfaction, we will discuss the rest of his incentive. By then," Kat said, gesturing to Ike, "I'm sure this man's employer will be eager to speak with you."

The chain-link fence rattled as a fourth member of their group came through the gate. The woman wore a pair of black driving gloves and carried a heavy black case. She nodded once at Kat, then began emptying the contents, placing a neatly folded plastic tarp and a roll of duct tape on the ground. One of the men climbed into the crane.

Kat checked her watch. "Shall I tell Mr. Zhirov we have an agreement?"

"No," I protested. "We do not have an agree—"

"May I have a moment to confer with my client?" Vero asked, dragging me aside. "Think about this, Finlay," she hissed.

"We are not putting ourselves further in debt to that man!" I whispered.

"If we say no, they will leave us here alone with the dead dude, and I do not know how to drive one of those," she said, thrusting a finger toward the crane.

"We have YouTube!"

Vero's head tilted. For a moment I think she actually considered it. "Even if we could move that stack of cars, do you really want to see what's under it?" I grimaced. "What that woman is offering is a lot more appealing than a ride in the back of a police car. And I am *not* talking about the back seat of Nick's!"

The thought of Nick finding out about this made my stomach turn. In a matter of days, Marco would start looking for his lost muscle and probably track him here. Once he did, what was to stop the loan shark from tipping off the cops to Ike's last known whereabouts?

"Nick said it himself," Vero pleaded, gesturing to the corpse. "Feliks can make almost anyone disappear, and I'm betting Flat Stanley here is no exception. You heard Kat. Feliks needs you to find *EasyClean* before his trial, and he isn't going to let the police or anyone else get in the way of that."

"So we find *EasyClean* and then what? Murder him, too?"

"We did *not* murder anyone," she said, pointing at Ike. "That man died at the hands of god. Or maybe gravity. And *definitely* too many trips through the late-night Wendy's drive-through. Whatever the reason, it was his own damn fault."

"So we're just going to cross our fingers and hope *EasyClean* chases us into a salvage yard?"

"I swear, I have a solution to the *EasyClean* problem. Just trust me." The plea in her eyes felt like a test of my faith in her. And I hated that because it didn't leave me any choice. "Please," she begged, "if we agree to Feliks's terms and leave right now, we can find Javi, make sure he's okay, and get him out of here before Kat's people do."

All my arguments died at the look on her face. Vero was right. If Kat's men found Javi here, Feliks would only see him as a witness to clean up. I didn't want to think about what Kat's methods might entail, but I was guessing the woman with the tarp and the duct tape would probably be involved.

With a quiet swear, I strode back to Kat's entourage. "Fine. I agree to your terms," I said, gesticulating around me. "If you make all this disappear *and* ensure that no one ever knows what happened here tonight," I added, parroting her own words back to her, "then I will figure out who *EasyClean* is. That's all—"

"All part of the deal," Vero finished for me as I gritted my teeth at her. "Yep, we'll handle *EasyClean*. No problem."

Kat nodded. The crane rumbled to life. Vero and I walked out the gate as a tarp snapped open behind us.

Vero and I jogged around the side of the garage, searching the parking lot for Javi's van.

"There!" I said over the hum of the crane. We rushed toward the white panel van at the far side of the lot. Vero wrestled with the driver's door as I tried the passenger side, both of us cursing when we found them all locked. I pounded on the window, calling Javi's name. Vero jerked the handle of the cargo door, stumbling backward when it flew open and she found Javi sprawled inside.

She climbed in and crouched beside him, shaking out her hands as if she wasn't sure where to touch him.

"Check his pulse," I suggested, keeping my eyes peeled for Feliks's goons as Vero placed two fingers on his neck.

Javi groaned. "Damn, your hands are cold."

"He's fine. Help me get him up." Vero slung one of his arms over her shoulder. I climbed in and took his other side, hauling him upright. He winced, running tentative fingers over the back of his head as we urged him out of the van onto his feet.

"What's your friend doing here?" Javi's head wobbled as he struggled to focus on me. "Were we drinking?" He glanced down at the button on his jeans, then back and forth between us. "Wait. Did we . . . ?"

"You wish you were that lucky," Vero said through a grunt as we ushered him toward my minivan.

"Do you remember anything?" I asked, breathing hard under his weight. Javi was nowhere near as big as Ike, but he was remarkably solid through his clothes.

He squinted. "All I remember is getting Vero's text. I was on my way to meet her. I opened the back of my van to grab a flashlight, and then . . . nothing."

"I bet you were mugged," Vero said with a pointed look at me. Behind his back, I felt her slip Javi's billfold and phone from his pockets. I didn't have the energy to point out the fact that she was breaking yet another law. We had just dropped a tower of cars on a man and sold our souls to the Russian mob. A little pickpocketing for the sake of selling our story to Javi to keep him from asking any questions didn't seem like such a terrible crime by comparison. The less he knew about what had happened here tonight, the safer we'd all remain.

Javi's reflexes were slow as he patted his empty pockets. "Shit," he muttered. His feet paused, jolting our procession to a stop. "What's that sound?" he asked. Vero and I exchanged glances behind his back as the crane's winch whined in the salvage yard.

"I don't hear anything," Vero said. We both flinched at the unmistakable crunch of metal on metal.

"Must be a side effect of your concussion," I insisted, urging him toward the minivan. Vero held him up as I opened the back door. Javi crawled inside and lay on the floor, his eyes closing as Vero slid the door shut behind him.

"I'll go delete the security footage from the computer in Ramón's office," she said quietly. "It'll only take me a few minutes. You stay here with Javi." I watched as she jogged back to the garage.

A yelp burst out of me when someone tapped me on the shoulder. I spun around, my hand clapped to my chest as I came face to face with Cam. "You scared the bejeezus out of me!" I whispered.

His put up his hands and took a cautious step back. "Sorry. I didn't mean to sneak up on you . . . this time," he clarified. "And just so we're clear, I totally didn't see you putting that dude in your van just now. I swear I won't tell anyone, so don't get any ideas about killing me or anything, okay?" I rolled my eyes. "I'm serious. That was some sick shit back there. I didn't think you had it in you, but damn . . ." He shook his head, splaying his fingers beside his ears. "Mind blown."

"What do you want, Cameron?" All I wanted was to get home, crawl in bed, and pretend this night had never happened.

He checked over his shoulder. "I can't stay long or they might notice I'm gone. I just wanted to tell you, I really was just trying to help when I came to your house the other night. And I didn't tell that Rybakov lady anything, I swear."

"What's done is done," I said irritably. "If you really wanted to help me, you could have just told me who *EasyClean* was." I had a strong suspicion the hacker knew more about *EasyClean*'s identity than he was letting on.

"If I knew who *EasyClean* was, I'd have told Mr. Z myself." At my withering look, he threw up his hands. "I already told you my theory. *EasyClean*'s a cop. That's all I know."

As often as Cam had been less than forthright, he'd never outright lied to me. I heaved a sigh. "Then give me *something,* Cam. A clue. A bread crumb. Anything. I just need someplace to start looking."

He scrubbed a hand over his closely shorn hair and swore under his breath, casting anxious glances toward the salvage yard. "Fine. You want to find *EasyClean,* start with the places where cops hang out." He pitched his voice low. "A dirty cop's always going to be looking over his shoulder to make sure he's not on anybody's radar, and the best way to do that is to stay in the mix, where he can listen to the gossip and know what's going on with everyone else's investigations. He'll make friends with the best detectives, the clean ones, the ones most likely to step in his shit. He'll hang close, go where they go, where he can keep an eye on them. If I was looking for *EasyClean,* I'd start where cops get together and talk about shit—the police station, their favorite bars, donut shops, whatever . . ." The crane's engine fell silent in the salvage yard. Cam backed toward the garage with an apologetic shrug. "Sorry, Ms. Donovan. I've got to go."

I watched him jog through the gate as I thought about what he'd said. He had a point. One that made a lot of sense. If *EasyClean* was a cop, the best way to find him was to get close to the detectives he worked with. My sister worked in Violent Crimes, but she was friends with a lot of the guys from Organized Crime and Narcotics, and if anyone happened to be working cases that might accidentally "step in *EasyClean*'s shit," it'd be the detectives from OCN.

The only problem was Nick was one of them.

CHAPTER 7

Vero and I paused inside the door of the bar as our eyes adjusted to the aura of the place. Hooligans was a far cry from the elegant cherry-woods and rich amber lighting of The Lush. The air in the upscale bar where I used to meet Julian after his bartending shifts had always hinted at designer perfumes and imported hops. This one felt more like the kind of bars Steven used to drag me to when we were in college, low-ceilinged rooms that smelled like hamburger grease and the cigarette smoke that trailed in from outside.

Cues snapped against balls and darts thumped into bull's-eyes mounted on the wall. The soft clatter of empty bottles being loaded into bins peppered low conversations, and a country song crooned from a jukebox near the back.

The bartender—a balding man with a bulbous nose and a ruddy complexion—glanced up as Vero and I eased into an empty booth. A server appeared, a woman with dyed auburn hair and deep smoker's creases around her mouth and her eyes. I offered her a polite smile, surprised by the wave of melancholy that washed over me as I ordered a vodka tonic with lime.

"Stop," Vero said after the server had gone.

"What?"

"Depressing yourself. You aren't missing anything you can't get with the right personal massager and an economy pack of double-As. Julian wasn't ready for you."

It wasn't me Julian hadn't been ready for, but everything that came with me—two young kids, a meddlesome ex, a history of questionable criminal behavior . . . I wasn't exactly the ideal partner for a twenty-four-year-old law student who worked nights at a bar. And if I was being honest with myself, I knew he wasn't the ideal partner for me. I loved my kids and Vero and my complicated, sticky life, and I wanted to be with someone who loved them too. It was one thing to have a separate identity to stamp on the cover of my books, but I was done compartmentalizing myself to fit in other people's neat and tidy boxes.

"I'm not depressing myself," I lied, busying myself with my phone.

"Sure you're not. What's the plan?" She cracked open a peanut from a bowl on the table, scattering dust and crumbs as she popped it in her mouth.

"We wait for Georgia to show up and pretend to be surprised. Then we ask her to introduce us to all of her friends." My sister had already told everyone she knew that I was an author. If anyone struck me as suspicious, I'd strike up a conversation and ask them if they'd let me interview them for research for a book.

I scrolled through a few local news sites on my phone, skimming the headlines.

"Any signs of Ike?" Vero asked.

"Nothing yet. Let's figure out who *EasyClean* is, get Feliks a name, and be done with it." My thoughts died as the door to the bar opened and Nick's partner, Detective Joey Balafonte, stepped inside. He nodded to the bartender, scanning the room as he slipped off his coat. His cool blue eyes made a brief pass over our table, then quickly doubled back. He froze, staring at me as if a breaker had tripped in his brain.

I offered him a small wave, doing my best to mirror his surprise, though I wasn't at all surprised Joey was here. Not just because he was Nick's partner. But because ever since that night when Nick had been shot and Joey was nowhere to be found, I'd had my doubts about him. If Mrs. Haggerty hadn't confirmed his alibi, stating that she had indeed spoken with a police officer who vaguely matched Joey's description in her driveway that night, I would have been certain that Joey Balafonte was the stranger on that dark country road who'd fired shots at me and Steven as we'd fled in the Aston.

The server handed him a beer. He accepted it with a congenial thanks, never once taking his eyes off me.

Vero looked up from her menu. "What's wrong?"

"Don't look now, but Joey's here and he's heading straight for our booth."

"First one to show up," she murmured as he approached our table.

"Ladies," Joey greeted us. "How was your Christmas?"

"Good, thanks," I said through what I hoped was a convincing smile. "How was yours?"

Joey shrugged. "A little lean this year, but you know how it is, right?" His eyes locked on mine, the same way they had over Nick's hospital bed the last time we'd seen each other, when every question had felt like a bullet fired at close range.

"Still moonlighting?" I asked.

He took a long pull of his beer as if he was rolling the question around. "It was seasonal work, the occasional odd job. Those kinds of gigs are harder to grab once the holidays are over." Vero kicked me under the table. "What about you?" he asked me. "How's the new book coming? Georgia mentioned it'll be out in a few months. I've been dying to read it."

I cocked an eyebrow. "I wouldn't have guessed you were a fan of romantic suspense."

"Don't suppose I am. But I do love a good mystery." He slid a toothpick in his mouth, his lip curling around it. Joey was the last to break our staring contest as a parade of off-duty cops strolled in.

My sister pulled off her hat and waved at Joey, then did a double take when she spotted me. Her smile was wide, her cheeks flushed from the cold as she headed for our booth. "Hey look, everybody!" she called over her shoulder. "This is my sister, Finlay, the one who writes the books I was telling you about." Her friends waved to us on their way to the bar. Joey drifted away from our table and melted into their group.

"Hey, Vero." Georgia nudged me deeper into the booth and sat down beside me, shucking her coat. "What the heck are you two doing here?"

"We heard the cheesy fries were good," Vero said, a little too enthusiastically.

"Hooligans has cheesy fries?" Georgia frowned as she reached for a plastic menu. "Huh. That must be new."

The server set an open beer in front of my sister. When she was gone, Georgia set down the menu and slid the bowl of peanuts toward herself. "Let me take a stab at what you two are really doing here." I opened my mouth to argue, but she held up a hand. "Look around you, Finn. No one comes here for the food." I shut my mouth, having no reasonable argument for that.

"I think you're here because you finally came to your senses about Nick," she said, cracking a nut. "But you were too chicken to call him and agree to a date, so you decided to play coy and show up here with your friend so you wouldn't be tempted to leave with him." She silenced my protest with a raised finger. "Don't pretend you didn't know we all hang out here every Thursday night."

"Damn, she's good," Vero whispered.

My face burned. "I didn't come to see Nick. He's not even here."

My sister smirked around her beer as she looked past me toward the door. Nick limped into the bar, leaning on a metal cane. Sleet dotted the shoulders of his coat, and he shook it from his hair as the door closed behind him.

"Whoa," Vero said, "Finlay's doing it again."

"Doing what?" Georgia asked.

"Manifesting dessert."

Georgia's face screwed up. "I don't even want to know what that means." She scooted sideways out of the booth, catching Nick's attention as he lifted his head. His cane rattled to a sharp halt when he spotted me. "You two lovebirds have fun," Georgia said, patting me on the shoulder. "Come on, Vero. I'll introduce you around. I could use a partner for doubles." I hardly noticed as Vero slid out of the booth.

Nick's smile was tentative, and my stomach did a little flip as he shuffled toward me. He inclined his head toward Vero's empty seat. "Mind if I take a load off?"

"Not at all." I stole glances at him as he maneuvered onto the bench. He looked just as good as he had when I'd last seen him. The fitted Henley under his coat hugged his muscular frame, and the dark waves of his hair had grown out a little, framing his face, doing dangerous things to my libido.

He leaned his cane against the side of the bench and waved to the server across the bar. "Can I get you anything?" he asked me as she made her way toward us.

I'd hardly touched my drink, but given where Nick and I had left things after Christmas dinner, I'd definitely need some liquid courage for this conversation. I tipped my glass to our server, and with a nod, she was gone.

"I called you a few times," he said casually. "Wasn't sure you got my messages. Vero said you've been busy."

I picked at the edge of my napkin. "I'm sorry I didn't call you back. After everything that happened with Steven, I just needed some time. I didn't mean to—"

"Hey," he said gently, calling a time-out with his hands as he ducked his head low, capturing my gaze across the table. "You've been through a lot these last few weeks, and if that's the reason you didn't call, I totally get it. No explanations or apologies necessary. I just figured you were upset with me."

I shook my head, confused. "Why would I be upset with you?"

"About all that stuff I said after dinner at your mom's house. I didn't mean to suggest that I was suspicious of you, or that you had anything to answer for. I should have kept my mouth shut. It wasn't the time to bring that stuff up."

I didn't know what to say to that. The answers to the questions he'd asked me under the mistletoe—about why my missing cell phone had turned up in Carl Westover's house, or what I'd been doing there with a fugitive witness the night Feliks decided to gun us all down—would have ruined more than just the moment between us. That night, Nick had said he didn't want to know the answers, but where did that leave us now?

As if he was reading my thoughts, he said, "I'm still hoping for that sympathy kiss."

A surprised laugh burst out of me. "Still?"

He laughed, too. "Why do you think I'm still using the cane?"

The server came with our drinks. The break in tension left a sticky grin on my face. "It's good to see you," I confessed when she was gone, surprised by how much I meant it. "How are you feeling?"

Nick rubbed his shoulder. "The doc did a nice job on my arm. Stitches are out and it's feeling pretty good. Leg's another story though. I'm in PT, pushing paper at work for another four weeks."

"I'm sorry."

"Could have been a whole lot worse," he reminded me. The gratitude in his eyes was hard to look at. Feliks's men may have been the ones pulling the triggers, but part of me still felt responsible for his injuries.

My guilty gaze slid away from him to the cops congregating by a table at the back of the bar. "I feel badly keeping you from your friends."

"You want to meet them?" he asked, taking my hand before I could answer. A thrill raced through me at his brief touch as he led me out of the booth.

Joey leaned against the wall, a toothpick tucked in his cheek as he watched the two of us pick our way across the bar toward him. I looked for Vero, but she and Georgia were engaged in a game of darts.

"Hey," Nick said over the chatter as we reached the cops' table. Someone called out to the server to bring Nick another beer, and they all scooted over to make room as they pushed an extra chair toward him. Nick's hand found the small of my back as he offered me his seat. "You all know Georgia's sister, Finlay?" The small group at the table waved. Nick pointed toward the others gathered around the dart boards behind them. "You already know Roddy." Officer Roddy's head towered over the others. He was an old friend of Nick's who'd provided security at my house on more than one occasion. "And that's his rookie-in-training, Tyrese," Nick said, gesturing to the fresh-faced recruit who was flirting with Vero. Nick returned his attention to the officers seated around the table. He pointed to the only other woman among them. She was willowy and elegant in a fitted pantsuit, her exaggerated cat eyes curling with her smile as she reached across the table to greet me. "This is Samara Becker. Sam works in High-Tech Crimes. She just came on as part of a joint task force with OCN. And you already know Joey," Nick finished.

Joey's smile was tight around his toothpick. I returned it, feeling the hair on the back of my neck prickle.

I waited through an awkward pause for Nick to introduce the last member of their group. When he didn't, Samara rolled her eyes. "And this is Wade," she said, hitching a thumb at the shaggy-haired man seated beside her. "He's a firearms instructor for the department." Wade nodded, his dark eyes aloof under the bill of a well-worn trucker cap. His arms were covered in two full sleeves of tattoos under a ratty old T-shirt that read I LIKE GUNS AND MAYBE THREE PEOPLE. His crooked smile seemed directed at Nick as he resumed slowly spinning his beer bottle in its pool of condensation on the table.

Nick lowered himself into an empty chair beside me. An electric current passed through me when our knees brushed. He murmured an apology as he maneuvered out of his coat in the tight space, his body angling slightly closer to mine as he turned to hang it on the back of his chair. He smelled as intoxicatingly good as he had the last time I'd helped him put it on, like warm leather and cloves, and I bit down on my tongue as I remembered the last thing he'd whispered in my ear that night as we stood under the mistletoe in my parents' doorway—that he'd wanted to kiss me. Then he'd left me with a chaste peck on the cheek and the nearly irrepressible need to tackle him and dry hump him in my mother's foyer.

"You're the author, right?" Samara asked, startling me from the memory. I cleared my throat and nodded, my palms a little sweaty. "What kind of books do you write?"

"Nick's kind, apparently," Wade said as he leaned back and scratched a rib. "Caught him reading one in the break room at the station last week." The table exploded in laughter.

"You ought to try reading one, Wade. You might learn a thing or two."

Samara gave a low whistle at Nick's comeback and the table erupted in laughter again. I glanced over at Nick, wondering how many of my six failed backlist paperbacks he had read and what kinds of things he might have learned from them. The first book in my new series—a book loosely inspired by Harris Mickler's murder, featuring a star-crossed romance between an assassin and a hot cop—hadn't gone to print yet, but it was already attracting more attention than I was comfortable with. Everyone in the police station had been talking about it since Sylvia had put out a press release, when a rumor began spreading through the department that the hot cop in my story bore a striking resemblance to Nick.

"Not all of us can be eye candy, Nick," Wade teased. "What else does the commander have you doing while you're pushing paper at the precinct? Posing for beefcake calendars like those hose draggers at the firehouse?"

"Nah," Joey chimed in around his toothpick, "Nick's too busy being the new poster boy for the FCPD." There was another round of laughter. Nick threw Joey a sharp look.

"Poster boy?" I asked. Nick shook his head, color rising in his cheeks.

"The department's had a lot of bad press," Samara explained. "Last year, a couple of dirty cops got caught working side hustles for the mob boss Feliks Zhirov. Zhirov skated—mishandling of evidence—and the local news outlets had a field day with it." A muscle tightened in Nick's jaw as she continued. "The PR rep at the department decided we needed to do something to improve community relations, so they came up with a plan to expand the annual citizen's police academy into some big dog and pony show—you know, win over the hearts and minds of the people we serve by letting them get a real hands-on, behind-the-scenes experience—only no one signed up. Then, after Nick's investigation led to Zhirov's arrest last fall and Nick's picture made it all over the news, PR got this wild idea to make Detective Hot Shit here the face of the new and improved FCPD Citizen's Police Academy. Suddenly, everyone and their grandmother started signing up, most of them women," she said with a wink.

"The rest of us got roped into teaching," Wade groused. "Now we all get to waste a week showing Rotary Club grandmas how to handle a gun and answering stupid questions for a campus full of horny soccer moms."

My sister smacked Wade on the back of the head as she returned from her game of darts. "It's going to be fun, Wade, and we're *all* going to be there to support Nick."

Sam turned in her seat and smiled up at my sister. "Now there's a thought," she said, tapping her chin with a French-polished fingernail. "Finlay should come to the police academy next week."

The color drained from Nick's face.

"That's probably not a great idea," I said quickly.

"What are you talking about? It's perfect!" Georgia said, her eyes wide with excitement. "You can ask us all your weird writer questions and get loads of ideas for your book."

"What do you say, Finlay?" Sam asked. "There are a few beds left in the academy dorm. If we register you tonight, we can probably hold you a seat on the bus. I can do it right now." She pulled out her phone.

"Bus?" I asked my sister.

"Think of it like a cop sleepaway camp."

Nick rolled his eyes at her.

"Georgia," I started, pretty sure I was speaking for both me and Nick when I said, "I really don't think now is a good time."

"It's only a week," she argued. "And you already said Steven has the kids. It's perfect. Vero should come, too."

"Come where?" Vero asked, returning from the dartboard with a very interested rookie cop in tow.

"Citizen's police academy," my sister said. "It starts next week. We're all going to be there."

"You're joking, right? A week? In cop school? With all of you?" Vero chuckled darkly as her scheming eyes circled the group. "That sounds *absolutely perfect,* Finlay! We'd have to be *idiots* to say no."

"No," I said firmly.

"We're in." Vero clapped her hands. "Someone sign us up."

"Already on it." Samara gestured for Georgia to take the empty seat beside her. My sister flushed as Sam scooted close, angling her cell phone so they both could see the screen.

Nick leaned toward my ear. "You don't have to do this," he said in a low voice.

"Come on, Nick." Roddy's rumbling baritone boomed over the table as he reached to scoop a handful of peanuts from the bowl. "It'll be a great PR angle. Think of the headlines! *Local suspense novelist gets hands-on with Fairfax County Police in preparation to write her next bestseller.*"

Vero wagged an eyebrow. "Finlay could definitely use a little *hands-on* research."

I shot her a look.

"Finlay's right," Nick said. "It's a bad idea. Tell 'em, Joe."

Joey's eyes caught mine across the table. The gleam in them made my insides squirm. "It's not a *terrible* idea."

"Done!" Samara said, dropping her phone in her purse. "We saved you two seats on the bus, but there was only one room left in the dorm, so you and Vero will have to bunk together."

"It's fine," Vero assured her, "I'll bring earplugs in case she snores."

"Would you excuse us for a minute?" I got up from my seat and steered Vero by the elbow to the ladies' room, throwing open the door and locking the bolt behind us. I checked for feet under the stall doors before rounding on her. "What are you doing?"

"Are you kidding me right now? You are looking a gift horse in the mouth. This is kismet."

"This is insane!"

"This is exactly the opportunity we need! Steven has the kids, I need a safe place to lie low until we can sell the Aston, and you need to find *EasyClean*. Problem solved. And think of all the research you could do for your book!"

"Research for my book is what got us into this mess in the first place!"

"And now, it's what's going to get us out." Mouths set, we stared at each other, each waiting for the other to cave.

I sank back against the sink and rubbed my eyes. Maybe it was kismet, but that didn't change the fact that Nick obviously wasn't a fan of the idea. Or that Joey seemed a little too eager, probably for the same reasons I should be—because we both suspected each other of something, and this was the perfect opportunity to keep an eye on each other.

Well, screw him. Two could play at that game. If Joey thought I was a criminal, he certainly wasn't going to prove it while I was stuck in a training academy surrounded by police officers. I, on the other hand, was hunting for a dirty cop, and this was as good a chance as any to get close to a whole lot of them and figure out which one it was.

"Fine," I said. "We'll go."

Vero jumped on her toes and hugged me hard enough to knock the wind out of me. "This is going to be so much fun! I swear, Finn, you won't regret it."

The scary part was, I already did.

CHAPTER 8

I stayed in the bathroom when Vero returned to the bar. Hands braced on the sink ledge, I hung my head, hiding from my own reflection in the mirror. Nick was right. This was a horrible idea. It didn't matter that it had been an accident; I'd killed a man while trying to sell a car which had been purchased for me with Feliks Zhirov's blood money. I had no business attending a citizen's police academy, much less sitting around their table in a bar. And a sympathy kiss was definitely out of the question.

It was too late to change Vero's mind about going. I would just have to avoid spending too much time with Nick.

My phone vibrated with a notification. A photo from Steven and the kids, the three of them making silly faces in their pajamas. I texted back a quick reply.

Finlay: *Thanks for the pic. Glad you're all having fun.*

Three dots rolled across the screen as Steven typed a response.

Steven: *Delia mentioned there's a drip in her bathroom faucet. Want me to go over to the house and fix it? I can change the air filters and replace the batteries in the smoke detectors while I'm there.*

As tempting as that was, Vero was probably right about setting boundaries.

> Finlay: *Thanks, but it can wait until I get home. Give the kids a kiss for me.*

I tucked my phone away and took a deep breath before returning to the bar. Vero was already chatting up Tyrese and Officer Roddy by the dartboards, and since we'd agreed it would be smart to spread out and talk to as many of our suspects as possible, I returned to the table we had abandoned.

Nick's chair was empty. Joey was sitting in mine, engrossed in a game of poker with Samara, Georgia, and Wade. I dragged over a chair, discreetly searching the bar for Nick as I sat down. I spotted him in a booth a few feet away, hunching over the table as he talked in low tones with an attractive, bookish-looking man in horn-rimmed glasses. I turned to Sam as my sister considered her cards.

"Who's Nick talking to?" I whispered.

She leaned around me to see. "That's Stu, our department's shrink."

Stu's ice water sat untouched on a napkin beside him. He hadn't even bothered taking off his coat. "Does he always hang out with OCN on Thursday nights?"

"Nope," she said, drawing a card and placing a peanut in the middle of the table. "*Dr.* Kirby's not really the cutting loose type."

"Then why's he here?" I asked. Joey glanced up from his cards at me, rolling his toothpick around in his mouth. I pretended not to notice.

"Feliks's attorney is playing dirty," Sam said, "trying to have one of Nick's witness statements thrown out, claiming the witness isn't competent to testify. Nick asked Stu for his professional opinion since Stu met with her a couple of times after her arrest." Stu pushed an envelope across the table to Nick. Nick opened it, skimming the contents. "I'm guessing Stu's letter to the prosecutor is in that envelope. Either that or Nick's clearance to get back to work."

I turned back to Sam, surprised. "I thought Nick was running the police academy thing."

"Only because he hasn't been cleared to do much else." At my puzzled look, she went on to explain. "Counseling is standard protocol after an officer-involved shooting. Hell, any of us would have needed a few extra sessions with Stu after what Nick survived."

"How about you two quit gossiping and deal." Joey threw down his losing hand as Wade dragged the pile of peanuts toward him. "Nick asked Stu to teach a couple of classes at the academy next week. I bet that's why he's here."

Samara raised an eyebrow at Joey. "I'll take that bet."

Wade pushed three peanuts to the center of the table. "My money's on Sam."

"Me, too," Georgia said, tossing in a few peanuts from her pile.

Sam shuffled the deck as Nick and Dr. Kirby rose from their booth.

Georgia called out to them. "Hey, Doc. Want to stick around and play a few rounds? We're just getting started."

Stu paused beside our table as he buttoned his coat. "Your stakes look a little rich for my blood," he said with a self-deprecating smile, earning a laugh from everyone, "but I'll see you all next week." He turned to Nick and lowered his voice. "I'll see you Tuesday evening after your classes let out."

Nick nodded once, his eyes dull as Stu left the bar. Joey, Wade, Georgia, and Sam all glanced up from their cards to look at him. I'd thought I couldn't feel more guilty than I had in the bathroom just now, but I'd been wrong. Less than an hour ago, Nick had been sympathizing with me over everything I'd been through, telling me I didn't need to apologize for needing time and not calling him back. I had been so afraid of what I might accidentally say to him if I did, I hadn't stopped to consider that he might have just needed someone to listen. The weight of a hundred crushed cars settled on my chest. It only grew heavier when he didn't sit down.

"I've got an early morning tomorrow, so I'm going to head out," he said, grabbing his jacket from the back of his chair.

"What'd Stu want?" Joey asked, reaching for the pile of peanuts.

Nick held up the envelope. "He says Theresa Hall is fit to testify. I want to get this letter to the prosecutor before Kat has a chance to dig her heels into this."

Sam raised her middle finger at Joey as she swept her winnings toward her.

Nick pulled a few bills from his wallet and left them on the table to cover his portion of the tab. "Drive safe," he said to no one in particular. A chorus of goodbyes rang out from various corners of the room. He paused beside me, his smile bittersweet. "It was good seeing you, Finlay."

I gave an awkward wave as he limped toward the door, angry and frustrated with myself as I watched it close behind him.

"You just going to sit there?" my sister muttered at her cards. She smirked as I jumped out of my chair and grabbed my coat.

"Nick, wait," I called out, rushing after him as his cane clicked across the parking lot.

He turned, hunched against the icy rain that had begun to fall as I caught up to him. For a moment, we just stood beside his car, staring at each other. "Do you want to get in?" His voice was husky, the air between us crackling, the same way it always seemed to whenever we were alone together.

"No," I said quickly. "I mean, I shouldn't." I shouldn't want to get in his car, but I did. And that was precisely the problem. "I just wanted to say I'm sorry for not calling you, and that I wasn't upset. Not with you." His eyes were intent on mine. His cheeks were flushed and his breath was warm. Our clothes were getting wet, and his offer was becoming more tempting by the second. I shivered, but I didn't think it was from the cold. "I should get back inside. I'll see you next week."

"I'm really glad you came tonight," he said as I backed away from his car.

It wasn't a lie when I said, "I am, too."

CHAPTER 9

Tyrese, Vero, and I were the last to leave Hooligans. An icy rain had begun falling in earnest and we pulled our hoods low, our chins tucked to our chests to fend it off as Ty held the door for us and we ducked out of the bar. I climbed into the van and stuck the key in the ignition, offering a prayer of thanks to the automotive gods when the engine started without much protest. A salt truck rushed past the parking lot, kicking up a spray of slush, its yellow roof light swirling, and I backed out of my parking space and eased onto the road, following behind it.

"What did you think?" Vero asked.

"You spent as much time with them as I did."

"Maybe. But your conversation with Joey felt a little on the nose."

The mention of it drew a chill out of me. Joey had been the first cop to show up tonight. Was that a coincidence, or was he just being thorough, careful not to miss any critical bits of conversations, same as we had been? And there had been all those perfectly vague references he'd made about odd jobs being hard to find after the holidays, how they were a little lean this year . . . *you know how it is, right?*

But Joey had been so convincing when he'd told me where he'd been the night of the shooting. And Mrs. Haggerty claimed she had indeed had a conversation with a police officer that night, specifically one that had been driving a sedan and had been talking with something in his mouth, like that damn omnipresent toothpick Joey was always chewing whenever he was somewhere he couldn't smoke. "I'm still not sure," I said, reluctant to let go of my suspicions. "What about Roddy and Tyrese? You spent a lot of time with them."

Vero shivered and cranked up the heat. "Tyrese is a definite no. He's greener than that stack of cash Kat was waving around. And he's too damn eager to please. *EasyClean*'s too confident to be a rookie; he's definitely been around the block. Now, Roddy," she said thoughtfully, letting his name sit a little longer on her tongue, "he might be worth checking out."

"Why do you say that?"

"Roddy was doing surveillance in front of your house the night of the shooting. If Joey's telling the truth, he was parked in front of Mrs. Haggerty's that night so Roddy could take a break and grab some dinner. But what if Roddy didn't go to dinner? What if he went after Steven instead?"

"Roddy?" I stole a sideways glance at her. Roddy was a middle-aged beat cop, and by the looks of the strained buttons at his waist, he'd been wearing the same uniform for quite some time. "Huh," I mused as I considered that. "Why do you suppose Roddy hangs out with all the big shot detectives from OCN?"

Vero put her fingertip to her nose. "I wondered the same thing about Wade. A firearms instructor would definitely know how to shoot." She raised an eyebrow. "And then there's Samara . . ."

"What about her?"

"Who's better equipped to find and manipulate an internet forum to her own advantage than someone who works in cyber forensics? She was probably the first person Nick called after Cam tipped him off to the website. Don't you think it's a little convenient that the forum had already *disappeared,*" she said, punctuating the word with air quotes, "by the time Sam tried to find it the next morning?"

"Feliks's people took it down overnight."

"Or did they?"

Vero had a point. Feliks had agreed to take the site down, but that doesn't mean he was the only one who'd had a hand in erasing it—or a reason to.

Salt from the truck in front of us peppered the hood of my minivan. I put on my turn signal, checking my mirrors as I switched lanes. The vehicle behind me switched lanes, too, pulling in close behind me. The driver's features were obscured by the bright shine of his headlights. All I could make out was the slap of his wipers and the Chevy symbol on the grill.

"What's wrong?" Vero asked as the light changed.

"I think we're being followed."

I accelerated around the salt truck and merged back into the right lane. Vero angled in her seat, watching the Chevy change lanes, too.

"We're definitely being followed, Finn. What if it's another one of Marco's guys?"

I sped up. "Maybe we should call Georgia."

"And tell her what? What if this guy knows what happened in the salvage yard last night?" Vero sank low in her seat, gnawing her thumbnail as I was forced to stop at a red light. My eyes leapt to the rearview mirror as the Chevy rolled to a stop behind us and the driver opened his door.

"Crap." I jerked the wheel hard, darting into the entrance of the strip mall beside us.

"What are you doing?" Vero braced herself against the dashboard as I cut through the parking lot, searching for another exit. I slammed on the brakes, skidding on the sleet as a black Camaro cut in front of my hood and jerked to a stop.

The driver's side door flew open and a hooded figure stormed out. He strode toward the passenger side of the van, his silhouette distorted through Vero's ice-crusted window.

"Put the van in reverse!" Vero shouted. I shifted into reverse and hit the gas. My tires whined, spinning uselessly on the ice. "Why aren't we moving?"

"My tires are bald!"

"Why the hell didn't you have them replaced?"

"Because tires are expensive and you gambled away all our money!"

The man pounded on Vero's window, cussing as the tires kicked sleet at him. He reached for the handle of Vero's door.

"Hell no, you don't!" She unbuckled her seat belt, put her right foot flat against the passenger door as she released the handle, and kicked the car door open. The doorframe bounced off the man's forehead. His hood fell back and his feet flew out from under him, dropping him on his ass in a pile of slush.

"Oh, shit." Vero ducked back in her seat, her eyes wide as she slammed her door. "It's Javi."

I lowered the passenger window. Javi's cheeks were flushed with anger and his lashes were dotted with ice. A goose egg–size bruise was already darkening the middle of his forehead and blood trickled over one irate eyebrow. Vero cringed and raised her window as Javi slowly stood up.

He slid the back door open. It smacked against the end of its track and bounced off his shoulder. Teeth gritted, he climbed into Delia's seat and slammed the door shut. A puddle was spreading from the hems of his jeans, and he did not look at all happy to be sitting in my daughter's booster seat.

I put the car in park and rummaged in my purse for a wet wipe. "Here," I said, passing one back to him. He took it with a begrudged "thanks."

Vero peeked over the back of her seat and gestured to his forehead. "A little rose hip and some vitamin E will help minimize scarring."

"You know what else minimizes scarring? Not beating the crap out of me when I'm trying to help you!"

"Help me?" Vero snapped as she rose on her knees.

"I've seen you three times in three days, and I've got a concussion, a soup burn, and I probably need stitches! If I thought you had it in you to kill someone, I might actually be worried!"

Vero whirled to me. "Not one word!" she warned me as a dark laugh bubbled out of me. "What the hell are you doing here anyway?" she asked, turning her glare back on Javi.

"I've been waiting outside that bar for you all night."

"How did you know I was at the bar?"

Javi pulled a phone from his pocket. His eyes bored into hers as he held it up and depressed a button. A faint ring started deep in Vero's purse. The ringtone wasn't Vero's, and judging by the slightly murderous expression on Javi's face, I was guessing he knew that, too. "Traced my stolen phone to the bar. You want to explain what it's doing in your bag?"

I dropped my head to the steering wheel.

"Not exactly," Vero answered. With a roll of her eyes, she fished his wallet and phone from her purse and dropped them in his outstretched hand. "You could have just come into the bar instead of running us down in your car like some kind of lunatic."

He pulled a face. "You're kidding, right? That place was crawling with cops. Figured I was better off waiting for the asshole who mugged me to come out. Didn't figure half the FCPD would be walking you to your car."

"I did *not* mug you, so don't you even go accusing me of that! Finlay and I found you that way. And just because a guy holds a door open for me doesn't give you the right to get all pissy about it."

Javi settled back against the booster seat, the tension in the van abating as he lowered his voice. "If you found me that way, then why'd you take my stuff?"

"Why do you keep so many condoms in your wallet?"

"Who's pissy now?"

Vero's mouth snapped shut. She turned around in her seat. "We emptied your pockets on the way to the hospital in case the doctors needed to cut off your clothes."

"For a concussion?"

"Happens all the time. If you watched *Grey's Anatomy,* you'd know."

Javi shook his head. "Are you going to tell me what really happened last night?"

"Do I have to?"

"You want me to ask Ramón?"

Sleet pinged off the car as Javi and Vero stared at each other.

"You might as well tell him," I suggested cautiously, hoping she'd read in my tone the details she should probably leave out. "We have to get rid of the car somehow. It can't stay where it is." Not anymore.

"What car?" Javi's eyes glinted as I met them in the rearview mirror.

Vero threw up her hands, deferring to me.

"How long would it take you to strip and sell off an Aston Martin Superleggera?" I asked him.

A low chuckle of disbelief started in Javi's chest. It died as he looked from Vero to me, then back again. "What the hell are you doing with a car like that?"

"It's a long story," Vero said.

"Does your cousin know?"

"It's in the shed in his scrapyard."

"If he knows about the car, then why all the secrecy the other night?"

"Ramón made me promise not to tell anyone." Javi slouched into the booster seat like the wind had been knocked out of him. He scrubbed a hand over his face, staring through the icy window beside him. "It's not what you think, Javi. He just worries. He doesn't want his garage tangled up with anything questionable."

Javi's laugh was cynical. "I've known Ramón my entire fucking life, V. I promise you, it's not the garage he's worried about." His eyes found mine in the mirror. "How much do you need for it?"

"As much as you can get without raising any red flags," I said. "We can't have it traced."

"I take ten percent off the top."

"So do the people I owe," Vero muttered.

Javi swore, shaking his head as if he was holding back a lecture. He leaned forward in his seat with a heavy sigh. "Give me the keys. I need to take a look at it before I make any calls." He held up a hand when Vero started to protest. "I'll go after hours. I won't say anything to Ramón. I promise," he added.

Vero unspooled the shed key from her key ring and passed it back to Javi with a quiet thanks. He slipped it in his pocket and pulled up his hood. "I'll come by Finlay's house in a couple of days and let you know how long it'll take to unload it."

"We won't be home," Vero said as he slid open the van door.

His face was unreadable under the shadow of his coat. He pulled his cell phone from his pocket and tossed it to her.

"Keep it on. I'll know where to find you." He got out and loped to his car before either of us could warn him not to come looking for us.

CHAPTER 10

Vero and I boarded the charter bus to the citizen's police academy just after sunrise on Monday morning. I fell into one of the last available seats toward the back, cradling my thermos of coffee, my eyelids already threatening to drift shut. I'd been up most of the night, staring down my revision for Sylvia, and while I had no problem envisioning the hot cop's very impressive assets (or what the heroine would like to do with them), whenever I began typing, the bad guys closed in and someone managed to die. Last night, it had been a huge, tattooed street fighter named Refrigerator Mike whom my heroine had mowed down with her car, and at four in the morning, before crawling into bed, I'd deleted the entire chapter.

Vero nudged me awake as she arched up in her seat, checking out the other passengers around us. "Did you know Mrs. Haggerty was coming?" she whispered.

I sat up, holding my thermos away from me as coffee dribbled from a leak in the top. "Where?" Vero pointed to a nest of gray hair a few rows in front of us. Great. The woman who'd been watching my house like it was a Netflix Original would be spending a week getting up close and personal with the detectives who were unknowingly investigating us.

"Who's her friend?" Vero asked as Mrs. Haggerty chatted up the tall, attractive gentleman seated beside her. He looked familiar, but it took me a minute to place him.

"I think that's her grandson." He'd visited her over the holidays, and I vaguely remembered a rushed and clumsy introduction as he was taking out her trash and I was emptying my mailbox.

I clutched my chest as a head popped up in the seat in front of me. A young woman in tortoiseshell glasses smiled at us over her headrest. She didn't look much older than Vero, and I wondered how she had afforded the police academy registration. The week of room and board hadn't been cheap, and after considering the meager funds in both of our accounts, Vero and I had charged the fees to my credit card. A young man with a shock of unruly red hair popped up beside her. He extended his hand over the headrest. "I'm Riley. This is Maxine," he said, hitching his thumb toward the girl.

"Call me Max," she insisted. "We're so excited for police academy! Aren't you?"

Vero jabbed an elbow in my ribs before I could answer that.

"What do you all do?" Max asked us.

"Finlay is a famous author—"

"I'm really not," I corrected Vero. Judging by the likely trajectory of my career, infamous was probably more accurate.

"And I'm her accountant. We're here doing research for her next romantic suspense novel."

Max's eyes went wide over her seat back. "Seriously? Riley and I are in the entertainment business, too. We're podcasters."

"True crime," Riley explained. "We're recording a behind-the-scenes series about criminal investigations. We're going to document everything we do this week for our show."

"We'd love to feature you," Max suggested. "You know, ask you some questions about why you came and what you hope to get out of your week here. I bet people would be really interested to hear how you get your ideas."

My smile was so tight, it hurt. "I bet they would."

"She'd be happy to," Vero said, throwing me on the altar.

The bus started moving and Riley and Max turned back in their seats.

"We're not talking to anyone this week," I whispered. "We have one job, and that's to find *EasyClean*."

"Correction. You have two jobs. One for Feliks and one for Sylvia. You're going to finish your revision so we can get paid."

"I can't do the revision."

"You *can* do it, because I'm going to help you."

"How are you going to help?"

"I'm going to kick you in the ass until you get it done yourself. And you never know," she said, reclining her seat as the bus bounced over the interstate, "a few days away from the kids, living in a dorm, doing hands-on research with a bunch of hot, fit police officers might inspire you."

I didn't need inspiration. I needed a new career. One that didn't involve police officers, corpses, or the Russian mob.

"So what's the plan?" Vero asked.

"Same as the bar. We spread out and get close to as many of them as possible. We ask a lot of questions and hope one of them lets something slip."

"When do I get to snoop?"

"I'll do the snooping."

"Why do you get to do the snooping? You're terrible at snooping."

"I'm not terrible at snooping."

"Last time you did the snooping, you needed an emergency extraction involving my cousin and a tow truck, and you still got busted sneaking out of Theresa's house. *I'll* handle the snooping."

"We'll discuss it." I turned toward the window, watching the traffic thin as the suburbs gave way to rolling fields and the smoky outline of the Blue Ridge Mountains on the horizon. The regional Public Safety Training Facility had been constructed on the grounds of a former detention center in rural Prince William County, a few miles west of the regional forensics lab Nick and I had visited last fall. I thumbed the tiny bullet in my pocket, the one we'd managed to retrieve from the Aston Martin after my run-in with *EasyClean*. Georgia had mentioned some of the forensic techs might be teaching classes this week. With any luck, maybe one of them could look at the bullet and tell us more about it.

The two charter buses slowed as we reached the campus, pausing at a security booth before proceeding through a gate. The grounds were ringed in forests and razor wire. Low brick buildings dotted the landscape, a running track and a handful of training fields visible just beyond them through the fence. A five-story tower loomed like a sentry in the distance. Through my window, I could just make out the fire department logo on its cinder block walls.

Vero and I followed the other ninety-six students off the charter buses into a nearly empty parking lot. A handful of older-model police cars occupied spaces designated for training vehicles, their paint scratched and their fenders dimpled with dents. A few ambulances were scattered among them, bearing the training center's logo. Beyond the parking lot, a skid-marked driving track was dotted in orange cones.

Vero and I huddled close to each other for warmth as we waited in line with the other academy students. We rolled our luggage beside us, our computer bags riding on top so they wouldn't absorb the puddles on the blacktop. The line moved slowly toward a folding table covered in welcome packets and lanyards with our names printed on them. A man in a gray sweatsuit emblazoned with the word INSTRUCTOR greeted us before we reached the table.

"Names?" he prompted, consulting his clipboard.

"Veronica Ruiz," Vero said. He marked a check by her name.

"Finlay Donovan." I tried not to stare at the thick raised scar that stretched from the right side of his mouth and disappeared under his FCPD beanie.

The man glanced up from his papers. A small smile tugged at the unblemished side of his mouth. "So you're the Finlay I've been hearing so much about. I believe you might owe me some money."

"But I already paid," I said, stretching up on my toes to find my name on his clipboard.

He tucked it behind him with a raspy laugh, his smile strained by the confines of his scar. "The day I turned in my badge, I bet Nick Anthony a hundred bucks that he'd never find a partner he liked better than me. The week he met you, he showed up on my front porch to collect, and he hasn't stopped talking about you since. Name's Charlie." He extended a hand to me.

A relieved sigh rushed out of me. "You're Nick's former partner," I said, shaking his hand. "I've heard a lot about you, too." Nick and Charlie had worked together for years, until Charlie was diagnosed with oral cancer. His treatment had forced him into early retirement, which was how Nick had ended up becoming partners with Joey.

"Nice work with the Molotov cocktails, by the way," Charlie said, checking my name off his clipboard. "Just do me a favor and try not to set anything on fire during your stay here, ladies."

Vero's laugh was dubious.

"We'll try not to," I assured him. His warm brown eyes crinkled with his smile, and I could see why Charlie's absence had been so hard for Nick.

Charlie pointed to the next check-in station. "Take your luggage to the uniformed officer and set your bags on the table to be searched so we can get you to class."

"Searched?" I asked.

"Students aren't permitted to bring personal firearms or weapons of any kind, and no alcohol or illegal drugs are allowed inside the facility. That's why we opted for the buses," he said, gesturing to the empty charter bus behind us. "Otherwise, the gate becomes a revolving door after classes let out every afternoon. It's easier on the staff if we only have to search everyone once." He pointed to a second set of tables. "After your bags are checked, pick up your welcome packets and name tags. Inside, you'll find your room keys, your schedule, a map of the campus, and your health and safety waivers. Sign your waivers, take your bags to your dorm, change into comfortable workout attire, and report promptly to the drill field. Leave your cell phones in your room." He checked his watch. "Your first session starts in twenty-two minutes. You might want to hustle, ladies. It's a push-up for every minute you're late."

Vero and I turned to find we were last in line. We grabbed our Rollaboards and dragged them across the pavement. Once we were through inspections, we followed the last of the stragglers to the dormitory, hefting our luggage up the two flights of stairs to the third floor.

Vero unlocked our room and flung open the door.

"This is it?" She dropped her bags at the foot of one of the metal-framed beds. The springs creaked as she tested the thin plastic mattress with her foot. A single pillow had been issued to each of us, along with a blanket and a set of starchy white sheets. But what I noticed most was what the room didn't have . . . no demanding toddlers or diapers to be changed, no dishes to wash or laundry to sort, no pushy ex-husbands, no demanding agents, and, best of all, no dead people. Maybe this week wouldn't be so bad after all.

I collapsed face-first onto the bed, wondering how long they might let us stay. "You think they were serious about the push-ups?" I asked.

Vero pulled back the blind and looked toward the drill field. "We'd better get changed. I don't want to find out."

We shed our jeans and boots, trading them for yoga pants and sneakers. Bundled in hats and gloves, we drew our lanyards on over our sweatshirts and hurried to the drill field. Nick's eyes lifted to mine as Vero and I caught up to the group. His subtle grin was only slightly reassuring as I looked past him and spotted Joey staring at me over crossed arms. Charlie glanced at his watch and gave us a discreet thumbs-up.

"Good morning, everyone." Nick spoke into a bullhorn, projecting his voice over the throng of students. "Welcome to citizen's police academy. I'm Detective Nicholas Anthony, your academy coordinator and an investigator in the Organized Crime and Narcotics division of the Fairfax County Police Department." A few excited titters rose from the group. I looked around me at the disproportionate ratio of women to men, certain I recognized some of the mothers from Delia's preschool among them.

"Your instructors this week are all current or former law enforcement professionals, all of them experts in their fields," he continued. "Please feel free to ask questions. The goal of this program is to help give you a taste of what it's like to be a police officer, so throughout the week, you will have opportunities to participate in some hands-on training." A woman in front of me let out a wolf whistle. A handful of others *whooped*, prompting laughter from the group. Nick's grin was indulgent behind his megaphone. "These exercises will require your undivided attention, so for your safety, we ask that you do not bring your cell phones to class." Nick waited for the chorus of groans to quiet. "Since you are not here in a professional capacity, you may sit out and observe any exercises that you wish. If you choose to participate, we will be awarding points to the top performers, and certificates will be presented to the winners on the final night of our program."

"What do we get if we win?" Vero called out.

"Bragging rights," Nick replied. "And the admiration of your instructors." A few of the instructors chuckled. Tyrese winked at her.

"I can live with that," Vero said, raising a playful eyebrow back.

Nick's cane clicked as he paced the front of our group. "We're going to start our training today by demonstrating the intense physical examinations new recruits are subject to before being considered for admission to the police academy. You will be completing the agility course with a partner," he said, pointing to the arranged orange cones behind him. "Learning to work with a partner is a critical part of what we do. Partnership is about trust and teamwork. A great partner can make or break a case, but they can also save your life in the field." Nick's eyes flitted to mine. Joey stared a hole through me over Nick's shoulder. I had the uneasy feeling he'd been watching me all morning, and I was liking it less and less. "You and your partner will be carrying a life-size dummy through a portion of the course. The dummy weighs one hundred and fifty pounds, so those of you with physical restrictions who wish to sit out the agility course may do so—"

Vero turned to whisper in my ear. "One hundred fifty pounds? That's nothing," she said. "Harris definitely weighed more than that. And don't even get me started on Andrei Borov— Ow!" she yelped as I stepped hard on her toe.

"After you've delivered your dummy to the finish line," Nick called out, "you will complete four laps around the track. Points will be awarded for the fastest completion times for each section of the course. Are there any questions?" He surveyed the class. "Then partner up and form a line beside the nearest set of cones. Those of you sitting this one out will be assisting the instructors. Take a clipboard and a stopwatch and report to Officer Roddy for instructions."

I spotted Roddy's head above the crowd and started toward him. Vero pulled me up short. "What are you doing?"

"I'm observing."

"No way," she said, pulling me toward the cones. "We are here to get the full experience."

"No," I corrected her in a harsh whisper. "*We* are here to find *EasyClean*."

"And *we* are not going to do it sitting on the sidelines. Even Mrs. Haggerty is getting in on the action." Vero pointed downfield at my elderly neighbor. Her bright pink running shoes matched her lipstick, and her sweatpants were emblazoned with the word JUICY on the ass. Her grandson held her hand as she attempted a few tame stretches.

"I don't think we have to worry about Team Neighborhood Watch," I said.

"Maybe not, but check out Riley and Max." Vero tipped her head toward the podcasters as they performed exaggerated lunges by the starting line. "Those two did not come to play. But I'm pretty sure they're in worse shape than you, so stick with me and try to keep up."

I rolled my eyes as Vero sat on the ground and reached for her toes. She smacked my leg and gesticulated for me to start stretching, too. Ty squatted beside her and leaned close to her ear. "Want a little pro tip?" he offered. Vero nodded, eager for an advantage. "Bend from the knees and let your legs do the work. Women carry most of their strength in their lower body, and the dummy's a lot denser than it looks."

"No kidding," she said, glaring after him as he jogged onto the course. "Did he just mansplain to me the most effective way to move a body? That's it," she said, getting up and rolling her sleeves. "Now we definitely have to win this thing."

"You don't have to do this, you know." I turned at the sound of Nick's voice beside my ear, coming face-to-face with the whistle hanging around his neck.

"Yes, she does," Vero said.

Nick smirked over his stopwatch. "Okay, then. Ready?"

"Wait," Vero said. "I have a question about the dummy. Does the body have to be in one piece when we move it, or is there some wiggle room in the rules for that? Because I was thinking—"

"We're ready!" I pushed Vero toward the starting line. "Are you nuts?" I whispered to the back of her head.

"It was a legitimate question!"

The whistle blew. Vero darted onto the course. She took a running leap toward a high wall made from smooth wooden boards, hooking one hand over the top and dragging herself up to straddle it. Perched on top, she craned her neck to find Riley and Max.

"Move your ass, Finlay!" she shouted down at me. "You can run faster than that! Breathe! In through the nose, out through the mouth!"

"This isn't Lamaze!"

"Come on, push!"

"What would you know about pushing!" I clasped her outstretched hand and pulled myself up the wall with a grunt, teetering like a seesaw when I reached the peak and nearly plummeting face-first down the other side. Vero vaulted neatly off the top, landing on her feet as I slid down the wall on my belly. By the time I made it to the bottom, Vero was already at the next obstacle, facedown on the ground, army-crawling on her elbows under a web of ropes.

"You've got to be kidding me," I said, panting as I watched her feet disappear under the nylon mesh.

"You can do it, Finlay!" she called over her shoulder. "It's just like the car at the salvage yard!"

"That's not helping!" With a resigned *fuck,* I ducked down on my knees and scooted on my belly under the ropes, following the soles of Vero's shoes and blinking away the dirt she was kicking into my eyes.

Vero scrambled out the other side. She rose on her toes, checking the progress of our competition. "We're gaining on them, Finn. Hurry!"

When I emerged, Vero hauled me to my feet. I ducked after her through a concrete tunnel. Then over a concrete tunnel. We high-stepped through a series of tires, then over a beam on a swinging contraption made of more ropes. When we made it to the end, filthy and exhausted, our CPR dummy was waiting for us, supine on the ground.

Vero and I took a moment, hands on our knees, breathing hard, sweat dampening our hairlines as we surveyed the competition. Riley and Max were already wrestling with their dummy, the deadweight of its loose limbs dragging on the ground as they tried and failed to surge ahead. Riley stumbled backward, holding the dummy's feet. Max's arms were hooked under the dummy's armpits as she struggled to hold the weight of its head and torso without tripping on the arms.

"True crime, my ass," Vero muttered.

Mrs. Haggerty's grandson jogged past us. Mrs. Haggerty's arms were around his neck, her spindly legs looped around his sides. She glanced over at me with a wild grin, holding fast to her grandson's neck as he bent to pick up their dummy. With a grunt, he hoisted it into his arms and forged ahead with Mrs. Haggerty bouncing like a jockey on his back.

The woman was being *carried* to the finish line.

"Give me the string from your hoodie," I panted, tugging my own through the hole in the neckline of my sweatshirt. I knelt beside our dummy's arms. Vero knelt beside its feet. A moment later, we had the dummy trussed like a pig. "Count of three," I said when she nodded she was ready.

We started walking in slow, coordinated movements. Together, we lengthened our strides, our pace quickening as we fell into a rhythm, the dummy swinging between us. The teams on either side of us paused to watch, their mouths falling open. Mrs. Haggerty's grandson did a double take as we passed him. "We really are exceptionally good at this, you know," Vero said through labored breaths. "It sort of reminds me of—"

"Don't say it!" We might as well have duct-taped the dummy to a skateboard and rolled him to the finish line for all the attention we were drawing to ourselves, but I'd be damned if I'd let Mrs. Haggerty win this.

The white chalk line came into view and Vero and I stumbled over it, dropping the dummy to the ground at Roddy's feet. He clicked his stopwatch, frowning at the restraints around the dummy's ankles.

Vero and I lumbered to the empty track, exhaling heavy ribbons of fog as we started our laps. Vero led the way to the inside lane, hopeful of holding the advantage as the other teams started to follow. I kept pace alongside her, letting my eyes wander to the bleachers, then over the sidelines as we fell into a brisk jog, unable to shake the feeling we were being watched. As we rounded the first turn, I glanced back toward the obstacle course. Joey stood over our dummy, hands on his hips, his narrowed eyes trailing us as we rounded the track.

CHAPTER 11

With stilted movements, Vero and I carried our lunch trays through the crowded cafeteria to an empty table in the back. My legs had felt like Jell-O by the time we'd finished our laps around the track, but the numbness had been short-lived, and I dreaded the sore muscles I was sure to have by the next morning.

Vero picked at the contents of her sandwich. She lifted the edge of her bologna and sniffed. "Are you sure we're not in prison? I'm pretty sure this is prison food."

"I wouldn't know." During the handful of hours I'd spent in a jail after Nick had caught me breaking into one, no one had offered me anything to eat. But the soggy PB&J on my tray was an excellent reason to never go back.

The door to the faculty lounge opened at the far end of the cafeteria, revealing a glimpse of the utopian smorgasbord on the other side. Tables were decked out with carafes of coffee, plates of cookies and breads, and trays of assorted cheeses, deli meats, and fruit. Samara came through the door, holding a chocolate chip cookie that could have doubled as a dinner plate, her heels snapping against the floor tiles as she cut through the cafeteria. She paused beside our table when she spotted us.

"Hey, you made it!" Her smile held a touch of pity as she took in our dirt-crusted sweats and the stray hairs slicked to our brows. "How are you two holding up?"

"I'll let you know in the morning," I said, rolling my sore shoulder.

"If it's any consolation, I heard you two killed it in the agility course today. We've got bets going in the faculty lounge."

"Is the food any better in there?" I asked.

Vero leaned across me and said in a low voice, "She means, is there any booze in there and who do we have to kill to get some?"

Sam laughed. "Sorry, no booze. I would offer to smuggle you some, except I hear the hard-ass who runs this academy frowns on that sort of thing." She tipped her head to me. "But if you play your cards right, I bet he would sneak you a bottle." She winked and I felt my cheeks warm. "I've got to return some emails before class. You all hang in there. The afternoon session's a doozy. Don't let Lieutenant Hamamoto rough you up too much." She took a huge bite of her cookie as she sashayed out the door.

"That's it," Vero said. "We're breaking into the faculty lounge tonight."

"No, we're not. Stealing cookies is—"

"Only a misdemeanor and a necessary survival skill. Screw your resolutions. We earned those calories." Vero finished the last of her chips and her milk, then tossed the contents of her tray in the trash. "You think Sam was serious about the afternoon class being rough?"

"What does your schedule say?" I asked around a bite of my sandwich.

"Only that we're supposed to report to the mat room after lunch."

I didn't know who Lieutenant Hamamoto was, but anything had to be better than crawling in the mud while Joey hovered over us, watching like a hawk.

The bench sank under my sister's weight as she dropped down beside me. "Does my hair look okay?" she asked, her eyes a little frazzled as she tried to smooth it down. "And how about my shirt? Does it match my pants?"

"You look fine, Georgia. What are you so worried about?"

"I'm teaching a class this afternoon. I just want to look nice, that's all." She darted furtive looks around the cafeteria. "How about my breath?" She turned abruptly and blew in my face.

I reeled back. "What is wrong with you?"

"Here, do me," Vero said, leaning across the table. Georgia blew between her cupped hands as Vero sniffed. "Not bad. What about your pits?" Vero grabbed Georgia's arm and held it high, leaning in. "You're good."

"You just missed Sam," I said casually. Blood rushed to my sister's cheeks, confirming my suspicions. "She's nice."

"And hot," Vero chimed in.

"When are you asking her over for dinner?"

My sister jumped up from her seat. "Wow, would you look at the time? I've got to run," she said, stealing half my PB&J as she climbed out of the bench. She slipped out of the mess hall before I could demand she return my sandwich.

"I have no idea what Georgia's so afraid of," I said. "Sam seems really great."

Vero shook her head at me. "Maybe it's genetic."

"What's that supposed to mean?"

"I could say the exact same thing about you and Nick. I just hope for your sister's sake, Sam isn't a killer."

My stomach soured at the thought. I hated the idea of snooping on my sister's crush. "How do we rule her out?"

"I don't know. We'll come up with something." Vero took a bite of the remaining half of my sandwich. "I should have gone for the PB&J, too. This is actually pretty good," she said, cramming the last of it in her mouth. She dusted crumbs from her hands. "Let's go. I might puke if they make me do push-ups after lunch, and I don't want to be late."

We followed the campus map to the mat room and filed in with the rest of the herd. Blue gym mats covered most of the floor and creepy training dummies had been positioned around the room. I suppressed a shudder at the disembodied torsos mounted on metal stands. They reminded me disturbingly of Carl Westover. Or, more specifically, the previously frozen piece of him that was still buried on my ex-husband's farm.

Vero and I nudged our way closer to the front of the room. I wedged between two sets of tall shoulders, freezing when I locked eyes with the instructor. Joey stood in front of the class, holding a pair of handcuffs.

"My name is Detective Joseph Balafonte." His voice ricocheted off the walls of the training room, no need for a bullhorn. His cuffs clicked softly, open then closed, as his gaze slid from mine to rove over the rest of the group. It wasn't until his back was to me that I noticed the second instructor in the room, a petite middle-aged woman of Asian descent, her dark hair streaked with gray. She smiled warmly at the class. Her feet were spread shoulder width apart, her hands clasped behind her back. It was a posture many of the officers here assumed when they were addressing us, but on this woman, in her soft heather-gray academy-issued sweatsuit, the pose felt more disarming.

"This afternoon, you will learn various arrest techniques," Joey said. "You'll have a chance to practice administering handcuffs with both compliant and noncompliant suspects." He gestured to the other instructor. "This is Lieutenant Hamamoto. She will be teaching you defensive techniques." The cuffs resumed their soft clicking as Joey changed direction, taking slow, measured strides toward the other side of the room. "Self-defense is one of the first and most critical skills we teach new recruits. I've lost count of the number of times I have come face-to-face with someone who wanted to hurt me or end my life." His penetrating gaze landed squarely on me. "And believe me, when the business end of a gun is pointed at your face, you're not thinking about being a hero. Your only thought is making it out of there alive." The room fell so deathly quiet, I could hear the soft rush of air through the soles of his sneakers as he paced. "*Survival* is what we teach here at the academy. Regardless of age or height or strength or gender, you are all capable of mastering the skills we will teach you through repetition and practice." Joey let the silence hang as he gestured to Lieutenant Hamamoto.

The lieutenant strode forward, her self-assured and measured voice commanding an attention that felt disproportionate to her stature. The class watched as she demonstrated how the handcuffs worked, using Joey as a subject. He turned his back, allowing her to snap the cuffs on, then off. Just when it seemed their demonstration was finished, Joey whirled, reaching for the lieutenant's throat. In a series of movements too fast to comprehend, she had Joey disabled and prone, his face pressed against the mat and his wrists secured behind him.

The class broke into applause. Lieutenant Hamamoto dipped into a short curtsy before unlocking Joey's cuffs and helping him to his feet. They repeated the exercise several more times, using different strikes from different positions, narrating each step in slow motion as they performed it. When they were finished, Joey retrieved a plastic bin full of handcuffs from the far end of the room.

"I need a student volunteer," he said to the class. A few hands shot up in the audience. "Come on up here with me, Mrs. Haggerty," he said, gesturing for her to join him. She approached the mat with determined steps. When she reached his side, he rested a hand on her hunched shoulder. "It's good to see you again."

She squinted up at him through the rims of her glasses. "Have we met?"

His eyes skipped to me, then quickly away again. "About a month ago, I carried your trash can to your curb, remember?"

"I remembered you being taller."

He chuckled politely. "I get that a lot."

Vero elbowed me in the ribs. "Did you hear that? She had no idea who he was," she whispered.

"Or she just doesn't remember," I whispered back.

"Ms. Donovan," Joey called out. My head snapped up. "Since you and your partner are having a hard time concentrating, why don't you come up and be my second volunteer."

The class parted for me. With a tight smile, I walked to the front of the room and joined Mrs. Haggerty on the mat. Joey dangled a pair of handcuffs in front of me. "Mrs. Haggerty is under arrest. You're going to attempt to restrain her."

"Do I have to cooperate?" Mrs. Haggerty asked, provoking laughter from the audience.

Joey grinned like the Cheshire cat. "Not at all."

I yanked the cuffs from his hand and smiled at Mrs. Haggerty. "Please turn around," I said sweetly. She held up two bony fists in response, circling the mat like she was Floyd Mayweather's grandmother. Students whispered behind cupped hands. I turned to Joey. "I can't do this. Her grandson is watching. What if I accidentally hurt her?"

"Either detain your suspect or forfeit your team's points." He slipped a toothpick in his mouth, probably to hide his smirk. Joey was doing this on purpose, making me into the bad guy, but I wasn't about to stoop to his level.

I pasted on a smile and held the cuffs out to Mrs. Haggerty. "Here. Why don't *I* turn around and you can handcuff me? How does that sound?"

She punched me in the arm.

Joey chuckled to himself as I stormed off the mat.

Vero caught me by the shoulders. "We are not forfeiting points!" she hissed as she turned me around. "Bag Estelle Getty and get on with it."

I took a deep breath as I stepped back onto the mat. I would just have to appeal to Mrs. Haggerty's sense of reason. "Mrs. Haggerty," I said calmly, "it's just an exercise. There's no need for violence. Please turn around and put your hands behind your—" I bent over double as she kicked me in the shin.

"That's it," I said, hopping on one leg. I grabbed her wrist as she threw an uppercut at me. She yelped as I slapped the cuffs around it. There were a few boos and dramatic gasps as I turned her around, took her other wrist, and secured them both behind her back. Vero was the only one applauding.

I glared at Joey as I dusted off my hands. Chin high, I proceeded to walk off the mat. Vero stopped clapping. Her eyes grew wide as she pointed at something behind me. Pain shot through my knee as someone kicked it out. I crashed face-first to the floor, my breath rushing out of me with a grunt as Mrs. Haggerty plunked herself down on my ass and shouted a triumphant "ha!"

The class erupted with cheers. Her grandson whistled.

Joey unfolded his arms and gave her a slow clap. "Nice takedown, Mrs. Haggerty." He unlocked her cuffs and helped her to her feet. His shoes appeared beside my face. "Rule number one," he said, addressing the class, "never underestimate your opponent. Rule number two, never let them out of your sight. Let's get started," he said, leaving me lying on the floor. "One set of cuffs per team. One team per mat. Lieutenant Hamamoto and I will be coming around to give you pointers and observe."

The knot of students dispersed, breaking into pairs and fanning out around the room. Vero hauled me to my feet, watching Joey askance as he made his way from mat to mat, offering advice.

"Joey's behavior toward you doesn't add up," she said. "You saved his partner's life. You haven't done anything wrong—"

"That he knows of," I corrected her.

Vero and I fell silent as Lieutenant Hamamoto approached our mat.

"Thanks, Lieutenant," Joey said in a low voice behind her, "I'll handle this one." My spine went ramrod straight as he came toward me with a set of open cuffs. I lifted my chin as we stared each other down.

"Turn around," he said quietly.

"I thought I was supposed to be the one practicing with the—" I gasped as he took my wrist and spun me around, his shoes moving between mine and kicking them gently but firmly apart.

The cuffs clicked shut. He leaned close to my ear. "I may not have figured out your game yet, but I am keeping an eye on you. Whatever it is you're into, you're in over your head."

"I don't know what you're talking about."

"Sure you don't. Because you're a nice person and everybody likes you, right? Well I have a lot of experience with nice people," he whispered, "and it's always the nice ones that have something to hide." The cuffs snapped open and I backed quickly out of his reach. "Better get some practice," he growled. "I'm betting you're gonna need it."

CHAPTER 12

The sun had set while we were in defense class, and the sky had darkened to the color of a bruise. Vero and I dragged ourselves up the stairwell to our dorm room. She keyed open the door and we both collapsed onto our beds.

"Whose idea was this again?" I asked, still short of breath. My yoga pants were drenched in places that should never sweat while you're fully clothed.

"Your sister's," Vero said, throwing an arm over her eyes, "and I'm never taking her advice again. *Go to the police academy,* they said. *There will be hot cops everywhere,* they said. Funny how no one bothered to mention the horrible food, the scarcity of hot water, or that we'd get our asses kicked on the first day by a woman half our size. The whole handcuffing experience isn't nearly as sexy as NCIS makes it out to be." We both quieted at a soft scratching sound. "If there's a rodent in this room, I'm out of here," she grumbled.

The scratching grew louder. Vero's arm slid away from her face. We both bolted upright when something thumped against the window. We got up and crept toward it, but I couldn't make out anything past our own reflections in the glass. I rushed to the wall switch and turned off the light. Vero reached for her pillow when something moved outside.

"What are you doing?" I whispered as she raised it behind her head.

"Improvising," she whispered. "Didn't you learn anything in class today? This pillow is a found weapon. If anyone tries to come in, I'm going to hit him in the face—you know, element of surprise. And then, while he's stunned, I'm going to suffocate him with it." We both gasped as a large hand pressed against the glass. "What are you standing there looking at, Finlay? Find a weapon and hide!"

I surveyed my side of our dorm room, frantically rummaging through my suitcase in the dark. My hair dryer was the only thing in it that remotely resembled a weapon. I unwound it from a tangle of clothes and flattened myself against the wall beside Vero. She rolled her eyes at me. Then her brow furrowed as she studied my hair dryer. She thrust her pillow in my hand and snatched my Revlon Volumizer, gripping it like a Smith & Wesson. I gaped at her as she pressed back against the wall and pointed it at the ceiling.

We both started as a shadowy figure filled the window frame. Metal scraped against metal.

"He's trying to jimmy the lock!" I whispered. "We should call my sister. Or Nick."

"No time," Vero said as the lock clicked open. "There are two of us and one of him. And we were in self-defense class all afternoon."

"He looks like a professional. That skews the odds," I hissed.

"Anyone can be a professional. For crying out loud, Finn, look at you!"

I sucked in a breath as the window slid open. The whites of Vero's eyes widened as a leg extended through it. I wound the pillow back. Vero raised my hair dryer as the intruder's sneakers landed softly in the room.

"Get him!" she yelled. I swung the pillow hard. The man swore as it connected with his face, knocking him backward into Vero. Vero jumped on his shoulders, one arm looped around his neck, the other smashing the hair dryer into his head as he pinwheeled to keep from falling on top of her. He staggered into the dresser, then the bed, eventually falling face-first over the end of it to the floor. Vero jerked his wrists behind his back, winding the hair dryer cord around them. She dug her knee into his spine and grabbed him by his hair. "We got him, Finlay! Turn on the light!"

I rushed to the wall switch and flipped it on.

Javi blinked at us, red-faced and livid. One of Vero's sweaty socks was stuck to his face and my hair dryer dangled between his butt cheeks. Vero let go, backing slowly away from him as Javi worked himself free of the cord.

"Sorry," I stammered, rushing to shut the window. "We thought you were someone else."

Vero bit her lip as he stood and she got a good look at the green and yellow bruises on his forehead. New ones were already blooming around them. "I might have overestimated the rose hip oil," she said in a small voice as he stalked toward her.

"You're trying to kill me, aren't you? Ever since third grade, when you ran over me with your bike."

"That was an accident."

"Or in middle school, when you pushed me off the high dive at the pool."

"Also an accident."

"How about homecoming night, when you spiked my beer with laxatives?"

"*That* was on purpose," she said, pointing a finger at him when they were nose to nose. "I hated your date, and you were being an ass."

He shoved my hair dryer into her hands. "I was worried sick! I called you a dozen times today. Why didn't you answer your phone?"

"We aren't allowed to have them in class."

"Do you have any idea how hard it was to get into this place? I had to bribe a food service delivery guy to let me hide in a truckload of bread! What the hell are you doing in a police training facility?"

"Lying low."

"From who?"

"People."

"And of all the places you could have chosen, you picked here?" He threw up his hands when Vero didn't answer. "Why are there bullet holes in the car, V?"

"That's kind of a long story."

"The only part I care about is if you were in the car while people were shooting at it!"

"Of course not!"

"Thank fuck," he whispered.

"They were shooting at Finlay."

Javi pinched the bridge of his nose as he sank onto Vero's mattress.

"So you saw the Aston?" I asked. "Can you get rid of it?"

He lifted his head. "I made a few calls. I know a guy who knows a guy who says he can unload it."

"How fast?" Vero asked.

"It'll take me a few days to arrange to have it moved."

"A few days!"

"I can't exactly strip it in Ramón's backyard, V! Not if we're keeping this a secret from him." They locked eyes in a silent standoff.

"Fine," she said, gesturing to the window. "Get as much as you can and let me know when it's done."

Javi stood. "So that's it? You're just going to hide out here with a bunch of cops until I get the money?"

Vero crossed her arms.

"Great. No pressure," he muttered. He moved to the window and put a finger between the slats in the blinds, peering at the campus below. Voices drifted up as students began migrating from the dorm to the mess hall. "Can't leave now. Not until all those people clear out. Mind if I crash here for a while?"

Vero made a show of studying her nails. "I don't mind. Do you, Finn?"

They stole furtive glances at each other from opposite sides of the room.

"I was just going to go find a hot shower and grab something to eat. Will you be okay here?" I asked her as I reached for my coat.

Javi leaned back against the wall beside her bed, one foot hitched behind him, his face a mask of casual disinterest as she surveyed him coolly and nodded.

"Good," I said. "Try not to kill each other until I get back." I grabbed my hair dryer off her bed and tucked it in my gym bag. It was probably safer not to leave anything to chance.

I set my gym bag in an empty shower stall in the shared bathroom at the end of the hall and tested the faucet. The pathetic trickle ran tepid for a moment, then abruptly cooled to a temperature that could probably preserve a body. Remembering the dense fog I'd seen earlier that day in the women's locker room, I collected my things and made the trek to the gym, weaving around crowds of students who were on their way to dinner. Judging by the quality of the offerings I'd seen in the lunchroom earlier, a hot shower alone seemed preferable.

I followed the signs to the locker room, relieved to find it empty. I turned on the shower and checked my phone as I waited for the water to warm.

Still no news of a squashed, tattooed wrestler from New Jersey turning up in any headlines.

I sifted through my notifications. Steven had sent a video a few hours ago while I'd been in class. I tapped it open. Delia was grinning in the back seat of his truck, his heavy tool belt draped across her lap. Zach brandished a plastic hammer with a maniacal laugh. The camera pulled back, catching Steven in the frame with them. He smoothed back his hair, adjusting the angle of his phone to capture his good side.

Wave hi to Mommy, he said.

Zach shook his hammer and squealed, *Mommy!*

A wide smile stretched over my face as Delia waved at me. *Daddy's taking us out to lunch and then we're going on an adventure to—*

The video cut off. A text from Steven had followed: *We miss you. How about family dinner at my place on Friday? Just you, me, and the kids.*

I frowned at my phone. Was this an olive branch to co-parenting or was he asking me on a date? I texted back a quick reply: *Family dinner sounds great. Let's plan for next week at my place. Vero and I will cook.*

I tossed my phone in my gym bag, pushing thoughts of Steven from my mind as I stripped off my workout clothes and stepped under the lukewarm spray. By the time I finished scrubbing, the locker room was thinly veiled with steam. I toweled off and dried my hair, my stomach rumbling through my sweatshirt as I dragged it over my head. I packed my dirty clothes and hair dryer into my gym bag and stepped out into the hall in search of a vending machine.

Voices rose from the basketball courts, the squeak of sneakers punctuated by the steady thump of a ball against the gymnasium floor. I slowed as I recognized one of the deep, booming voices through the double doors. Rising up on my toes, I peeked through the small window.

Joey was light on his feet, hunched over the ball as he defended it from Roddy. Roddy towered over him, making grabs at it until he eventually swiped it and pitched it to Charlie. Charlie dribbled it down the court for an easy layup. Nick leaned against his cane behind the court, catching the balls that flew under the backboard and pitching them to his friends. He smiled, throwing out the occasional trash talk along with them, but as the play moved to center court, Nick's attention drifted toward the door. I ducked out of sight, hoping he hadn't noticed me.

The promising glow of a vending machine guided me down the hall. I fed what little cash I had into one of the snack machines. My fingers hovered between the buttons that would release a pack of Oreos or a Twix, but it was only seventeen days into the new year, and while there wasn't much to be done about Ike, I was determined to salvage this one resolution. I opted for the Cheez-Its instead.

The coils inside the machine turned on, spinning its meager offerings closer to the ledge, but apparently not close enough. The cheese crackers tipped, catching on the glass. With a swear, I threw my shoulder against the vending machine. The Cheez-Its didn't budge. I dropped to my knees and thrust my arm into the receptacle, feeling for the opening on the other side.

"I should probably point out that if you stop now, you're only guilty of a second-degree misdemeanor."

I froze as Nick's cane clicked steadily closer. "Is that bad?"

His reflection shrugged back at me through the glass. "Sixty days in jail and a five-hundred-dollar fine. That's a pricey bag of Cheez-Its, if you ask me."

The metal compartment banged shut as I jerked my hand free. "I missed dinner," I said defensively. "And my purse is in my dorm room with Vero, and I can't go back in to get it because she's probably . . ." Nick raised an eyebrow. ". . . sleeping," I finished. "And that damn vending machine ate my only dollar."

He bit back a smile. "I was just getting ready to grab some dinner myself. I've got a key to the kitchen. Want to come with?"

I tried not to look too eager at the prospect of a hot meal. "That'd be nice. Thanks."

"Great." His grin spread wide. "I just need to grab my things from my locker. Back in a sec."

I gave the vending machine one last shove as Nick disappeared into the men's locker room, leaping back like a thief when the gymnasium door flew open behind me. Joey stumbled backward through it, as if he'd been pushed. Charlie followed him into the hall, a basketball tucked under his arm as he pressed a hard finger to Joey's chest.

"Don't think I don't know who you are or what you're all about," Charlie said, his scar twisting with his scowl. "If you know what's good for you, you'll back the hell off, Balafonte. I worked with Nick Anthony for six years, and that man is no fool. If he hasn't seen through you yet, he will."

Joey batted Charlie's hand aside. "The way he saw through you?"

My Cheez-Its chose that exact moment to slide down the vending machine with a *thump*. Charlie and Joey stepped abruptly apart, both of them turning toward the sound as my crackers dropped into the tray.

"Sorry," I said, breaking the tense silence. "Didn't mean to interrupt. I was just getting something to eat."

The locker room door nudged open. Nick hobbled a few steps into the hall and paused, his eyes sweeping over the three of us. "Everything okay?"

Joey cleared his throat. "Yeah, I was just gonna run out and grab some dinner. Figured maybe you'd want to come with. We can swing by the lab on our way and pick up those reports you've been waiting on."

Charlie chuckled quietly, bouncing his ball with a cocksure smile. "Thought you were a detective, Balafonte. Read the room."

Joey glanced at the duffel in Nick's hand, then the gym bag by my feet.

"Sorry, partner," Nick said as he limped toward me. "I've already got plans for dinner. But do me a favor and text me if you hear back from the lab before I do. I can drop by and pick up the reports in the morning."

Joey's eyes narrowed. "You're taking her off campus?"

"Never said I was."

"You never said you weren't."

Nick turned to his partner. "What's the matter with you?" he asked in a low voice.

Joey shrugged. "Nothing. Your program, your rules. I just don't think it looks good to go bending them because you want to get in her pants. That's all."

Charlie's ball stopped bouncing. Nick's knuckles tightened around his cane.

"Hey," Joey said, throwing up his hands, "I'm just being honest with you, Nick. That's what partners do." He pierced Charlie with a cold glare before disappearing into the locker room.

Charlie dropped his ball. He came up beside me and gave the vending machine a hard shake. A pack of M&M's dropped into the tray alongside my Cheez-Its, and I was pretty sure I hadn't paid for them. He handed both snacks to me with the tip of an imaginary hat. "The lady's hungry, Nick. If you don't take her to find something to eat around this place, I will." Charlie clapped Nick on the shoulder, scooped up his ball, and dribbled it into the locker room.

"Sorry about that," Nick said, frowning at the door as it drifted closed behind them. "I don't know what the hell's wrong with Joey. I'll understand if you want to pass on dinner. I can walk you back to your dorm."

"No," I said quickly. The last thing I needed was for Nick to see Javi in our room. Or worse, shimmying down the drainpipe outside it. I glanced over his shoulder toward the locker room. I could either dine on vending machine snacks and risk another run-in with Joey, or I could go to the kitchen with Nick for a hot meal and maybe ask a few questions of my own. I hoisted my gym bag over my shoulder. "I'm starving. Let's go."

CHAPTER 13

Nick and I made our way at a leisurely pace toward the building that housed the cafeteria. We paused at a crosswalk, allowing a police car to pass us. I watched as it rolled slowly toward the exit lane and proceeded to the gate. I could just make out the night duty officer inside the security booth. He glanced up from his cell phone as the cruiser approached, pushed a button to open the barrier, and waved the driver through it.

Leaving the training facility seemed simple enough.

"Is it really such a big deal for a student to leave the campus?" I asked.

Nick thought about that as his cane clicked over the crosswalk. "In theory? No. If you did leave, you'd be searched when you got back."

"So why was Joey so upset about it?"

"Joey didn't have an issue with you leaving. He had an issue with you leaving with me."

"Why?"

"If I didn't know better, I'd think he was jealous."

I choked on a laugh. "Why would you think that?"

"He's just a little too interested, you know? He's been asking a lot of questions about you."

The hair on my neck stood on end. "What kinds of questions?"

Nick was quiet for a moment, as if he was considering how to answer that. "Mostly questions about you and me. How long I've known you. How we met. If we were ever a thing."

"A *thing*?"

"He wanted to know if we'd ever been . . . intimate." He risked a sidelong glance at me.

I tried not to sound as curious as that question made me feel. "What did you tell him?"

"I told him it was none of his business." An awkward silence dragged between us. Did that kiss we shared in his car three months ago count? Did I want it to? And, more important, why did Joey care?

"I probably shouldn't have brought it up," Nick said, shamefaced. "I don't think Joey meant anything by it. I think he was just trying to . . . I don't know . . . connect with me about something other than work. I think he senses that I still haven't entirely warmed up to him yet."

"Why not? I thought you two got along."

Nick's head swayed indecisively. "I can't put my finger on it, Finn," he said in a voice too low to carry. "Joey's a stand-up guy and a decent partner. I don't think he tries to be a dick."

"It just happens naturally?"

A smile broke over Nick's face. He didn't bother to deny it. "Joey can be a little too direct. It rubs people the wrong way sometimes."

"What's Charlie's beef with him?" I asked.

"You caught on to that?"

"It was hard to miss."

He shrugged as we rounded the corner to the dining hall. "Charlie's beef is the same as everyone else's, I guess. Joey asks too many questions. They come off as a little intrusive. I think it's just his way of trying to fit in. It's tough being the new guy. It's natural to cling to your partner when you don't have anybody else, and Charlie's shadow is a long one to walk in. I don't think I was off the mark when I said Joey's probably jealous."

"I can see why. Charlie's pretty great."

"So are you." Nick paused under the awning to the dining hall. He turned to me. His lips parted around a thought, then closed again. "Come on," he said, running his card key through the scanner and holding the door open for me. "You can warm up inside while I find us something to eat."

I wondered what he'd been about to say, as he led the way to the kitchen. He flipped on a single wall switch, forgoing the bright overhead fluorescents in favor of a handful of dim spotlights over the counters. He took my coat and hung it on a hook on the wall beside some aprons. "Make yourself at home. Can I get you something to drink? Juice box? Milk?" His cane clicked toward a gigantic stainless steel fridge that could probably fit a half dozen bodies. "Sorry, it's not as classy as Feliks's restaurant."

I laughed. "I'll take this over Feliks's any day. Got any coffee?" I asked, rubbing my eyes.

"You planning on staying up?"

"I've got a deadline for Sylvia."

"Check the faculty lounge. There's probably some left over in the carafes, but I should warn you, it's not exactly Starbucks."

"Noted." I slipped through a set of doors into the darkened cafeteria, following the emergency lighting toward the faculty lounge at the far side. The smell of cooked broccoli lingered in the room, the only clue it had been occupied a little more than an hour ago.

The faculty lounge was unlocked and I flipped on the light switch. My name caught my attention, printed in red on a dry-erase board on the opposite wall. A table had been drawn on it. Each team of students had been listed in the leftmost column, followed by a tally of their points. The next column also contained a number—a ranking, but not the one we'd earned through our scores. These were odds, and Vero and I seemed to be leading the pack.

Sam hadn't been kidding. The faculty were literally betting on us. While a few of the instructors had placed bets on other teams, most had gambled on Vero and me. Only one instructor had bet against us—Joey Balafonte had bet we'd lose the whole damn thing.

Unsettled, I searched the cabinets for a mug and helped myself to a cup of coffee. The dregs in the silver carafe were bitter but still warm. I sipped as I turned for the door, pausing beside a tray of desserts. With a quick glance at the door, I pulled aside the plastic wrap and snuck two chocolate chip cookies from the tray, stuffing them into my sweatshirt pockets. I rearranged a few oatmeal raisins to cover the gaps before turning off the lights.

My phone vibrated with an incoming call. My mother's name flashed on the screen.

"Mom?" I answered on my way back to the kitchen. "It's not a good time. Can I call you back?"

"Hi, Mommy."

I halted in my tracks, checking my screen to be sure I had read it right. How was Delia calling me from my mother's phone? "Hi, baby. Did Nana come to visit you at Daddy's?" Why would Steven invite my mother to his house? The two hadn't stepped foot in the same room since we'd divorced.

"No," she said. "Daddy, Zach, and I went on a secret mission to *our* house. Then we came to visit Nana and Pop Pop."

"A secret mission? That sounds exciting." A little too exciting. Vero had confiscated Steven's house key three months ago. "How did Daddy get into the house?"

"That was the most funnest part," she said, her tongue slipping on her *S*'s between her missing front teeth. "We sneaked around the backyard so no one would see us. Then Daddy opened a window with one of his screwdiapers—"

"He used a screwdriver?"

"Yes! But Daddy was too big to fit in the window, so he held it open and I got to be the one who climbed in. Then I ran and unlocked the back door for Daddy and Zach. Zach and I were pretending to be spies so Mrs. Haggerty wouldn't see us," she finished in a stage whisper.

"Ooooh, that does sound like fun." Almost as much fun as murdering my ex-husband with a screwdriver. "Was Daddy spying, too?" I asked sweetly.

"Mostly, he was cussing," Delia said. "First, he used the *D* word when he looked under the bushes and his special key was gone." Because I'd disposed of the one he'd kept hidden there for Theresa after I'd caught him cheating and kicked him out of the house. "Then, he used the *S* word when he got stuck in the window. And then," she said with a dramatic rise of her voice, "he used all the bad words when Zach poured chocolate syrup on the carpet in the playroom while Daddy was upstairs working in the closet."

"In the closet?" I paused. What could Steven have found in my closet that would have prompted him to take the children to my parents' house? "Delia, is Daddy there with you now?"

"No. We're having a sleepover at Nana and Pop Pop's tonight."

"Can I talk to Nana?"

"She and Pop Pop are watching the news and Zach and I can't watch anything fun. Nana said I'm not allowed to use my iPad until I'm thirty. She says computers are full of bad people."

A sharp laugh burst out of me. "She would know." I pressed a hand to my temple as I carried the phone a safe distance from the kitchen. "Put Nana on the phone, sweetheart."

There was a rustling on the other end of the line, then my mother picked up. "Finlay, is that you?"

"Why are the children with you? Where's Steven?"

"I don't know."

"What do you mean, you don't know?"

Her voice fell to a whisper. "I swear to god, Finlay, he was breathing when he left."

I pinched the bridge of my nose. "What was he doing at your house to begin with?"

I heard the swing doors swish closed behind her as she carried the phone into her kitchen and lowered her voice. "He called me this afternoon and asked if he could come over. He sounded upset. At first, I was worried that he might know about the whole . . . you know . . . *incident*," she whispered. "But then he asked if he could bring the children. He said an emergency came up and he needed someone to take the kids for the night. I told him they could stay with us."

Damnit, Steven. "Do you have any idea where he went?"

"He wouldn't say. Only that it was very important."

I pulled the phone from my ear to check the time. "I'm sorry Steven dumped the kids on you like this. I can come get them. I'll call an Uber and be at your place before their bedtime." If I asked Nick, he'd probably even drive me. Vero could stay here. She'd be safer in the dorms until Javi was able to get the money from stripping the car.

"Don't be ridiculous," my mother said. "We're delighted to have the children. Stay at your police thing. You can pick them up when you get home." The phone became muffled as my father's voice called out from the next room. "I should go. Your father's back is bothering him and he can't find the heating pad."

"Tell Dad I hope he feels better. And give the kids a kiss for me. Thanks, Ma."

As soon as she disconnected, I dialed Steven's number. It rang to voice mail. "Steven? It's Finlay. I just talked to my mother—and Delia," I added pointedly, "and they said you had some kind of emergency. I hope this emergency had nothing to do with your visit to my house this afternoon. Call me when you get this."

I shoved my phone in my pocket and carried my coffee to the kitchen. The mouthwatering scent that greeted me almost made me forget Steven altogether. A pan of beef, onions, and garlic hissed on the stove. Nick stood with his back to me, the sleeves of his Henley rolled to his elbows and the sash of a red apron tied around his waist. One hand leaned on his cane, the other stirred.

He glanced over as the door swung shut behind me. "You were gone for a while. Thought maybe you got lost looking for the coffee."

"Sorry, my mom called."

He put down his spoon. "Everything okay?"

"Everything's fine. It's just . . . Steven." I waved off Nick's concern. The children were safe at my parents' house and Steven was the last person I wanted to be thinking about right now. "What's for dinner?" My stomach rumbled as I peeked around him into the pot of boiling water on the stove.

"It's not exactly chili and biscuits at my place, but for tonight, spaghetti will have to do."

"Sounds perfect. How can I help?"

He smiled at me over the shoulder of his apron, and the effect was a little staggering. "You can relax and keep me company." He gestured to a makeshift table he'd set with two stools, a tablecloth, napkins, and utensils. A pitcher of grape juice rested in the middle, a portion already poured into two clear plastic cups. I pulled one of the stools up to the counter, resting my head on my hand as I watched Nick slather slices of bread in garlic and butter. My eyelids drifted closed, the stress of the day easing as the coffee left a warm trail down to my stomach.

"How was your first day?" he asked, setting the bread in the oven.

"Exhausting," I confessed. "Lieutenant Hamamoto kicked my ass. I might never recover."

Nick laughed as he limped to the fridge. "If it's any consolation, you and Vero did really well today."

I took a moment to appreciate the view as he dug around inside the vegetable bins. Maybe it was fatigue, or the fact that he was far too easy to talk to, or maybe it was just how good he looked in that apron that made me ask, "Why didn't you want me to come this week?"

He turned from the refrigerator to frown at me, one arm laden with a head of lettuce, a cucumber, and a tomato. "What do you mean?" he asked, his brow heavy as he limped back to the cutting board beside the stove.

"When Sam and Georgia suggested the idea, you were the only one who tried to talk me out of coming."

"No." He set down the produce with a shake of his head. Hooking his cane over the lip of the counter, he leaned back against it to face me. "That had nothing to do with you, Finn. That's not it at all. It's just . . . this whole thing," he said, gesturing around him, "the desk jockeying and paperwork and publicity junkets . . . none of this is me." He braced his arms on the counter and frowned, as if he was trying to figure out how to explain. "I hate watching other detectives take my cases. I hate going to counseling and PT every week, waiting for doctors and shrinks to decide when—or *if*—I can get back to work. I hate looking at Charlie and thinking one day that could be me." Guilt flashed across his face as he said it, but I found his honesty endearing, this vulnerable side of him I'd never seen before.

He turned to the cutting board, accidentally knocking his cane to the floor. He bent to retrieve it, suppressing a wince. I rushed off my stool to pick it up for him. His eyes caught mine as I pressed it into his hand.

"Thanks," he said, his voice gravelly.

"Don't mention it," I whispered, forgetting to let go. For a long moment, neither of us moved.

A timer trilled by the stove.

I cleared my throat, releasing his cane as the spell between us broke. "Sounds like the spaghetti's done. Want me to make the salad?"

"Sit," he insisted, reaching for the timer. "It'll only take me a minute."

I pushed my stool to the table, wishing there was something stronger than grape juice in my cup as I took a long, cool sip of it. I offered again to help, but Nick seemed as confident in the kitchen as he was everywhere else, expertly moving between the counter and the stove as he prepped the salad, drained the pasta, and retrieved the tray of garlic bread from the oven. He refused to let me lift a finger, carrying the salads and plates to the table in small trips he could manage in one hand.

"This looks amazing," I said as he set a heaping plate of pasta before me. "Where did you learn to cook?" I tore into a bite of garlic bread. It was crispy and warm, the center dripping with butter, and I think I might have moaned in bliss.

"Trial and error, mostly," he said, easing onto his stool and setting down his plate. At my inquisitive look, he explained, "My mom worked two jobs when I was a kid. I made dinner most nights for me and my little sister."

"Where was your dad?" I asked around a mouthful of pasta.

"He left when I was eight. We never heard from him much after that."

I glanced up from my meal, feeling a stab of sympathy for him. Steven had left me, but at least he was committed to raising his children. "That must have been hard."

"You sound a little like Stu," he teased me. "If you start billing me by the hour, I might start to worry."

"Are you kidding? You just cooked me dinner. I should be paying you."

Our laughter quieted as we took turns stealing glances at each other between bites.

"So," he said, breaking the silence, "I've been meaning to ask you how your book turned out."

"My book?"

"The one you were working on in December, about the missing attorney. Did you finish it?"

I felt the blood rush to my cheeks. "Not exactly," I said into my pasta. "Sylvia thinks I still have a few things to work on. She wants me to revise the ending." I tried not to think about her (or her taxi driver's) suggestions. After watching Nick prep dinner in that apron, it was far too easy to envision the scenes my agent was expecting me to write.

Nick's frown was thoughtful. "Last time we talked, you said the end of the story didn't come together the way you'd hoped. You think the attorney's going to show up in the new one?" I raised an eyebrow. We both knew which attorney he was curious about, and it wasn't the one in my book. "Not that I'm looking for a spoiler," he rushed to add. "I was just curious if the guy was still around."

Nick had never known Julian's name, only that I'd been seeing an attorney and the attorney's mysterious disappearance in my book held certain parallels to our real-life relationship. I smiled at my empty plate. "That story line's over. My heroine has moved on. It's just her and her trusty sidekick now." *Holding hands as they plummet off a cliff.*

I reached across the table for his dishes. "You cooked. Let me clean up."

He rose from his seat to help. "I had to do something to save face.

Last time I asked you to have dinner with me, it wasn't much of a date." Our shoulders brushed as he nested our plates. There was a tentativeness to the word *date,* as if he was feeling out my reaction to it.

"Because it *wasn't* one," I reminded him.

"Date or not, it was a pretty fantastic night."

"We got kicked out of Feliks's restaurant and ended up in his dumpster. I think your memory of that night might be a little fuzzy."

Nick caught my wrist as I reached for our forks. His hand was warm, his teasing smile close to mine. "My memories of that night are very clear, and Zhirov's restaurant isn't where I wanted to take you."

I swallowed. This was the part of the story when the cop's gaze was supposed to fall to the assassin's lips. Her eyes would drift closed. The air would grow thin. Her heart would race as she imagined how it would feel to be with him . . .

She'd been on the run for so long, all the while he'd been close behind her, wanting her. Chasing her. But now, his hand cuffing her wrist in its gentle embrace, there was nowhere left to run.

She didn't want to run. Not tonight.

She pressed a finger to his lips, silencing his sweet promises of a future she knew she could never have with him. He couldn't swear she would never go to prison; she was far from innocent. And he couldn't keep her safe. Not from his friends, and not from her enemies.

But maybe they could have this one night.

Here, far from home, where no one knew who she was.

She grabbed hold of his shirt and pulled his mouth to hers, their first kiss since their last fateful night together, desperate and—

"Finn? You okay?" Nick hovered over me, his brow creased with worry.

I blinked up at him. Then at my hands, which were clutching the front of his apron.

"I'm fine," I said, clearing my throat. "Just a little light-headed. Probably all the carbs."

Do not think about dessert. You're not thinking about dessert. You do not need or want any dessert.

He pressed a hand to my forehead. "Maybe you should sit down. You're flushed, and your pulse is a little quick."

"No kidding."

A door smacked open somewhere in the cafeteria. "Nick!" Joey's voice echoed through the cafeteria. I let go of Nick's apron, leaving sudsy, wrinkled handprints on the fabric, still a little weak in the knees as the kitchen door flew open. Joey didn't even notice me as he made a beeline for the stove. "Smells good. What's cookin', partner?"

Nick's cane clacked hard against the floor as he limped after Joey. "What the hell's so important?"

Joey shoved a file against Nick's apron. "Tox reports are in."

"We can go over them tomorrow," Nick said, trying to hand them back.

Joey lifted the lid on the saucepan and tested the sauce with a finger, searching the counter for a plate. "Get this . . . four of the victims had traces of weed, opioids, coke . . . the usual suspects. But vic number five— "

Nick snatched the lid and dropped it back on the pot. "I said, it can wait until tomorrow." He tipped his head toward me.

Joey's swung around, stopping short when he saw me. His eyes raked over the kitchen, taking in the dim spotlights, the tablecloth, and the juice glasses we hadn't gotten around to cleaning up yet. He turned slowly to Nick. Nick stared back, daring him to say something.

I hitched my thumb toward the exit. "I should probably go."

"Stay," Nick said. He shoved the file at Joey. "Detective Balafonte has somewhere he needs to be."

"Sam can handle it," Joey argued.

"It's not Samara's name on the schedule."

A muscle worked in Joey's jaw. He glared at the wet handprints on Nick's apron. "See you in the morning, *partner.* The report will be on my desk if you manage to get your head out of your ass before then." He took the file from Nick, slamming the door into the wall on his way out.

CHAPTER 14

Nick was quiet as we washed our plates and put away the leftovers. Whatever spark had kindled between us during dinner had extinguished the moment Joey had burst in. I could sense Nick's frustration still simmering under the surface as he gave the kitchen a quick once-over before locking it for the night. I should have been relieved for Joey's interruption, which had probably saved me from ripping off Nick's apron and doing unspeakable things in a public place, but I couldn't deny feeling a little frustrated, too.

My eyes climbed the brick wall of the dormitory as Nick escorted me back to my room. The light was on in our window. I sent Vero a quick text, warning her that I was on my way with Nick, then slipped my phone back in my pocket, hoping Javi was already gone.

Nick stopped at the entrance of the building. We waited through an awkward pause while a group of academy students filed out the door. I bit my tongue, resisting the urge to tease Nick when several of the women in the group (and at least one man) turned to ogle him as they walked by. Max and Riley were the last to exit, and I tucked myself behind Nick, hoping to avoid them.

I cringed when Max spotted me. "Hey, Finlay! Are you and Vero coming to movie night? Officer Roddy's making popcorn."

"Movie night?" I asked Nick.

"*Silence of the Lambs* in the auditorium. Starts in half an hour."

I shuddered as I called out to Max, "Thanks, but I'll pass."

Nick bit down on his grin, waiting for the last of their group to disappear from view before reaching for my hand.

"I'm sorry about tonight," he said in a low voice, probably so we wouldn't be overheard. "For what it's worth, I was having a really good time before my partner showed up."

"I had a nice time, too. Thank you for dinner."

He pressed a chaste kiss to my cheek, and it took every ounce of willpower I had not to turn my head and catch his lips. He smiled as if he knew. "You've got a long day tomorrow. Get some sleep."

"You, too," I said, a little breathless as he pulled away.

He watched me scan my lanyard, waiting until I slipped inside and the locks snapped closed behind me before he limped from the building. I raced up the two flights of stairs to our room, listening with an ear to the door before throwing it open.

Vero bolted upright in bed. "Oh, it's just you." She dropped facedown against the mattress and used the pillow to cover her head.

"I brought you dinner," I said, fishing the cookies from my pockets.

"Not hungry."

"All they had was chocolate chip."

Vero shot up, the pillow dropping to the mattress beside her. I set both cookies in her lap. "Where's Javi?" I asked.

"Left," she said around a mouthful of crumbs. "He said he'll call when he has the money. Where'd you disappear to?"

"I missed dinner. Nick took me to the kitchen and made us something to eat."

She stopped chewing, a hopeful gleam in her eyes. "Please tell me that included dessert."

"Joey came and I lost my appetite." I kicked off my shoes and flopped down on my bed. "He's been increasingly hostile to me ever since we got here. It's like he doesn't want me anywhere near his partner."

"More like he doesn't want you anywhere near his *work*. Probably because he's hiding something."

I stared at the ceiling as I considered that. What if Vero was right and it wasn't my proximity to Nick that Joey was worried about? What if it was just my being here at the academy?

I sat up and swung my legs over the side of the bed. Each of the instructors had been issued a temporary office for the week so they could keep up with their cases and their regular job responsibilities while they were here. "Do you have your schedule?" I asked.

Vero frowned at my sudden urgency. She reached in her backpack and handed me her class schedule. I skimmed it for Joey's name, remembering what Nick had said in the kitchen about Joey having someplace he was supposed to be this evening. I paused over the listing for movie night. Roddy and Joey were scheduled to staff it.

The report will be on my desk if you manage to get your head out of your ass . . .

Meaning Joey's office door would likely be open. The movie would run at least two hours. I turned the schedule over, studying the campus map.

"Where are you going?" Vero asked as I got up and shrugged on my coat.

"Snooping."

Vero narrowed her eyes at me as I tugged on my shoes. "If you're going snooping, what the heck am I supposed to do?"

"How do you feel about *Silence of the Lambs*?"

I peered into the window of the auditorium. The movie had already started. Joey sat with his arms crossed in the aisle seat of the back row. Roddy walked up and down the steps, handing out paper bags full of popcorn. "You promised I'd get to snoop," Vero said as I nudged her to the door.

"You can snoop and go hungry, or you can do reconnaissance and have snacks." Roddy had taken the microwave from the faculty lounge and wheeled it to the auditorium on a kitchen cart. He'd plugged it into an outlet in the hall, beside a folding table packed with soda cans and a case of microwave popcorn.

Vero eyed the snack cart and snagged herself a Coke. "Fine. You do the snooping. I'll handle recon. What's the code word?"

"What code word?"

"The one I'm supposed to text you to warn you if Joey's coming." She peeped in the window. "How about Hannibal Lecter? He kind of looks like Hannibal Lecter. He gets that same crazy look in his eyes when he stares at you, like he's thinking about eating your liver with—"

"Go!" I whispered, shoving her through the door. "We don't need a code word. The movie just started. I have plenty of time."

I started briskly toward the faculty offices, checking the room numbers against the ones listed on the map, praying none of the instructors were working late tonight.

Joey's office was at the end of the dimly lit hall. His door was closed and I tested the knob, not sure if I was relieved or terrified to find it unlocked. I slipped inside and shut myself in, my heart racing as I pressed back against the door. I rushed to the window to close the blinds before turning on the light.

I'm in, I texted Vero.

She texted me back a photo. The image was dark and a little blurry. I held it close to my face to decipher what I was looking at. Joey slouched in his seat, his head tipped back and his eyes closed. His mouth hung open as if he'd fallen asleep, and some of the tension slipped out of me.

I tucked my phone in my pocket and turned a quick circle in the room, wondering where to start.

Joey's laptop sat open on his desk. My phone vibrated again as I reached for the keyboard.

Vero: *Hope you remembered gloves.*

Finlay: *Shit.*

Vero: *Told you I should do the snooping.*

Finlay: *Shut up and eat your popcorn.*

I dug my mittens from the pockets of my coat and drew them on, wishing I had been prepared with something more Temperance Brennan and less Bernie Sanders. I poked the spacebar with thick, woolly fingers. A password prompt appeared on the screen, and I abandoned the laptop with a whispered swear.

I slid Joey's desk drawer open. The contents were spare, the barest essentials someone might need for a week—a stapler, a sticky note pad, a box of toothpicks, a handful of pens, an opened pack of chewing gum . . .

"He has to be hiding something," I whispered as I turned away from his desk.

His leather jacket hung on a hook behind the door. I patted it down, retrieving a key ring from one of the pockets. Fanning the keys across my mitten, I singled out the smallest one. I scanned the room. A file cabinet was wedged between the desk and the window. When I worked the key inside the lock, I was rewarded with a soft *click*.

The metal drawer slid open. I pushed aside a carton of cigarettes to see the items underneath: class schedules, faculty emergency numbers, student rosters, a handful of unfinished police reports, and a stack of files. I read the names on the tabs, pausing over the only one that was familiar—Charles Cox.

Why would Joey have a file with Charlie's name on it?

I pulled it free of the drawer and opened it, skimming the contents, surprised by the amount of personal information inside: employment history, promotion letters, retirement records, the details of Charlie's cancer diagnosis and treatment, copies of commendation letters and a handful of minor disciplinary ones, spanning nearly twenty years. A few handwritten notes had been scribbled in the margins. Dates.

Phone numbers. Most of them hardly legible and none of them making much sense to me.

I returned the file to its place with the others, remembering what Nick had said about Joey having a big shadow to walk in. Maybe this was Joey's way of trying to one-up Nick's old partner, by learning as much as he could about him. Whatever rivalry was brewing between them, I didn't have time to concern myself with it now.

I slid the drawer closed and returned the keys to Joey's jacket. If Joey Balafonte had any secrets, he wasn't keeping them in here.

My phone vibrated. I slipped off a mitten to check Vero's text.

Vero: *Tow truck.*

Finlay: *???*

Vero: *Your code word if you need an emergency extraction.*

Finlay: *Very funny.*

Vero: *Find anything?*

Finlay: Noth . . .

I paused, my fingers hovering over my screen. I thumbed off my phone and returned it to my pocket, reaching for the file on Joey's desk. It was the same one he'd tried to push on Nick in the kitchen.

Curious, I used my mittens to open it. The five toxicology reports inside had been ordered by Ekatarina Rybakov, Feliks's attorney. Each report corresponded to an autopsy. Four of the victims had died from gunshot wounds to the head. The fifth had been a victim of carbon monoxide poisoning. A chill drew up my spine as I read the positive findings on the tox screens, recalling what Joey had started to tell Nick in the kitchen.

. . . four of the victims had traces of weed, opioids, coke . . . the usual suspects. But vic number five—

Victim number five had tested positive for ketamine.

I didn't have to read the victim's name. I already knew it. Because I had been the one who'd roofied him. It was Harris Mickler, Feliks's accountant, the very first body Vero and I had ever buried after I'd discovered his corpse in my minivan.

No. No, no, no, no.

Feliks's trial was starting in a matter of weeks. What was Kat planning to do with this?

I stiffened at the sound of footsteps approaching in the hall.

Shit, shit, shit! My hands shook in my mittens as I shoved the reports back in the file and returned it to Joey's desk. I whirled at a soft rap on the door, my heart thundering as I searched for a place to hide. There was no closet. No furniture to crawl behind.

The knob began to turn. I leapt behind the door as it opened. Breath held, I pressed flat against the wall.

I stood stone still as the door swung closed again, too terrified to breathe as I stared at Nick's back, three feet in front from me. I leaned closer to Joey's jacket, ignoring the thick smell of cigarette smoke as I tried to melt into its sleeves. Nick reached for the toxicology reports as he sat down in Joey's chair. He rifled through the pages. I could hear the exact moment he got to victim number five, the quick exhalation of his whispered swear.

My phone vibrated in my pocket. Nick lifted his head. I didn't dare breathe as he reached out with one hand and slowly adjusted the angle of the sleeping laptop screen.

This was it. He was going to spot my reflection and catch me and cart me off to jail.

He tipped an ear in my direction. His chair began to swivel. I stifled a gasp as the office door swung open and smashed into the end of my nose. My eyes watered furiously as it started to throb.

Please let it be Vero.

"Surprised to see you here," Joey said, a lingering prickle in his tone. "Thought you said the lab reports could wait until tomorrow."

The desk chair creaked. "Didn't mean to make myself at home. Figured you'd be at the movie for a while."

Joey grunted. "Ty offered to cover when he heard Vero was there. Rookie's been following her around all week like a damn puppy."

Very slowly, I reached into my pocket and silenced my phone. I pulled up Vero's last text.

Vero: *Hannibal Lecter just left the auditorium.*

I typed out a frantic reply: TOW TRUCK!!!

Vero: *Seriously???*

Finlay: *Get me out of here NOW!!!*

I squeezed my eyes shut, praying Joey didn't close his office door before Vero could come up with a distraction.

"What do you make of it?" Joey asked.

Nick blew out a long exhale. "The only leg the defense has to stand on is reasonable doubt. If I know Kat, she's going to latch on to these reports like a bulldog and use them to plant doubt in the jury. If she can persuade them to consider the possibility that this one death could have been attributed to someone else with an equally compelling motive, that would blow a hole in the prosecution's case. If they question one of the murders, they'll have to question all of them."

"Unless you can prove Zhirov had a hand in Mickler's murder, too."

"After reading this, I'm not convinced he did." Nick sounded tired, defeated when he said, "According to Mickler's wife, ketamine is the drug Harris was using to abduct his victims. Investigators found bottles of it in his office and in his car. Which begs the question . . . who drugged him, then poisoned him? The ketamine suggests the motive for Mickler's death was revenge. The nonviolent manner of death? Probably a woman. Someone reluctant to use a weapon, probably because they'd never killed before. I'm thinking Harris was murdered by one of his victims."

"Then how did he end up in a grave with four of Feliks's victims?" Joey asked.

"Maybe Feliks's men came for Mickler but he was already dead. They could have taken the body and dumped it with the others, just to keep anyone from finding it."

My stomach grew queasier the longer I listened. It was a plausible theory because it was partially correct. I could see Joey and Nick following it to an even bigger truth. *What if someone else killed Harris Mickler? And what if that same someone buried him on the sod farm, knowing those bodies were already there because she had somehow been involved with them?*

I jumped out of my skin at the piercing wail of a fire alarm.

"Damnit!" Nick said. "What now?"

Nick and Joey rushed out of the room. I peeped around the door and slunk out of Joey's office when they disappeared from sight, my mittens pressed to my ears against the blare of the alarm. The faint smell of smoke drifted through the hall. I yelped as I rounded the corner and smacked into Vero.

"Please tell me you didn't start an actual fire," I said.

She pinched two fingers together and closed one eye. "Just a really little one."

The alarm cut off. Nick's and Joey's raised voices carried down the hall, urging the academy students to return to their dorms. I dragged Vero with me into the women's bathroom, checking for feet under the stall doors before asking, "How did you set a fire without anyone seeing you?"

"I didn't," she said, perching on the counter. "I asked Ty to make me a bag of popcorn. When his back was turned, I added a few minutes to the timer, then I distracted him until the microwave caught on fire."

"Do I want to know how you distracted him?"

"Believe me," she said, "it didn't take much. What kind of dirt did you dig up on Joey?"

I leaned back against the counter beside her. "More like, what did Joey manage to dig up about us?"

CHAPTER 15

Vero and I huddled in a corner of a table over breakfast the next morning. The cafeteria was buzzing with chatter about the classes for the day. I sucked down a second cup of coffee. I hadn't slept a wink or written a word last night, consumed with worry over those damn toxicology reports.

Vero dusted toast crumbs from her mouth. "Nothing on those reports is going to matter if we don't find *EasyClean,* because Feliks will be pissed and he'll tell the police about Ike, and we'll both go to prison anyway. We've been here two days already and we've got nothing to show for it. I say we broaden our search. So what's the plan?"

I unfolded my schedule, holding it between us. "We have seminars all day. Apparently, we earn points for every class we attend. My sister's teaching a class on investigative procedure, Joey's doing search and seizures, Stu's giving a talk on victims' advocacy, Sam's offering a class on cybercrimes—"

"I'll go to that one. What else?"

"There's a forensics presentation in the auditorium, a K-9 demonstration on the drill field, and an arson presentation scheduled in the fire tower."

Vero shuddered. "Pretty sure we've both seen enough of that. When do we get to the fun stuff?"

"Looks like we get to pick two hands-on classes tomorrow. A few patrol officers are offering ride-alongs," I said, tapping Roddy's name on my schedule. "I'll sign up to ride with Roddy. That'll give me a few hours with him at least." We could affirm him as a possible suspect or scratch him off our list.

"Nuh-uh," Vero said, snatching the schedule from me. "You've been on three ride-alongs with Nick already. I'm signing up with Roddy. You can take firearms training with Wade. You still have the bullet we dug out of the Aston?"

"It's in my gym bag."

"Bring it with you. Maybe he can tell you something useful about it."

"Where am I supposed to tell him I found it?"

"You're the storyteller. Make something up."

We both clammed up as Max and Riley exited the food line with their trays, searching the bustling cafeteria for two empty seats. Max gave us a broad grin when she spotted us, making a beeline for our table.

She and Riley dropped into the seats across from us. "We missed you at the movie last night," Max said to me, breaking the seal on her carton of milk. "Sucks that we couldn't stay to watch the end, but at least we got to practice using the extinguishers. It took two of them to put the fire out."

"Two? For popcorn in a microwave?" I shot Vero a look. "Must have been a pretty big fire."

Vero smiled. "No hotter than your next book."

"Speaking of your books," Max said between spoonfuls of oatmeal, "we researched some of your earlier publications last night in preparation for our interview. *And* we read all twenty-four of your Amazon reviews."

Vero nudged my elbow. "Hear that, Finn? You got one more. I wonder who wrote it?"

Riley consulted his notes. "Some guy calling himself *FarmerSteven.*" *Great.* My ex-husband had resorted to leaving me book reviews.

Vero rolled her eyes. "And what did FarmerSteven have to say?"

"He said your work is 'a fine example of contemporary American literature.' And he said the sex was good, if a bit unrealistic."

Vero slammed her hands on the table. "*Good?* He thought the sex was *good*? That man wouldn't know good sex if it was happening in his own damn pants!"

"We also read that article in the gazette about your new series," Max said. "The one about the assassin. That must be so challenging to write from the point of view of the villain." She and Riley each uncapped a pen. Were they taking *notes*?

"She's not a villain. She's the hero," I corrected her.

"She's really more of an antihero," Vero said. "Admit it, Finn. Your lady killer is deeply flawed."

"She's not *deeply flawed*. She has a very strong moral compass, thank you very much. She's just . . ."

"An opportunist," Vero said as I said, ". . . misunderstood."

Riley nodded, scribbling furiously. "Max and I were curious," he said. "What kind of research do you do to put yourself inside the head of a killer?"

Chocolate milk shot out of Vero's nose.

I kicked her under the table. "Mostly Google."

Max looked up from her notes. "Too bad there aren't any forensic profilers on the faculty. You know, like Clarice Starling from the movie last night? Someone who could help you really understand who your assassin is and what makes her tick."

I set down my coffee. Curious, I reached for my schedule, skimming the classes. Vero frowned suspiciously as I bolted to my feet.

"Would you look at the time! We don't want to be late for Dr. Kirby's seminar." I scooped up my tray, urging Vero to follow.

"But our interview!" Max called after us.

"Later!" I promised.

Max was right . . . there were no forensic profilers at the academy, but a department psychologist just might do.

* * *

Vero and I had agreed to split up at the stairwell. Vero went to Samara's class on cybercrimes and I had made it to Stu's class just as it was starting. I'd slid silently into a seat in the back of the room, strategizing a list of questions I planned to ask him and, more important, how to frame them, when I'd become engrossed with his lecture, nearly forgetting why I was there. His presentation on victims' advocacy covered a broad swath of dark terrain, from human trafficking to domestic violence to sexual assault, including accounts of actual cases and his experience working with both the victims and the law enforcement professionals who'd been involved. I couldn't help wondering what he and Nick talked about every week, or the kinds of traumas Nick had been a witness to.

I lingered in the classroom as the other students filed out after Stu's lecture. He smiled when he spotted me, as if he knew who I was. I introduced myself and extended a hand.

"It's good to meet you, Finlay," he said, confirming my suspicion as he set down his messenger bag to shake my hand. "Nick speaks very highly of you."

I wasn't sure how to return the sentiment. Everyone seemed to like Stu, but Nick had been pretty tight-lipped about his counseling sessions. "Thank you, Dr. Kirby. I was hoping you might have a few minutes to help me with a question."

"I'm happy to try. And please, call me Stu." He gestured to a chair in the front row, waiting for me to settle into it before perching casually on the edge of his desk.

"I'm not sure if Nick told you," I continued, "but I'm a suspense novelist, and I'm working on a new project. I'm actually here this week doing research for my next book. One of my characters in the story is a . . ." I hesitated. Was there a clinical term for a dirty cop? ". . . a police officer who's become involved in criminal activities."

Stu's eyebrow rose over the rim of his glasses. "Not the hot one, I hope."

"No," I stammered, blushing at his wry grin, wondering how much Nick had already told him about my books, "not that one. See, the villain in my story is also a cop, only he's secretly working for some pretty bad people on the side. I'd like to portray his character as realistically as possible, and I was wondering if you could tell me anything that might help me understand who he is?" I felt a small stab of guilt. Lying to a therapist felt a lot like lying to a priest, but if Stu sensed I was fibbing, he didn't let on.

"That's a hard question to answer," he said thoughtfully. "I've worked with a few police officers who've found themselves on the other side of the law for one reason or another, but every case was different, each influenced by that individual's own unique struggles."

"What do you mean?"

"People who work in law enforcement see a lot of things most of us couldn't stomach, and their job is pretty thankless. It isn't always easy to be the good guy. Most days, playing the bad guy probably feels like the easier option."

I bit my lip as I pondered what else to ask. By the sound of it, *Easy-Clean* could be any of them.

"So if I was writing a mystery, what specific clues might reveal the identity of my dirty cop?"

Stu pushed his glasses up the bridge of his nose. "Well, from a practical standpoint, money is usually a motivator. There's a reason they gamble with peanuts," he said with a compassionate smile. "May I ask, does any of this have to do with Nick?" At my puzzled look, he said, "I know you said you're trying to understand a character in your book, but it seems that maybe you're asking something else."

"What do you mean?" I asked cautiously.

"The use of metaphors can be a safe way for our minds to explore subjects that are hard to talk about. If you were hurt in your last relationship, it makes sense that you might be searching for clues that a new romantic partner could secretly be a bad guy, to protect yourself from being hurt all over again. Creating a character can be a cathartic way to explore our own fears and traumas. It can also help us identify what we need to move beyond them." He paused, considering me as he let that sink in. "I can't divulge anything of a clinical nature, but I don't think it's a breach of confidentiality to say that Nick's one of the good guys. He's been through an ordeal, but he has a strong support system here and he's doing all the right things. And it would probably mean a lot to him to know that you care." He arched an eyebrow, hinting at a suggestion.

I nodded, quiet as I unpacked all that. In the space of a moment, we'd gone from dissecting the killer's heart to mine, and my insides felt both hollow and jumbled, as if someone had opened me up and dumped me out, then left me with a mess to fold and put away.

Stu's smile was sympathetic as he glanced at the clock. "I should probably head to my next session. And you should probably get to yours—that is, if you don't have any other questions?"

"Not unless you can tell me how to get my two-year-old to stop playing hide-and-seek in public bathroom stalls and my five-year-old to stop tackle-hugging people." Stu studied me with a curious tip of his head. "My sister has been reading parenting blogs and she's convinced my son is expressing an unhealthy avoidance of potty training and that my daughter is developing attachment issues as a side effect of my divorce." My laugh was unconvincing as I waited for affirmation that I hadn't screwed up the one part of my life that meant more to me than anything else.

"I can't say I'm much of an expert on potty training," Stu confessed, "but games like hide-and-seek can be a way for children to reinforce their sense of object permanence—their confidence that even when they can't see something, it still exists in the world. As for the tackle hugs, it's not necessarily unusual, or concerning, for children to be uninhibited when expressing themselves. Your son's willingness to put space between you, trusting he'll be found, and your daughter's unreserved passion for the people she cares about . . . those aren't unhealthy qualities, Finlay. If anything, we could all learn something from them."

"That's a metaphor, isn't it?"

Stu's smile creased the corners of his eyes as he took up his messenger bag. "Children are remarkably resilient, Finlay. Grown-ups can be, too."

The door swung closed behind him, muting the hum of conversations in the hall, leaving me alone in the empty classroom and yet oddly reassured that there was hope for my heroine after all.

CHAPTER 16

Vero was waiting for me in the hallway when I left Stu's classroom. "What did he say?" she asked, falling in step with me as I navigated around clusters of academy students searching for their next seminars.

"Nothing that will help us narrow our list of suspects. Did you get anything out of Sam's class?"

"Aside from a girl crush?" Vero shook her head. "That woman is beautiful, smart, and sassy as hell. And she has great taste in shoes."

"Remember what Cam said. Anyone can be anyone online, and designer pumps don't come cheap." Money was a powerful motivator, but it was also a universal one. Any person here might be swayed to do the wrong thing for the right price. "Just because she's a woman doesn't mean she isn't our guy. I only saw *EasyClean* from a distance. Sam's tall enough to have been the shooter I saw and, in the right coat with her hair pulled back, I could easily have mistaken her for a man in the dark."

"I don't know, Finn. I'm not getting serial killer vibes out of her. Sam's studied every kind of cyber-fraud that exists. She takes down bad guys with a keyboard, not a firearm."

"That doesn't mean she doesn't know how to use one."

"True. But she's definitely more Lord and Taylor than Smith and Wesson. She wasn't even wearing a holster under her jacket. Probably because it would have clashed with her suit."

"We can't rule her out just because she's well dressed."

"No, but we can rule her out because she's smart. If Sam wanted to use her cyber powers for evil, why would she have bothered getting her hands dirty by actually murdering people when she could have just hacked their accounts or scammed them out of their money? Think about it," she said in a low voice as we wound around a group of oncoming students. "*EasyClean* could have blackmailed Feliks as soon as he discovered the forum. Instead, *EasyClean* chose contract killing for a revenue stream. Probably because he wasn't secure enough in his own computer skills to think he could hold his own against Feliks's cyber guys."

She had a point. "Fine. We'll rule her out. For now. But I reserve the right to reopen our investigation if she asks my sister out. What's your next class?"

Vero turned her schedule toward me. "That's why I came up here to find you. Check out the seminar in the auditorium. It starts in thirty minutes."

I read the title of the class aloud as we walked. "Crime Scene Forensics: Impressions and Pattern Evidence."

"No, the instructor." She tapped the names listed beside it. Dr. Mohammed Sharif, Tool Marks Examiner, and Peter Kim, Lab Technician. "Isn't that the same Pete you met at the lab? The one who reads your books?"

I drew the schedule closer and read the brief bio under Peter Kim's name. I'd never asked Pete for his last name, but how many Peters could there be in one lab who worked in soil analysis and impressions? "It must be."

"Still have that bullet with you?" Vero asked. I nodded. "If we hurry, maybe we can catch him before his lecture starts."

Vero and I drew open the door to the auditorium and peeked inside, relieved to find most of the seats were still empty. A projection screen rested on the stage between two podiums. Pete looked up from his notes as the door clicked shut behind us. He nearly tripped, his note cards scattering to the stage floor in his rush to get out from behind his podium to greet me.

"Wow! Finlay, I didn't know you were going to be here." He met us at the side of the stage, took my hand, and shook it enthusiastically. "I mean . . . that's not entirely true. Nick told me you'd be here this week. I just didn't know you'd be at my lecture." He did a double take as he noticed Vero beside me.

"Sorry," I said at his dumbfounded look. "This is my nanny, Vero."

"Accountant," she corrected me.

"Oh, wow, an accountant," Pete said, reaching to shake her hand, too. "Numbers are great. I like numbers." His eyebrows shot up. "I mean, not *your* number, because that would be inappropriate. And probably awkward. You know, for both of us. I just meant numbers in general." Pete took his hand back, clamping his arms tightly against his sides, probably to hide the damp rings that had begun forming under them. "You're the first ones here," he said, ducking to retrieve his note cards from the floor. I knelt and scraped up a few stray cards for him. "We're not supposed to start for another ten minutes, but you're welcome to sit wherever you like. Preferably somewhere I won't be able to see her . . ." He shook his head. "I mean you, because sometimes when I get really nervous, I sort of freeze up, and once it was so bad, I even—"

"Pete," I said, bending low to catch his eye as I handed him the cards. "We came early because we were hoping to ask you for a favor." The instructor at the other podium—presumably Dr. Sharif—glanced over at us between stern looks at his notes. I lowered my voice, gently pulling Pete aside into the shadow of the thick red folds of the stage's curtain. Vero followed, tugging it closed behind us as Pete gave his armpit a discreet sniff. His arm fell back to his side as I retrieved the bullet from my backpack. It didn't look like a bullet—at least none I had ever seen. It was shaped more like a wilted flower, but Pete seemed to recognize it immediately.

He reached for it, squinting at it under the low lights. "Where'd you find it?"

I looked to Vero. We hadn't come up with a story. "We . . . didn't. A friend of ours did. We were curious if you could tell us anything about the weapon that might have fired it."

Pete looked skeptical. "Where did your friend find it?"

"She . . ."

"Found it at a school playground," Vero improvised. Pete nodded, as if this didn't surprise him. "I told Finlay it would make an excellent opening for her next book. A suburban mom finds a key piece of evidence while her kids are playing innocently on the playground, and she takes it upon herself to investigate where it came from."

"Whoa." His eyes ping-ponged between us. "That would make a great story. She wouldn't be able to uncover much on her own though. She'd need a professional to examine it. You know, a firearms examiner."

"Like Wade?" I asked.

"Wade Coffey? The firearms instructor?" Pete looked stung. "No, he just teaches people how to shoot. She'd need a forensics expert, someone who knows how to analyze tool marks."

"Someone like you?" Vero asked eagerly.

"Yes. I mean, no," he corrected himself. "Not exactly—"

"Can you tell us anything about the bullet?" I asked as the auditorium began to fill with the hum of voices.

"I'm really not an expert in this sort of thing," he said, trying to hand the bullet back. Vero slipped a piece of notebook paper from her backpack and scribbled her phone number across it. His eyes flew open wide as she held it out to him. "But I might know someone who could take a look at it," he said quickly, taking her number.

"Thanks, Pete," I said, zipping my bag shut. "And let's keep this between us, okay? I'd rather no one else know about it."

An awed wonder dawned slowly across his face. "Oh, I get it. You don't want this to get back to Nick because the hero in this book is going to be the lab guy and not the cop. Because everyone in the department knows the hot cop from the first book was modeled after Nick, and his ego would be bruised if he thought he was upstaged by a hot scientist!"

Vero stifled a snort. I pinched her before it could escape.

Pete's grin was triumphant. "Your secret's safe with me," he said, holding up the bullet. "That's what heroes do. You know, save the day and . . . stuff." He glanced sidelong at Vero. I could guess the *stuff* he was imagining. He hitched a thumb over his shoulder, stumbling backward into the curtain. "I should put my cards back in order before the lecture starts." The bullet slid from his fingers as he waved. It hit the wooden floor with a ping and he scrambled to pick it up. He slapped at the curtain, searching for an opening in the fabric.

Vero shook her head as he disappeared through it. "Don't take this the wrong way, Finn, but I don't think Pete is qualified to save us."

"We don't need him to be a hero. We just need him to tell us about the gun that fired that bullet." And hopefully keep his mouth shut.

CHAPTER 17

After breakfast the next morning, Vero walked to the front gate to meet up with Roddy for her ride-along, and I followed the map to the shooting range for my handgun class with Wade. A few other students were already waiting in his office, peering through a small window into the empty firing stalls on the other side. Mrs. Haggerty's grandson stood beside her, offering her his arm for balance as she rose up on her toes to see. Charlie leaned casually against the wall, chatting with a handful of other officers. He greeted me with a nod as I pulled off my mittens and claimed a space against the wall in the crowded room.

A blast of cold air whipped my hair as Wade rushed in. The acrid scent of cigarette smoke trailed from his clothes as he brushed past me toward the desk. His eyes flicked over us as he stripped off his denim jacket and dropped it over the arm of his chair. He wasn't wearing a shoulder or belt holster like the other detectives wore under their coats, just a ratty T-shirt and two full sleeves of brightly colored ink. He raked back his windblown hair, revealing the ghost of a faded tattoo on his neck that looked like it had been lasered off.

"Listen up," he said, gesturing to one of the instructors to hold up his sidearm. "That is a Sig Sauer P226. It's a full-size service pistol and the preferred service weapon of many law enforcement agencies."

"Is that what we'll be using today?" one of the students asked. A few of the instructors laughed as the officer holstered his gun.

"You," Wade said, handing each of us a plastic tote, "will be using these. In your kit, you'll find a training pistol, protective gear, and one box of .22 caliber ammo. You will be working one-on-one with an instructor." He handed off a stack of clipboards to Charlie. "Please follow your designated instructor to the range, complete your waivers, and await further instructions before handling your firearms."

I stayed behind as the rest of the class filed through the door into the shooting range.

Wade sat on the edge of his desk, checking off boxes on what I presumed to be my clipboard. I cleared my throat when the silence became awkward. "Hi, Detective Coffey. I'm—"

"It's Wade. Or Coffey. Take your pick," he said without looking up.

"Right, sorry. I don't know if you remember me. I'm—"

"Georgia's sister and Nick's piece. Got it. Sign this." He turned the clipboard toward me and dropped it on the desk. I opened my mouth to object to being objectified as Nick's anything, but Wade was already rummaging in a drawer.

I reached for the clipboard and began skimming the waiver but gave up after reading the same line three times. Something about Wade rattled me. It wasn't just his gruff demeanor or his tattoos, or the fact that he was the only instructor in this place that didn't feel at all like a cop. It was the way his eyes darted around me instead of over me. There was a shiftiness about him that felt out of place here. All the other instructors insisted on being addressed by their rank or "detective." They all had the same direct gaze, had mastered the same stillness—the assured walk, the *shoulders back, legs apart* way of holding themselves. Everything about Wade felt evasive. Frenetic. And yet, as I stared down at the words on the waiver—as he dragged a tin of chewing tobacco from his back pocket and shoved a wad into his gum—I still had the sense I was being closely watched.

I signed my name on the form and passed the clipboard back to him.

"Let's go." He walked fast, forcing me to keep up as he pushed open the door to the shooting range. There was an oddness to his gait, something between a swagger and a limp. Without slowing, he grabbed a set of earmuffs and goggles from a hanging rack and dropped my tote on a waist-high shelf in the only empty booth. He passed me the ear coverings and goggles from inside my kit. "Put these on."

"Then how will I hear the instructions?" He didn't bother to answer as he slipped on his own set of earmuffs. "You're a man of few words. Got it," I said, donning my protective gear. I glanced through the plexiglass barriers separating the stalls and found Mrs. Haggerty in the one right beside me. She grinned up at Charlie as he loaded bullets into the magazine of her gun.

Wade slapped the box of ammo onto the shelf as if he'd rather be anywhere else.

"So you're . . . not a police officer?" I asked as he removed the gun and its magazine from my tote. If my intrusive questions were going to piss him off, better to figure that out *before* he loaded it.

Wade's jaw tightened around his chew. He angled the magazine so I could see the rapid, fluid movement of his fingers as he filled it and slapped it into the gun.

My mouth went dry as he held the pistol out to me. I stared at it, jumping at the sudden pop of gunfire from another stall.

"You seen a handgun before?" His voice was surprisingly clear, if a bit echoey, through the earmuffs.

I nodded. The last time I'd been this close to one, it had been pressed to the side of my head. I could feel Wade watching me, waiting for me to take it, but I couldn't seem to make myself reach for it.

"Ever held one? Fired one?" he asked.

I shook my head.

With slow, careful movements, Wade placed it in my hand, using his own to show me where and how to hold it. His voice softened as he corrected the position of my fingers and thumbs. "I *was* a cop, for fourteen years," he said.

"Why'd you leave?" I asked, welcoming the distraction.

"Bad knee. Among other things." He raised my hands until the pistol was pointed straight out in front of me.

"Were you with OCN?"

"For a while." He pressed a button on the wall that sent my hanging paper target racing backward on a track. "Started in a uniform, like everybody else. Made detective and rotated around for a few years. Spent the last four in OCN. Deep cover. Got made. Jumped out a window trying to save my own ass and busted my knee when I hit the ground. The rest is history."

The nose of my gun dipped a little. Wade hadn't just been undercover, but deep cover. That explained the tattoos and wild, unkempt hair, but it explained a lot of other things, too. My sister had told me about the deep cover cops, though never by name. I wasn't even sure she knew who they were. They worked alone, no partners to watch their backs, no contact with family and friends as they submerged themselves in a world of criminals. One misstep and they'd end up in a shallow grave before anyone knew they were gone.

"Spread your feet," Wade said, adjusting my stance. "Bring your shoulders forward. Relax your knees. Now extend your arms straight out in front of you. You're going to line up your sights with the center of the target. Middle of the chest."

"Not the head?"

"Center mass. You're more likely to hit your target. When you're ready to shoot, move your finger to the trigger, touch, and pull."

I drew in a slow, shaky breath and let it out slowly, bracing myself for the sound as my finger slid to the trigger. My eyes slammed shut at the muted but familiar pop.

"Good," Wade said. "Your nose was a little high, but not bad for your first try. Keep your eyes open next time." I stole a glance at Mrs. Haggerty's target as he recorded my score. "Eyes on your own paper," Wade scolded me. "Try again."

I emptied the rest of my magazine as Wade offered quiet corrections. I managed to keep all my bullets on the paper, though only half of them landed within the target. Wade showed me how to reload, and as I fed bullets into the channel, I peeked once more at Mrs. Haggerty's paper. She'd fired every one of her rounds and hadn't put a single hole in it.

Charlie took her empty training gun and set it aside. He reached into his holster and withdrew his own. The range fell silent as he loaded the chambers of the largest revolver I'd ever seen, snapped the cylinder in place, and passed the pistol to Mrs. Haggerty.

"Holy shit," said one of the other instructors. "Charlie's giving her his Magnum." A few of the instructors huddled together, laughing quietly to themselves as Mrs. Haggerty hoisted the massive revolver.

"Is that really a good idea?" I asked Wade as she closed one eye, staring down the wobbling length of it.

Wade's lip twitched around a mouthful of chew as Mrs. Haggerty pulled the trigger. The sound was deafening, even through the earmuffs. Charlie caught her as she teetered backward on her heels.

"Hooo! That's got some kick!" she said as Charlie set her on her feet. The instructors laughed, breaking into applause. Charlie leaned over her shoulder, pointing out the lone hole she'd shot in her paper. Mrs. Haggerty squinted downrange, trying to find it.

"Why does Mrs. Haggerty get a big gun?" I asked. "That hardly seems fair."

"Don't let the size fool you," Wade said. "The bigger the gun, the more surface area to grip, the easier it is to control."

Charlie grinned through the divider at Wade, a challenge in the crooked slant of his lips.

Wade eyed Charlie over the rim of his Coke can as he spit. He set it down and took my training pistol from me before I could finish loading it. His shirt rode up as he reached behind him into the waistband of his jeans, revealing a slender holster hidden inside it. He withdrew his gun, checked the magazine, and placed the weapon in my hands, adjusting my grip around the Glock logo.

The range fell quiet again as Wade pushed a button and my target zoomed another fifteen feet toward the opposite wall. "Double or nothing," he said, loud enough for Charlie to smirk.

"What are you doing?" I sputtered. "I can't hit that. It's too far."

"You can hit it. Keep your eyes open."

"But everyone's watching."

"Which means they'll all be talking about it in the faculty lounge when Mrs. Haggerty shows you up." He nodded to the paper. "Center mass. Take him out."

I gritted my teeth and adjusted my grip. The instructors murmured as Wade issued quiet commands and I lined up my shot. I pulled the trigger, eyes open this time. One of the officers let out a low whistle. Charlie tipped an imaginary hat to me as Wade recorded my score, awarding extra points for the added distance.

"Show's over," Wade called out. "Everybody back to work. Finish your boxes of ammo, tally your scores, and leave your clipboards with your instructors."

"Why do you use a smaller gun than the other instructors?" I asked him when the pop of gunfire around us resumed.

"Did you know I was carrying before I showed you?" he asked. I shook my head. I hadn't noticed the Glock in the back of his jeans until he'd reached under his shirt to remove it. "You can tell a lot about a person by the way they handle—or don't handle—a weapon," he said, the subtle inflection of his voice suggesting he'd been making a few observations of his own. "Cops carry big guns where everyone can see them. My cover would have been blown the first day I went under if I'd been caught wearing one of those," he said, jutting his chin toward the other officers. "You can't look like a cop, talk like a cop, carry yourself or your weapon like a cop. The bad guys have to believe you're just another bad guy."

"Were you? A bad guy?" I asked, surprised and a little terrified that I had voiced the question aloud.

His lips quirked behind his spit can. "You asking me if I'm a bad guy or if I've done some bad things?"

I thought about that as I pulled the trigger. "Is there a difference?"

He seemed to consider that as he set down his can. "You do the job long enough, gets harder to tell. We're all liars," he said, taking the gun and reloading the magazine with a snap. "Some of us are just better at hiding it."

I was still processing what he'd said, sifting through the nuances of it, as he returned the Glock to me.

"So who else do you teach besides PTA moms and Rotary Club grandmas?" I asked, parroting back his comment from the bar the night we'd met.

The corner of his mouth hitched up. "Why? Are you going to put me in one of your books?"

"Will you answer my questions if I say yes?"

"You shoot, I'll talk," he said, inclining his head toward the target. He waited until I'd discharged a few more rounds before answering. "Mostly, I handle testing and training for the department," he said between pops of the gun. "Occasionally, I teach civilians and department employees who want to apply for a concealed carry permit—judges, secretaries, lab rats, the occasional attorneys."

"Who's the best shooter here?" I asked as I worked through my remaining rounds. "Besides you."

He leaned in to correct my grip. "If you asked me a couple months ago, I would have said Sam."

"Samara?" I asked, not bothering to mask my surprise. "I thought she specialized in cybercrimes."

"She goes through the same training as everyone else. Joey's not bad either. He looked pretty sharp the few times I've seen him out here. But it's easy to hit a stationary target on a lighted range. It's another to take out two active shooters through a smoke line in the dark. Damn near impossible after you've been shot twice."

I lowered the empty gun. "Nick?"

Wade reached for it, his voice low in my earmuffs. "Don't go telling him I said it. The asshole's cocky enough."

"Don't go telling Nick what?" came a voice behind us. I turned and saw the last of the students filing out of the range. Charlie stood with his arms crossed behind us, watching Wade load the last of his bullets into the Glock.

"Nothing," Wade said as he handed it back to me and gestured for me to keep shooting.

"Good," Charlie said. "Wouldn't want to have to tell him you were giving his star pupil a hard time, but it sounds like he's got nothing to worry about."

Wade grunted. "Tell that son of a bitch I never gave a woman anything she didn't like." Charlie guffawed. "What do you want, Charlie?"

"Need the keys to one of the training cruisers. Got emergency vehicle training this afternoon. Thought I'd take the class out to the skid pad and let Mrs. Haggerty do a few donuts. Finlay can ride shotgun."

My finger slipped. Wade ducked as the shot rang out and a plastic light cover shattered in the ceiling downrange. I lowered the weapon, quickly moving my finger off the trigger as a piece of plastic dropped to the floor with a soft plink.

A chuckle started deep in Wade's chest, growing louder in stereo as Charlie laughed, too. "That's not funny!" I said. "Mrs. Haggerty can't see far enough in front of her to read the odometer!"

"It's a closed course," Charlie said. "The most she can do is burn a little rubber. It'll be the most excitement she's seen in years. Don't worry, I won't let her do anything I wouldn't do." He winked, and I had the feeling that left Mrs. Haggerty quite a bit of wiggle room.

"I'll get the keys. Keep an eye on my shooter," Wade said to Charlie. "And you," he said to me, "go easy on the lights."

"What was that all about?" I asked Charlie once Wade was gone. I watched him through the small window of his office as he dragged open the top right drawer of his desk and rummaged around inside.

"Just poking at an old bruise," Charlie said. "A few years ago, Wade and Nick had a falling-out over a woman, and Nick hasn't gotten around to forgiving him yet." Charlie jutted his chin toward the target. I tried to ignore the feeling that settled uncomfortably in my chest as I turned and fired my last few rounds. "If it's any consolation, Wade seems to like you," he said when I was finished. "And I can probably count on one hand the people in this world Wade Coffey likes."

"How do you know?"

"He bet on you."

"You mean that whiteboard I saw in the faculty lounge?" I asked dryly.

Charlie narrowed his eyes at me. "And what was a nice lady like you doing sneaking around in the faculty lounge? Not sampling from the fine collection of confiscated liquor, I hope."

"There's liquor hidden in there?"

"Third cabinet from the right, below the fire extinguisher."

"Nick neglected to mention that."

"I bet there's something else Nick didn't mention. And since I've got a cool hundred riding on you, I might be inclined to tell you." He dipped his head close and lowered his voice. "If I was you, I'd get to bed early tonight." Before I could ask him why, he turned for the door. Wade dropped a set of car keys in Charlie's hand as they passed each other. "See you on the track, Donovan," Charlie called over his shoulder.

Wade held his hand out for his gun. "How do you feel?" he asked, tucking it back in his waistband.

"Better," I admitted as I stripped off my earmuffs and goggles and dropped them in my tote. Wade pressed the button on the wall. My target raced toward me with a startling whine, light shining through the bullet holes as it jolted to a stop in front of me. Some of the confidence I'd felt waned. The holes were haphazard and scattered, far less organized than they'd looked from a distance.

"You did good today," Wade said as he tallied my points. He plucked the paper from its hanger and held it out to me. "Just remember, don't put your finger on the trigger unless you're willing to pull it. When you do, don't second-guess yourself. Aim straight for the chest." His eyes caught mine and held as I reached for my target. It was the first time I saw the glimmer of a detective inside them, and I hoped he hadn't seen the glimmer of a criminal in mine.

CHAPTER 18

When I opened the door to our dorm room after class, Vero was sprawled on her belly on her bed, reading from my open laptop.

"Hey!" I slapped it shut.

"A tsunami, Finn? Are you kidding me right now!" She sat up on her knees, grabbing my computer as I reached for it and holding it hostage behind her head. "The assassin and the cop were having a moment—a very hot one, I might add. They were just about to get naked and do it on the beach, and you had to throw a *tsunami* at them? What kind of cockblock is that?"

"It's not a cockblock! It's a natural disaster."

"Do they even have tsunamis in Mexico?"

"I don't know! I've never even been there." The most exotic place Steven and I had ever done it was in the bed of a pickup truck in the parking lot of his frat house in college.

"Tonight, you're going to rewrite this scene, Finlay. You're going to get rid of the tsunami—"

"Fine, I'll make it a tropical storm."

"No storms! Your assassin is going to stay on that beach and confess her feelings to the cop. She's going to be bold and brave and face her fears, and she's not going to freak out and go running in the other direction when he does the same. She's going to throw caution to the wind, Finlay—"

"You told me to delete the wind."

"She's going to lose herself for one night of pleasure and passion."

"And then what? They're only going to get hurt."

"So they get a little sand in their nether regions. What's sex without a little chafe?"

She held out my laptop. I took it with a begrudged sigh. She didn't understand. It had been different with the attorney. The stakes had been low. There'd been no risk in being intimate with him because he didn't have the power to arrest her.

The cop was different. What happened to the assassin in the morning? Was she just supposed to wipe the sand from her ass and turn herself in? There was no resolution to their story that didn't end in a shitstorm of pain and aloe vera. "I'll figure something out." I kicked off my shoes and collapsed onto my mattress. "How was your ride-along with Roddy?"

"Bo-ring." She rolled onto her back and stared at the ceiling. "He wouldn't let me drive. He kept blathering on about rules and policies. *Blah blah blah*. He wouldn't even let me put the lights and sirens on. We spent two whole hours clocking radar and he didn't give anyone a ticket. He let every one of them off with a warning and I fell asleep twice. Roddy felt bad that it was a slow day, so we bought a box of Twinkies to split between us and hung out in the parking lot with a few of the other patrol officers."

"Talk to anyone interesting?"

"No one of note."

"What about Roddy? You think he could be *EasyClean*?"

"Hell. No. The guy's way too boring to be *EasyClean*. I'm serious, Finn," she said at my cynical look. "Case in point, I asked him why he isn't a detective after twenty years in the department. Want to know what he said? That he never really cared about getting promoted, he just likes the job. His wife's a cosmetic surgeon in McLean. He drove me past his McMansion in Clifton. He doesn't need money; his wife's loaded. There's no way he's *EasyClean*."

"Did you ask him anything about the night of the shooting? Were you able to corroborate Joey's story?"

"Yes and no." She rolled onto her side to face me and propped herself on her elbow. "Roddy definitely remembered calling Joey and asking him to cover our house that night so he could grab dinner and do a little last-minute Christmas shopping for his wife. He said he left as soon as Joey's car arrived. They flashed their headlights at each other, but they never got out of their cars. And according to Roddy, Joey was gone by the time he got back."

"Meaning he has no idea how long Joey was actually there. Or if the person who covered for him was even Joey."

"Precisely."

"Which means Joey is still high on the list. And you're sure there's no way Roddy could possibly be our guy?"

She blinked at me. "He put his roof lights on and stopped four lanes of traffic to help a turtle cross the road, Finn. I think we can safely scratch him off our list of suspects. How about you? What did you get out of Detective Coffey?"

"He's not a detective. Not anymore." I relayed both of my conversations with Charlie and Wade, including everything I'd learned about him—why he carried a different gun than most of the other cops here and why he behaved differently. I told her about his competitive streak and his rivalry with Nick. And yet, while every clue seemed to point to Wade as a likely suspect, it wasn't Wade who had left me feeling ill at ease.

"What do you think of Charlie?" I asked, turning to Vero.

She looked me up and down. "Don't get me wrong. He's a little old for you, but you do you."

I tossed my pillow at her head. "I mean, do you think Charlie could be *EasyClean*?"

Vero hugged my pillow to her chest. "He seems too nice," she said doubtfully.

"Maybe, but consider the facts. He and Nick still see each other every week. Nick practically said he tells Charlie everything. Charlie was a cop who was forced out of his job before he was ready, which probably left him hurting financially. The pieces all fit." But more than that, something Wade had said kept replaying in my mind.

We're all liars. Some of us are just better at hiding it.

Charlie was charming, but he was also a rule bender. Not a breaker, per se, but he seemed to have no problems pushing boundaries. Like when he'd sneakily revealed the location of the booze in the faculty lounge while admonishing me for being there. Or when he'd suggested I get to bed early tonight, for what reason I didn't know but Nick clearly hadn't felt was appropriate to share with me. How he'd encouraged Nick to take me to dinner even though Joey had been adamant that it was a flagrant violation of a rule that didn't exist but probably should.

I thought back to two nights ago in the gym, to the argument I'd overheard between Charlie and Joey.

Nick Anthony is no fool, Charlie had said as he'd shoved Joey. *If he hasn't seen through you yet, he will.*

The hair on my arms stood on end as I remembered Joey's response. *The way he saw through you?* He'd implied that Nick hadn't seen something he should have—that Charlie was hiding something.

It's always the nice ones that have something to hide, Joey had warned me during his class.

But if Charlie and Joey were both liars, which one of them was the bad guy?

CHAPTER 19

I shot upright in bed, jolted awake by a series of loud thumps. Blinking away the fog of sleep, I scrambled to catch my open laptop before it could slide off my thighs to the floor. The screen awoke, illuminating my manuscript. The cursor blinked behind the last words I must have typed before I'd drifted off. Vero dragged her blanket over her head, burrowing deeper under her pillow as someone pounded on our door.

"Wake up, trainees!" The booming voice sounded disturbingly like Joey's. "You've just been called to a crime scene. This homicide isn't going to solve itself. You've got ten minutes to get to the drill field. Let's go, let's go, let's go!" More banging, more shouting, the noise becoming muffled as he made his way down the hall.

I closed my laptop and swung my legs over the side of the bed, shaking Vero by the shoulder. "Get up and put on some clothes. We have to be at a crime scene in ten minutes." When she didn't respond, I grabbed the corner of her blanket and flipped it away from her.

Vero curled into a ball, clutching her pillow. "If you make me get out of this bed, this room is going to become a crime scene."

"Fine. You can do the push-ups." I shucked my pajama pants and dragged on a pair of jeans.

She rolled over to glare at me when I switched on the light. "What time is it?"

"A little after one."

"Someone had better be dead."

"I'm pretty sure that's the point," I said, pulling on my coat. "Here, put these on." I grabbed a sweater and a pair of warm pants from Vero's suitcase and tossed them on her bed. Grudgingly, she got up and dressed, following me into the hall where we melted into the pack of bleary-eyed faces filing out of the dorm. By my rough head count, only half the teams had bothered getting out of bed.

"What's this all about?" Vero asked, tying her sleep-mussed hair back into a loose ponytail as we reached the drill field. The instructors were all there, steam on their breath as they talked amongst themselves, holding clipboards and sipping coffee from Styrofoam cups.

Nick leaned on his cane in the middle of them, entirely too bright-eyed for the hour. "Just a little role-play."

Vero rubbed her eyes. "For the record, Detective, this is not the kind of role-play I expect when a man bangs on my door and wakes me up after midnight."

Tyrese's eyebrows shot up, his cup jolting to a stop halfway to his mouth and splashing coffee down the front of his coat.

Nick suppressed a wry smile as Ty used his sleeve to mop himself. "Noted, Miss Ruiz." He raised his voice so the students in the back of the group could hear him, waiting for their hushed speculations about our reason for being there to quiet. I avoided making eye contact with Riley and Max, who were practically buzzing. "Listen up, everybody! It should come as no surprise to you that most violent crimes are committed at night. The graveyard shift is when many of those crimes are reported and detectives are woken from a nice, peaceful sleep to investigate a crime scene, like you were tonight. In order to give you the full hands-on experience, that's precisely what you all will be doing for the next ninety minutes." My sister began distributing hand-drawn maps to each team. "Dispatch just requested an officer to respond. A body was spotted by someone claiming to have been walking his dog in a remote wooded area. The caller did not provide his name, but he gave the approximate location of what may be an expeditious grave. Your job is to proceed to the location and investigate. The first team to locate the body—if one does indeed exist—will be awarded twenty points. They will also be responsible for securing the crime scene. The instructors will then assign various investigative tasks to the other teams. I recommend you take notes and handle your evidence carefully. Each piece of evidence you find will be used to obtain an arrest warrant and indict a suspect before the end of the week. Any questions?" Someone yawned in response.

"What time are you going to wake us up for class tomorrow?" another student asked.

"Your first classes won't start until ten. If you all hustle through this exercise tonight, you can be back in your dorms before three and get a decent night's rest."

"How many points do we get if we solve the case?" Vero asked, suddenly wide awake.

Charlie and Roddy exchanged a silent high five. Joey crossed his arms, looking annoyed as the other instructors murmured in small huddles, probably adjusting their bets for the whiteboard in the faculty lounge. I looked for Wade, but he wasn't among them.

Nick spoke over the rising chatter of the teams. "The instructors staged the crime scene while you all were at dinner tonight. Every piece of evidence, including any obtained through witness statements, has a designated number of points attached to it. Detective McDonnell and Officer Governs will be keeping score. Bonus points will be given to individual teams that follow the best practices and investigative procedures you learned in your classes today. Points will be deducted for improper searches, mishandling of evidence, and breaks in the chain of custody. Any other questions?" Nick passed his clipboard to Georgia. "Good. Please proceed to the wooded area designated on your maps. As soon as you arrive, you may begin your search. If you or your partner locates the body, call out to the nearest faculty member and we'll provide instructions from there."

Vero ushered me ahead of the other teams, pretending not to notice

Riley and Max when they waved to get our attention. "What are you waiting for? Let's go," Vero said, dragging me by my coat as the instructors looked on.

"Maybe we shouldn't seem so eager to go looking for a body."

"Don't be so uptight. It's just like an Easter egg hunt, only better."

"It's twenty-eight degrees out here, it's dark, and I don't see any chocolate. Tell me how this is better."

"Because this time, we don't have to worry about getting caught." She hustled farther ahead of the pack. I blew out a stream of fog as I struggled to keep up with her. "Let's start looking there." She pointed at the edge of a shadowy tree line and handed me the map. I drew my phone from my pocket and turned on the flashlight. She yanked it from my hand and turned it off. "What are you doing with that? You know we're not supposed to bring our phones to class! The instructors will deduct points if they catch you with it, and I am not losing this thing to Mrs. Haggerty." She shoved my phone back in my pocket and pulled a standard flashlight from her coat. She shone it in front of us, sweeping it in broad strokes over the ground as we walked.

"Why are we stopping to look here? The other teams are all moving deeper into the woods." Riley and Max's flashlight was little more than a speck through the trees. Even Mrs. Haggerty and her grandson had nearly disappeared from sight.

"Nick said we're looking for an expeditious grave. Expeditious means quick—"

"I know what expeditious means."

"If you were hauling around a body and you wanted to get rid of it *quick*, how far into the woods would you want to drag it? I say we start close to the trail."

I didn't argue, mostly because I didn't feel like walking any farther. We picked our way through the brush, the beam of her light intersecting with the others in a filmy kaleidoscope of patterns as the rest of the class searched in the distance. Vero knelt beside an uneven stretch of ground, shining her light into a pile of sticks and debris.

"Look," she said, ducking closer and angling her head. "Do you see that?" A flicker of white showed through the dead foliage. I plucked a loose branch from the pile, revealing a mannequin's arm underneath.

"Detective, we found it!" Vero called out, hauling away another branch.

A chorus of resentful moans sounded through the woods. Footsteps crackled through the brush, beams of light converging as the other teams formed a semicircle behind us and leaned close, eager to see.

Vero and I tossed away the last of the ground cover, unveiling a shallow dip in the dirt. The plastic limbs of a CPR dummy protruded from the hole.

"Nice job," Nick called out as he hobbled toward us. "Did anyone check to see if our victim is breathing?"

"I don't think that's necessary, sir," Riley said behind me.

Nick laughed as the teams parted to let him pass. "You know what they say about assumptions. They make an ass of you and . . ." Nick paused in front of the gravesite. His eyes narrowed at the pile of disconnected limbs. "Very funny, guys," he said, throwing accusing looks at each of the instructors. "Which one of you knuckleheads dismembered my mannequin?" The teachers barked out a few surprised laughs.

"Check it out, Detective." Max circled around to the far side of the grave, aiming her flashlight at the dummy's face. "There's a name written on the victim's forehead."

"Let me see that." Nick hobbled around the grave and reached for her flashlight. He leaned on his cane over the shallow hole. "Really hilarious, guys." Nick's light lifted to a group of chuckling instructors. "Apparently, the deceased has a name," he said dryly. "Obviously, we can't confirm the victim's name is *actually* Carl without further investigation."

Vero and I stiffened. She elbowed me in the ribs.

"I know!" I hissed.

"But I'm awarding thirty points to Officer Donovan and Officer Ruiz for locating the deceased," Nick continued. "They will now be responsible for clearing and securing the area while the rest of you wait for the ME. That role will be played by Peter Kim, our forensic tech volunteer." Pete trudged through the brush, carrying a plastic tote in one hand and his flashlight in the other, his lab coat peeking out from under his puffy parka. Vero and I lingered beside the grave while Pete met with the other teams outside the crime scene.

"Nice job," Nick said, handing me a roll of yellow tape. His hand brushed my back as he went to join the rest of the class.

Bracken crackled under our feet as Vero and I got to work, stretching yellow tape around the bases of the trees. "The dummy is hacked to pieces," I whispered. "And someone named the victim *Carl.* That can't be a coincidence."

"It has to be," she whispered back. "There's only a handful of people in this world who know how Carl Westover died, and not a single one of those people would be stupid enough to tell anyone that he was chopped into bits and stuffed into a freezer. We should stay cool," she insisted as she tore the last of the tape from the roll. "None of the detectives seem concerned. And tons of people are named Carl, right? You saw how the instructors reacted. I bet one of them was just trying to screw with Nick. They probably watched too many episodes of *The Walking Dead*. That whole show is just eleven seasons of Andrew Lincoln dodging dismembered body parts while he shouts, '*Carl!*'" Vero bellowed the name in a raspy voice, doing her best impression of Rick Grimes while she staggered and made zombie faces.

I shushed her as a few heads turned our way, most of them giggling.

The teams began fanning out, dividing the crime scene into a grid and searching for evidence. Nick joined the other instructors with a begrudging smile as they razzed him about his desecrated dummy, each of them pointing the finger at someone else. Maybe Vero was right. No one seemed terribly disturbed by the discovery except Vero and me.

"I don't know about you," she said, "but I did not drag my sleeping ass out of bed at oh dark thirty to watch some other team win the prize. I'm going to grab us a piece of this action before all the good clues are taken. Are you coming or not?"

"I'll be right there," I assured her.

As Vero picked her way back to the crime scene, I retreated farther from the search parties, ducking under the yellow tape toward the razor-wire fence. I kept my back to the other teams, concealing my phone as I dialed Steven's number again. Again, it rang to voice mail.

"Steven, it's Finlay," I said in a low voice, checking over my shoulder to make sure I was alone. "You know that . . . parcel I asked you to hold on to for me? The special one I asked you to keep at the farm for a while? I just need to know if it's still there. That you didn't move it or . . . open it for anybody. Call me when you get this." I disconnected, feeling anxious and off-balance, unable to shake the feeling that the dismembered dummy was no coincidence as I started back toward the group. Ahead, shouts of *I found something* or *Should I bag this, Detective?* were answered by encouraging comments from the instructors while my sister called out the point values.

I paused, my phone light shining on a crumpled piece of paper in my path. I bent to pick it up. The paper was dry, which meant it couldn't have been out here long. The sleet and freezing rain we'd had the night before would have turned it into frozen paste by now. I smoothed it out and held it under my light. The sales receipt was dated earlier that day from a hardware store not far from here. Three items had been purchased with cash: a pair of work gloves, a hacksaw, and a permanent marker.

I hurried through the brush, ducking back under the yellow tape to find Vero. "Hey, I think I found something," I said, holding the receipt out to her.

Her eyes widened as she took it. "Where was it?"

"Past the yellow tape, about a hundred feet that way," I said, pointing loosely to where I'd found it.

"Too far," she said, handing it back to me. "That's outside the crime scene. The instructors said they only dropped clues within fifty feet of the grave. Probably so we're not out here searching all night. Why? What is it?" she asked when I refused to take it.

"Look at the items they bought."

Vero frowned at the receipt. "If this was part of the exercise, why'd they leave the clue so far from the crime scene?"

"Unless it wasn't part of the exercise at all."

"Let's wrap it up, everybody," Nick called out. "Bag and tag the last of your evidence and sign it into the chain of custody with an instructor."

I took the receipt from Vero and stuffed it in my pocket.

"But we still haven't found the murder weapon," Mrs. Haggerty's grandson pointed out.

"Sometimes we don't," Nick said frankly. "Head back to your dorms and grab some shut-eye. Tomorrow, a few volunteers from the Commonwealth Attorney's Office will be coming to assist us with a mock trial." The announcement was met with excited chatter as teams began filing back through the woods toward the dorm.

Vero arched up on her toes, searching the crowd. "I'm going to catch up to Pete and see if he's had any luck with our bullet. I'll meet you inside."

I lagged behind the rest of the herd, hoping to avoid Riley and Sam, my thoughts still stuck on the dummy we'd found. Between Harris Mickler's toxicology report and the dummy named Carl, it was starting to feel like the ghosts of my past were coming back to haunt me.

A cane clicked down, blocking my path, and I clutched my chest, sucking in a gasp.

"You really shouldn't walk alone in the woods at night. You never know who might be out here." Nick reached for my hand, helping me over a fallen branch.

"Like the axe murderer who hacked up your CPR dummy?"

He shook his head and sighed. "Yeah, exactly like that. When I find out which one of those assholes did it, I'm sending them a bill." The path ahead of us was reasonably clear, but he held my hand anyway, both of us ambling slowly to the rhythm of his cane. "And now I'm going to be up all night correcting tomorrow's handouts, because the autopsy report I prepared for our mock trial says our victim was strangled. And her name definitely wasn't Carl."

I forced out a laugh, determined to push thoughts of Carl Westover from my mind. Nick and the other cops weren't taking the dummy seriously. I was probably overthinking this. "If it's any consolation, it was a pretty fun class. You know, minus the whole *being dragged out of bed in the middle of the night* thing. You could have warned me about that, by the way."

"That wouldn't have been fair to the other teams. Besides, I told Charlie."

I narrowed my eyes at him, remembering Charlie's warning about getting to bed early. "That hardly counts."

"Precisely." He paused beside a tree, resting his weight against the trunk as he pulled me into the space between his legs. He smelled like coffee and his leather jacket, and faintly of the spicy cologne that he wore. The three together were a deadly combination, and my breathing became shallow as he reached for the zipper on my coat. "You know," he said in a seductively low voice as he dragged it down. He reached inside my breast pocket, somehow managing not to touch me as he withdrew my cell phone from it. "You're not supposed to have this in class. I should probably confiscate it, but I'll let you off with a warning." He grinned as I snatched it away from him. His expression grew serious as I checked to make sure the screen was locked before tucking it away. "Everything okay? I saw you leave to make a phone call. It's not the kids, is it?"

"No, nothing like that. It's just . . . Steven being Steven," I said through an infuriated sigh.

Nick nodded. A sobering silence drew out between us. Somehow, even after Steven had walked out on our marriage, he still managed to make everything in my life revolve around him. I pressed a hand to my temple. "Can we just . . . not talk about him?"

Nick drew my hand from my face with a tentative smile, holding it between us as he ducked low to meet my eyes. "There is actually something else I've been wanting to talk to you about. We didn't really finish the conversation we started in the kitchen last night."

"What part?" I asked cautiously.

"The part when I was telling you how much I like spending time with you." He stroked a thumb over mine, his voice falling soft. "I'm glad you came this week. I'm sorry if anything I did or said made you doubt that. When the citizen's academy is over, I thought maybe we could—"

"Nick!" My sister's shrill shout carried like a Harpy's through the trees.

Nick's head dropped back, a ribbon of frustration spooling into the sky with his heavy exhale. "Be right there," he shouted back. I started to pull away, but he cupped my hands between his. "You're freezing. You want to come inside and get something warm to drink? There's hot chocolate in the faculty lounge, and I'll be up for a while fixing all these damn reports anyway. I'd love some company."

"I shouldn't." Hot chocolate sounded a little too much like dessert. This week was supposed to be about resolutions and deadlines: find a killer, eat healthy, don't murder anyone, and fix my book. I backed away, nearly tripping over a root. "I was up late last night working on this revision for Sylvia. I should try to get some sleep. And you should probably get your work done. I'll see you in class tomorrow."

"You sure you don't want me to walk you?"

"The dorm's right there," I said, hitching a thumb at the smattering of lights across the drill field. "I'll be fine. This place is crawling with cops."

He laughed, masking a wince as he pushed himself off the tree and put his weight on his leg. "I'll be alone in my office if you change your mind." There was a twinkle in his eye as he limped off to find my sister.

I pulled my coat tighter around me, quickening my pace as I crossed the dark length of the drill field. The wind that whipped over it was sobering, bringing the chilling events of the night back into crisp focus. Nick hadn't been alarmed by the dismembered dummy, I reminded myself. It was all one big joke as far as the instructors were concerned. Just a coincidence. And the wind had probably blown the hardware store receipt away from the crime scene. I probably should have turned it in to Georgia for the points.

A gust tossed my hair over my eyes. As I brushed it aside, I caught the faint hint of cigarette smoke. I turned, spotting a flicker of red out of the corner of my eye, but as I scanned the buildings around the drill field, they were all quiet and dark. I started toward the dorm when I caught the tiny flash again. The bright cherry of a cigarette burned on the uppermost deck of the fire tower. Just as quickly, it dimmed, but the smell of it grew stronger as if the wind had carried it right to me. All I could make out was a shadowy figure on the roof, leaning against the low wall, watching me.

I hurried the rest of the way across the drill field and waved my lanyard over the scanner to the dormitory's front door. The lock didn't budge. I peeked inside, but it was two thirty in the morning, and the vestibule was empty. Everyone had already returned to their rooms for bed. I walked around the side of the building, searching for another entrance, pausing in my tracks when I heard a hushed conversation around the next corner.

"If you're fucking with me—" Joey's gruff voice was unmistakable.

"Would I have come here just to mess with you?" I tipped my head as I recognized the second voice, too. It was Cam. "I found it myself," Cam said. "Exactly like I told you."

A ripple of panic washed over me. What had Cam found—or

claimed he'd found? Before Cam began hacking computers for the mob, he'd been working off his petty crimes as a confidential informant for Joey. I couldn't be sure who he was loyal to now. Was he reporting something to Joey as an informant? Or was that a ruse to conceal a job he was doing for Feliks Zhirov? Either way, Cam had enough dirt on me to land me in hot water with both of them.

I peered around the bricks. Joey had Cam's back against the wall, his fist wound in the front of Cam's jacket, their faces close. "You must be crazy sneaking in here."

"Don't get your panties in a bunch. I came through the woods. No one saw me cut the fence."

Joey shoved Cam hard against the bricks. "You're walking a very fine line."

"I'm just trying to help you!"

I stepped around the corner before I could think better of it. "What's going on here?"

They leaped apart. Cam's leather jacket was shredded. Blood dripped from the crease of his hand where the fence must have cut through it. He glanced at Joey, like he was looking for some cue to run. Or lie. Joey held fast to the collar of Cam's coat.

"What are you doing out here?" Joey snapped at me. "You should be in your dorm."

"The front door's locked and my card isn't working. I was on my way to try the other door, but apparently I interrupted something." I looked between them.

"It's nothing," Joey said. "Just some punk kid who thought it'd be smart to sneak in. He's lucky I'm feeling generous. I was just about to escort him off the grounds." He jerked his chin toward the dorm. "Go inside. There's nothing to worry about here."

"It's late," I pointed out. "His parents are probably worried sick. I could take him to the infirmary. Get him some bandages for his hand. Maybe some hot chocolate." All I needed was a few minutes alone with him to make sure he wasn't in danger with Joey and figure out what he was doing here. I held my cell phone out to Cam. "You can use my phone if you need to call your mom or dad to pick you up." Cam lived with his grandmother, but revealing I knew that could land us both in a heap of trouble.

Cam glanced once more at Joey.

"He can use mine," Joey said.

"Are you sure you don't want to come with me?" I prompted Cam. "I'm happy to wait here until you and the detective have finished talking."

He gave a quick shake of his head. "I'm fine. You don't have to worry about anything."

"Let's go." Joey shoved him toward the parking lot. Cam pulled his hood over his head, dragging it low to conceal his face. His eyes caught mine, then darted to the dormitory windows above me before he turned away.

I gnawed my thumbnail as I watched them walk briskly toward the gate. Joey waved off the duty officer as they maneuvered past the barricade. Brake lights flashed as Joey depressed his key fob and deposited Cam roughly inside his unmarked sedan. He wouldn't hurt Cam, I told myself—not after I saw them together. I tried to convince myself Joey would never be that callous—or that foolish—as his car disappeared from sight.

CHAPTER 20

After Cam and Joey left, I hurried through the back door of the dormitory and raced up the stairs to my room. Vero was in her pajamas, sitting cross-legged on her bed, staring at my computer on her lap. She tapped a key with a dramatic flourish, looking up at me with a triumphant gleam in her eyes.

Her face fell as I rushed to the window and pulled back the blind. "What happened to you?"

"What do you mean?"

"You look like you've seen a ghost."

The window was unlocked. No sign of forced entry. But there was a faint red smear on the frame inside. "Did you lock the window after Javi left the other night?"

"No. Why? What's going on?"

"You're never going to guess who I just ran into outside." At Vero's blank stare, I said, "Cam was here. He snuck through the fence and Joey caught him."

Vero set my laptop aside. "You think he was here looking for us?"

"I don't know. I couldn't exactly ask him. I only caught a little of their conversation before they got in Joey's car and left."

"What did he say?"

"Cam told Joey that he found something. I didn't hear what."

Vero stiffened. "You don't think that little sneak blabbed to Joey about Ike, do you?"

"I don't think so," I said, remembering the last words Cam had spoken to me before Joey carted him off. *You don't have to worry about anything,* he'd said, right before he'd glanced up at the windows of our dorm. "I think he might have been in our room. Help me look for anything out of place."

Vero scrambled off her bed to help me search. We shuffled around the room, tossing aside blankets and clothes, searching under mattresses and pillows, opening drawers . . . At first glance, nothing appeared to be missing. My computer was on Vero's bed. Vero's phone was right where she'd left it while we were in class, charging on her nightstand. Our wallets were both present and accounted for. And as far as I could tell, nothing was out of . . . place.

I reached into the open gym bag beside my bed, withdrawing the notebook I'd been using to take notes during classes. A bloody handprint stained the cover. A torn sheet of paper slipped free of its pages, folded into a square around a tiny, hard lump. Cautiously, I opened it.

A gold tooth fell into my hand, bits of dried bloody tissue still clinging to its roots.

I dropped the tooth, stifling a gag. It plinked off the tile floor and skittered toward Vero.

"What the hell is that?" she said, leaping back to avoid it.

"I'm pretty sure it's Ike's."

"I know that! Why would Feliks send it to us?" Vero rummaged through her toiletry bag and handed me a disinfectant wipe.

My skin crawled as I frantically rubbed the wipe over my fingers. "I don't know. What does the note say?"

Vero pinched the corners of the paper and held it between us. Cam's message was written in blocky, rushed letters.

The Big Man's Losing His Shit. If You Think You Know Who Ez Is, You'd Better Come Out And Say It Soon Or Heads Are Gonna Roll. He's Got Dirt On You And He's Not Afraid To Use It. Also, Please Don't Kill Me For Saying That.

With Gravitas (I looked it up),
C

"Something tells me we're not getting any tomatoes," Vero said, passing me the note.

With a grimace, I used my wet wipe to retrieve the tooth from the floor. I crumpled it inside Cam's note and dropped it back in my bag, unsure what else to do with it.

"That's disgusting," Vero said.

"That's insurance," I said, rubbing my hands up and down my jeans. The tooth was obviously a message from Feliks, leverage to make sure we fulfilled our end of the bargain we'd made with Kat. "She promised to handle Ike if we handle *EasyClean,* but we haven't figured out who he is yet, and she clearly hasn't disposed of Ike's body. At least, not all of it." I shuddered.

Vero patted my shoulder. "Look on the bright side. Cam said all we need to do is cough up a name."

"So?"

"So we'll give Feliks a name, Kat will make Ike go away, and we'll find some other way to pay off Marco. Problem solved."

"How are we supposed to give Feliks a name if we can't figure out who *EasyClean* is? Did you talk to Pete?"

"I caught up to him after class," she said, dropping onto her bed. "He talked to the guy who specializes in this stuff, but Dr. Sharif says he won't look at our bullet because he only works on official cases for the police. And you want to know the worst part? The asshole kept our bullet. He says students aren't supposed to have ammunition on the grounds."

"That bullet was the only tangible evidence we had!"

"Pete said he'll try to get it back for us. Meanwhile, I've been working on that whole second part of our plan, and I have some news about the money." The eager gleam had returned to Vero's eyes. I'd seen it before, and it never boded well.

"Should I be worried? Because I'm definitely worried."

"Do you want the good news or the bad news?"

I peeled off my coat and tossed it on my bed. "What's the bad news?" Might as well get it over with first.

"Javi called. He found a buyer. They're meeting at Ramón's later tonight to move the car. He should have the money by Friday."

I frowned as I kicked off my shoes. "That's the bad news?"

"He could only get a hundred and fifty grand out of the guy, minus Javi's ten percent."

"What's the good news?" I asked cautiously, remembering the look on her face when I'd come inside the room. She'd been on my computer. On the training center's Wi-Fi. I hoped, whatever she'd been doing, it didn't involve any wheeling and dealing with loan sharks or the Russian mob.

"Sylvia loves your new ending."

I froze, poised on one leg, my right sock peeled halfway down my foot. "I haven't even written the ending. How could she love my new ending?" My stomach dropped at Vero's smirk.

"Sylvia texted you this morning to ask how your revision was going. You were in the bathroom, so I texted her back for you. I told her the new ending was brilliant and that your characters were currently on a hot beach in Mexico, drinking margaritas in a state of postcoital bliss."

"No, they're not!" I cried, tearing off my sock and throwing it at her. "They can't be in bliss, they're in the middle of a—"

Vero dodged my sock and held up a finger. "If the word *tsunami* comes out of your mouth, I will finish the rest of this book myself. The cop and the assassin will hump each other for three hundred pages, I'll write a velociraptor orgy into the ending, and I'll send the whole damn thing to your agent." She waited for me to shut my mouth before lowering her finger. "I just sent Sylvia a summary of the changes you *are* going to make," she said sternly, "and I asked her to extend your deadline. You're welcome."

My blood pressure was so high I could feel it pulsing in my head.

"You know what you need?" Vero asked me.

"A paycheck?"

"That, too. Come on," she said, tossing me my sock and dragging on her coat.

"Where are we going?"

"To the faculty lounge for cookies and booze."

Vero and I cracked open the door to the dining hall. The cafeteria looked like a graveyard in the dark, its empty tables forming neat rows like tombstones and stacks of chairs casting eerie shadows against the walls. We tiptoed toward the faculty lounge, pressing our ears to the door before peeking inside.

I reached for the light switch, but Vero slapped my hand from the wall. "Are you crazy? Someone might see." She pulled her flashlight from her coat and switched it on. "Where did Charlie say they kept the liquor?"

"The cabinet below the fire extinguisher."

Vero circled the buffet table in the middle of the room, dropping to her knees in front of the cabinet in question. "It's locked. Look for a key."

I searched the cabinet above my head, recalling the fireproof key box I'd noticed when I'd been looking for a mug the other night. I pried it open, digging through a stack of card keys. "Try this one," I said, passing her a tiny metal one.

Her grin was wicked as the lock popped open. She rifled through the contraband and withdrew a bottle of whisky. I pulled two mismatched mugs from the shelf, and we sat on the floor with our backs to the cabinet, the drape on the buffet table shielding us from view of the door.

Vero poured a few fingers in each of our mugs and set the bottle between us. My eyes watered as I took a deep swig. When I opened them, Vero was stealing a handful of cookies from the buffet. She set two in my hand. "Don't give me any bullshit about New Year's resolutions. It's been a day, and I don't want to hear it." She rested her head against the cabinet as she nibbled, grinning at my quiet moan when I gave in to temptation and tore into my cookie.

"I can't believe Joey's betting against us," she said, shining her flashlight at the dry-erase board. "You want to know what I think? I think he's just been giving you a hard time and talking shit about you to Nick because he's trying to make you look bad, so that when you finally prove he's a dirty cop, no one will believe you."

"We're doing a fine job of making ourselves look bad." We held the top score for moving a body and unearthing a corpse, and my high-speed maneuvers had raised more than a few eyebrows during my driving class yesterday.

Vero grinned behind her mug. "We might actually win this thing if Mrs. Haggerty doesn't steal it."

For the life of me, I couldn't figure out what it was Vero was so eager to win. It's not like we were competing for a cash prize or an all-expenses-paid trip to Bermuda. And I highly doubted Nick's admiration—or Tyrese's for that matter—were high on her list of motivators. And yet, she'd been so determined to master every test they'd thrown at us.

I thought back to that day Vero had interrogated Aimee in Macy's, when she'd pretended to be a cop. Then the night Nick was shot and Vero had called for an ambulance, claiming to be a police officer, reciting some ridiculous lines she'd probably heard while watching an episode of *Brooklyn Nine-Nine*. Maybe I wasn't the only one who wished I was on the right side of the law.

"There is such a thing as forensic accounting," I suggested.

Vero choked on her liquor. I patted her back as she recovered. I didn't think it was such a far-fetched idea. She was young and fit, stubborn, and intelligent, teetering between fearless and confident to a fault. She'd be a great investigator.

"I'm pretty sure they're looking for candidates that *haven't* committed felonies."

"It's not like there's a warrant out for any of them." At least, not yet.

She took the bottle and refilled our mugs. "Speaking of hot pursuits," she said, deftly changing the subject, "are you going to spill the beans about where you and Nick disappeared to after class?"

"Are you going to tell me why the letter *J* is tattooed on your ass? And don't tell me it has nothing to do with Javi." She gasped as if I'd revealed a state secret. But she wore crop tops and low-riding pajama bottoms to bed, and she had a habit of throwing her covers off when she got hot in the middle of the night. I'd seen the top half of the letter peeking out of her waistband, high on her left butt cheek, just before she'd rolled out of bed for the crime scene exercise tonight.

She hiccupped and leveled a finger at me. "For your information, a lot of people's names start with the letter J, like . . . Jimmy Fallon. And Jesus. And Jack Daniel's," she said, holding up her mug. "Don't look at me like that. I was eighteen and stupid when I got that tattoo, and my stingy boss doesn't pay me enough to have it lasered off."

It was my turn to gasp. "Or maybe you just don't want to."

"Puh-lease."

Voices carried through the door from the cafeteria. Vero snapped off her flashlight and scrambled under the tablecloth with our cookies and mugs, remembering the bottle of whisky as the lounge door opened and the room flooded with light. I reached under the drape, dragging it under the table with us a second before a pair of shoes and a cane rounded it toward the coffeepot.

"Then who sent it?" Nick's voice was tense. A cabinet door slammed.

"No idea," Joey answered. "When Georgia, Roddy, and I staged the crime scene after dinner, the dummy was in one piece, no markings on it. I talked to every instructor after the exercise. No one copped to it. They all said they had no idea how it got that way."

"But someone dug it up, dismembered it, and emailed a photo of it to Feliks Zhirov. And you know this how?"

"One of my CIs was screwing around trying to find a back door into Zhirov's network. He claims he saw an email with an attachment."

"Jesus, not Cam." I could practically hear Nick shaking his head. "And you believe him?"

"He described the crime scene to a T, Nick. He even knew the name written on the dummy. He gave me the time, subject line, and the email address of the sender. It came from a Google account registered under a bullshit ID. Tell Nick what you told me, Sam."

Vero and I glanced at each other. Samara had been so quiet, neither of us had realized there'd been another person in the room.

"I called in a favor from a friend at Google. The CI's story checks out. An email was sent to Feliks's address from the same Gmail account the CI gave us. I asked her to verify the contents of the attachment, but my contact refused to open it without a warrant."

"And we have no idea who sent it?" Nick asked.

"No," Samara answered. "All we know for sure is that it was sent from an IP address in our network."

"Here? You're telling me this was an inside job?"

"Or someone who had access to the campus's Wi-Fi. It's not bulletproof," she admitted, "but it's locked down pretty tight. Whoever it was, they were definitely here on campus when they sent that email. I have no reason to believe our network was hacked."

"Did you check the arrival and departure logs at the gate?" Nick asked.

Joey answered. "No one signed in today who wasn't supposed to be here."

Nick's cane tapped an agitated beat against the floor. "What did the email say? Anything other than the photo?"

"Sam printed a copy."

Paper rustled. Nick read aloud, "You're taking too long and you know what I want. Pay up before I give them all your buried secrets."

"Any idea what it means?" Samara asked.

"Someone's blackmailing Zhirov," Nick said thoughtfully, as if he was working through a puzzle. "Sounds like they're threatening to turn over evidence if he doesn't comply with their demands. But evidence of what?"

"I wondered the same thing," Joey said. "A body in a shallow grave could be a reference to Zhirov's upcoming trial, but none of those bodies were hacked up like that dummy."

"What about the name . . . Carl?" Nick asked.

"I did a quick search of the files from Zhirov's investigation," Joey said. "The name Carl only yielded one hit—Carl Westover, Theresa Hall's stepfather. According to public records, he died last year. Stage four cancer. He was buried at home on a family plot."

Vero squeezed my hand. Only part of that was true. Carl was presently buried at his home on a family plot—or at least, most of him was—but it hadn't been his cancer that killed him. And one very large piece of him was still buried on my ex-husband's farm.

The paper rustled again. My skin prickled at the renewed sense of urgency in Nick's voice. "You think this message to Feliks has something to do with him?"

"Only one way to know for sure," Joey said. "It's a long shot, but if there's something in that man's grave that could implicate Zhirov—something big enough to be worth blackmailing him over—it might be worth checking out."

Vero covered her mouth to stifle a gasp.

"We'll never get a warrant to exhume him on a hunch," Nick said. "We need something solid we can take to a judge."

"What about his wife?" Joey asked. "You think Barbara Westover would mind if we poked around her property?"

"She hates Feliks Zhirov almost as much as I do," Nick said. "It's worth a try. Classes don't start until ten tomorrow. I can head to the Westovers' first thing in the morning and be back before the mock trial. Sam, can you go back through our network traffic and see if there were any other outgoing emails to that same address? It's possible this wasn't the first."

"I'm on it."

"Want me to do a search of the area where we buried the dummy?" Joey asked. "See if I can find anything?"

"Don't bother," Nick said. "Whoever staged that photo was smart. They knew dozens of students would be tromping all over those woods tonight. You'd be better off picking through the clues the students found. See if anything jumps out that wasn't part of the exercise."

I touched the hardware receipt in my pocket as the door to the faculty lounge shut behind them.

"This is not good," Vero said.

"We have to get to Mrs. Westover before Nick does. If they dig up that grave and find Carl in pieces, they'll open an investigation into his death. That will lead them straight to Barbara Westover and her daughter, and Theresa will lead them straight to us." Feliks had been responsible for murdering Carl, but we'd all had a hand in covering it up. "Come on, we have to go."

"Go where?" Vero whispered, chasing me out of the lounge through the dark cafeteria. "We can't go anywhere. We don't have a car!"

"We need Barbara Westover to move her husband's body, and we can't call her from here."

I threw open the exit door and paced under the awning, shaking out my hands. It had begun to rain, a nasty wet mix of icy, slushy drops. I ran a hand down my face, willing myself to sober as the reflection of the parking lot beyond the fence blurred against the pavement. We couldn't sign ourselves out; there would be a record of us leaving the campus. Somehow, we had to slip past the duty officer at the gate and find a car.

"What if we sneak out and ask Javi to meet us near the road?" Vero suggested.

"You said he's meeting with his buyers about the Aston tonight." Besides, Javi already knew too much. We'd have to do this on our own.

An unmarked police car turned into the parking lot. The officer on duty waved it past the security booth. The sedan didn't even have to come to a full stop before entering the gate.

I pulled my phone from my pocket and hunched over the screen.

"What are you doing?" Vero asked.

"Texting my sister."

You awake? I typed.

Three chat dots appeared, then, *What's up?*

Need to run to the pharmacy for tissues and cold medicine. Can I borrow your car? Georgia was practically a germophobe. There was no way she would offer to drive me.

Sorry. Had an emergency. I'll be back in the morning. See if Nick can take you.

My laugh was almost hysterical, and probably a little drunk. I shielded my face from the rain with my sleeve, pushing up on my toes to peer out over the parking lot. Sure enough, my sister's car was nowhere in sight. My arm fell away from my face as I did a double take at the rows of retired police cars.

The training cruisers . . . Wade kept the keys in his top right desk drawer.

"I think I can get us a car," I said. "Can you find us a uniform? You know, like the sweatshirts and hats the instructors have been wearing?"

"Where am I supposed to find one of those?" Vero asked.

"Try the locker room or the laundry. We just need something official. Something a cop here would wear. And make sure it's warm," I said as she turned to go. I had a feeling it was going to be a very long night.

CHAPTER 21

I wasn't sure what I had expected when I'd scanned the card key I'd stolen from the metal box in the cabinet of the faculty lounge, but the soft *click* of the lock releasing still took me by surprise. The air inside Wade's office smelled faintly of stale tobacco. A pale glow filtered through the window to the shooting range where a light had been left on in one of the stalls. A paper target dotted with tightly packed holes hung below it like a ghost.

"Hello?" I called out, just in case I wasn't alone, my mind already spinning a story to explain what I was doing here with a stolen key at three in the morning. My voice echoed back to me as I tiptoed through the office. I checked the corners of the room for cameras, but the only ones I remembered seeing the day before had been inside the shooting range, directed toward the stalls. I crept toward Wade's desk and slid open his top right desk drawer. Rummaging under a can of chewing tobacco, a soft pack of Marlboros, some notepads, and a lighter, I found a handful of key rings at the bottom.

The key chains had all been labeled with a permanent marker. I squinted at the makes, models, and years, looking for the oldest one. Hopefully no one would notice if a well-worn training sedan came back with a near-empty tank of gas or a little extra road grime.

I chose a set of keys and hurried to the exit.

As I reached for the door handle, I paused, certain I'd caught a trace of cigarette smoke in the air. I glanced back at Wade's office, then through the window into the shooting range at the lone paper target. With a shudder, I slipped the keys in my pocket and closed the door behind me.

Thirty minutes later, I was freezing my butt off in a beat-up, geriatric training cruiser behind the shooting range. Sleet spattered the windshield and an icy draft seeped through the vents, but I was too afraid to turn on the engine for fear that someone might notice the exhaust.

I jumped at a knock on my window. A dark coat with an FCPD insignia filled the frame, the gold name badge pinned to the front obscured by the layer of ice on the glass. The officer hiked up his belt and knocked again.

Shit.

I rolled down the window, struggling to come up with a reason for being here as the officer ducked to peer inside.

"Vero?" Her name burst from my mouth on a held breath.

She scowled at the interior of the sedan as freezing rain bounced off the shoulders of a police coat that was at least two sizes too large for her. She opened my door and held her hand out for the keys. "This is the last time I let you pick our stolen car. This thing is a junker. I'll be shocked if it starts."

"At least if we wreck this one, we won't have to kill anyone to pay it off."

"Again . . . not our fault."

"Never mind the car. Where did you get that uniform?"

"Borrowed it from Tyrese," she said, blinking away sleet and gesturing impatiently for me to get out. "Don't worry. He won't miss it."

"What do you mean, you borrowed it? How is he not going to miss his uniform? You're wearing his badge, Vero!"

She arched up on her toes, picking a wedgie out of her ass. "Can we please get on with it? My uniform is getting wet, and these polyester pants are chafing the hell out of my lady bits. Ty's boxers kept falling down so I took the damn things off."

"Why were you wearing his underwear?" I sputtered.

"Because he was wearing mine." She rolled her eyes as if the answer should have been obvious. "Move over," she said, shouldering me aside. I contorted myself over the center console, sliding into the passenger seat as Vero got in and shut the door.

I gaped at her bagging sleeves as she started the car. "Do I even want to know?"

"It was easy. I showed up at Ty's room with the bottle of Jack Daniel's and told him I really wanted to see him in my panties. Next thing you know, we were swapping clothes."

"Are you crazy! What if he reports you?"

"Believe me, he's not going to say a word about this to anyone."

"How can you be sure?"

She held her hands in front of the vents and adjusted the dials. "You really think he wants to tell his partner he woke up handcuffed to his bed, wearing nothing but a push-up bra and a lacy pink thong? Don't worry," she said as I buried my head in my hands, "I left him the key. It just might take him awhile to find it. And I promised to send him a lewd picture of me in his uniform if he let me hold on to it for a while."

I was pretty sure my heart stopped.

She drew on a pair of mirrored sunglasses and turned on the defroster. "Get in the trunk."

My head snapped up. "I'm not riding in the trunk!"

"What if the cop in the security booth sees you?"

"Then *I'll* drive and *you* get in the trunk!"

"I'm the one wearing the uniform." Vero pulled a lever and the trunk popped open. She stared at me, waiting for me to get out.

I climbed out of the car with an exasperated huff. "Whatever you do, do not stop at the security booth," I warned her. "Do not make eye contact or attempt a conversation with the duty officer. Just wave and keep driving when he opens the gate."

"Where?"

"Head to the nearest town and stop at the first all-night convenience store you can find. We're going to buy a prepaid cell phone so we can call Mrs. Westover. We'll tell her to move Carl, and then we're bringing the car right back." I climbed inside the trunk, shoving aside a stack of orange training cones and contorting myself to fit beside them. The last thing I saw was Vero, her hair pulled back in a severe bun, a pair of mirrored sunglasses obscuring her face, and her petite frame swimming in Tyrese's starchy uniform as she shut me inside.

My phone started to vibrate. I twisted sideways, working it free of my pocket. Vero's name lit on the screen, filling the trunk with an eerie blue light.

I tapped the screen to accept the video call. Vero's phone was propped on the passenger seat beside her, angled toward her to catch her profile in the frame. The windshield wipers slapped a steady beat across the glass.

"I figured you might get claustrophobic back there. See? It's almost like a ride-along," she said as the car bounced over a speed bump. Water splashed against the undercarriage as the cruiser jostled through puddles.

"I think I'm going to be sick." I shut my eyes, breathing through my mouth. The smell of highway tar and plastic cones was thick in the cramped, dark space, and if Vero didn't let me out soon, I was certain I was going to vomit.

"Don't worry, Finn. We'll have you out of there in no time." She plucked the handheld microphone from under the dash.

"What are you doing?" I asked, my nausea suddenly overshadowed by raw panic.

She pressed the *Talk* button and held it to her lips. "Pretending to look busy." Her voice boomed out across the parking lot, projected by a set of speakers in the grill. She rushed to turn it off, flipping switches and buttons at random. A country song blared over the radio. Blue lights swirled over her shocked face and the siren whooped twice before she managed to shut it all off.

I dropped my head back and shut my eyes. We'd been involved in the murder and disposal of four men, but we were going to prison because of Vero's thong.

"Stay cool," she said. "We're coming to the security gate."

I held my breath, my eyes glued to the screen as Vero dimmed the headlights and turned off the wipers. The cab, dark a moment ago, filled with the diffuse light from the security booth. It reflected off Vero's shades. "What's happening?" I asked, my heart suspended between beats as the car slowed.

"The officer is opening his window." She dragged down her shades with a low whistle, angling to get a better look at him.

"Do not stop this car, Vero!"

"Relax," she said, "it's pouring out here. He can hardly see through the windshield. Oh . . . it's working! The gate's going up. He's waving me through."

I didn't start breathing again until the car began to accelerate. My head bounced painfully off the floor of the trunk as we bumped over a pothole.

Vero winced. "Sorry."

"Just hurry up and let me out!" I closed my eyes and concentrated on not puking as the minutes ticked by. The car made a sharp turn, throwing me against the cones. A moment later, the engine cut off. Then the phone. I pounded on the lid of the trunk.

Cold air rushed in and I drew it deep into my lungs. I grabbed Vero's hand, clamoring over the lip to the damp ground. Her tennis shoes glowed white against the slick dark pavement, the hems of Tyrese's black uniform pants rolled in sloppy cuffs around them.

I got up and leaned on the rear bumper, struggling to get my bearings. We were behind a building. A gas station, judging by the smell of it.

"I'll go inside and get us a phone," Vero suggested.

"No!" I nearly fell over as I rushed to my feet. "You can't go in there wearing that. Stay with the car. I'll do it." I drew my hood up to cover my face and circled the building, my feet tripping to a halt as I recognized where we were. The charter bus had driven through this intersection three days ago. The small stretch of shops between traffic lights had consisted of one gas station, a grocery, a bank . . . and a hardware store.

I dug the crumpled slip of paper from my pocket. The name on the sign over the hardware store across the street matched the one printed on the receipt I'd found during the crime scene exercise in the woods.

I walked around to the front of the convenience store. Two security cameras were mounted high above the doors, one angled toward the gas pumps, the other toward the road and (with any luck) the hardware store beyond it.

Bells on the door jangled as I stepped inside the store. A scruffy young man in a trucker hat hunched behind the counter, flipping the pages of an adult magazine, the crumbs from the MoonPie he was eating scattering over the centerfold. He sipped from his Coke can, swishing soda in his mouth, his throat bobbing around his swallow just before he released a belch. I found a cheap prepaid phone on a display beside the counter and set it in front of him. He looked up from his magazine, stuffing the rest of his MoonPie in his mouth as he rung up the charge on his register. I paid cash and took the phone, not bothering to ask for a bag as I left.

I rounded the building to the training cruiser and knocked on the driver's side window. Vero started, clutching her chest as she rolled her window down. "Come on," I said, tossing the phone on the seat beside her and gesturing for her to get out.

"I thought you didn't want anyone to see my uniform."

"I changed my mind." Vero wanted to pretend she was a cop. Here was her chance. "You're going to go inside the convenience store and ask to see their security footage from yesterday morning," I said, unfolding the receipt I'd found and pointing at the time stamp. "This hardware store is directly across the street. The cameras out front might have picked up *EasyClean* or his car when he came to do his shopping."

"You seriously think the convenience store clerk is just going to let me see his security feeds without a warrant?"

I took her by the arm and dragged her out of the car. "You talked Tyrese into wearing your bra. This should be a piece of cake." I walked her around the building and pushed her toward the door. The clerk glanced up as the bells jangled and Vero walked in. He straightened, slapping his magazine closed, nearly dropping his Coke as he hid the can under the counter.

"Hey, Officer," he said, his cheeks flushing a guilty shade of red as I melted into the candy aisle and peeked over the display.

Vero stripped off her mirrored sunglasses and hitched her thumbs in her belt, her dark eyes roving over the crumbs on the counter. The clerk turned the magazine over as Vero sidled up to the register. "You pay for that soda?" she asked, staring down her nose at him.

The clerk began to stammer. "I . . . no . . . not yet . . . I usually don't pay until—"

"So you've done this before?" she said, holding up the plastic wrapper from the MoonPie and waving it in his face. He reached for his magazine as Vero slid it from the counter. She flipped it open, giving him a heavy dose of side-eye when the pages stuck together. The clerk swallowed. "Tell you what?" she said, dropping it back in front of him. "You help me with a matter of public safety, and I won't tell your boss you've turned his candy aisle into a free buffet."

His cheeks flushed. "What kind of help do you want?"

Vero leaned over the counter, speaking in hushed tones. The kid glanced through the window at the empty parking lot and motioned for her to follow him. They disappeared through a door marked EMPLOYEES ONLY.

A McDonald's commercial played on a TV mounted on the wall.

My stomach grumbled as I perused the Hostess selection while I waited for Vero. The commercial gave way to a newscast as I hovered beside the Twinkies.

"*. . . The vehicle was discovered yesterday morning in a privately owned field off a remote rural road west of Culpeper after witnesses reported smelling smoke in the area. Tonight, investigators think they may have a break in the case . . .*" I glanced up at the TV, doing a double take at the photo on the screen. "*. . . The vehicle is believed to have been registered to Ignacious Grindley of Pleasantville, New Jersey, known more commonly as Ike. His wife reported him missing three days ago, telling authorities in Pleasantville that he had traveled to Northern Virginia for a work-related trip and she became concerned when he neglected to answer his cell phone . . .*"

Vero emerged from the back room. She jolted to a stop beside me, slack-jawed, her eyes glued to the screen.

"*Police are asking anyone who may have seen this man to contact their local authorities. Mr. Grindley's wife and his employer were both unavailable for comment . . .*"

"Let's go," I said, pulling my hood low to cover my face as I turned for the door.

"They were supposed to make that guy disappear," Vero hissed as we rushed to the car. "His face is all over the news!"

"I told you we shouldn't trust her." We ducked inside the cruiser and shut the doors. I stared out the window, reeling in my racing thoughts. "The car was burned. And they didn't say anything about a body. There's probably no evidence in that car connecting him to us."

"Marco has to know Ike is dead by now. What if he tells the police Ike was at my cousin's garage?"

"Given the kind of work Ike was doing for Marco, I seriously doubt Marco wants the police involved. We'll stay calm, find *EasyClean,* and hope Kat holds up her end of the bargain. Did the clerk show you the security footage?"

"Yes, but the camera didn't capture the entrance to the hardware store. All I could make out was the parking lot out front. I checked a ten-minute window before and after the time stamp on the receipt. I didn't see any police cars."

"What about unmarked ones?"

"None that stood out. If *EasyClean* was in the store, he must have parked someplace else."

I pried the prepaid phone from its packaging and dialed the cell number Carl's wife had given me a month ago, the night we'd all sat around her kitchen table and agreed never to tell the police what had happened to Carl. No one answered.

"Maybe she's screening her calls," Vero suggested.

I stared at the phone. Leaving a message felt too risky. Nick would recognize my voice if Barbara's voice mail messages ever became evidence. I checked the time. The clock on the dashboard said it was a little after four.

"We still have a few hours before sunrise," I said. "The Westovers' house isn't far. Let's see if Barbara's home."

CHAPTER 22

The sleet had relented to a meek drizzle by the time we'd reached the peeling clapboard siding at the rear of an old country market adjacent to Barbara's property. The Westovers' family plot was a short walk through the woods from where we'd parked.

"What's the plan?" Vero asked. She'd ditched the sunglasses at least, but she still looked like a kid in her big brother's Halloween costume.

"We'll go to the house first and see if she's home." Barbara kept a rifle in her kitchen, and it probably wasn't wise to leave anything to chance.

"And if she's not?"

I didn't think Vero really wanted an answer to that.

We headed into the woods, in what I hoped was roughly the same direction we had taken the last time we'd been here. Vero aimed her flashlight at the ground and I followed close behind her, careful not to trip over fallen logs as we descended the sloping hill toward the Westovers' house.

"The lights are out," Vero said.

"It's four thirty in the morning. She's probably asleep." I climbed the porch steps and knocked loud enough to wake the dead.

Vero peered in the window. "Maybe she's staying with Theresa," she said through chattering teeth.

"We can't just show up at Theresa's. She's got twenty-four-hour surveillance on her town house since she violated her house arrest."

I turned, rubbing my arms, staring at the shed beside Barbara's empty driveway.

"Don't say it, don't say it, don't say it," Vero chanted.

With a heavy sigh, I plodded down the porch steps. "Let's check her shed. Hopefully, she has a shovel."

"I knew you were going to say that."

We found a heavy-duty shovel and a pair of gardening gloves inside, and we trudged them back up the hill to the small graveyard behind Barbara's house.

"Give me some light," I said.

Vero aimed her flashlight at the dirt in front of Carl's grave marker. I paused, one foot poised on the head of the shovel. Everything about this felt foolish and futile. I had moved Steven's key from its hiding spot, but that hadn't kept him from breaking into my house. If anything, it had only fueled his determination to get inside. Moving Carl's body would be no different. Nick would know the grave had been tampered with as soon as he laid eyes on it, and it would only make him more determined to get a warrant.

I tossed the shovel to the ground. Plucking off a glove, I pulled out my phone.

"What are you doing?" Vero asked. I walked between the handful of graves, typing the names of the deceased into my browser as Vero aimed her light at the headstones. "I thought we were moving the body."

"Not the body. Just the marker." Maybe the solution wasn't moving Carl, only creating the illusion that his body was somewhere else.

"I don't follow."

"If we dig Carl up, we have nowhere to put him. The soil will be loose when Nick gets here tomorrow and he'll have all the justification he needs to pull a warrant. All we need to do is slow him down a little. If we switch two of the headstones, Nick will come tomorrow and find a marker in place and the ground intact. And even if he does manage to get a warrant to exhume the grave—"

"He'll find someone else's body inside it."

"Here," I said, kneeling beside a plot that was smaller than the rest. I held up my phone to show Vero the death record.

Her forehead wrinkled. "Doris Westover? But she's a woman."

"Her obituary was published by a crematorium. Her plot is probably smaller than the others because they didn't bury a coffin."

"Just the ashes," Vero finished.

Carl wouldn't have had a memorial or a public obituary. Barbara wouldn't have wanted to draw that kind of attention to his death. According to Barbara, she'd simply told his family and colleagues that he'd been buried during a small, private ceremony at home. All we had to do was move the grave marker and make sure she corroborated that one small detail—that he'd been cremated and these were his ashes.

"Whatever we're doing, we'd better do it fast," Vero said. "It'll be light in a few hours, and we should get the car back to the academy before sunrise."

Vero and I worked quickly, using the head of the shovel to leverage the two heavy markers off the ground. Vero hoisted up one side and I lifted the other, both of us bickering and tripping over the landscape as we carefully switched the positions of the headstones. The exercise was reminiscent of the obstacle course we'd tackled two days ago, with a lot more cussing and a few more stubbed toes. By the time we'd finished, our hands were calloused and our noses were red and dripping from the cold.

We kicked the scattered dead leaves back in place around the graves, panting steam as we surveyed our handiwork. Every inch of me hurt.

Vero's lips had turned blue. "My lady bits are frozen."

"Let's put this stuff back where we found it and get out of here."

Ty's pant legs dragged on the ground as Vero plodded along beside me down the hill toward the shed. I used an old rag to wipe dirt and fingerprints from the shovel as Vero slipped off the gloves and hung them back on their hook. Bright slashes of light cut through the cracks in the siding. Vero and I went still as tires crunched over the gravel.

I peered through the cracked door of the shed in time to see Nick's car pull into the driveway. My heart leapt into my throat as he killed the headlights.

"Is it Barbara?" Vero asked hopefully.

"No. It's Nick and Charlie." By the faint moonlight, I could just make out Charlie's profile in the passenger seat.

"I thought Nick wasn't supposed to come until the morning!" Vero whispered.

"I guess he got antsy."

Nick squinted through the windshield at Barbara's house. If we opened the shed door now, he'd spot us. "When they get to the porch, we'll make a run for it."

Vero looked at me like I'd just described a scene from *Mission: Impossible*. "Have you seen yourself run?"

"Thanks for the vote of confidence."

A car door opened. I peeped through the crack as Nick and Charlie got out of the car and Charlie followed him to the front porch. Nick's cane thumped up the steps. A series of loud knocks rattled the door. I tip-toed out of the shed and peeked around the side.

"So this is where it happened," Charlie mused, staring over the porch rail at the blackened scorch marks that stained the front yard. A smile tugged at his scar. "Molotov cocktails, huh? I can see why you like her."

Nick leaned on his cane beside him as he waited for Barbara to answer. "I'm glad," he said with a smile. "She seems to like you, too. Now if I could just get Joey to come around."

"What do you mean?"

Nick shook his head. "He and Finn have been acting strange ever since the shooting. Suspicious of each other. Both of them dancing around it."

"Kind of like you and Joey?"

Nick choked out a laugh. "Why the hell would I be suspicious of Joey?"

"Why don't you tell me?" Charlie asked. "Why'd you bring me out here instead of your partner, Nick?"

"Because I couldn't sleep, and I didn't feel like waiting until the morning. I texted you and you were up. That's all."

"Did you even tell him you were coming?"

Nick looked away.

"You already know how I feel about him. I've never held back. And Georgia's sister is smart. You said it yourself, she's got good instincts. If she suspects there's something off with Balafonte, I'd pay attention if I was you."

Nick frowned at the yard.

"What is it?" Charlie asked.

"It's just . . . I don't know, Charlie. There's something about that night that doesn't sit right with me. I read Finlay's statement a million times. She said she found this address in Steven's calendar that afternoon when he went missing, and she came out here looking for him."

"So?"

"So he wasn't here. Theresa was. And so was Finlay's missing phone, which means the two of them must have been together a few days before. But why? Theresa and Finlay can't stand each other."

"Maybe what's not sitting right with you isn't Finlay's relationship with Theresa, but Finlay's relationship with her ex-husband. Whatever she was doing here, she was obviously doing it to protect him, and now there's a little green monster eating away at you, and your mind's working overtime trying to invent some other reason she might have come, because you don't want to admit you're jealous." Charlie held up a finger as Nick opened his mouth to protest. "And don't bother telling me you're not. I know you better than that."

Nick sighed and shook his head in defeat.

Charlie dropped a hand on his shoulder. "No one's home, so why don't you and I go find that graveyard and take a look around. It'll be like old times."

Nick smiled and tapped his cane. "Sure you can keep up with me, old man?"

"I've had six months of chemo and radiation, and I'm still in better shape than you."

They laughed as they descended the porch steps. I leaped back into the shed, pulling the door closed a second before they rounded the corner, their shoes crunching against the frozen grass.

I waited for their voices to fade. "We should make a break for it now," I whispered. "We can take the long way through the woods and find our way back to the car."

Vero nodded. I slunk out the shed door and held it open for her. As she stepped down, Ty's pant leg caught on the handle of a rake, sending it crashing to the floor. The rattle of its tines echoed through the yard.

"Did you hear that?" Nick's voice was faint but clear at the crest of the hill.

"Sounded like it came from the house," Charlie said.

Vero and I sprinted from the shed, underbrush snapping as we darted into the woods. Flashlights clicked on behind us, their beams breaking over the landscape as Vero and I ducked behind two trees, breathing hard.

"Police!" Nick called out. "Who's out there?"

Vero and I pressed back against the trunks as their footsteps crackled closer through the bracken. I pressed a hand over my mouth so their lights wouldn't catch the fog of my breath. Charlie's shoes paused a few feet beside me. My pulse ratcheted higher. I was certain he could hear the slam of my heart against my ribs.

"See anything?" Nick called out to him.

"Nothing," Charlie said, kneeling in the brush. "Probably just a couple of raccoons making trouble. Come on." His light swung away, his footsteps fading with it.

Nick's light made another slow pass before clicking off again. Vero and I waited until they disappeared up the hill before breaking into a run.

CHAPTER 23

Vero and I stumbled out of the woods, breathing hard.

"That was close," I panted.

"You think they saw us?"

"I don't know, but let's get out of here before they decide to come looking." I sagged against the passenger side of the training cruiser, clutching a cramp in my side as Vero rounded the hood. She paused beside the driver's door and looked at me over the roof. "What?" I asked. "What's wrong?" I hurried around to her side of the car and stopped in my tracks. "Oh, god. That's . . ."

"A whole lotta penis." Vero and I both took a few steps back to absorb the entire image. The giant blue phallus spanned the length of the car. Its testicles had been artfully spray-painted around the rear wheel well, encircling the tire treads and dripping down the lug nuts.

"Jesus."

Vero reached for the door. "Come on, we've got to go."

"Go where? We can't drive it back to the academy with a giant penis painted on it!"

"We have to take it somewhere. Nick and Charlie could come rolling by any minute, and we do not want to be sitting in the Oscar Meyer Weinermobile when they . . ." Her face fell as she patted the pockets of Ty's pants.

"No. No, no, no! Do not tell me you lost the keys!"

"They must have fallen out while I was running! I told you running was a bad idea!"

"What do we do?" I asked, trying the handle of every door. We were miles from the nearest town and my purse was under the passenger seat.

Vero stared at the car. With a swear, she leaned over the hood and pulled the windshield wiper toward her. Prying back the soft black cover, she extracted a thin metal rod from underneath.

"Don't judge," she said, ignoring my dubious look as she bent the end of the rod and slipped it through the gap between the car door and the window frame. She worked it down the side, wiggling it into place. After a few tries, she gave a sharp, upright pull. "Get in," she said, hauling her door open.

By the time I made it to the passenger side, Vero had the driver's seat slid all the way back and the plastic cover removed from the dashboard under the steering wheel. "I can't believe we're hot-wiring a police car." I gnawed my thumbnail as she fiddled with the wires. "It feels like we're stealing it."

"We stole the car three hours ago."

"We didn't steal it. We borrowed it. We had a key."

"Like we had a key to the Aston Martin?"

She had a point. "Did Ramón teach you how to do this?"

"Ramón would kill me if he knew I knew how to do this. I watched Javi do it. Twice." Vero held two wires together. The car started with a cough. She slapped the plastic cover back in place and eased onto the road as she tossed me her phone.

"Find me the most scenic route you can to Ramón's. The fewer cars and traffic lights, the better."

"But the garage isn't open."

"Exactly. And he might have something in his shop that will get rid of the spray paint."

I directed Vero along the most rural routes I could find. The trees rushed by in hypnotizing patterns as the adrenaline rush of the last hour began to wane.

Vero's attention was split between the road and her rearview mirror. "Don't you think it's strange that Nick didn't tell his own partner he was coming out here?"

"Nick obviously didn't want to wait until the morning. And Joey's a stickler for the rules."

"Is he really though? Or does he just want people to think he's all virtuous and righteous. Maybe it's all just a show. Charlie seems suspicious of him."

"Charlie also seemed eager to go poking around without a warrant."

"I don't know, Finn," Vero said with a thoughtful shake of her head. "The more time we spend around Joey Balafonte, the more convinced I am that he's *EasyClean*."

I couldn't necessarily argue with that. Nick obviously had reservations about his partner. And Charlie was openly skeptical. Still, I wasn't ready to sic Feliks's dogs on Joey. Not until we had proof.

We fell silent as unmarked rural roads gave way to painted lines and traffic lights, checking every side street we passed, anywhere a real police car might be waiting to pounce. Vero eased to a stop, parking along the curb a block away from Ramón's garage. She killed the headlights and left the engine running.

"Why'd we stop?"

Vero pointed at the gate to the salvage yard. A familiar black Camaro was parked in front. A sleek black Cadillac SUV idled alongside it. "Javi's here," she said, squinting through the windshield, "but I don't know those two guys he's talking to."

The men's expressions were severe under the glare of their headlights. One of them threw up his hands and shouted at Javi.

"Didn't he say he was meeting with his buyer for the Aston Martin tonight?"

"Doesn't look like it's going well. Hand me the binoculars." I withdrew them from my purse and passed them to Vero.

"What about the car across the street. You think he's with them?" I asked, pointing at a dark blue Audi. Its headlights were off, its pale yellow license plate clearly visible between them. Vero adjusted her focus. "Definitely not with them," she said, thrusting the binoculars in my hands. "His plates are from New Jersey."

I raised the binoculars to my eyes. The driver hadn't seemed to notice us. His huge camera was aimed at Javi and his buyers as their argument began to escalate. The camera panned over Ramón's parking lot, then the street, swinging slowly toward us. The photographer did a double take through the windshield, staring at me through his lens. I pulled the binoculars from my face. "Shit, I think he saw me."

The Audi's high beams came on. Vero and I shielded our eyes from the glare.

"So that's how you want to play it," she said, reaching for the buttons on the dash.

"Vero, this is not a good idea!"

Her grin was wicked as she began flipping switches. Our high beams turned on. Blue lights flashed and the siren whooped. There was a flurry of movement by the gate to the salvage yard. Javi's buyers tripped over each other as they fled to their SUV. Javi started to backpedal toward his Camaro, his eyes narrowing at the giant penis on the side of our car. He gaped at us, ignoring the fleeing SUV as it climbed over the curb and sped away. Tires squealed as the Audi peeled out after it.

Vero gunned the engine. Javi watched as we tore off in pursuit. Through the cruiser's back window, I saw him clutch his head as if it might explode.

"Vero, slow down and turn off the roof lights! Someone might see us."

She held her foot on the gas until our blue lights flickered off the rear end of the Audi. "Quick," she said over the siren, "get a picture of his license plate."

I braced one hand on the dash as I snapped a picture with my phone. "I got it. Let's turn around and go back to the garage." I pressed back into the seat as Vero urged the cruiser faster.

"We can't just let him get away. He was staking out the garage, Finlay! And he took pictures of Javi."

"There's nothing we can do about that now!"

The traffic light ahead of us turned yellow. Brake lights illuminated like dominoes in front of us. The Audi accelerated, swerving around lanes of slowing cars.

"Shit," Vero said through her teeth. Her foot came down hard on the gas as the Audi surged through the intersection.

I gripped the door as the training cruiser charged after it. "Vero, the light!"

"I can make it."

Vero pushed the cruiser faster. The light turned red. Cars began crossing the road in front of us. One of them paused abruptly in the middle of the intersection, confused by our siren and lights.

Vero jerked the wheel, narrowly avoiding the other car's hood. My stomach dropped as we hit a bump and caught air. I yelped, peeling one eye open when our wheels reconnected with the ground.

The road narrowed to two lanes. A long, dark ribbon of asphalt stretched out in front of us. "We're gaining on him," Vero said, picking up speed as she straddled the center line.

"What are you doing?"

"I'm going to make him pull over."

"And then what?"

"I haven't figured that out yet!" The cruiser swerved as Vero reached for the microphone under the dashboard. "Turn it on for me."

"No! He's not just going to pull over because a speeding penis tells him to!"

"Who's wearing the uniform, Finlay? Me! I'm wearing the uniform!"

"Fine!" I flipped on the speaker.

Vero pushed the talk bar and held the microphone to her lips. Her next words boomed out over the landscape like the voice of god. "This is the police. Reduce your speed and pull your vehicle over." The Audi slowed by a fraction. "See? It's working." Vero kept to the center of the road, urging the Audi toward the shoulder. It wavered a little, slowing a bit more as the driver stretched across the front seat and reached into his glove box. "Look, he's getting his license and registration ready. I know exactly how to handle a traffic stop. I watched Roddy do it during our ride-along."

The driver's window came down. He kept one hand on the wheel. His other stretched out toward us.

"Vero, he has a gun!" We ducked as he fired at us. Vero let off the gas and jerked the wheel to the right, falling in directly behind the Audi's bumper.

"Put down the weapon and stop your vehicle!" she shouted into the mic. I gripped the door handle as the driver fired again. "Asshole! What part of pull over did you not understand!"

The driver leaned out his window and pointed his pistol right at us. Vero cut the wheel hard as he pulled the trigger. We both screamed as the cruiser skidded off the road. It bounced into the weeds, rolling to a stop at the edge of a field.

The Audi's taillights shrunk in the distance. Blue lights swirled over the sea of weeds around us. My hand shook as I switched the siren off.

"Are you okay?" Vero's knuckles were white around the steering wheel.

"Yeah." My voice was hoarse from screaming. "You?"

"Uh-huh." She turned off the roof lights. Our high beams stretched across an open field, catching the wide yellow eyes of animals in the dark.

Vero's door flew open. She shrieked as someone grabbed her by the arm and hauled her out of the car. I threw open my door and scrambled out, clutching my heart in relief when I saw it was only Javi.

His eyes raked over every inch of her. "Jesus, Veronica! You could have been killed."

"I'm fine," she insisted, muffled by his jacket when he dragged her against his chest into a bone-crushing hug.

My legs felt like Jell-O as I leaned against the trunk. "I'm fine, too, by the way, in case anyone was wondering."

Vero wriggled out of Javi's arms, hiking up her belt and pushing up the huge sleeves of Ty's uniform.

"What the hell are you wearing?" he asked her. "And where the fuck did you get this car?"

"I borrowed it," she said.

"You borrowed it," he repeated, as if that might make sense of any of this. "From who?"

Vero put her hands on her hips. Ty's sleeves sagged around them. The hem of his shirt had come loose from her waistband, hanging almost to her knees. "None of your business."

Javi stared at Ty's name badge and gritted his teeth. "Do you mind telling me what that was all about back there?"

"I do, actually."

A bitter laugh burst out of him. "I was this close," he said, bringing his thumb and forefinger together, frustration sparking in his eyes. "This close to closing the deal on the Aston."

"Didn't seem like it. Looked to me like they were balking."

"Because I was trying to get a few thousand more for you! And if you hadn't shown up when you did, they would have come around. After your crazy light show back there, I'll be lucky if I can talk them into coming back."

He raked back his hair as he paced the side of the car. He shut Vero's door, shaking his head at the paint job. "We should get this off the road."

"We need to get it back to the training center before sunrise. Preferably without the . . . you know." I gestured to the penis.

Javi's sigh was heavy as he opened the door. He frowned at the steering column and turned slowly to Vero.

"I lost the key," she said defensively.

He fought a reluctant grin as he held the door open for her and watched her get in. "Help me push it," he said to me.

Vero put the car in reverse and Javi and I leaned against the hood, giving it one final heave until the car climbed over the grass onto the shoulder of the road. Javi got in his Camaro and followed us the short distance back to the garage. He unlocked a bay, ushered the cruiser inside, and closed the door behind us.

"Paint thinner's on the shelf," he said. "I'll go find some more rags."

Vero watched him disappear through the office door. When he was gone, she switched on a single light over her cousin's workbench and rummaged in his cabinets.

"Here," she said, passing me a rag and a bottle of something that smelled like nail polish remover.

I knelt beside the car and poured some on the cloth, leaning away from the fumes. The garage was creepy in the dark, disturbingly reminiscent of the night Feliks Zhirov and I had first met in this very spot. I scrubbed fast, eager to be gone. Vero took a second rag from the workbench and knelt beside me. She chuckled to herself as I rubbed circles in the paint.

"What's so funny?" I asked.

"This might be the closest you get to a penis this week. You do realize we've only got two days left of police camp, and you still haven't jumped Nick's bones yet."

"Jumping Nick won't fix anything."

"Neither will ignoring the fact that you want to."

"You're one to talk," I said, gesturing to the door Javi had disappeared through.

"Javi and I are ancient history."

"I don't buy it. The guy's obviously still in love with you."

"He's just a flirt. It doesn't mean anything. It never did." I detected a hint of melancholy in this last bit, as if I'd pulled a bandage from a festering wound.

"What happened between you two?"

"Who the hell knows?" she said, scrubbing harder. "It was the summer before I left for college. We were together, and then the summer ended and suddenly we weren't. He disappeared the week before I left for school. Just . . . *poof.* No texts. No calls. Ghosted me without a word. Didn't speak to him again until I came home for Thanksgiving break. I got home a day early and surprised my cousin at the garage where he was working. Javi was there."

"What happened?"

"He pretended everything was fine. Like nothing had ever happened between us. He showed up for dinner the next night at my mother's house with Ramón, but my mom wouldn't let Javi through the door." She laughed quietly as she remembered it. "I'd never seen her so angry before. She told him he didn't deserve me. That he wasn't good enough for her daughter." Vero's smile faded. "I didn't have the heart to tell her it may have been the other way around."

She stood back and surveyed our work. I could still make out the faint outline of a penis where we'd scrubbed and blue paint clung to the treads of the tires. I hoped there would be a healthy film of road grime to cover it up by the time we got back to the training center.

Javi returned through the back door, carrying a handful of rags and a used Goodyear tire he must have pilfered from the salvage yard. He peeled off his coat and unbuttoned his flannel, stripping down to a thin white undershirt. Vero and I stood back, giving him room. He worked fast, the dark shadows of ink on his back and shoulders visible through the fabric as he set a jack under the frame and cranked the rear of the cruiser off the floor. He stripped the blue tire off the car and rolled it aside, fitting the gently used one in its place. When he finished, he knelt beside the front panel, rubbing out the last of the blue paint. I glanced over at Vero, but she was too busy watching Javi to notice.

When he finally stood, sweat dampened his hairline and his shirt. He peeled it off, using it to catch a bead of perspiration at his temple before dropping it on the hood and reaching for his flannel. Javi was covered in ink. Hardly an inch of bare skin remained on his arms or his back, but his chest was a blank canvas with the exception of a single tattoo. A small *V* adorned Javi's left pectoral, close to his heart, the tip of it just visible as he buttoned his flannel closed. It was suspiciously similar to the *J* on Vero's backside.

I turned to her, drumming my fingers over my smirking lips, holding back every *I told you so* I badly wanted to utter.

"So what now?" Vero asked him, her cheeks flushing.

Javi used his undershirt to wipe the tire grime from his hands. "I'll call the buyer and offer him ten percent off our original deal. Maybe I can convince him to come back." Vero opened her mouth to protest. "Relax," Javi said as he tossed his shirt on the workbench, "I'll take it from my cut."

"I don't want any handouts from you."

"Then what do you want, V?" He stared her down, the dark fire in his eyes mirroring the intensity in hers. She was in denial if she thought for one minute Javi didn't still have feelings for her.

The temperature in the garage seemed to climb a few degrees. I cleared my throat. "Thank you, Javi. We'll take whatever you can get for it." It was almost five thirty, and we weren't likely to avoid notice if we returned the police cruiser after sunrise. "We should get back to the training center while it's still dark." I nudged Vero toward the car. Before the two of them killed each other. Or kissed each other. Neither would get us back to the academy any faster. And despite Sylvia's deadline and Vero's persistent badgering, neither of us had time to waste rewriting our romantic dramas. We only had two more days to figure out who *EasyClean* was and get Feliks off our backs.

CHAPTER 24

The sunrise was little more than a promise on the horizon when we returned to the training center just before dawn. We'd pulled over a mile from the academy and I'd climbed into the trunk. Vero had propped her phone up in the front seat and I listened, breath held, as she narrated our precarious return through the gate. The officer in the booth had glanced up from his phone as our headlights approached, took one look at the roof lights, and waved us through. Vero parked the training cruiser alongside the others and helped me out of the trunk.

"You should get back to the dorm and get out of that uniform before anyone sees you wearing it," I said, dusting myself off. It was almost seven, and I was sure a few cops would be surfacing from their rooms to squeeze in a run before class or an early morning workout. "The cafeteria should be opening in a few minutes. I'll grab us some breakfast and meet you back in our room."

Vero hunched into Ty's coat, her teeth chattering and her steps brisk as she disappeared into the back door of the dormitory. I hurried toward the mess hall, dreaming about a hot cup of coffee and the possibility of a donut, grateful there was still time to shower and catch a few hours of sleep before classes were scheduled to start.

"Finlay!" My sister's voice rang out behind me, punctuated by the patter of running feet. I turned as Delia crashed into my legs. Zach took a running leap into my arms, both of them showering me with kisses.

I held them to me, drinking them in. They were still warm from my sister's car, and their hair smelled faintly of my mother's kitchen. "What on earth are you two doing here?" I pressed my lips to their foreheads as my sister rolled their luggage over the sidewalk.

Delia scrunched up her nose. "You smell funny, Mommy."

My sister dropped their bags, giving me a suspicious once-over. "What happened to you?"

I set Zach down on the sidewalk and brushed my tangled hair back from my eyes. There were pine needles in it. Thorns stuck to my coat and my shoes were covered in mud. I hid them behind my children. "Too much cold medicine," I said. "I crashed pretty hard after the crime scene class in the woods last night. Didn't get a shower." My sister took a cautious step back as I faked a sniffle. I hoped it was far enough that she couldn't smell the paint thinner on my hands. "Why aren't the kids at Mom and Dad's?"

"Ma called me a few hours ago. Dad's got a kidney stone, and apparently it's the size of a small planet. She asked me to watch the kids so she could take him to the hospital, but they admitted Dad through the ER this morning and she doesn't want to leave him. I tried calling Steven to see if he could cover the kids, but he didn't answer his phone. I'm scheduled to teach a class at ten, so I packed their bags and brought the little buggers with me."

I wrangled Zach as he tried to dash away, slinging him onto my hip as he wriggled. "Is Dad okay? Should we go to the hospital, too?"

"He's fine. Mom's there fussing over him, and the urologist is on his way to blast the thing with a laser. The last thing Dad needs is a peanut gallery waiting for him to piss asteroids into a cup. He'll be good as new in a few hours. What about you? Feeling any better?"

I stifled a yawn. "Nothing a hot shower and a nap won't fix."

"Great." She passed me the kids' Rollaboards and diaper bag. "I'm starving. I'm going to grab something to eat and catch some sleep before class. Try not to be late. Nick's got some good sessions planned. See you in a couple of hours."

"But, Georgia," I called after her as Zach started crying for his blanket, "what am I supposed to do with . . . the kids?" I sighed as she disappeared into the cafeteria.

Delia tugged on my sleeve. "Mommy, can we go inside? I'm cold."

"Sure, sweetie. Come on." I took both Rollaboards in one hand and slung the diaper bag over my elbow, clutching Zach to one hip as I led Delia into the gym. I used my foot to haul open the door, my body running on what was left of my adrenaline as I ushered the children into the women's locker room, relieved to find it empty. I handed Delia a coloring book and a box of markers from her overnight bag and gave Zach a bag of dry Cheerios to distract him as I searched the luggage for his missing blanket, swearing quietly when I couldn't find it. I set him down on the floor in front of the showers and sent a quick text to Vero while they were occupied.

Kids are here with me. Long story. Can you bring me a change of clothes to the gym?

Haha, you're very funny, she replied.

"Say cheese," I said to the kids. They looked up at the camera with wide eyes and gap-toothed expressions, marker ink staining their hands. I snapped a mug shot of my children and sent it to Vero.

WTF?! I'm on my way.

I pulled up Cartoon Network on Delia's tablet and set it in front of the kids, making sure they were fully engrossed before calling my mother.

"Finlay? I'm sorry about the kids," she answered. "Your sister has them. I had to go to the hospital with your father." Hospital noises quieted in the background, as if she'd stepped outside.

"Delia and Zach are actually with me."

"What? Where's Georgia? She promised she would help with the children!"

So had everyone else since my divorce. "Don't worry about me. I've got everything under control. Is Dad okay?"

"He's fine. Just cranky. The urologist is stuck in traffic on the beltway. I called the nurse's station and asked them to bring some morphine."

"He's in a lot of pain?"

"No, I am. The man's driving me crazy."

I laughed. "Try to get some rest. And give Dad a kiss for me. Call me when he's out of surgery, okay?"

The children were still playing quietly when my mother disconnected. I dialed Steven again. His phone rang straight to voice mail, just like it had last night.

"Where are you?" I asked his recording. "The kids are with me at the police academy. Call me." I jabbed the red button, swearing an oath to myself that if he wasn't already dead in a ditch, he would be after I found him.

I stripped out of my dirt-caked clothes, turned the water on high, and ducked under the warm spray, drawing the curtain shut. Muddy brown water swirled down the drain. I pumped a handful of shampoo from the wall dispenser, peeking through the curtain between rinses to make sure the kids were still where I'd left them.

"Finlay?" Vero called out.

"In here!" I shut off the faucet and wrapped a starchy white towel around me.

The kids squealed, cartoons and snacks forgotten as they scrambled to greet Vero. She dropped my gym bag on the bench in time to catch Zach as he jumped. She spun him around, giving them both a squeeze. "What are you two nuggets doing here?" she asked in an overly sweet voice, the question clearly directed at me.

"Dad's in the hospital with a kidney stone, so my sister brought them here," I said, wrangling on a bra and dragging a clean sweatshirt over my head. When the kids had settled back in front of their cartoons, I whispered, "Did you return Ty's uniform?"

She nodded. "Sent a naughty photo to his phone first and left his uniform in a trash bag outside his door. Don't worry," she said, clearly amused by my chastising look, "I didn't include any identifying features. How about you? I thought you were bringing breakfast." She stuffed a handful of Zach's Cheerios in her mouth.

"Didn't get a chance. Apparently, my sister needed a nap."

Vero's answering laugh was wry as I rummaged in the gym bag for the rest of my clothes.

"Where's my underwear?" I asked, tossing aside a pair of jeans.

"Forget your underwear. Where's Zach?"

Delia glanced up from my phone. "He went that way," she said, pointing to the exit.

"Shit!" I dragged on my jeans, zipping them as I tore out of the locker room. I shouted Zach's name, following a trail of Cheerios across the hall to the entrance to the men's locker room. My son's maniacal laughter echoed from inside.

I closed my eyes with a whispered "*Fuck!*"

I took a deep breath and pushed open the door. A wall of steam greeted me and the unmistakable sound of a shower turning off. Zach giggled. I whispered his name as loud as I dared, speed-walking down the aisle between the banks of lockers until I spotted his coat. He ran fast in the opposite direction, my panties clutched in his chubby hands as he grinned at me over his shoulder. I started after him, jolting to a stop as a man emerged from the showers. Nick limped into the dressing room, his hair damp, his chest bare, and a small white towel tied low around his hips.

Zach squealed as I lunged for his coat. It slipped through my fingers as he bolted toward Nick. The rest seemed to happen in torturous slow motion.

"Whoa! Hey, buddy. *Ooof!*" Nick scrambled to catch my son as he leapt. Zach's shoe caught on Nick's towel, pulling the knot at his waist free. Nick made a grab for it as the towel slid from his hips.

He held it with one hand, covering his groin, clutching Zach to his glistening chest with the other.

Vero rushed into the locker room with my daughter in tow. She skidded to a halt and slapped a hand over Delia's eyes. Her own were fixed on Nick, shamelessly wide with appreciation. "That's . . . impressive," she said in an awed voice.

"Cop reflexes," he said, clearing his throat. Zach rested his head on Nick's chest, holding my panties under his chin like a blanket, momentarily content and probably long overdue for a nap.

"Hi, Nick!" Delia said from behind Vero's hand.

"Hi, Delia." Nick cringed. "You mind?" he asked me.

"Oh, right! Of course!" I stammered.

"There you go, buddy," he said, lowering Zach into my arms.

"Why don't I take the kids to the vending machines and get them a snack," Vero said, still a little breathless, "while you . . . you know . . . do whatever it is a grown, single woman might do when presented with a truly, *truly* spectacular research opportunity." She leaned close to my ear as she plucked Zach away from me. "I want to hear all of it. Every. Single. Detail."

"I'm still here," Nick said.

"Right. We'll wait for you outside." Vero paraded my children out the door. The locker room fell abruptly silent in their wake.

"I am so sorry," I said, turning my back to give him a moment of privacy only to catch his reflection in the full-length mirror on the opposite wall. His eyes found mine in the mirror as he secured his towel, and I dropped my gaze, my cheeks catching fire. "I know the kids shouldn't be here," I said to my bare feet. "Steven was supposed to have them, but something came up and he left them with my parents, and then my dad got a kidney stone and Mom called Georgia to watch them, but she's teaching a class at ten and—"

"Hey." He touched my shoulder, turning me gently around to face him, bringing me distractingly close to parts of him that made it increasingly difficult to think. "I know about the kids. Georgia called me this morning from your parents' house and asked if it would be okay to bring them. I told her it was fine."

I blinked up at him in surprise. "You did?"

"It was either that or let you leave." Nick's hair was darker, longer when it was wet. The damp waves fell over his warm, mahogany eyes, making them far too hard to look away from.

"I should probably go." I stumbled backward into a locker. The tantalizing smell of his bodywash wasn't helping my sense of direction. Or my traitorous hormones. "You've got class in a few minutes and you aren't dressed . . . like, at all."

The corner of his mouth twitched with amusement as he snapped open a locker. He pulled a dark blue dress shirt off the hanger inside and slipped it over his shoulders, leaving it open over his towel. "I think you mean *we've* got class," he said as he buttoned the sleeves. "I expect you to be there on time, shoes on and everything."

"I don't have anyone to watch the kids," I pointed out. "It wouldn't be fair to ask Vero to miss class to babysit for me."

His locker clanked shut. His eyes narrowed with purpose as he came to stand in front of me. "You're right. You shouldn't have to ask Vero, or your parents, or your sister, for that matter. What's not fair, Finn, is your ex shirking his responsibilities and dumping them back on you. They're his kids, too. You should be able to count on him, and it's not fair to *you* that you can't."

A knot formed in my throat. "I'll be sure to remind him of that if he ever decides to answer his phone. Meanwhile, I should probably take the kids home."

Nick held up a hand, a muscle working in his jaw. "Just . . . wait here."

He opened his locker and withdrew his cell phone. He picked a number from his contact list and held the phone out in front of him, putting it on speaker. "Hey, Roddy."

"Go 'head, Nick."

"I've got a 10–41 at the gym. Actually, make that two. Think you and Ty can help me out for a few hours with a couple of unattended minors?"

"Copy that."

"And swing by the mess hall for some juice boxes on your way."

"Roger."

Nick tossed his phone on the bench. "See? Problem solved."

"Thank you," I said as he started to button his shirt, mourning the loss of the view and at the same time relieved he had covered it. His intoxicating man-smells were scrambling my brain, and after his heroic display on the phone just now, I couldn't be trusted to stick to my resolutions when all he was wearing was a dress shirt and a towel. "You really didn't have to do that."

"I freely admit, my motives weren't entirely selfless." He leaned back against the bay of lockers across from me, his smile kicking up on one side as he arched a brow. "So what was that Vero was saying about research?"

I felt every ounce of blood turn hot in my body. "It's nothing. I'm just . . . having some trouble with a scene."

"What kind of trouble?" His grin was a little rakish, as if he knew.

This was the part where the heroine was supposed to be bold. Where she was supposed to admit how hard she was falling for him. How much she wanted him. That she was tired of running. She was supposed to be fearless and take his hard, wet body to the ground and get a sand-rash in her nether regions while the storm raged around them.

"I should probably go," I croaked, backing out of the locker room. The knot in his towel looked as precarious as my willpower. "I should probably find Roddy. And Ty. And my shoes. And Georgia will probably make me do push-ups if I'm late. I'll see you after class." I turned and ran through the door, fleeing into the hall where Vero and the kids were waiting for me.

CHAPTER 25

I burst out of the men's locker room like my ass was on fire. Vero was waiting with the kids by the vending machines, my gym bag slung over her arm and the children's luggage propped against the wall. She frowned and checked the clock on her phone.

"We still have fifteen minutes until class. What are you doing out here? I was expecting a long and detailed report."

"You'll have to settle for the SparkNotes." I took my bag from her, picked Zach up off the floor, and slung him onto my other hip.

"What the heck have you been doing for the last ten minutes?"

"Arranging for someone to watch the kids so you and I can go to class."

"Great. Who's babysitting?"

I nodded toward the vestibule doors as Roddy's patrol car pulled into the emergency fire lane in front of the building.

"Oh, shit," Vero muttered as Tyrese stepped out of the passenger side. Ty was moving slower than usual, his FCPD-issued sweats a stark contrast to Roddy's crisply pressed uniform as he followed his mentor into the hall.

Roddy peeled off his sunglasses. "Ladies, I understand we have two delinquent minors in need of surveillance."

"Right here, Officers." Vero patted Delia's head. Zach burrowed his face into my shoulder, wiping donut crumbs on my sweatshirt.

Roddy knelt in front of Delia, bringing them almost eye to eye. He held two apple juice boxes out to her in one of his massive hands. "Okay, kiddo. You'll be hanging with me and my partner for a few hours while your mom and Vero go to class. Think you can handle that?"

She narrowed her eyes at him. "Can I have one of those?" she asked, ignoring the juice boxes and pointing to his badge.

"Nope. But how about one of these?" He took off his police hat and dropped it onto her head. The bill slipped down her forehead, covering her eyes, and Delia pushed it up to squint at him.

"Can we ride in your police car and chase bad guys with the sirens on?"

Roddy smiled sideways at his partner. Tyrese hung back, darting covert glances at Vero. He shifted discreetly, making me wonder if he might still be wearing her undergarments. "Officer Governs has a pretty bad headache this morning, so maybe we should skip the sirens. How about we play in the gym instead?" He handed Delia a juice box. Her hat bobbed back over her eyes with her satisfied nod. Zach reached for the other juice box as I set him on his feet.

"You're pretty great with kids," I told Roddy.

"I've got two of my own. Sixteen-year-old twins," he said. "You've got nothing to worry about, Finn. This isn't anything we can't handle."

Ty didn't look entirely sure as Zach squealed and sped off down the hallway. "What are you staring at, Rookie?" Roddy barked.

"They didn't cover this sort of thing in the Academy," Ty stammered.

"What do you need, a manual? The kid's a 10–80. Get on it!"

Ty loped down the hall after Zach. I caught a flash of pink lace over the waistband of his sweatpants. Roddy tipped his head, squinting at his partner's backside.

"We'd better go. We're going to be late for class. Thanks, Roddy," I said, grabbing my gym bag. Tyrese returned, carrying Zach by the back of his jacket like a sack of potatoes. He held Zach aloft in front of me as

I knelt before my children. "I need you two to be on your best behavior for Officer Roddy and Officer Governs. Can you do that for me?"

Delia nodded. Zach laughed, his feet dangling a foot off the ground. I gave them each a kiss, handing over their luggage and diaper bag to Roddy as Ty herded my children into the gym.

Vero and I hurried to the academic building, consulting her schedule.

"What's our first class?" I asked.

"Mock trial in the courtroom," she answered, leading us around a corner, where a line of students was filing into a classroom.

"Hey," Max said, abandoning her place in line to join us at the back, "did you two see the news about that burned car out near Culpeper yesterday?" I gave a noncommittal nod, wishing she would keep her voice down as we entered the mock courtroom. "Riley and I were talking to one of the forensic techs here. He knows a guy who knows a guy who's an investigator in Culpeper County. Apparently, the guy who owned the car worked for some seedy casino in Atlantic City."

Riley nodded fervently as he joined the conversation. "I'm getting major foul play vibes. We're going to see if Detective Anthony can help us land an interview with the investigator on the case."

"Speaking of interviews," Max said, "we never got to finish yours, Finlay. Maybe we could do it over dinner?"

I kept my head down as we slunk into the last two empty seats behind them. "Wow, I wish we could, but we have other—"

"We'd love to," Vero said. Max and Riley gave us two thumbs-up as they turned around to face the front of the room.

"Why did you agree to that?" I whispered to Vero.

"They seem to know an awful lot about Ike's case. If we play our cards right, we can interview them, too."

"Good morning," Nick said, addressing everyone as he counted out handouts and passed them down the rows. The classroom had been made to resemble a courtroom, complete with a witness stand, two tables from which the defense and prosecution could present their cases, and a dais for the judge's bench at the front of the room. "I hope you all got some rest after your crime scene exercise last night. As police officers, we spend a lot of time in courtrooms, usually as witnesses for the Commonwealth. Some of you will be presenting testimony in today's criminal trial based on the discoveries made during last night's investigation. As promised, we have some volunteers from the Commonwealth Attorney's Office with us today to assist us with our mock trial."

Vero elbowed me in the ribs as Nick invited the volunteers to join him. A blond man in a suit and tie rose from his seat in the front row. A red-haired woman stood beside him, smoothing back her chignon. They shook Nick's hand as he thanked them for coming. Then Julian Baker and his roommate, Parker, turned around to face us.

CHAPTER 26

"Everyone, please welcome Parker Keller and Julian Baker to our citizen's police academy." Nick swept an arm toward our guest instructors as the class broke into polite applause. "Ms. Keller is a practicing prosecutor with the Commonwealth Attorney's Office. And Mr. Baker is a third-year law student at George Mason University, where he's pursuing a concentration in criminal law."

I ducked low in my seat. Julian wasn't just any law student. Up until two months ago, he was the one I'd been sleeping with. And Parker was his very protective roommate. Judging by how much she hated me, I was pretty sure she was in love with him.

"Officer Donovan." Nick searched the faces in the room until he found me. "As the first officers on the scene, you and Officer Ruiz will be the prosecution's first witnesses in our role-play. Finlay, we'll have you start. Come on up," he said, gesturing to the witness stand.

Julian's smile fell away as I stood and navigated between the tightly packed chairs to the front of the room. Parker glanced at Julian, whispering to him in a low voice. He dismissed her question with a tight shake of his head, refusing to meet my eyes as I entered the witness box.

"The Commonwealth Attorney was scheduled to be our judge," Nick explained. "Apparently, he was called away on an emergency this morning and won't be able to join us, so I'll be playing the part instead. Which of our attorneys will be playing the role of prosecutor?"

"I will," Parker said, as Julian said, "I'll do it." He snatched up a copy of his script, taking a seat behind the prosecutor's table before Parker could argue. She raised an eyebrow as she set her briefcase on the defense's side and settled into her chair.

Nick stepped onto the dais, hooking his cane over the arm of the bench as he sat. "Will the bailiff please swear in our first witness?"

Joey leaned on the wall beside the door to the classroom. Arms crossed, he pushed himself upright and approached the witness stand, his toothpick rolling from one side of his tight mouth to the other. He pulled it from his cheek, raising his voice so the class could hear him when he asked, "Will the witness please state their name for the court?"

I cleared my throat. "Finlay Donovan."

"Raise your right hand," he said brusquely. "Officer Donovan, do you swear to tell the truth, the whole truth, and nothing but the truth, so help you god?"

Julian's whisky-gold eyes met mine across the room. It felt like there was a warning inside them. It was only a role-play, I reminded myself. I had a script. I was only answering a few questions about a CPR dummy. This had nothing to do with Carl Westover. "I do."

Joey stared at me as he put the toothpick back in his mouth and departed the witness stand, resuming his post beside the door.

Nick addressed the class from the dais. "For the sake of time, we're going to skip ahead and assume you've already heard the opening statements of each side." He turned to Julian. "The Commonwealth Attorney will now call its first witness."

Julian smoothed down his tie, checking his script as he approached the stand.

"Officer Donovan," he began in a formal tone, careful not to make eye contact with me. This was a different Julian than the bartender I'd known. His shirt was pressed, his dress shoes polished, his silk tie cinched tightly below his throat. The smile lines beside his eyes had turned to stern creases, and the full mouth he used to kiss me with was pursed in concentration. "Is it correct that you and Officer Ruiz found the deceased?"

"Yes," I answered, consulting my script.

"Can you please describe what happened when you arrived at the park?"

My voice came out flat as I read my next line. "Upon a preliminary search of the area, my partner and I saw what appeared to be a human hand, loosely covered by leaves and dirt."

"What did you and your partner do next?" he asked without looking up.

"I removed a branch to get a better look, confirming the presence of a body."

"Would you describe what you saw to the court?" Julian gestured to the class. Their attention was rapt, students in the back rows arching taller to see. Mrs. Haggerty sat in the center of the front row. She squinted and pushed her glasses higher on her nose as Riley and Max took furious notes behind her.

"The deceased appeared to have been dismembered and left in a shallow grave," I said, repressing a shudder.

"And what did you do when you located the remains?"

I checked my next line. "I called Dispatch and informed them of my findings. Then I secured the crime scene and waited for a homicide detective to arrive."

"Thank you, Officer Donovan." Julian nodded before turning to the dais. "No further questions for the witness, Your Honor."

Nick addressed the class. "We'll now hear cross-examination by the defense."

Parker rose and approached the witness stand, offering Julian a close-lipped smile as he passed her. She tucked a red lock of hair behind her ear as she sauntered toward me, her grin lifting on one side, just enough to make me squirm.

"Officer Donovan," she began, skimming her lines, "you said you waited for a detective to arrive. Which detective responded to the call?"

"Detective Nicholas Anthony," I answered.

Parker set her script beside her briefcase on the defense's table, her hands clasped behind her as she paced. "Was it your understanding that Detective Nicholas Anthony was the lead investigator on this case?"

"Umm . . ." I looked to my script for the answer to Parker's question, then up at Nick when I couldn't find it on the page. He gave a small nod. "Yes," I said.

"Was this your first time working with him?" she asked.

"No," I said tentatively. "Nick and I have worked together before."

"By *Nick,* I assume you mean Detective Anthony?"

"Yes."

"Would you say you know him well?"

A hard cough came from somewhere in the audience. I was pretty sure it was Vero.

I scanned our lines, certain I must be missing a page. "I guess . . ."

"Do you have a personal relationship with him?"

I dropped my script.

"Does anyone know what page we're on?" Mrs. Haggerty called out.

"Objection, your Honor," Julian said, glaring at Parker. "I fail to see how my client's personal relationships are any of the court's business."

"Really?" She turned to him with a hand on her hip. "I assumed the answer to this question would be of particular interest to you."

"If it mattered, I would have brought it up during discovery, not ambushed her in court."

Nick rapped his gavel, silencing the class's murmurs. "I admit, I'm curious to hear Officer Donovan's answer to that question myself. But in the context of this case, I'm going to have to sustain the prosecution's objection. And I'll remind you, Counselor, you were provided with a script."

"Of course, your Honor." Parker retrieved her script from the defense table. She rolled it in her hands as she paced back to the witness stand, her smirk still in place as she addressed me. "Officer Donovan, would you say Detective Anthony is honest?"

I flipped through my papers, completely lost. "Yes, but—"

"Have you ever known him to misrepresent facts or conceal evidence to protect someone?" Nick's eyes narrowed at Parker before darting to mine. We both knew of a time he'd concealed evidence—the night I broke into the jail, he'd covered for me and let me go—and Parker knew it, too, because she'd been there.

"Objection, Your Honor," Julian said. "Outside the scope of the direct."

"Sustained," Nick said sternly. "Let's keep the line of questioning relevant to the case, Counselor."

"Then let me ask a different question." Parker gestured toward Julian. "Officer Donovan, is this your first time meeting the prosecution's attorney?"

"Objection!" Julian snapped. "You don't have to answer that," he said, locking eyes with me across the classroom.

Nick held up a hand. "Where is this going, Counselor?"

Parker turned to the dais. "I'm only trying to rule out any conflict of interest, Your Honor. There are ethical considerations if the prosecution's attorney has a personal relationship with a witness that might negatively affect my client." She turned back to me. "You're under oath, Officer Donovan. Is this or is this not the first time you've met Mr. Baker?"

"No," I said through my teeth, "this is not the first time I've met him."

Riley raised his hand. "I don't think this is how a cross-examination is supposed to work." Max slapped a hand over his mouth, sitting forward in her seat.

"I've definitely never seen this on *Law and Order,*" Vero muttered.

Parker raised her voice over the murmurs of the class. "Officer Donovan, please tell the court when you first met Mr. Baker."

Julian shot to his feet. "Objection, your Honor!"

"Overruled." Nick's knuckles tightened around his gavel as his eyes bored into me. "The witness will answer the question."

"*Oh, shit,*" Vero sang under her breath.

I slapped down my script. "You really want to know? I've known Mr. Baker since October of last year."

Vero stood up. "Can I declare a mistrial?"

"I'm lost," Mrs. Haggerty called out. "What the heck is happening?" The class erupted in confused chatter.

Nick stood and banged the gavel. "Our volunteers will take questions from the class while the court takes a recess! Bailiff, you're in charge." Nick dropped the gavel on the desk, abandoning his cane as he climbed down from the dais. He shouldered his way past Parker and Julian, taking my hand as he limped past the witness stand and towed me from the room.

He pulled me behind him down the hall, checking the locks on every door we passed until one finally flew open. He dragged me inside the maintenance closet, closing us inside and flipping on the light, his dark eyes furious. I backed into a set of metal shelves, knocking over a broom. Bound stacks of paper towels spilled to the floor around me.

"Julian Baker? He's the attorney you were involved with? For how long?"

"I don't see how that's any of your business."

"I'm not talking about your love life, Finn! I'm talking about the Mickler case! You knew I was investigating Harris Mickler's disappearance! You knew I was talking to the bartenders at The Lush, and you never said a word! Were you seeing him then, too?"

"No!" I crossed my arms. "Seeing him isn't exactly the right word."

Nick laughed darkly as he rocked back on his heels. "Right. I forgot. The lawyer from your book. Is this the part where you tell me it was all just research for a novel?"

"Is that a rhetorical question, or do you really want me to answer that?"

The heat kicked on, warm air whistling through the vent in the ceiling. He shoved a finger over the knot in his tie and wrestled open the top button of his dress shirt. Bracing a hand on the shelf behind my head, he leaned over me and pierced me with a stare. "Do you swear to tell me the truth, and nothing but the truth, right here, right now?"

I nodded, thrown off-balance by his nearness.

"Were you at The Lush the night Mickler disappeared?"

"Yes."

"Wearing that wig I found at Ramón's garage?"

"Yes."

A muscle tensed in his jaw, his voice low and tenuous when he finally spoke. "When I asked Julian if he remembered a blond woman in the bar that night, he said only one stood out to him and she left the bar alone. He said he talked with her outside before she left. A busboy and a patron said they remembered seeing them together in the parking lot. Was it you?"

My throat thickened. "Yes."

"Why did you tell him your name was Theresa?"

My eyes burned with tears but I refused to blink as I raised my voice. "Because he was gorgeous and charming and interested in me, and I didn't want to tell him that I was a broke, single mother whose husband had abandoned her for someone else! For one night, I wanted to know what it felt like to be Theresa!"

Nick took a step back. He rubbed a hand down his face. "Did you meet up with him that night?"

I shook my head. "He followed me out to my van to make sure I was sober enough to drive home. He asked me if I wanted to stay until the end of his shift, but I was late to pick up the kids at my sister's. He gave me his number and told me to call him sometime. Things just sort of happened from there." I hadn't had to think about my answer. Every word I'd spoken was the truth.

Nick nodded, his relief palpable, making me realize where his line of questions had been leading from the beginning. None of this was about my fling with Julian. Nick was establishing my alibi, confirming Julian's story that I had nothing to do with Harris Mickler's disappearance. That I couldn't have been the same blond woman Harris left the bar with. Because if I was, it would change everything.

Nick's voice was gravelly when he asked, "Do you still have feelings for him?"

"Maybe. Sometimes. I don't know," I said through a frustrated sigh. "Julian made me feel desirable and sexy and smart. Like all he saw was me. None of the rest of it mattered to him—the kids, the divorce, my failing career. None of it . . ." I frowned at the floor as those words sank in. As I finally answered the question that had been gnawing at me for weeks. "None of it was important to him," I finished under my breath.

Nick tucked a finger under my chin, pulling my reluctant gaze to his, holding my head up. "You *are* desirable and sexy and smart. But you're also resourceful, resilient, and courageous as hell, and any partner who doesn't see all of you isn't seeing the most amazing parts." His full lips were close, dusted in dark stubble, and my heartbeat quickened as I remembered how it had felt to kiss them. He eased back and let me go, but it did nothing to quell the sudden tension between us. His mouth thinned as a fist pounded against the door.

"Nick!" Joey's voice boomed outside. "You in there?"

Nick called out, "Not a good time, Joe!"

"Get your ass out here. We need to talk."

Nick dropped his head as the doorknob rattled. "I swear to god, I'll kill him and they'll never find the body," he muttered. He limped to the door and threw it open. Students hovered in the hall, whispering behind cupped hands as a handful of officers looked on in amusement. Nick pulled the door closed behind him, leaving it cracked. I spotted Vero in the crowd. Our eyes caught through the narrow opening.

I peeked out as Nick grabbed Joey by the collar. "The next words that come out of your mouth had better be the most important ones you've ever spoken."

Joey answered with the only two that mattered. "Zhirov escaped."

CHAPTER 27

I braced myself against the doorframe of the maintenance closet, mirroring Nick's shock as a hush fell through the hall.

Nick blinked at his partner. "What did you just say?"

Joey lowered his voice. "They think Zhirov escaped early this morning. Correctional officers said they saw him in his cell before lights out last night. This morning, he refused to get out of bed, claiming he had a headache. The officer on duty said he never got a good look at whoever was in the bunk, but when they opened his cell this afternoon, the guy wearing Zhirov's jumpsuit didn't match any of the inmates on record. They're still trying to ID him, but they suspect he's a Russian national."

I felt the blood drain from my face.

Nick released Joey's collar. "Has anyone talked to his attorney?"

"Kat's slinging the usual crap. Claims she had no idea. She's spinning it around, citing negligence on the department's part, crying to anyone who'll listen that her client had been receiving threatening letters and was probably abducted while he was in custody. She's demanding an investigation."

Nick raked a hand through his hair as he paced. "She's full of shit. She and Zhirov are working this whole blackmail angle to their advantage. It's all smoke and mirrors. Kat probably orchestrated the whole damn thing."

"Careful," Joey said, darting glances at the other cops lingering in the hall. "She'll sue you for slander and take you for every cent you have."

"Thanks for the advice."

"Want some more? Button up your shirt and fix your goddamn tie. The commander called. He'll be here in an hour."

Nick shot Joey a look as he fastened his button. "What's he coming here for?" he asked, cinching his tie around his throat.

"He probably wanted to be the one to break the news to you. He knows how hard you've worked on this case."

"Zhirov could be anywhere by now. There's no way we'll get him back in custody before his trial date."

"Everyone's looking for him," Joey assured him, "including the feds. If he's still on US soil, they'll find him. Here," he said, passing Nick a folded piece of paper. "This ought to make you feel better."

"What is it?" Nick asked. I angled closer to the gap in the door, struggling to hear them as they lowered their voices.

"Sam's been monitoring all the network traffic, looking for outgoing emails to that same address the crime scene photo was sent to last night. She found this one today."

Nick's eyes brightened as he read it. "There must be fifty businesses listed here."

"Shell companies. All local."

My fingers tightened around the doorframe. Shell companies. Like the one that owned the Aston Martin. The one Feliks set up in my name. Was *FD Consulting* on that list?

"What's this number?" Nick asked.

"Sam thinks it's an offshore bank account number. Looks like someone's getting impatient. The blackmailer threatened to mail the list to you if Zhirov doesn't comply."

"When was this sent?"

"Around midnight last night. Whatever Feliks saw on this list must have spooked him."

Nick shook his head. "Feliks doesn't get spooked. He gets angry. Our blackmailer will be lucky if he's not dead by morning."

Joey's phone buzzed. He glanced at the screen. "I need to grab this call. I'll ask Roddy and Georgia to help cover your next class. Take a few minutes and pull yourself together before the commander gets here."

"Thanks, Joe. And hey," Nick said as his partner turned to go, "I'm sorry I flew off the handle just now. I shouldn't have."

Joey's eyes skated to mine through the crack in the door. "We've all done a few things we probably shouldn't have."

His footsteps retreated down the hall. The closet door opened abruptly, and I fell through the opening into Nick's chest. He looked down at me, one eyebrow raised. "Did you get all that?"

I nodded, mustering a sympathetic grin. "Kind of hard not to."

He held the door open for me, turning off the light and closing the closet behind us. The hall had emptied with the exception of a few stragglers. Vero stood off to the side with Roddy, their heads bent close, their faces sober.

"Where do you think Feliks will go?" I asked Nick.

"Not far. Zhirov's too cocky to tuck tail and run. He'll want to stay near his business."

I wrapped my arms around myself. This was exactly what I feared he'd say. Not only was Feliks free, but he was probably close. And Feliks was far too proud to let *EasyClean* get away with playing these games with him. He would want this resolved quickly. The citizen's police academy was over in less than two days, and if I didn't deliver *EasyClean* soon, I was certain Feliks would come looking for me.

"Hey," Nick said, dipping his head to look me in the eyes, "I don't want you to worry about Feliks. You and the kids are safe here. I promise."

"Detective Anthony?" Nick and I turned as a uniformed officer rounded the corner, his face ruddy from the cold. "Sorry to interrupt, sir, but there's a problem at the front gate. Some guy showed up, claiming he's registered for the citizen's academy and demanding to come in. I checked his ID but he's not on the roster. The guy gave me a bogus license and he's driving a rental car from New Jersey." Vero and I locked eyes across the hall. "A couple of officers attempted to escort him off the grounds, but he got belligerent. When we searched him, he was carrying."

Nick rubbed his eyes. "Where is he now?"

"Detained at the front gate."

"I'll be right there."

"I should go find the kids," I said. Nick took my hand as I tried to slip away.

"Hey," he said in a low voice, "are we going to talk about what just happened in there?"

"Later," I assured him, backing out of his reach. Someday, maybe we would talk about everything that had happened today—all the small truths I spilled and the big ones I probably should have but didn't. For now, all I wanted was to find my kids. Nick was wrong. None of us were safe here.

When I left Nick by the maintenance closet, Vero and Roddy were nowhere in sight. I rushed across campus toward the gym. Police lights swirled by the security gate. Beyond the fence, a group of uniformed officers was gathered beside a patrol car. A large man was detained in the back seat. His eyes found mine through the window, trailing me as I pulled my hood over my face and hurried to find my kids.

I threw open the gymnasium doors, nearly dizzy with relief when I heard the unmistakable sound of my son's peeling laughter echoing down the hall. I followed the sound to the basketball court. Zach's diaper strained the fabric of his overalls, a trail of empty snack wrappers in his wake as he chased a bouncing ball down the court. Roddy and Vero stood at the sideline, staring up into the bleachers. Ty was stretched across a bench. One of his arms dangled over the side, his fingernails stained a garish shade of red. Delia sat on her knees beside him, her tongue poking out of the side of her mouth, her eyes narrowed in concentration as she colored his cheeks with a magic marker. A smear of blue blanketed the closed lids of his eyes, and black lines radiated from them like exaggerated sunrays. He snored softly.

Vero's shoulders shook with silent laughter. I clapped a hand over my mouth, terrified to wake him.

"I'm so sorry," I whispered to Roddy.

"Don't be." Roddy shook his head as he watched his partner sleep. "I had to call him three times just to get him out of bed this morning. He'll learn a valuable lesson from this."

"The correct application of lip liner is an important lesson for all of us." The laughter Vero had been holding back burst out in a loud snort.

Delia looked up, blinked at us, and smiled. "Look, Roddy! Isn't Ty pretty?"

Roddy flashed her a proud thumbs-up as Ty began to stir. Vero hid the last of her giggles behind her hand as he opened his eyes.

Delia patted his chest. "You're all done," she said, putting the cap on her marker. Ty sat up fast, the spider legs drawn around his eyes stretching wide as he put a hand to his face. "Remember to ethfoliate and moithturize. Vero says it's very important."

"It's water soluble," I called up to him as Vero laughed silently into her fist.

Roddy gave a startling clap of his hands. Ty looked up from his nails. "Nap time's over, Rookie. We've got a class to cover. Let's go, let's go, let's go!"

Ty sprinted down the bleachers.

"Thanks, Roddy," I said as he followed Ty to the door.

Roddy tipped his hat. "No thanks necessary. It's a pleasure to serve."

"You're right," I said to Vero as I watched them go. "There's no way that man is *EasyClean*." It was the only thing I felt certain of. And that after spending the afternoon with my children, Ty would probably never want kids of his own.

I turned back to the mess my son had made of the basketball court. His ball sat abandoned by the back wall.

"Where's Zach?" My eyes darted to every corner of the gym. Delia glanced up from her markers and shrugged.

"Come on, Dee!" Vero grabbed Delia's hand, towing her after me as I raced to the rear exit. It was the only door Zach could have escaped through without any of us noticing.

I shouted his name, catching a glimpse of his coat as he followed a group of students through a side door to the lecture halls, completely unnoticed. I chased after them, impatiently swiping my card key and waiting for the locks to slide open. Vero scooped Delia into her arms and followed me inside. We called Zach's name, dodging groups of students chatting in the hall.

I skidded to a stop beside Mrs. Haggerty. "Mrs. Haggerty! Have you seen . . ." She squinted up at me through the thick lenses in her rose-gold frames. "Never mind."

Flashing lights caught my attention down the hall. Over her shoulder, I spotted Zach's blinking sneakers as they disappeared into a classroom. I navigated around Mrs. Haggerty and sprinted down the hall. Vero's sneakers squeaked on the tile behind me as we skidded to a stop inside the classroom door.

A familiar man stood at the front of the room, the same man we'd seen standing behind a podium on the stage of the auditorium two days ago, right before his lecture with Peter. The name printed on the whiteboard behind him read DR. MOHAMMED SHARIF—FIREARMS EXAMINER.

"That's the asshole that stole our bullet," Vero whispered.

Dr. Sharif's Adam's apple bobbed as Zach stared at him across the room. He watched the blinking lights on my son's shoes with a look of abject horror.

"I'm so sorry if he disturbed you." I grabbed hold of my son to keep him from tackle-hugging the doctor's legs. Zach giggled and the man flinched. Tiny beads of perspiration had begun forming on his forehead. "Dr. Sharif? Are you okay?"

The doctor's eyes lifted to mine, recognition sparking. "You?"

I read his name again and glanced down at his shoes. "Mo?"

He backed into the whiteboard.

A police radio squawked and Roddy appeared in the doorway behind us. "I've been looking everywhere for you," he said, hiking up his belt. "Steven's here."

"Thank god," I whispered.

Roddy plucked his mic from his vest. "Nick?"

"Copy."

"Found 'em. I'll have everyone escorted downstairs."

Mo cried out. "Whatever this woman told you, Officer, I swear to you that I did nothing inappropriate in the restroom of the Walmart!"

Roddy frowned at him, his eyes ping-ponging between us.

I interjected before Mo could regale Roddy with our drama in the men's room. "I'll be down in a few minutes, Roddy. Dr. Sharif has generously offered to help me with some very important tool mark questions. Right, Doctor?"

Mo nodded emphatically. "I am happy to cooperate with this woman—and the police—in any way I can. Just please don't make me go with you."

"That was easy," Vero muttered. "Roddy and I will go find the kids' luggage and wait for you in the lobby." The classroom door closed behind them as she led the children out.

Mo sagged, clutching his chest.

"The bullet Pete gave you," I said, still a little out of breath, "I need to know anything you can tell me about the gun that fired it." This man was my last hope for giving me anything . . . *anything* at all that would help me identify *EasyClean*. Feliks was loose and Marco clearly knew we were here, but if I could find out whose gun fired that bullet, there might still be time to give Feliks a name and negotiate with Kat for that duffel bag full of incentive money.

Mo searched frantically through the loose papers and books on his desk, plucking the bullet from a small plastic tray. He carried it to a lab table, turned on a microscope, and set the bullet on the stage. Wiping a bead of sweat from his brow, he leaned over the eyepiece and adjusted the dials. He studied it, using a set of tweezers to turn the bullet this way and that before removing it from the stage and passing it to me. "The caliber is 9mm," he said, gesturing for me to leave. "There's quite a bit of damage."

"That's it?" I asked, refusing to budge. "Can't you tell me anything else . . . a model number or something?"

He held open the door and nudged me through it. "Lots of models are compatible with 9mm rounds," he said irritably. "All I can tell you is the name of the manufacturer. The rifling marks suggest it was fired from a Glock."

CHAPTER 28

When I descended the stairs toward the main entrance of the building, Vero, Roddy, and the kids were nowhere in sight. Steven was pacing in front of the vestibule, arms crossed, casting impatient sideways looks at Nick, Georgia, Samara, and Joey, who were huddled close, having a tense conversation at the edge of the hall. Nick glanced up, his eyes trailing me as I crossed the lobby and tapped Steven on the shoulder.

Steven whirled. "Hey," he said, spreading his arms wide to hug me. I held him back by the chest.

"Where have you been?" I asked in a harsh whisper.

"Look, I'm sorry I had to leave Delia and Zach with your mom. An emergency came up."

"Didn't you get my messages?"

"I did, but I was a little busy." He held up a hand and dropped his voice to a whisper. "And before you ask, the package you left with me is fine. Carl is right where we left him." Steven grimaced. "Or at least that one part of him anyway. I checked as soon as I got home last night. What the hell's going on? You sounded worried."

Obviously, I hadn't sounded worried enough for him to bother calling me back. "Nothing. I'm handling it."

"Where are the kids?"

"Vero's bringing them."

His eyes grew wide. "She's here?" He looked over my shoulder toward the knot of cops across the room. "We need to talk about your babysitter," he said urgently. "That girl is a criminal."

"*She's* a criminal? What the hell were you doing breaking into my house?" The low hum of the cops' conversation quieted. They all turned toward my raised voice. Steven put an arm around my shoulder and ushered me down the hallway. As soon as we were out of earshot, I shook him off.

"I went to the house to handle those repairs we talked about. Since when do you keep a vibrator in your nightstand?"

"You were snooping in my room!" I whispered.

"I wasn't snooping. I was looking for a flashlight. Does that thing really need so many goddamn batteries? There were enough Duracells in that drawer to power a Tesla."

"You have exactly ten seconds to explain to me what you were doing in my house."

"I know you said the repairs could wait until I got home, but I wanted to surprise you."

"Oh," I said through my teeth, "you definitely surprised me."

"While I was there, I found something suspicious in Vero's room. She's been lying to you, Finlay. Ruiz isn't her real name. Her last name is actually Ramirez. I saw it on her college acceptance letter. Did you know she dropped out of the University of Maryland last—"

"*That's* why you broke into my house? So you could *spy* on her?"

"I own that house, Finlay! I have every right to know who's living under my roof. That cash I saw in your freezer last fall was definitely stolen, and whatever she spent it on is probably illegal."

"You're being ridiculous!"

"I'm protecting our children!"

"They don't need your protection, Steven. They need a father!"

His mouth twisted into a snide grin as he gestured toward the cops in the lobby. "Is that what you're doing here? Looking for one?" I drew a slow, steadying breath through my nose as Steven paced away from me with his hands on his hips. "Fine," he said once he had calmed, "if you won't listen to me, then ask Nick to look into Vero." An incredulous laugh burst out of me. "There's a warrant for her arrest in the state of Maryland, Finn! Didn't you do a goddamn background check before you hired her?"

My laughter died. I stared at him, gobsmacked, my jaw practically touching the floor.

"Of course, I did!" I did not. "And I know all about what happened in Maryland." Though apparently not all of it. Vero had neglected to mention anything about a warrant, which was arguably the most important part. I glanced past him as the vestibule door opened. Vero came in, carrying Zach on her hip and holding Delia's hand. Roddy toted their luggage behind her. "You don't have all the facts, Steven. Vero lost that money. She didn't steal it. It was all just a big misunderstanding."

"Then it shouldn't be a big deal if I tell Nick and Georgia about it." He turned away from me and started walking toward the lobby.

"If you do this, the children will never forgive you," I called after him. "*I* will never forgive you, Steven." He stopped, his hands clenching and unclenching at his sides as he slowly turned to face me. "I will handle this with Vero when we get home," I promised. "But right now, Nick and Georgia have more important things to worry about."

"More important than the safety of our kids?"

"Feliks Zhirov escaped from jail this morning, so yes, Steven, they are worried about the safety of our kids. Are you taking them home with you or not?"

The anger drained from his face. "I'm taking them."

"Thank you."

"But when you get done with your little training camp," he said, closing the distance between us as he stirred the air with a finger, "we're going to discuss this as a family." He reached in his pocket and thrust a business card at me. "This guy's a therapist. My attorney gave him my number a few months ago. I think he can help."

I crumpled the card in front of him, looking around me for a trash can. "I don't need a therapist, Steven!"

"He's a family therapist, Finlay, and we're both going! Guy agrees it's a good idea." I threw the crumpled card at him. Steven shoved it in the pocket of my coat. "When you come to your senses, the children and I will be at my house," he growled.

I followed him back to the lobby, pasting on the practiced smile I wore for my children as they scrambled into his legs, nearly knocking him down.

"Wow, Steven," Vero said over their heads. "You finally made it. Nice of you to show up." A vein bulged in Steven's temple. I drew a line across my throat to get Vero's attention, silently begging her to stop, but she was too busy goading Steven to notice. "Delia was telling me all about your little B and E lesson at Finlay's house the other day. You're quite the role model."

"They don't know anything about you, do they?" he said, his voice filled with venom as he grabbed the kids' bags. His eyes skated to Roddy over her shoulder as he leaned close to her ear. "Give me one reason. Just one good reason to tell them about your little problem in Maryland. I'm begging you."

Vero's grin fell away. She cast an anxious look at the cops across the lobby, paling when I slipped the diaper bag off her shoulder. "We'll talk about it later," I whispered. She stared at the floor as I took the children's hands and nudged Steven through the vestibule. By the time I'd buckled the kids into his truck and hurried back inside, Vero was nowhere in sight.

"What was all that about?" Nick asked, catching me by the elbow as I rushed past him through the lobby.

I rose up on my toes, searching for her head over the growing crowd of students who were filing out of their afternoon sessions. "Nothing. Did you see where Vero went?"

He pointed to an emergency exit at the end of the hall as Ty came up behind him. "Sir, Commander Ortega's here asking for you."

Nick did a double take at the faint lines radiating from Ty's eyes and the lingering red scribble around his lips. "Tell him I'll be right there," he said, shaking his head as if he didn't have the capacity to wrap it around one more thing.

"You going to be okay?" he asked me. When I nodded, he checked his watch. "The mess hall's opening in a few minutes. Why don't you and Vero grab something to eat. I'll find you after dinner." His eyes flicked over my shoulder. "There are some things we need to talk about."

I turned in time to see Julian and Parker carrying their messenger bags toward the lobby. By the time I turned back to Nick, he was gone.

I burst through the emergency exit, searching the walkways for Vero, pivoting when I heard the door sling open again behind me. Julian called out to me as he jogged to catch up.

"Now's not a good time," I said, agitated and hurried.

"I know." He stopped in my path before I could run off. "I know you have a lot on your plate right now. I just wanted . . ." He raked his curls back from his forehead, the dusky light of the sunset casting shadows over his cheeks. "I wanted to apologize for what happened in the mock trial. Parker's boss asked her to volunteer, and she didn't want to do it alone, so I offered to come. Neither of us realized you or Nick would be here. If I'd known, I never would have let her sign us up. She had no idea what she was doing, Finn."

I hated that he was defending her. It was one thing to see the good in people; it was entirely another to be ignorant about who they were once they showed you. "She knew *exactly* what she was doing, Julian. She's in love with you, and she was trying to make me look like a liar to prove I'm not good enough for you. She obviously didn't get the memo that we're not seeing each other anymore."

"I'm sorry," he said quietly.

I blew out a sigh. "It's not your fault." The fact that I was guilty of the same—that I had given Vero the benefit of the doubt, knowing she hadn't been honest—wasn't lost on me. "You and Parker are friends,

I get it. She was only trying to protect you. But you should probably make it clear to her that you and I have moved on."

"Have you? Moved on?" The fact that he'd never told Parker we'd broken things off made me wonder if he was asking something else, if there was still hope for us. I thought I caught a flash of regret in his eyes as he turned away. "You don't have to answer that. It's none of my business."

"I have to go," I said softly as a streetlamp flickered on. Vero was alone and scared. And the secret she'd been keeping from me probably weighed a million pounds on her conscience by now. Vero and I may have had a lot of problems, but we were invested in each other. We were raising my kids together. Burying bodies for each other. And I had to believe that counted for something.

"Wait." Julian reached for me, drawing back before he could touch me. He jammed his hands in his coat pockets as he wrestled with what to say. "I know you probably don't want my advice, and I'm probably the last person who should be giving it, but there are some questions you shouldn't answer, Finn. It's okay to hold back. You don't have to tell Nick everything. You know that, right?"

"I know." Julian and I looked at each other for a long time. It felt like we'd come to the end of a chapter, and there were so many things about our story I wished I could have rewritten. His smile was bittersweet, as if he knew.

"Be careful," he said, the sun slipping below the horizon as he walked away.

CHAPTER 29

I took the steps to our dorm room two at a time, relieved to find Vero's luggage was still there. I'd called her cell no less than a dozen times, but all my calls had rolled to voice mail. She wasn't with all the other academy students in the cafeteria. All the classrooms were being locked for the night, and the shooting range was closed. The only building I hadn't tried was the gym.

I called her name as I drew open the gymnasium doors. The basketball courts were dark. So were the training and mat rooms. I cracked open the door to the women's locker room. The lights were off and the changing room was empty. I was just turning to go when I heard a sniffle.

I let the door fall closed and headed to the vending machines, praying I wouldn't have to commit a misdemeanor as I fed a handful of crumpled dollar bills into the snack machine. The last packet of Pop-Tarts dropped into the dispenser. Feeling lucky, I tried the drink machine. A Dr Pepper fell with a satisfying thump.

I carried the snacks back to the locker room and flipped on the lights, following the sounds of Vero's sniffles to the only closed bathroom stall. I lowered my head, tilting to see underneath the partition, and spotted a familiar pair of pink-and-white Skechers in front of the commode. I knocked on the stall door.

Vero's voice was muffled as she blew her nose. "I'm not coming out unless you have a warrant."

"Vero, it's me. Open the door."

"So your sister can arrest me?"

"She's not going to arrest you."

"Then your boyfriend will."

"He's not my boyfriend." And I was pretty sure he never would be after the conversation we were likely to have later. "Nick's not going to arrest you either. Neither is anyone else here, for that matter."

"They have to. I'm a wanted fugitive."

I rolled my eyes and thrust the Pop-Tarts under the partition.

"Are you seriously pulling a Zach on me?"

"Are you seriously making me? Let me in."

"I can't," she said.

"Why not?"

"Because I handcuffed myself to the toilet paper dispenser."

With a heavy sigh, I dropped down onto my belly to slither under the door. "You know, I'm getting really tired of crawling around on public restroom floors."

"Are you alone?"

"Were you expecting a posse?" I asked, dragging myself into the stall.

Vero sat on the toilet lid, her wrists cuffed around the dispenser beside her. Her nose was red and her eyes were puffy. I sat on the floor by her feet with my back against the wall.

"Where did you get the cuffs?"

"From the mat room down the hall."

"Where's the key?"

"In the toilet with my phone." At my raised eyebrows, she said, "I accidentally dropped it while I was trying to call Javi to come pick me up."

I rolled onto my knees and opened the stall door. "I'll go get someone to help."

"No!" She leaned back on the seat lid and kicked the door shut, holding it closed with her sneaker. "I'm not leaving this bathroom. And I'm not going back to Maryland."

"No one is taking you to Maryland. Steven didn't tell anyone but me about the warrant. Unless you get yourself arrested again, you probably have nothing to worry about."

"That's a comfort," she deadpanned.

I shoved her foot out of the way and sat back down, holding a chunk of Pop-Tart where she could reach it. "Eat this. You're missing dinner." When she took it, her sleeve was wet with snot.

"We're both missing dinner." She leaned forward to nibble off a corner. "Did you bring anything good to drink?"

I laughed. "Under the present circumstances, I didn't think stealing liquor from the faculty lounge would be the wisest choice." I opened the soda can and held it to her mouth. "Why didn't you tell me there was a warrant out for you?"

"Because you were letting me live in your house—with your *kids*—and I didn't want you to change your mind and kick me out."

"Let me get this straight," I said, pulling the soda from her lips. "You show up in my garage and find me standing over Harris Mickler's lifeless body, and you're, like, *Sure, I'll help you bury the dead guy. Where's my forty percent? While we're at it, let's become serial killers. There's a sale on chest freezers at Lowe's and I've got three thousand feet of Cling Wrap in the trunk of a sports car I bought with money I negotiated from the Russian mob.* But you thought the fact that you were wanted for petty larceny—of a *sorority house treasury fund,*" I emphasized, "was the most concerning part of all that?"

"Because I didn't do it!" she said adamantly.

"I know that!"

She looked surprised. "You do?"

"You told me you didn't steal that money. Of course I believe you." Some of the tension left her shoulders as I held the soda out to her. "Is there anything else I should know?" I asked, tipping the can for her as she sipped.

"You know as much as I do now. I only found out I'd been formally charged because the cops went to my mother's house looking for me and she freaked out." She rested her head against the side of the stall.

"She called my cousin and told him there was a warrant out for me, and I haven't crossed the state line since."

I offered her another piece of Pop-Tart, perplexed by Maryland and New Jersey's geography. "If you never went back to Maryland, how did you get to Atlantic City?"

"Drove around it," she said with her mouth full. A laugh started deep in my chest. "What's so funny?" she asked, spraying crumbs at me.

"Nothing," I said, attempting to stifle it. "It's just . . . you went to all that trouble for a year, evading an erroneous theft charge, only to meet me and get wrapped up in all this." I waved my hands around, gesturing at everything.

"All this," she said, mimicking my gesture with her head, "would make a pretty great story, you know."

"If a little far-fetched."

"Are you kidding me? It's a recipe for a blockbuster hit!" Her handcuffs rattled as she counted on her fingers. "It's got courtroom drama, car chases, deep cover agents . . . not to mention a pretty tricky mystery to solve. And I bet Sylvia would love that hot little make-out scene you were working on in the closet."

"There was no making out in the closet."

Vero shook her head like she wasn't buying a word of it. "I saw him when he came tumbling out of there with his hair all mussed and his tie undone, like he'd gone from giving you the third degree to giving you something else." She wagged an eyebrow, but the only thing Nick had given me was a guilty conscience, raging hormones, and a need for a cold shower.

"We talked. That's all," I said irritably.

Her cuffs clanked against the toilet paper dispenser as she shook a reproving finger at me. "You know what your problem is? You don't think you deserve him. That's why you're keeping him at arm's length. Because you've got this ridiculous idea that you're a terrible person. You feel responsible for what happened to Harris and Andrei and Carl and Ike, even though you didn't kill a single one of them. Everything you did, you did to protect someone: your kids, your mom, your ex—god only knows why . . . hell, you even went out of your way to protect Theresa! If that doesn't qualify you for sainthood, there isn't a damn bit of hope for the rest of us. So you told a few fibs, big deal! Nick doesn't want *perfect*. If he did, he would have lost interest in you a long time ago—"

"Thanks."

"—He just wants *you,* Finn. So quit telling yourself you're not worthy, take off your big girl panties, and jump him before your deadline so we can finish this book and get paid the rest of our—" A door slammed. Our eyes locked as it echoed through the locker room.

"What was that?" Vero whispered.

"Sounded like it came from the basketball court." I set down the soda and peeked out from under the stall. We'd been talking as if we were alone. Talking about things no one should overhear. I rose to my feet and unlocked the door. "I'll go see who it was. You wait here."

Vero held up her wrists. "Like I have any choice?"

I crept past the showers toward the door to the basketball court, pausing to listen before cracking it open. The court was still dark. Diffuse light filtered through the windowpanes in the doors to the hallway.

Cam's back was hunched, his body restless as he paced the center line. The soft crack of his knuckles ticked through the room like the second hand of a clock.

"Finlay!" Vero hissed from the bathroom. "Finlay, what's going on?"

Afraid Cam might hear her, I slipped through the door into the gym and let it close behind me, ducking under the metal bleachers and peering through the slats. Cam whipped around as the hallway doors were thrown wide.

Joey stormed onto the court. "What the hell are you doing here? I thought I told you not to come back!"

Cam raised his hands. "I'm sorry, Joe! I swear, I didn't have any choice!"

The rear door of the gym flew open. Joey went rigid as two armed men dressed in black strode in.

CHAPTER 30

Joey surrendered his hands as Feliks's men approached him. One of them frisked him, taking his gun from its holster. The other called out an all clear. I sucked in a breath as Feliks entered the room. His long strides were imperious, the scruff on his jaw and the length of his hair the only hints that he'd been behind bars less than a day ago.

"You've got a lot of nerve coming here," Joey told him.

"Perhaps," Feliks admitted, adjusting the cuffs of his suit, "but I have a rather urgent situation that must be dealt with once and for all, and since my attempts to delegate the matter were not as fruitful as I would have liked, I had no choice but to remove myself from custody and handle the unpleasantries myself." One of the men placed Joey's gun in Feliks's outstretched hand. Cam flinched as Feliks checked the magazine and snapped it back in place.

"Ms. Donovan," Feliks called across the gym, "if you would be so kind as to join us." I yelped as a meaty hand closed around my arm and hauled me out from under the bleachers. A huge man dressed in Feliks's standard-issue bodyguard black deposited me roughly in the center of the court. "Where is her friend?" Feliks demanded.

Onc of his bodyguards smirked and said something in Russian. The others laughed. Vero rattled her handcuffs, shouting a string of expletives from the locker room.

"Leave her," Feliks told them, unamused. "I don't have a lot of time,

Ms. Donovan, so pardon me for getting right to the point." He gestured to Joey with his gun. "Is this the man you've identified as *EasyClean*?"

"What . . . how . . . how could you know that?" I stammered. The clanking and swearing in the locker room grew louder.

"This is the last time I will ask you, Ms. Donovan. Do you or do you not suspect Detective Joseph Balafonte of being *EasyClean*? Did you and your nanny not discuss these suspicions on more than one occasion over the last eighteen hours?" He flicked off the safety.

My heart thumped wildly in my chest. Eighteen hours was a strangely specific window of time. My mind raced back to eighteen hours ago. It would have been the middle of the night, while Vero and I were at the crime scene exercise in the woods, just before I'd walked back to our dorm and found Cam under our window . . .

I touched my cell phone through my pocket. I'd had my phone with me that night. But Vero . . . she had left hers in our room.

I whirled to Cam. "You bugged Vero's phone?" He winced.

Feliks raised his voice. "Ms. Donovan, my patience has limits."

"Yes . . . I mean, no! Yes, I suspected Joey might be *EasyClean,* but I never said I was sure! I can't prove it's him! Whatever it is you're planning to do, I don't think—"

Feliks's hot breath fanned my face as he leaned close and whispered, "You are not here to think, Ms. Donovan. You are here to do what I hired you to do. And now that I've made the task simple for you, you will cease this pointless stalling and finish the job." He shoved the gun in my hand and stepped aside, his arm sweeping toward Joey, presenting me with a clear target.

I kept the gun pointed at the floor, my head swinging frantically back and forth. "I can't do this! I could be wrong. And even if I'm right, he doesn't deserve to die just because he tried to blackmail you!"

"I'm surprised by your lack of enthusiasm, Ms. Donovan. I assumed you would be eager to punish the man who attempted three times to murder your children's father, yet here he is, standing before you, and you are unwilling to put him down." When I didn't speak,

Feliks clasped his hands. "Very well. I have presented you with an opportunity for retribution. Do you decline?"

"Yes, I decline!"

"Then I will present you with an order. Kill him. Now, Ms. Donovan. We are running out of time."

One of his men pressed a gun to my temple. My whole body tensed against the shock of cold steel. I lowered my eyes to Joey's gun. It grew impossibly heavy in my hand as Joey backed away from me toward the bleachers. His eyes darted to the exits, but Feliks's men had them covered.

Feliks stole up behind me and whispered, "Ekatarina has expressed her doubts about you from the beginning." His arms came around me, lifting my hands until the gun was pointed straight out in front of me. My heart lurched as he moved my finger toward the trigger. "I told her I knew that you weren't what you claimed to be. And yet, there is a facet of you I find fascinating, a glimmer that makes me curious," he said into my hair as he adjusted the direction of the barrel, "and I think, if I turn you just the right way in just the right light, you might prove yourself to be valuable." His hands drew slowly away from me, leaving me holding the weapon.

Joey's silhouette drifted in front of me like a paper target. Hot tears wavered his outline.

"I won't do this," I said through the painful knot in my throat. Vero and my mother would take care of my children. Steven would surely step up if I was gone. "Shoot me if you want, but I won't kill him." I took my finger off the trigger and held the gun out to Feliks. I closed my eyes and swallowed hard. I'd predicted in seventh grade gym class I was going to die wearing sweats on a basketball court, but I'd thought I was being melodramatic. I never dreamed I'd be right.

A gun cocked beside my ear.

"Stop! I'll do it!" Cam ripped the gun away from my hand. He pointed it at Joey, level with his head, his voice shaking when he said, "I've got as much of a reason to kill that asshole as anybody."

Feliks looked on with a curious lift of his brow.

I clapped a hand over my mouth. I wanted to shout at Cam in my mom voice, to tell him to put the gun down and think about what he was doing, but I was terrified of shattering the tension in the room. Cam's jaw was set, his body shaking.

Joey put up his hands. "You don't want to do this," he said in a low voice. "Not like this. Lower the gun." Cam's finger slid toward the trigger. "Someone taught you better than this. I know they did."

Cam clenched his teeth. "Shut up."

"You don't point a gun at someone unless you intend to shoot them, and I don't think you really want to hurt me." Cam's face twisted, confused, as if that last part ached sinking in. "There's another way through this. A better way than the one you're aiming for. It'll be okay. Just listen. Look at me, Cameron," Joey pleaded. Cam's eyes lifted reluctantly to Joey's. "Lower the gun."

They stared at each other. Joey gave a small, encouraging nod as the nose of the gun dropped a fraction. I sucked in a sharp breath as Cam's finger moved over the trigger. Joey's eyes flew open wide as the gun fired.

I braced for the earsplitting pop—for the police to rush in, the sirens and lights, the chaos that would inevitably follow—but the sound of the bullet ripping into Joey's chest, the crack of his head against the bleachers behind him as he fell, was all muffled by the roar of blood in my ears. Cam lowered the gun, his face slack with shock, as one of Feliks's men came forward and gently took the weapon from him.

The sound of my name came to me as if through a fog. "Ms. Donovan," Feliks snapped his fingers, tearing my attention from Joey's motionless body. "Make sure it's done." He checked his watch, gesturing for me to hurry.

I hurried to Joey on trembling legs and dropped to my knees at his side, my hands pressed to the floor as I listened for breaths. A faint pulse fluttered in his throat, but for how much longer? Blood was spreading quickly from a cut behind his head. It trickled over my fingers. I pushed aside Joey's coat, leaving thick, red smears on his shirt as I searched for an entrance wound, but the tiny hole in the fabric was dry.

I slid a finger through it, over the sturdy layer of Kevlar hidden underneath.

My mind rushed back to his last words to Cam.

It'll be okay . . . lower the gun.

Not drop the gun. *Lower* it.

Cam must have figured out what Joey was trying to tell him—that he was wearing a vest. I nearly cried out with relief. Cam's eyes were glassy and pleading when I stole a look at him over my shoulder, the warning in the shake of his head so small, it was almost imperceptible.

I stood, my hands raised as I returned to the center of the court, letting Feliks get a good look at the blood on them.

"He's dead." I didn't bother to hide the quiver in my voice. "You've done what you came to do. *EasyClean* is no longer a problem for you. The police are probably already on their way. You should leave while you still can."

Feliks nodded, satisfied. He put an arm around Cam, bringing their faces close. "I'm sorry your induction to our family had to be such a difficult one, but eliminating your uncle was a necessary task."

Uncle?

Feliks cocked an eyebrow at my gasp. "You seem surprised, Ms. Donovan. I assumed you, too, would have made this discovery by now." I stared at him, baffled, as he explained. "After you and your nanny discussed Detective Balafonte last night, I had my people do a bit of digging to confirm your suspicions. In doing so, they came across a rather interesting connection. It seems Cameron's father was a police officer, one who used to do odd jobs for me from time to time. It was during one of those jobs that he met an unfortunate end." Cam stared at the floor, his expression numb, as if he already knew. "Detective Balafonte requested a transfer to this jurisdiction after his brother's death, presumably so he could keep a closer eye on his brother's illegitimate son—and me."

Feliks dropped a possessive hand on Cam's shoulder. "Cameron's Uncle Joey arrived here last year, just in time to negotiate a deal to keep his nephew from being lost to the juvenile justice system. By making

Cameron his very own confidential informant, Joseph could more easily keep the boy under his thumb. However, that wasn't the only secret Joseph was keeping from his colleagues here. You see, he was granted a transfer here in exchange for his participation in an Internal Affairs investigation. Under the guise of rooting out corruption in the department, he's been quietly surveilling the police officers I've employed. Apparently, he's been using the information he gleaned to exploit my vulnerabilities." Feliks's gaze dipped thoughtfully to the blood on my hands. "If Joseph blamed me in some way for his brother's death, I suppose it makes sense that he was secretly out to ruin me. Though, given his pristine employment record, I'm surprised that blackmail was his weapon of choice; I would have expected a nobler pursuit."

I stood there, dumbstruck as I tried to reconcile everything Feliks had just said. Joey was Cam's uncle. All this time, he'd been working for Internal Affairs, lying to Nick—lying to his entire department—about all of it. Had he really been using his job only to uncover Feliks's weaknesses and exploit them for revenge? Had my suspicions about Joey been right all along? It seemed easier to believe now, in light of these revelations, and yet I couldn't shake the last thing Feliks said, about Joey's character and his choices, the hint of doubt I detected . . .

The faint slam of a car door outside shook me from my thoughts. Feliks signaled to his men. Weapons drawn, they moved quickly to the rear exit. Feliks paused in front of me. The thumb of his leather driving glove traced the curve of my cheek. "How disappointing that our time together is up while we have so much unresolved business to discuss."

He put an arm around Cameron and ushered him out.

When the door closed behind them, I rushed back to Joey. "Wake up!" I shouted, slapping his face. Buttons popped free as I tore open the front of his shirt. The bullet was lodged in his vest, just to the right of his sternum. I pulled at the straps, Velcro shrieking as I yanked them loose. Joey moaned. His eyelids fluttered, his pupils doing strange things in the low light. He blinked at the blood on my sweatshirt, his hands groping his chest for a wound that wasn't there.

"You're alive, you idiot. But you have so much explaining to do."

Shouts came from the women's locker room. Then the men's. The gymnasium doors flew open. Nick, Georgia, Roddy, Wade, Ty, and Charlie all swarmed in with their weapons drawn. Vero rushed in behind them, a broken toilet paper dispenser dangling from her handcuffs. Wade flipped a series of switches on the wall and light flooded the room. The barrel of Nick's gun shifted to each corner of the gym as he limped toward us.

"That way," I said, pointing to the rear exit. Roddy, Ty, Wade, and Charlie rushed out the back door in pursuit, though I was sure they wouldn't find anyone. Feliks would never have stepped foot on the campus without ensuring he had an exit strategy.

Nick holstered his gun as he reached my side, his eyes and hands frantically searching my clothes, my hair, my face. "Are you hurt?"

"I'm fine," I insisted, "but Joey hit his head pretty hard." Georgia was already kneeling beside him, her phone pressed to her ear, calling for an ambulance. As Nick went to check on his partner, Vero threw her arms around me, the toilet paper dispenser swinging hard against my back.

"You're okay! I thought Feliks was going to kill you!"

I hugged her back. "For a minute, I thought he was, too."

Joey groaned as he tried to sit up. Nick held him down, checking his head. Joey lay back, his eyelids drifting shut again. "Where's his Glock?" Nick asked me.

His Glock. Vero and I exchanged a look. I hadn't thought to look carefully at the gun Feliks had put in my hand. "Feliks took it," I said.

"Feliks was here? You saw him?" Nick asked.

"I already told him," Vero interrupted with a pointed look at me, "that you and I were in the bathroom and we heard a commotion in the gym. I was indisposed," she said, holding up her wrists, the toilet paper dispenser swinging between them, "so you came to check it out. By the time I got free, Zhirov's goons had already dragged you into their soiree with Joey, so I ran for help. And that's *all I told him.*"

Nick's eyes skated between us as he withdrew a key ring from his pocket and unlocked Vero's cuffs. "Why do I get the feeling there's something you're *both* not telling me?"

Vero pressed her lips shut.

Better to stick close to the truth, I reminded myself. Nothing Vero and I had said so far had been a lie. It just hadn't been the whole story. "Feliks was here looking for Joey," I said cautiously. "He said something about a photo. He thought Joey had emailed it to him last night."

Nick narrowed his eyes. "Joey? But that's not possible. Joey couldn't have sent that photo. He was . . ." Nick's thoughts trailed. I could see him trying to work through it—the timelines, the possibilities.

An EMT brushed past us. Two more came right on his heels, wheeling a gurney. The gym erupted in chaos as Wade, Ty, Roddy, and Charlie burst in, breathless and sweating. Roddy shouldered his way through the crowd, red faced and panting.

"Anything?" Nick asked him.

Roddy shook his head. "The media are here. They're looking for a statement from you about Zhirov's escape. I could use a little help getting their vans clear of the gate."

Nick scrubbed a hand over his face as the EMTs put a neck brace on Joey. "We can't let the press get wind of what happened here today. If Feliks thinks Joey's dead, then Joey's only safe if it stays that way."

"Good luck keeping it quiet. The ambulance rolled in with lights and sirens, and now every reporter out there is frothing at the mouth. Commander Ortega wants the campus locked down."

"Great," Nick muttered. "Where are the students now?"

"Sheltering in place in the mess hall."

"Have them escorted to the dorm. I want an officer stationed on every floor."

"What are you going to tell the press?" Roddy asked.

"As little as possible." Nick put his hands on his hips, frowning as he watched the EMTs strap Joey on a gurney. Joey's eyes were closed. An oxygen mask covered his mouth. Nick reached in his partner's pockets and collected Joey's wallet and phone. He tapped Georgia's shoulder on his way back to us, beckoning her to follow. "Stay here with Joey," he told her. "I want the EMTs to leave quietly through the front gate. No lights. No sirens. Roddy, I want you to leak word to the press that the ME is on his way. Then have the EMTs circle around and pick up Joey from the back. Georgia will ride with him. When they get him to the ER, make sure he's listed as a John Doe."

"We're going to fake his death?" Georgia asked.

"For as long as we can," Nick answered.

Vero looped her arm in mine and turned for the door. "You heard the man, Finn. We'd better get to our room."

Nick caught us by our elbows. "Not so fast. You two are staying here with Roddy. We'll need statements from both of you." He drew me aside, tipping my chin up. "You okay?"

I was not okay. None of this was okay. I nodded into his hand.

"Stay close to Roddy and Ty. I'll find you later," he promised before he disappeared into the crowd.

CHAPTER 31

It was well after nine o'clock that night when Vero and I were finally escorted to the dorm. After three hours, Nick hadn't returned to the gym. The EMTs and Joey were long gone, the parking lot already cleared of reporters by the time Roddy had relented to let us wait in our room. Someone would come for us later, he'd said, once Nick was finished putting out fires and had time to take our statements. Roddy had called him and offered to handle it, but Nick had insisted he be the one to do it.

Our escort followed us upstairs, unlocked our door, and did a quick cursory check of our room before retreating to the hall, where he would presumably remain until Nick was ready for us. The officer's radio squawked outside, his voice low and muffled through the wall.

Vero kicked off her shoes and shucked her coat with a shiver. She whipped a blanket from her bed, swinging it over her shoulders like a cape. "It's colder than a bag of frozen body parts in here."

"The heat must not be working." I rubbed my hands together and dragged my blanket from my unmade bed. I froze, the blanket draped halfway around my shoulders as I gaped down at my mattress.

"What is it?" Vero asked, creeping up behind me.

A black duffel bag rested in the middle of my bed, the zipper straining around its contents. Vero rushed to the window and pulled back the blind. The lower sash was open and an icy draft whipped into the room.

Vero tossed her blanket aside and reached for the duffel bag. The zipper whined open and she stared into it with a look of awe. Or maybe lust. I wasn't entirely sure. "Oh, Javi, you beautiful, sexy beast," she whispered.

I shut and locked the window as she pulled a brick of cash from the bag and fanned it under her nose. "I thought you said Javi wouldn't have the money until tomorrow."

"He must have worked something out. I told him we were in a hurry." She dumped the cash onto my bed, counting the stacks. Her brow furrowed as she counted them again.

"What's wrong?" I asked.

She removed a rubber band from one of the bricks, licked a finger, and quickly thumbed through the bills. "There are two hundred and fifty thousand dollars in here," she murmured.

"How was he able to get so much for the car? You don't think he sold it in one piece, do you?" I sank down on my bed, queasy at the thought. "He was supposed to make it impossible to trace."

"We don't have time to worry about that now," she said, zipping the money back into the bag and stuffing it under her bed. She sat down on the mattress, taking deep Lamaze breaths as she wiped her hands down the front of her yoga pants. "Nick's going to be here any minute, asking for our statements. What are you going to tell him?"

I hugged my coat around me. I had to tell Nick something. At some point, Joey was going to wake up in that hospital and give a statement, too. I replayed the events of the night, from the moment I'd first recognized Cam in the gym to the moment the police came barreling through the doors. Joey would have heard me accuse Cam of bugging Vero's phone. And Feliks hadn't said anything that could incriminate me, at least not out loud. He had only whispered to me the handful of words that could put me behind bars. *You are here to do what I hired you to do.* But I had refused to kill Joey. Several times. And I'd covered for him in the end, faking his death so he could escape with his life. Anything Joey had learned about me would be far less incriminating than the secrets he had been hiding. "I'll tell Nick the truth. I'll answer any direct questions he asks." I only hoped he wouldn't ask too many.

"What are you going to tell him about Joey? Do you think he's really *EasyClean*?"

"I don't know." I'd always known Joey had the means and opportunity to be *EasyClean,* but now I knew he also had a motive. All the circumstantial evidence pointed to Joey as our killer. His gun was the same make as the one that had fired the bullet into the Aston. He'd known where the CPR dummy was buried. He could have cut it up, marked it with Carl's name, and taken the photo after the other instructors had left. He could have sent the email to Feliks, knowing Cam would find it, then turned it over to Sam to conceal his own involvement. And yet, I had the nagging feeling there was a piece of the puzzle I wasn't seeing, just beyond my grasp—a taunting clue that was hiding right in front of me.

I glanced down at Vero's feet. Then at the duffel bag behind them. "I'm not sure who *EasyClean* is, but I think I know a way to find out."

"How's that?"

"The same way we get Zach out of the men's room."

Vero frowned as I dragged the duffel bag out from under her bed. "With fruit snacks?"

"With bait."

Vero unzipped the duffel bag and took an artfully arranged photo of the cash. Using the dark web browser we had installed on my laptop last fall, we set up a bogus email account and typed a message to *EasyClean*, to the same address he had used to communicate with us twice before.

To: EasyClean
From: Assistant2Z
Subject: Ready to do business

Message: You've made your point. However, the significant sum you require poses a challenge, as my employer's assets have been frozen and it will take time to arrange a transfer through alternate

> channels. As a gesture of good faith, we are prepared to deliver a partial installment. Assuming you keep your end of the bargain, the rest will be deposited into your account within seventy-two hours. You'll find the location and time of the drop and proof of funds attached.

Vero read the message over my shoulder. "It's been two months since the forum shut down. You think *EasyClean* still uses this address?"

"It's the same address he used to send that blackmail letter to Feliks in December. He's probably still using the same one." It was almost eleven o'clock. With any luck, he'd get the message in time. We'd leave the duffel bag on the roof before the scheduled drop at three A.M., then wait to see who came looking for it.

"What if the police are monitoring *EasyClean*'s email account?" Vero asked.

"We've got a clean line of sight to the fire tower from here. We'll keep a close eye on it over the next few hours. If we suspect anyone's watching when it's time to set up the drop, we'll back off and let the police take him down." If everything went according to plan, *Easy-Clean* would show up to discover a duffel bag containing stacks of bundled brown paper towels we'd stolen from the bathroom maintenance closet.

We held our breaths as I clicked send. I passed my laptop to Vero and paced our room, unable to sit still through the silence that followed. I nibbled my thumbnail as I stood in front of the window, staring at the dark shadow of the fire tower, listening for a chime or a notification indicating the message had failed to reach its recipient, but the computer remained quiet.

I held Vero's binoculars to my eyes, adjusting the focus. From our window, I could clearly make out all five sets of zigzagging metal stairs that led to the roof of the fire tower. A bright half-moon shone between the clouds, its light glimmering off the railings. It was the perfect location for a setup.

"What if nobody shows to pick up the money?" Vero asked.

"Then we can safely assume *EasyClean* is Joey." Presumably, Joey was still in the hospital without access to a secure computer, and Nick had taken his phone and wallet from his pocket in the gym. As long as Joey was stuck in a hospital bed and Nick was here, Joey would have no way to know about the drop, and no way to get here. But if *Easy-Clean* was one of the others—Charlie, Wade, or even Samara—two hundred and fifty thousand in cash should be more than enough to draw them out.

We both jumped at a loud knock on the door. Vero slapped my laptop shut. She zipped the cash inside her suitcase and kicked the duffel back under the bed as I shoved the binoculars under my pillow. I smoothed down my hair and opened the door, expecting to find Nick on the other side of it. Samara smiled, her arms weighed down by two paper bags and the shoulders of her trench coat dotted with rain.

"Heard you two had an interesting night," she said, pushing her way into the room and setting the bags on the dresser. "Roddy thought you might be hungry since you missed dinner." She proceeded to unload one of the bags. "Looks like the kitchen staff prepared quite a feast. I've got two club sandwiches, some coleslaw, potato salad, and a couple of brownies for each of you." She handed each of us a soda.

Vero wrinkled her nose at the can. "You couldn't have brought anything stronger from the faculty lounge?"

Sam crumpled the empty bag and pitched it in the trash can. She turned to us with a smirk, untying her trench coat and opening it with a flourish. A pint of whisky was tucked in the inside pocket.

"Bless you and the white horse you rode in on," Vero whispered. She reached for the bottle like it was the last one on earth. "I knew I loved this woman for a reason."

Sam laughed, the long ties of her open coat swaying against her red leather pumps. "Considering the day you've had, I figured there wasn't any harm in bending the rules, but do me a favor and don't mention it to Nick. He's in a pretty shitty mood. He practically took my head off when I tried to deliver a few sandwiches to his room just now." She held up the second bag. "Said he wasn't hungry."

My smile faltered. "Nick's in his room?"

"Apparently, he's brooding, but you didn't hear it from me." She stole a brownie on her way to the door. At the last minute, she turned, her voice tentative when she asked, "You don't by any chance know where I can find Georgia, do you? Silly to let Nick's sandwiches go to waste."

"She's probably in her room," I said absently. I should have been relieved that Sam was looking for my sister rather than sitting behind a computer, planning a raid on the fire tower, but my mind hung stubbornly on what she'd said about Nick. If he had already finished working for the night, why hadn't he come to find me and take my statement?

"Georgia's room is down the hall," Vero supplied helpfully. "Room three nineteen. Take an extra brownie," she suggested with a wink. "Georgia's got a sweet tooth."

I hardly noticed as Sam took an extra brownie and showed herself out.

"If your sister doesn't marry that woman, I might." Vero cracked open the whisky and took a long swig, her eyes watering as she passed me the bottle. When I didn't take it, she studied me with a suspicious tip of her head. "Oh, no. What's that look? I know that look."

I checked the time on my phone. All night long, I'd assumed Nick was too busy to come. That he was tied up in meetings with his commander and writing reports. When he'd said good-bye in the gym, he'd said he would find me when he was done, but that had been almost five hours ago. So why hadn't he brought our dinner himself? And why was he alone, brooding in his room?

I took the bottle of whisky from Vero and passed her the binoculars. "Keep an eye on the drop site. I'll be back in an hour."

CHAPTER 32

I told the officer standing watch outside our door that I needed to use the bathroom. When his back was turned, I darted down the stairwell at the end of the hall. Nick's room was on the first floor. I'd seen the number printed on the back of his lanyard when he'd stood over me that morning in the maintenance closet, and I'd committed it to memory for reasons I hadn't been ready to think about.

I checked to make sure the hallway was clear as I slipped out of the stairwell and searched for Nick's room. I rapped on the door, starting when it opened almost immediately. His hand was braced against the doorframe, his eyes shut and his free hand pinching the bridge of his nose as if he was fighting a headache.

"I told you, Sam, I'm fine. Losing perps is just part of the job, and I really don't feel like talking about—" Nick's hand fell away. The collar of his dress shirt was loose, unbuttoned to his sternum, the rumpled fabric framed between the leather shoulder straps of his holster. He frowned down at me, the bright light of the hall casting harsh shadows under his eyes.

I swallowed my nerves. "If you're not up for company, I can go."

"No, I just . . . I wasn't expecting you." He glanced over my shoulder, as if he was waiting for his commander to pop out from around a corner. "You probably shouldn't be down here."

"Probably not." I pulled Sam's pint of whisky from under my sweatshirt and held it out to him. He took my wrist and pulled me into his room, checking to make sure the hallway was empty before closing the door behind us.

Nick's room was dimly lit by a small lamp on the desk beside his bed. The confined space smelled like him, like soft, worn leather and the spicy musk of his cologne. The faculty accommodations were nicer than the student dorms, more like a cheap motel room. The warm lamplight, his partially made bed, his shower towel slung carelessly over the open closet door . . . it all felt intimate, and suddenly I understood his hesitation to let me in.

We did an awkward dance, maneuvering around each other in the tight space as he scooped his jacket and cane off the bed, tossing them onto his open suitcase on the floor to make space for me to sit. I perched on the edge of his mattress, watching him as he peeled two Styrofoam cups from a stack beside the coffeepot on his dresser. He opened the whisky, pouring a generous splash into each cup.

"How's Joey?" I asked.

Nick's eyes pinched at the corners as he passed me a drink. "He's fine. Just a concussion and some stitches. The hospital's keeping him under observation tonight. They'll probably discharge him tomorrow." He downed most of his drink in one deep swallow, his jaw clenched against a wince as it went down. He pulled out his desk chair and turned it to face me, favoring his leg as he eased down into it. He stared into his cup, his elbows resting on his knees.

"I thought you were coming to take our statements," I said between sips.

"I thought I was, too. But then the hospital called and said Joey was asking for me, so I went to see him." His eyes lifted to mine. "He wanted to give me his statement."

I swallowed a gulp that left my voice hoarse. "Joey hit his head pretty hard. Did he remember much?"

"Why don't you tell me what you remember first?"

"Are you asking for my statement?"

"I'm asking for the truth."

A week ago, I'd told Vero she should face her fears and speak her truth. That anyone who assumed the worst about her wasn't good enough for her in the first place. But now, as I sat on the edge of Nick's bed, looking into his eyes, I understood why she would circumnavigate an entire state just so she wouldn't have to.

And yet, what kind of future could I hope to have with Nick if I couldn't do it?

"Ask me anything," I said cautiously.

"Why did you suspect Joey of trying to kill Steven?"

I licked my lips, willing the liquor to make it easier to speak. "Do you remember the night you were shot, when I left the Westovers' house, right before they put you in the ambulance?" Nick's brow furrowed, his eyes darting back and forth between mine. "I went to find Steven. His business partner told me Steven's vehicle had broken down on his way to the Westovers' house. I knew the killer was still out there looking for him, and I wanted to get to him before anything happened. I found him stranded on the side of the road a few miles away. As he was getting in my car, someone pulled over and started shooting at us." Nick tensed, his frown deepening as he straightened in his chair. "We managed to escape without seeing who it was. All I knew was that the shooter was driving a sedan, they were reasonably skilled with a gun, and that Joey wasn't with you at the Westovers' that night because he was supposed to be out looking for my ex-husband."

"Why didn't you tell me when you came to see me at the hospital?"

"Because Joey was your partner. And because I couldn't be sure it was him. I had no proof."

Nick was quiet as he took it all in. "Did you know he's with Internal Affairs?"

"Not until tonight. Feliks said he thought Joey got himself assigned here as part of some revenge scheme. That Joey was trying to blackmail him. Was he?" I asked, watching Nick for a reaction.

His hand rasped over his stubble. "I asked Joey the same thing. He denied it. He swears it wasn't him."

"Do you believe him?"

He shook his head. "I don't know what I believe, Finn. I thought the guy was my partner, but he's been keeping secrets from me for months. How do you trust someone after that?"

I looked down into my cup, wishing I knew the answer. "What else did Joey say?"

"He said you saved his life tonight, and if it wasn't for you, he'd be dead."

A thick silence blanketed the room. It was the truth, and yet it only skimmed the surface. There was so much more buried in the murk underneath. "Joey wouldn't have been in danger if I hadn't suspected him in the first place."

"That wasn't your fault and Joey knows it. He told me about the bug in Vero's phone. You didn't do anything wrong." Nick downed the last of his drink. He set down his cup, his eyebrows knitting together as if he was searching for the right words to say. "Joey said you're not here doing research for a book. That you only came this week to find the person who tried to kill Steven."

"That's not the only reason," I argued.

"I'm not judging you, Finn. After everything Steven put you through, I think it's admirable that you want to protect him."

"He's my children's father. Of course, I want to protect him, but that's not the only reason I'm—"

"I know." Nick rose from his chair, blowing out a long sigh as he limped across the room. His hands were heavy on his hips, his voice rough when he finally spoke. "When Steven was here to pick up the kids, he told me you two are trying to reconcile. That you're going to start seeing a marriage counselor."

My jaw dropped. I set down my cup to keep from crushing it. "He told you that?"

"I feel like such an asshole for not seeing it before. I was so wrapped up in how I feel about you that I didn't stop to think that maybe you wanted something else. It all makes sense now, the way you pull away every time we're alone together. Like something's holding you back."

"That's not it," I said, launching to my feet as he paced. "I didn't pull away because of Steven!"

"You don't have to explain, Finn. I get it. He's Delia and Zach's father, and this is about them as much as it is about you. You had a house and a family and a life together before Theresa came along. And now she's out of the picture and you feel like maybe the two of you have a chance at working things out, and I don't blame you one bit for wanting to protect him, or for wanting to have your family back." He turned to face me, his hand on his chest. "I just wish you'd been honest with me about how you felt."

I opened my mouth, but nothing came out. Nick thought I was here at the academy because I was still in love with Steven. Because I wanted him back. Nick couldn't be more wrong about that. But he'd been right about one thing—I hadn't been honest with him about how I felt.

"You're right," I said in a steely voice. "I am here to find the person who tried to murder my ex-husband. Because he is the father of my children, and for that reason alone I will always want him to be safe. And maybe even happy. But I have no plans of going to counseling with him, and I would rather rip my own toenails out than welcome Steven back into my bed." A spark lit in Nick's eyes as I took a bold step closer. "But Joey was wrong if he told you that was my only reason for being here. I did come to do research for my book. I have writer's block," I said, confessions spewing out of me like a dam had finally broken. "Sylvia says my manuscript sucks, and my publisher is refusing to pay me because I can't write a goddamn sex scene."

Nick frowned. "You lost me."

"I don't know what the hell I'm doing with this book!" I said, throwing up my hands. "The cop and the heroine are supposed to be together—I know that—but every time I put them alone in a scene, I freeze up and I can't finish it." I looked up at the puzzled creases around his eyes, struggling to figure out how to explain. "The last book was different. The heroine's romance with the lawyer was easy," I admitted. "There were no strings attached and she had nothing to lose, because she could never picture a future with him anyway. But with you . . ." My mouth went dry at the intensity of Nick's stare. "With you, the stakes feel higher, because this feels like it could be something more. And I think I'm holding back because I'm terrified of ruining it."

His voice was husky. "What are you saying?"

What was I saying? That I was done waiting for everything to be perfect. For *me* to be perfect. I was done trying to contort myself to fit everyone else's expectations of who I should be. I was done feeling guilty for things that weren't my fault. Mostly, I was done denying myself my own happy ending.

I wanted dessert, to hell with the consequences.

I took Nick by the straps of his holster and kissed him. His body went still.

I drew back, afraid I'd gone too far. That maybe, after everything I'd confessed over the last twelve hours, he didn't want this anymore. "I'm sorry. I shouldn't have—"

"Don't." He slid a hand through my hair and pulled me close, his breath whisky-sweet on my face, our foreheads almost touching. Eyes closed, he said, "Don't apologize for this."

His mouth sank into mine, a teasing brush of five o'clock shadow and soft lips. He deepened the kiss with a maddening patience, the slow sweep of his tongue achingly thorough as I curled my fingers into the front of his shirt and drew him to me.

My body hummed with the buzz of whisky and adrenaline. With the warm leather smell of his clothes. Maybe it was this room or this place or the near-death experience I'd had only hours ago. Maybe it was the way he'd looked in a shower towel, with my son pressed to his chest. Or the way I'd thought about him every single night since he'd left me standing under the mistletoe. But when Nick kissed me, I felt it everywhere.

My fingers fumbled over his buttons.

"You sure about this?" he asked as I pushed his holster over his shoulders and dropped it on the floor.

"Uh-huh." Our breaths started coming fast. All the frustration that had built over the last two months was cresting like a tsunami inside me.

"Finn . . ." I nipped his bottom lip and he swore under his breath. His muscles tensed under my fingers, his skin hot, his chest pebbling with goose bumps as I pushed his undershirt over his head. "Maybe we should set up some ground rules so we don't get carried away. I can wait as long as you need. I don't want you to rush into anything you're not ready for—"

"Please stop talking."

The sound that came from him was almost feral. He backed me to the wall, pinning me by the hips, our kisses becoming fevered and desperate. I grabbed on to his shoulders, my palm brushing the raised scar there, a remnant of the shoot-out at the Westovers' house.

A vibration started somewhere in his pants. "Your phone," I panted as his mouth moved down my neck.

"Not answering."

"But what if it's about Feliks?"

"Don't care."

I worked the button loose on his pants.

"You okay with this?" he asked, gripping the hem of my sweatshirt.

"Definitely, completely, totally okay with this." He tugged it over my head as we limped backward across his room. My heel connected with the bed and I fell into it. Nick fell with me, every gloriously solid inch of him landing between my legs.

"Oh, wow," I said, a little breathless at the thought. "That's . . . a lot of research material."

He grinned against my ear. His hair tickled my collarbone, then the rise of my chest as his mouth moved down to my bra, teasing me through the fabric. "We don't have to cover it all tonight."

"I wasn't objecting." I arched against him, the sensitive skin of my belly jumping at his touch. I felt his fingers unfasten the button on my jeans. Felt the zipper hum down. Felt Nick moan against my navel as he realized, the same moment I remembered, that I didn't have any underwear on.

"Ground rules?" His voice was strained and urgent, his hands still where they gripped my jeans, waiting for me to decide how far I was willing to go. But I was so far beyond caring about the rules anymore. It was only a month into the new year, and I was throwing my third resolution into the fire like a cheap champagne flute.

"No rules," I said. I was only destined to break them. And I refused to feel guilty about any of this.

CHAPTER 33

I was distantly aware of the vibration of a cell phone. I burrowed deeper into the bed, fighting off a shiver. When the rattling didn't stop, I threw an arm out of the blankets, swatting out blindly for my nightstand. My hand came down on a smooth, warm curve that was definitely not my cell phone.

I blinked open one eye. My cheek was pressed against Nick's side and my outstretched hand rested on one truly spectacular pec. I peeled my drool-slicked face from his bare skin to peek at him. His lips were parted, shadowed in dark stubble. His worry lines were softened by sleep and the pale moonlight filtering through the window blind.

My phone started buzzing again. Nick stirred, his arm curling tighter around me. A soft moan rumbled in his chest as I pushed up on one elbow and reached across him for my jeans. I dug inside the pocket for my phone and hurried to dismiss the call, silently opening the string of text messages Vero had sent from the prepaid phone we'd purchased yesterday.

11:58pm: Where are you?

12:11am: The power's out all over campus.

12:12am: I can't see a damn thing and it's cold in here.

12:32am: Please tell me you're doing research for a steamy bestseller and you haven't been dismembered by the Russian mob.

12:45am: Finn?

Shit! How long had I slept? The clock on my phone said it was almost two. *EasyClean* would be arriving soon to pick up the money and we hadn't made the drop.

I pried Nick's arm from my hip, careful not to wake him as I backed out of the blankets and gathered my clothes from the floor. I hurried to dress, pulling back the edge of the blinds to see the glare of moonlight on freshly frozen sidewalks.

An eerie hush seemed to hover over the campus. Vero was right; every window in every building was dark. The fire tower was a hulking black shadow in the distance, the crisscrossing stairwells impossible to make out.

Shit. Shit. Shit!

I found my shoes and tucked them under my arm. My toe caught the edge of Nick's suitcase on my way to the door. I bit back a swear, but Nick didn't stir. His chest rose and fell in a steady, deep rhythm, his arm still curled around the empty dip I'd left in the bed. I wondered how long it had been since he'd truly gotten any rest, and I hoped for Vero's and my sakes he'd stay asleep for a few hours more.

I typed out a quick message to Vero. *On my way up. Be there in a minute.*

Her response was immediate. *If you do not bring the whisky back, I'll murder you myself.*

I grabbed the bottle off the desk, careful not to make a sound as I closed Nick's door behind me.

* * *

A chill had settled over the dormitory while I'd been in Nick's room. I snuck back upstairs, using my phone to light my way up the pitch-black stairwell to the third floor. I jumped as a flashlight beam caught me square in the face.

Roddy lowered his light. He fought back a grin as he checked his watch. "You've been down there for hours. That must have been quite a statement."

"Very funny," I said, willing my heart rate to slow.

"Where's Nick? Why didn't he walk you back?"

"He fell asleep, and I didn't have the heart to wake him." Roddy gave me a scolding look. "It was only two floors. I was perfectly safe. I never left the building."

"You should be more careful," he said, shaking a finger at me. "Ty's watching your room for the next few hours. You should get some sleep. I left some extra blankets for you and Vero. Power lines must be down from the ice storm. Might not have heat for a while. Try to stay warm."

"You, too. Thanks, Roddy."

When his flashlight bobbed down the stairwell, I exited the stairwell and found Ty reclined in a borrowed classroom chair beside the door to my room. His head was tipped back and his eyes were closed, his long legs stretched out in front of him. He cracked open one eye with a smirk as I scanned my card key, slipped inside, and quickly shut my door.

Vero was waiting inside, wearing her hat, coat, and shoes, the black duffel bag ready beside her feet, the contents zip-tied shut.

"It's about damn time," she whispered, snapping a blanket off her bed as I put on my coat.

"Sorry, I didn't hear my phone."

She grumbled something unintelligible that sounded a lot like *I bet.* "Here, help me tie these." She passed me a blanket from a folded stack and grabbed another for herself. "So . . . ? How was dessert?" At my mortified look, she said, "Oh, please. Don't even tell me you didn't sample the menu."

"I might have had a little taste," I admitted.

"And?"

"And . . . it was really good."

She narrowed her eyes at me as she took my knotted blanket and tied it to the end of her bed frame. "Really good? That's all you've got? You've been gone for hours, Finn! He'd better have treated you to one of those fancy chocolate fountains and an all-you-can-eat dessert buffet!"

"The buffet was incredible," I blurted.

"How were the serving sizes?"

"Vero!"

"You promised you would tell me everything!"

"Fine," I said, unlocking the window. "If you must know, the serving sizes were huge, I went back for seconds, and his biscuits were utterly spectacular."

"I knew it!"

"Keep your voice down." The last thing we needed was to attract any attention. I lifted the lower sash of the window, shivering as an icy breeze poured into the room. The grounds below us were empty, the campus disconcertingly quiet. I tossed out the makeshift rope we'd made from the blankets and leaned out to watch it fall, a little queasy as I stared down the three flights to the bottom. The rope was barely long enough to brush the ground.

Vero slung the empty duffel bag through the window. It landed with a soft thump.

"You go first," she said.

"Me? Why do I have to go first?"

"So if we fall, you can catch me."

"What do you mean, *if we fall*?"

"Knots aren't my strong suit."

"I can't believe this was your idea."

"You have a better one?"

"Ty's probably asleep by now. We could probably sneak right past him."

"You want to take that chance?"

I gritted my teeth, remembering Ty's smug grin moments before. I put one foot out the window. My heart leapt into my throat as I took hold of the blanket-rope and straddled the sill.

"Hurry," Vero nudged, "or we'll be too late to make the drop."

"Don't push!" I hissed as I eased the rest of my body out the window. I began sliding down the rope in short increments, gripping it between my feet as I felt for the knots. I couldn't believe I was doing this. I'd survived my run-in with Feliks in the gym only to plummet to my death from a rope that could have doubled as my son's woobie.

My fingers fumbled over the last knot, dumping me flat on my bottom in the frozen grass. I got stiffly to my feet and brushed myself off, wincing at the throb in my tailbone.

I looked up at our window and gestured for Vero to hurry.

She checked the knot on the bed frame twice before straddling the sill and sliding over the ledge. She reached back up, trying to close the window behind us. Her body gave a sudden lurch. We both gasped as the knot slipped and suddenly, Vero was hurtling toward me. I held out my arms, determined to catch her, and at the same time unsure exactly how that would work. My mind flashed back to the tower of cars that had squashed Ike. I was certain this was karma crashing toward me just as Vero's body jolted to a stop. Her glove clung to the sill of the second-story window. She hovered for a moment, looking down at me with wide eyes as her fingers slid to the edge of the brick. With a squeak, she plummeted backward into my arms, and my lungs emptied in a painful burst as we smashed into the ground.

Vero lay sprawled on top of me, breathing fast as she stared up at our window. "You okay?" she whispered.

"I should have stayed in bed with Nick," I said into the back of her coat.

She rolled off me and helped me to my feet. I limped after her, carrying the duffel bag, as she tossed the blanket-rope into the dumpster behind the dorm.

We hurried across the drill field, careful not to linger too long in the open. Ducking into the first stretch of trees we could find, we hunched in the shadows, watching the tower. Vero held up her binoculars and scanned the fire escape, making a slow pass up the side of the building to the roofline.

"It's too dark up there. I can't make out a damn thing," she whispered.

I checked the time, weighing the risks. *EasyClean* wasn't due to arrive for another thirty minutes. And if Samara had intercepted our email, I'd know. She would have banged on Nick's door hours ago to wake him up. "I'll take the bag to the roof," I said. "You stay here and keep an eye on the stairs. Text me if you see anyone coming."

"Be careful," she whispered as I crept to the first rung of the fire escape. The metal was slick. I hoisted the bag onto my shoulder and climbed as fast as I dared, avoiding the glittering patches of ice on the landings. By the time I reached the final flight, my lungs were on fire, the steam on my breath whisked away by a cutting wind. I glanced over the metal handrail. Moonlight glinted off the lenses of Vero's binoculars through the trees. I gave her a quick thumbs-up, hoping she could see me. Her phone light flashed in response.

I took a steadying breath and climbed the last few steps to the roof.

Wind whipped over the waist-high ledge surrounding the deck, tossing my hair over my eyes as I looked for a place to hide the bag, somewhere out of sight, where only someone who was looking for it might see it. The landscape of the roof deck was sparse. The shallow jogs in the low wall didn't leave many options, but the large concrete enclosure in the center of it . . . that might work.

There were no windows in it, just a heavy steel door and a sign that read PUMP HOUSE. A giant spool of fire hosing was mounted to its side, and the nook behind the hoses seemed just big enough to conceal the duffel bag. I hurried toward it, eager to hide the bait and get back to Vero, when a shuffling sound came from the far side of the pump house.

"Damnit, where the fuck are you?" someone whispered.

I backed slowly away from the pump house and spotted movement in the dark. A man was on his hands and knees behind the spool, his denim-clad legs sticking out as he searched for something. Ice crackled under me as I crept along the edge of the roof to see more of him. My breath caught as Wade stood and reached above his head, his jacket riding up as he searched the eaves under the pump house roof. The slender handle of a familiar Glock peeked out of the waistband of his jeans.

"There you are, you sneaky bastards." He turned, a silver Zippo in one of his hands and a pack of Marlboros in the other. We both froze, staring at each other across the narrow slice of the roof.

"You're not supposed to be here," I said, a tremor in my voice.

His grin was crooked. "Neither are you."

CHAPTER 34

Wade shook a cigarette from his pack and hunched over his lighter, dropping the tip of it to the bright orange flame. He sucked in a drag, watching me as he expelled smoke through his nose. "You can put your hands down, unless you're confessing to something." I lowered my hands, surprised to realize I'd been holding them up. He glanced at the duffel bag. "Does your boyfriend know you're here?"

I tucked it closer to my side. "Should he?"

Wade shrugged. "Guess that depends on why you followed me. Look," he said, flicking sparks into the wind. "I've got nothing against you, but I didn't come up here looking for a hookup. I just came to find my stash." He waved his pack of Marlboros at me. "It's my last pack. Ortega's got the whole place locked down. Can't leave to go to the store."

"You were up here looking for *cigarettes*? At three in the morning?"

"We all have our vices. Mine's no worse than whatever you came looking for." He took another lazy drag as his eyes made a slow pass over me. "So what'd Nick do to piss you off? Must have been something pretty shitty to make you pack your bag and move out of his room at this hour of the night."

I followed the jut of his chin toward the duffel under my arm. "Oh! No, this isn't my bag . . . I mean, it is my bag, but it's not what you're thinking," I stammered. "Nick didn't do anything wrong. I just . . . couldn't sleep."

"Welcome to the club." He held his cigarettes out to me.

"I don't smoke."

One corner of his mouth hitched up. "And I don't screw other cops' girlfriends on icy roofs in thirty-degree weather. So what the hell are we doing up here?"

"I wish I knew." I slumped against the back of the pump house beside Wade and checked my phone. *EasyClean* should have been here by now, and there was still no word from Vero. No one was coming. I should have been relieved to have my suspicions confirmed, but if Joey had really been *EasyClean* all along, why did I still feel so uncertain about him?

I dropped the duffel bag by my feet. "You won't tell Nick I was here, will you?"

"If I tell Nick I was up here with you, he'll probably shoot me, and I prefer to keep my ass in one piece."

"Thanks."

He gave a shallow nod, blowing smoke through his nose as it was whisked off by the wind. I remembered back to two nights ago, when I'd caught a whiff of it as I'd crossed the drill field. I wondered if Wade came out here every night. If he didn't sleep well, the same way Nick hadn't been sleeping well. *Welcome to the club,* Wade had said, as if this was a curse they all suffered. No wonder so many of them were in therapy. As much as Stu complained about how little money he made as a department shrink, he probably had no shortage of patients who were . . . cops.

My mind raced back to the day I'd first met Dr. Stuart Kirby. Nick had thanked him for writing a letter stating Theresa was competent to act as a witness in Feliks's trial. Sam said Stu had met with Theresa a few times after her arrest. How much had she divulged to him behind closed doors? What details had she confessed to him, assuming the information would be held in confidence between therapist and client? Had she told him about what had happened to Carl? Where she and Barbara had hidden his body?

I pushed myself upright. I couldn't believe I hadn't put it together before. Nick had been seeing Stu for weekly counseling sessions since the shooting. They probably talked about the case. About Feliks. About me and Steven.

Steven . . .

I reached inside my pocket for the crumpled business card he'd pushed on me yesterday. My hands shook as I read the therapist's name. STUART KIRBY, PHD.

This guy's a therapist. My attorney gave him my number a few months ago.

A few months ago . . . around the same time *EasyClean* would have been vetting Steven as a target.

The facts began to crystallize into something tangible and sinister. The longer I sat with them, the more horribly right they felt. Stu had access to the campus Wi-Fi. He had clients and friends here; he could move through this place as easily as any cop. He didn't have to go to the bar to glean information from Nick's peers. He gathered all the information he needed in private sessions, one-on-one.

Wade's posture shifted as he registered the look on my face. During our class, he'd said he taught civilians who worked for the department. If anyone knew what kind of gun Stu carried, it would be the person who had probably shown him how to use it. "Does Stu carry a Glock?"

Wade nodded once. "He's got a permit. What about it?"

"It was Stu," I said. "He was the one who sent that photo of the dummy to Feliks."

I was dimly aware of a vibration in my pocket. At the same moment, footsteps thumped softly up the fire escape. Wade crushed out his cigarette, growing tense as he watched me. We both turned as Stu rounded the side of the pump house.

He froze when he saw us, his eyes wide enough to catch the moonlight. The tails of his trench coat billowed in the wind, the loose cut of it making his shape difficult to define. In hindsight, I could see it all so clearly now. This was the same silhouette I'd seen get out of the sedan on that dark country road. I had no doubt that the rifling patterns made by Stu's Glock would match the ones on the bullet in my pocket. And I also had no doubt he was carrying that Glock somewhere under that coat.

"'Sup, Doc?" Wade said, his eyes making a furtive pass over Stu. "It's a little late for a walk, isn't it?"

Stu's eyes darted between us. Then down to the duffel beside me. His throat bobbed with a swallow. "I . . . I remembered I left something up here today. I just came to find it. What are you two doing up here?" The fingers of his right hand twitched. Wade draped his arm casually around me, tucking me close to his side.

"You know me." He gave my shoulder a squeeze. "Came up for some air. We didn't think anyone would be here." When I glanced up at him, he gave me a lascivious wink.

Why wasn't he doing something? Confronting Stu? Why wasn't he whipping out his gun and arresting him? That's what Nick or Joey or Georgia would have done. But as I caught sight of the ghosts of the tattoos on Wade's neck, I remembered why. He wasn't like the other cops. He played the bad guy to survive, and if he was acting the part now, with someone who *knew* him, it was because he sensed that Stu was a threat.

Stu pushed his glasses up the bridge of his nose and gestured to the duffel bag. "I think that might belong to me. I'll just take it and be going."

Wade stepped in front of him as Stu took a few steps toward it. "Pretty sure you're mistaken, Doc. That bag belongs to—"

Stu pulled his gun and pointed it at Wade's face. "Step away from the bag."

Wade slowly raised his hands as he backed us away from the pump house.

Stu reached down blindly for the duffel, dragging it toward him with one hand, his gun steady in the other. He hesitated over the zip tie Vero had fastened around the zippers, darting panicked glances toward the fire escape.

Wade stood in front of me and laced his fingers behind his head. "You want the bag? Take it and go. I've got no beef with you." His fingers wiggled, catching my attention. His right thumb pointed down, toward the exposed waistband of his jeans. His coat and shirt had ridden up, revealing the butt of his Glock.

"Seriously?" I whispered.

Wade lifted a thumb in response.

Great. I'd had one hour of target practice. What could possibly go wrong?

With slow movements, I reached into his pants. "If you ever mention this to Nick, I will murder you in your sleep," I whispered.

Something pelted off my cheek. A chunk of ice no bigger than my thumbnail dropped to the concrete beside me. I turned and spotted a figure crouching by the side of the pump house.

Joey shook his head and held a finger to his lips. I let go of the Glock. I had no idea whose gun Joey was holding, but I was guessing he was as grateful as I was that I wouldn't be the one doing any shooting tonight.

He slunk along the wall, attempting to peer around the edge of it, but the angle was all wrong. There was no way he'd get a clean shot without exposing himself.

"Finlay," Stu snapped. I peeked over Wade's shoulder and found Stu watching me. "Wade's gun . . . the one he keeps in the back of his pants. Put it on the ground and kick it to me. Do it slowly, or I'll shoot him."

"Fucking great," Wade said under his breath as I removed the gun from its holster and set it on the ground. I kicked it toward Stu with my sneaker, only clearing half the distance. Stu left it on the deck between us as he knelt over the bag, his gun pointed loosely in our direction as he struggled to free the zipper.

Wade's knuckles tensed behind his head, as if he was considering something stupid.

"Joey's here," I whispered as quietly as I could. "Just keep him talking."

"Whatever's in that bag must be hella important," Wade called out. "You gonna tell us what it is, or are you going to make us guess?"

Stu worked at the zip tie with increasing frustration. "Keep quiet. Unless you have a knife," he added as an afterthought.

"Why don't you come frisk me and find out?"

"I'm not an idiot. It would be safer just to shoot you."

"If you wanted to shoot me, you would have done it already. Why don't you put the gun down so we can talk?"

"Talk?" Stu laughed.

"That's what you're good at, isn't it? Talking?"

"Don't bullshit me, Wade. You hate talking. You told me as much when the department made you sit on my fucking couch." He jerked the zip tie with a wince. "I taught the class on hostage negotiation, remember? I wrote a book on it!"

"Then how about you save us both a lot of time and skip to the part where you take the bag and run?"

Stu shot to his feet, shaking his gun at us. "Just shut up and let me think!"

My heart thundered in my chest. This was not the same Stu I'd met with two days ago. This Stu was a cornered criminal who was almost out of options. He could flee, but that would leave two witnesses behind—two people who could connect him to crimes far worse than blackmail.

"What was that?" Stu asked in a low voice, cocking his head toward the quiet crackle of footsteps on ice. His eyes panned the deck. "Who else is up here?"

Wade shrugged. "I don't know what you're talking about."

A loud *thwack* echoed from the other side of the pump house.

"I got him!" Vero shouted. "I caught Joey! It's safe to come out, Finn!" She rushed around the corner, holding Joey's gun.

CHAPTER 35

Vero dropped Joey's gun as Stu turned his Glock on her. Wade dove for his weapon, his fingers almost grazing it as Stu whirled and pulled his trigger. We all scattered as the shot rang out. Another ricocheted off the roof deck.

I yelped as I came face-to-face with Vero behind the pump house. "What do we do?" I whispered.

"If we try to make it down the stairs, he'll shoot us both in the ass."

"Find a place to hide. We'll split up and confuse him."

Vero darted into the shadows one way. I crept the other. I peered around the side of the pump house. Stu was leaning over the roof ledge, checking the fire escape below him. I snuck out from behind the wall and ducked behind the nearest shelter I could find, squeezing myself into a dark corner of the roof while his back was turned.

"Finlay! Wade!" Stu called out. "I know you're up here."

"Still here, asshole!" Wade answered. I peered around the corner, looking for him. His voice was breathless and strained. It seemed to echo from everywhere. I couldn't be sure where it was coming from. "You always were a lousy shot."

"Only because I didn't want to hurt you," Stu called back. I held perfectly still as he retrieved Wade's gun from the ground and tucked it into his coat. He turned, searching the deck for the one Vero had dropped, his voice becoming frantic when he couldn't find it. "Finlay!"

he called out, grabbing the duffel bag. "You and your friend, get back where I can see you! Both of you!"

I pressed back into the wall. The campus was full of cops, I reminded myself. Someone would have heard the gunfire. Any minute, someone would come to check it out. We only had to stay alive long enough for them to get here.

"What the hell is so goddamn important in that bag anyway?" Wade panted.

"Enough to start over." Stu's voice broke. I held my breath, listening to the crackle of ice under his shoes. "My future is in that bag."

Vero's voice rang out from the far side of the pump house. "Must not be worth very much if you're sending blackmail letters to Feliks Zhirov." Stu's footsteps paused. "Is there a DSM code for being an idiot?" she taunted. "Because he's going to kill you when he finds you."

"Hide-and-seek is over! Come out where I can see you!" Stu's footsteps retreated.

I peeked out from my hiding spot in time to see him stalk around the pump house, searching for Vero.

"Wade?" I whispered. "Where are you?"

His answer came as a soft grunt from the opposite wall. I rushed toward it and spotted the tips of his fingers clinging to the roof ledge. I looked over the side and gasped. "What are you doing down there?"

Sweat bloomed on his brow. The toes of his boots were braced on the windowsill below him, his knuckles white where they gripped the edge of the concrete. "It seemed preferable to getting shot."

"What do I do?" I whispered, afraid to touch him. The ground below him was dizzyingly far, solid asphalt. It's not like I could run down the fire escape and catch him.

Wade cocked his head as Stu's footsteps started moving in our direction.

"Find my gun and hide," Wade whispered. "And keep your mouth shut."

I didn't have a chance to tell him Stu already had his gun. Or that keeping my mouth shut wasn't exactly my forte. But hiding was something Vero and I knew how to do. I scurried behind a raised concrete slab as Stu rounded the pump house.

My heart pounded as I waited for him to find me.

"What do you care if I'm blackmailing Feliks?" Stu snapped. Panic gripped me as the slow crush of his shoes suggested he was moving in Wade's direction. "He's a despicable human being. It was about time he suffered a loss. He doesn't care about anyone else's pain. He's never helped anyone. Healed anyone. He doesn't deserve the kind of wealth he's amassed at the expense of innocent victims."

"And you do?" I called out. I squeezed my eyes shut as I listened to Stu pivot toward me.

"I can hardly afford a car payment after my mortgage in this county! What's a couple million to a guy like Feliks Zhirov? It's pocket change to him. I deserve that money more than he does."

Wade choked on a laugh. "You deserve to be in a prison cell with him."

"I can still kill all of you and take the bag!" Stu shouted.

"Wouldn't be the first time you killed someone for cash," I called out. A heavy silence fell over the deck. "You're *EasyClean,* right? The same *EasyClean* Sam and Nick found on that women's forum the night it disappeared." My skin prickled through the silence that followed. I didn't like that I couldn't hear him move. That Vero wasn't responding. That Wade's struggling grunts had gone eerily quiet.

I poked my head out of my hiding spot and froze.

Stu's gun was raised, less than ten feet away, pointed right at me. I scrambled back on my hands as he stalked toward me, holding the duffel bag. My back smacked into the roof ledge; nowhere else to go.

"How many people have you murdered for money?" I asked, desperate to keep him talking.

"I'm not a monster like Feliks. I didn't do it for the money."

"You charged a fee for it."

"I provided a service for which I charged fair market value! The jobs I chose were all carefully vetted, and believe me, their transgressions were far worse than mine. They all deserved what was coming to them."

I stared up at him. How was he defining these *transgressions* he'd vetted? "What do you mean, *worse*? I don't understand—"

"No, you *can't* understand," he corrected me. His voice shook with barely contained rage as the nose of his gun came terrifyingly close to me. "You're here for fun, playing at a citizen's academy, making up stories as part of some big PR circus! When it's over, you'll go home and write some bad guys into your book, but you don't actually know any of those bad guys—not like I do. You've never actually seen real crime scenes or real bodies. You live in a world of metaphors. Of simulations and dummies. I can't explain my reasons to you; you can't possibly understand them!"

"Then explain them to me," a voice called out.

Stu's body went rigid. I peered around his legs toward the fire escape, but all I could make out was Nick's silhouette as he limped into view. His gun was extended, trained on Stu's back. "I'm listening, Stu. I want to understand. Put the gun down and talk to me."

Stu's finger hovered over the trigger, his voice growing thick. "Do you have any idea how many perpetrators I've interviewed for this department? How many victims I've counseled?" He shook his head as if he couldn't fathom the answer to his own question. "I've listened to hundreds of mothers and wives recount the details of their abuse. Watched their husbands and boyfriends released and returned home on bullshit technicalities. I've attended funerals for their children, knowing I'd done all I could and it would never be enough. There are people out there who need help, Nick. The kind of help police and social workers can't give them, but *EasyClean* could. You, of anyone, should understand why I did it. You've watched Zhirov hurt people over and over, and every time he's walked away unscathed."

"Doesn't excuse it." Nick's arms were steady as he limped closer.

"We both took oaths when we signed on for this, Stu. You swore to do no harm."

Stu whirled, swinging his gun toward Nick. "You swore to protect and serve!"

"I swore to uphold the law! I never once stooped to Zhirov's level!" I held my breath as they circled each other, guns extended, twenty feet apart. "You used Feliks's forum to conduct your own illicit business. You used your clients—you used *me*—to advance your own agenda. You murdered people and took money for it, same as Zhirov. Don't make that same mistake now." Nick lowered his voice. He looked Stu in the eyes. "Put the gun down. Let's go inside and talk."

Stu's finger shook as it slid away from the trigger. After a long moment, his elbows bent. He dropped the duffel bag and lowered his gun. I only started breathing again when it clattered to the deck. I scrambled for it and tossed it away from him.

Nick's voice was gravelly when he said, "Put your hands on your head and turn around." Stu's expression was mournful as he slowly turned to face me. "Get on your knees," Nick said.

Stu kept his hands on his head as he eased himself down. His resigned calm made me uneasy. He didn't look angry or confused or even scared anymore. He seemed sad, as if he'd come to a decision he'd hoped he wouldn't have to.

Nick holstered his gun. He limped forward, reaching into his pocket for his cuffs.

A gust of wind caught Stu's coat. One side of it blew open; the other seemed held in place, weighed down by something in the pocket. My eyes shot wide as I remembered Wade's gun.

I shouted Nick's name as Stu reached inside his coat. He pulled the gun and turned it on Nick. With the uninhibited conviction of an impassioned five-year-old, I hurled myself toward Stu and threw my arms around his legs, remembering the lessons I'd learned that week, about survival and size and not second-guessing yourself when you're ready to pull the trigger. About not holding back. The force of my tackle hug sent us crashing to the ground. Wade's gun flew from Stu's outstretched hand and skittered across the roof deck.

Nick's shoes skidded to a stop beside me. He pulled me off Stu and cuffed Stu's hands behind his back.

"Any other guns I should know about?" Nick asked, grinning at me with an awestruck expression as I dusted off my hands and caught my breath.

"Just that one." I gestured toward the one protruding from the back of Vero's pants. She had a foot braced on the half wall as she dragged Wade over the ledge.

Stu wrenched his head off the ground as Nick frisked his clothes. "You know me, Nick. We've worked together for years. I'm not one of the bad guys. You don't have to handcuff me—"

Wade tumbled onto the roof deck and sprawled on the concrete. "Now would be a really good time to shut up and wait for your attorney," he panted.

Someone groaned behind the pump house. "Jesus, my head... what the hell... ?" Vero cringed as Joey started shouting. "Someone get these cuffs off me! And where the hell is my gun?"

Wade rose stiffly to his feet. "Relax, you cranky bastard. I'm coming." Vero looked sheepish as she offered Joey's gun to Wade. Wade waved her off. "If Joey gives you a hard time, you have my permission to shoot him."

I threw her a dark look as she tucked the pistol gleefully back in her pants.

Roddy thundered up the fire escape with Ty on his heels. Nick took a moment to debrief them before they escorted Stu from the roof.

"Wait," I said, running to catch up to them. I stood in Stu's path and asked in a low voice, "When you said the people you vetted had all done worse things than you, what did you mean?"

Stu lifted his chin. His glasses had broken when I'd tackled him. They sat crooked on his nose, the lenses cracked, but he seemed to see right through me when he said, "What is it you're really asking, Ms. Donovan?"

"Why did you agree to kill my ex-husband?" I whispered.

He turned away from me. "I'm not saying anything more until I speak with my attorney."

"*Now* you decide to listen to Wade's advice?" I dropped Stu's arm, backing away as Roddy nudged him toward the stairs. Stu's perspective on right and wrong had become so warped. The man was clearly disturbed. I was probably worrying for nothing.

Nick limped across the deck toward me. He took me by the shoulders, holstering me snugly in his arms as he whispered into my hair. "When I woke up and you were gone, I called Ty to make sure you'd made it back to your room. He said you were fine. Jesus, Finn, if I'd known you were up here, I would have called a SWAT team."

"How did you know where to find me?" I asked into his coat.

He drew back to look at me, brushing a few windblown strands from my eyes. "The hospital called and said Joey was missing. A few minutes later, I got a voice message from him, telling me to call Roddy and Ty and meet him on the tower roof." He pressed his lips to the top of my head. "What the hell were you thinking, coming up here?"

"I might be able to answer that." Joey massaged his scalp, looking a little woozy as he knelt over the duffel. He cut the zip tie with a pocketknife and unzipped the bag, turning it upside down. Twenty-five bound stacks of paper towels tumbled out of it. Joey looked up at me with an incredulous smile. "Looks like someone was pretty determined to catch her ex-husband's would-be killer."

Wade grinned around his cigarette as he hunched over his lighter. "We should all be lucky enough to have an ex-wife like that."

"Don't encourage her," Nick said. "She could have been killed."

"Cut her some slack," Wade said. "You have to admit, that was some pretty impressive detective work. She'd make a hell of a vice cop."

"What's the going salary for that?" Vero asked.

A slightly hysterical laugh bubbled out of me. I was ready to go home, cuddle my kids, and get back to worrying about fictional bad guys. Though maybe I could make room in my life for a not-so-fictional good one.

Wade gave me a furtive wink as he shouldered his way past Nick on his way to the fire escape. Nick stopped him with a hand to his chest. Wade looked down at it and exhaled smoke through his nose, as if he was too tired to do much else about it.

"Do I want to know what you were doing up here in the middle of the night with my girl?" Nick asked through a smirk.

Wade glanced over Nick's shoulder at me, a wicked gleam in his eye as he flicked his ash. I shook my head, furiously mouthing the word *no*. "Are you asking me for an official statement about it?"

"No," Nick said.

"Then I ain't tellin'."

Nick laughed to himself, satisfied. "Fine, but don't go anywhere. I am going to need a statement about everything else. Want me to call down for a first aid kit?" he asked, gesturing to the blood on Wade's forearms.

"Just a couple of scrapes." Wade hitched a thumb toward Joey. "The snitch might need a few stitches though."

Joey touched the crown of his head as he scowled at Vero.

"Don't look at me like that," she warned him. "Wade gave me permission to shoot you."

Nick pulled Joey aside before a fight could break out. Vero and I hovered close, listening to their conversation. "What the hell are you doing here?" Nick said. "You're supposed to be in the hospital."

"Cam must have hacked the hospital computers. He found me and called my room. He said it wasn't safe to talk, but he was monitoring the blackmailer's email address and something was going down on the fire tower at three. He said Feliks's blackmailer would be here."

"You should have called me," Nick said. "I would have handled it."

"I would have, but I wasn't exactly sure what I was walking into. Or who." Joey and Nick exchanged a long look.

A long sigh billowed from Nick as he leaned back against the half wall. "You thought you'd find Charlie up here. And you were afraid I might choke and let him off the hook."

Joey leaned on the wall beside him. "It was a bad hunch. I'm glad I was wrong. Gotta admit, I never even considered Stu for a suspect." He turned to me and Vero. "When did you two figure it out?"

"Around the same time you did," I said ruefully. "Let's just say we had a few bad hunches along the way as well. Sorry about that."

Joey rubbed the back of his head. "Me, too."

A light bulb hummed to life over the fire escape. An indicator panel flashed on the side of the pump house, glowing green in the dark. Sidewalk lights and security spotlights flickered on across the campus in sections as the power came back to life. "It's about time," Vero said, rubbing her hands together. "I could really use a hot shower."

Joey drew an exaggerated breath through his nose. Nick did, too. "You smell that?" he asked Joey, pulling a face.

"That's not funny," Vero snapped.

I started to laugh, but then I smelled it, too.

The sulfurous reek of propane was thick in the air. That was all the warning we had before the green light on the indicator panel turned red and smoke began to pour over the roof.

CHAPTER 36

Nick checked the indicator lights on the side of the pump house, squinting against the smoke. He waved it from his face as he moved quickly to the roof ledge, frowning down at the tiny outbuilding below. He pulled out his phone and thumbed in a number.

"What's happening?" I asked, coughing into my sleeve.

"This building is used to train firefighters," Nick said, as he waited for someone to answer. "The whole tower is one giant simulator. It's designed to withstand an actual blaze. It's all run by computers from a control room in that outbuilding down there. The power surge must have triggered the training simulators when the electricity came back on."

My eyes watered as I swatted at a band of smoke. "Why isn't anyone shutting them off?"

"It's four in the morning. The whole campus is asleep." Nick tried another number as black clouds billowed from the windows below us.

Wade rushed up the fire escape, his clothes and face stained with soot. "The fourth floor is already engulfed. Stairs are too hot," he called out to us.

Joey paced the ledge, looking for another exit. "Unless somebody's got rappelling gear, that fire escape is the only way down."

"Roddy and Ty aren't answering their phones." Nick hurried to the pump house and tried the door but it wouldn't budge. He checked the glowing numbers on the indicator panel. "The fifth floor is already at six hundred degrees," he called to Wade. "Help me get this door open and turn on the pumps."

Wade knelt and rolled up his jeans, unstrapping a disturbingly large knife from a sheath around his calf. He wedged it under the doorknob of the pump house and began prying at the lock.

"Finlay, call your sister," Nick called out to me. "Joey, call Sam. I'll try Charlie. Someone has to pick up."

The urgency in Nick's voice was making me nervous. Nothing about this felt like a simulation anymore. I dialed my sister's cell phone. It rang straight to voice mail.

"Finn, look!" Vero dragged me to the ledge and pointed across the drill field to the dormitory. A light was on in one of the third-floor windows. "I think that's Mrs. Haggerty's room."

I pulled up my contacts list and dialed Mrs. Haggerty's cell phone. "It's ringing," I said, blinking at her window through the smoke. I nearly cried out with relief when she picked up on the third ring. "Mrs. Haggerty?"

"If this is about my car's extended warranty, I'm hanging up."

"Don't hang up! It's Finlay Donovan. Thank god, you're awake!"

"Not that it's any of your business, but I'm on a new medication for my cholesterol and it makes it hard to—"

"I'm sure it does, Mrs. Haggerty, but this is an emergency! I need you to look out your window."

Vero gripped my arm, our eyes watering from the smoke as we waited. After what felt like four hundred years, Mrs. Haggerty's window got brighter, as if she'd opened her blind.

"I can't see anything. I don't have my glasses on. Hold on a minute. I'm sure they're here somewhere."

"We don't have time for you to find your glasses!"

"It's not polite to shout."

"I'm sorry. Just . . . forget about the glasses," I said, fighting back a cough. "I need you to go to my sister's room down the hall. Room three nineteen. I need you to knock very loudly on her door and tell her to call me. Tell her it's an emergency."

"Well, okay then. I'll just get dressed and—"

"No, Mrs. Haggerty, please! There's no time to get dressed. Just hurry. It's a matter of life and death."

"Well in that case—" The call disconnected.

"What happened?" Vero asked as I stared at my phone.

"I don't know! She cut me off."

There was a loud smash as Wade kicked the doorknob loose and disappeared inside the pump house. His phone light glowed through a thick haze of smoke as he studied the pumps.

Nick watched the numbers rise on the indicator panel, his phone pressed to his ear.

My cell phone rang. "It's Georgia!" I said as I connected the call. "Georgia—"

"Do you have any idea what time it is?" she mumbled. "And why is Mrs. Haggerty in her nightgown in my room?"

"I need you to have someone turn off the simulator in the fire tower!"

"The what?"

"The fire tower!" I shouted, swatting at the smoke. "We need someone to turn it off!"

"What the hell are you talking about?"

"Look out your damn window!"

There was a prolonged bout of grumbling, then the screech of her blinds. Georgia swore. "Who the hell's running a simulation in the middle of the night?"

"I don't have time to explain."

"Where the heck are you?"

"On top of the fucking fire tower, Georgia! Turn it off!"

"I'm on my way!" The line disconnected. I covered my mouth with my sleeve.

Wade burst out of the pump room. "Nine hundred degrees!" he

called out to Nick. "The emergency shutoff isn't working and the pumps won't start."

A dull roar came from the floor below us. Nick swore at his phone.

"Georgia's coming!" My lungs burned as I leaned over the roof ledge looking for her. Vero appeared beside me, carrying the fire hose over her shoulder. She dragged it to the half wall, unwinding it from its spool.

"What are you doing?" I shouted. "The pumps aren't working."

She tossed the hose over the side. "I'm getting us off this roof. We're climbing down. Just like we did from our dorm room."

"We're five stories up, Vero! And we didn't climb down, we fell!"

"Don't worry, I'll go first," she said eagerly, slinging a leg over the ledge.

A tiny flashlight beam bounced over the drill field, catching my attention. Others followed close behind it. Red and blue lights swirled in the distance.

"Eleven hundred degrees!" Wade shouted. "Everybody down!"

Nick appeared like a ghost through the haze. He grabbed Vero by her hood, dragging her off the ledge as he tackled me to the ground. Glass shattered as the windows in the floor below us blew out. A hatch in the floor shot open, ripped from its hinges. Fireballs spewed through it, coloring everything orange and black. I lost sight of Wade and Joey as Nick sprawled on top of Vero and me, sheltering us under his body, his coat spread over us to protect our faces from the smoke. The roof was hot through my clothes, the air hard to breathe.

Sirens wailed beneath the roaring wind. I heard my sister holler five stories below us. Heard her pounding against the control room door. A gun fired. Glass smashed. "I'm in!" she shouted.

The pumps kicked on with a loud rumble. The flames drew back through the hatch with a *whoosh*. Fans hummed somewhere below. Beyond Nick's shoulder, the wall of smog began to thin.

His body was heavy on top of us. He waited a moment before lifting his head.

"Detective," Vero said, her voice husky from the smoke. She waggled her eyebrows at him. "I think we're having a moment." I shoved my elbow into her ribs and pushed Nick off of us, starving for air.

He rolled over onto his back, black rivulets of sweat trailing down his neck. "Joey! Wade!" he called out through a raspy throat. "Everyone okay?"

Joey groaned. Wade coughed. I rolled onto an elbow and spotted them lying a few feet away, the duffel bag still smoking beside them. Charred paper towels tumbled in the wind.

Wade shook a cigarette from his pack and slid the filter between his lips. His Zippo scraped as he lit it. Joey reached out blindly for the pack and Wade passed the lighter to him.

"Finn!" Footsteps boomed up the fire escape. Georgia burst onto the roof deck, her eyes wild as they swung over the smoking landscape. She rushed to me through the blackened puddles. "Thank god you're okay. Mom would have killed me." She clasped my hand and hauled me upright. Her hand was slick with blood.

"What happened to you?" I asked her.

She glanced down at herself, surprised by the cuts. "The control room was locked. Didn't have a key. I had to shoot out the window and bust in. Must have cut myself," she said, wiping it on her flannel pajamas.

A fire truck rounded the corner and two ambulances screamed through the gate. More footsteps pounded up the steps. Roddy, Ty, and Samara rushed onto the deck, carrying first aid kits, blankets, and extinguishers. A winded Charlie dragged himself up the last few steps behind them.

"We thought you all were cooked!" Sam said, kneeling beside Wade. He batted her hand away as she yanked the cigarette from his mouth and snuffed it out. He dropped his head back onto the deck, muttering to himself as she flipped open her first aid kit.

Ty wrapped a blanket around Vero and helped her to her feet.

"I'm sorry, Ty," she said, her face a mask of smoke-smudged sincerity. "It's been fun, but I'm afraid you and I have no future together. I'm pretty sure Detective Anthony and I just made a baby." She patted him on the shoulder. "If it makes you feel better, you can keep my underwear as a token of our fleeting relationship."

Ty backed away from her, darting odd glances between her and Nick as he handed Nick a blanket. "I'd better go see if anyone else needs any assistance," he muttered.

Nick shook his head as he wiped a smear of sweat from his brow. He draped the blanket over my shoulders and leaned back against the ledge, opening an arm to me. My blanket pooled around my ankles as I waddled to his side with a shiver. He pulled me in close.

"Where's Stu?" he asked Roddy.

"Cuffed in one of the classrooms," Roddy said. "I saw the flames through the window and we came back as soon as we could. What the heck happened up here?"

"No idea," Nick said. "The power came back on and the simulators started a second later."

"The control room was locked." Georgia winced as Sam plucked a piece of glass from her arm. "No one was inside it and I didn't see anyone on the ground when I got here. It's a mystery."

"About as mysterious as that power outage," Sam said as she reached for some gauze.

"What do you mean?" Nick asked.

"I called the power company a few hours ago for an update. When I asked them how much longer they thought it would be out, they had no idea. They said this entire section of the grid was down and it wasn't from the weather. They said it was a network problem."

"Like a computer network?" I asked. Sam nodded.

Vero locked eyes with me. "Can the simulator be controlled remotely, from a computer somewhere else?" she asked Sam.

"Sure, if it's accessible through a network and runs on a program."

"Then it can be hacked." I stepped out from Nick's arm. This entire night had been planned. The power outage, the fire . . . there was no way this had all been a coincidence. These events must have been coordinated by someone who knew what was happening on this tower tonight. Cam had alerted Joey that *EasyClean* would be here, but I was certain Feliks was pulling the strings.

"You think Feliks was behind this?" Sam asked them.

"Not unless he hacked us from the air," Nick said. "That phone call I got earlier tonight . . . the one I didn't answer," he said, casting me a brief but meaningful look, "it was our task force contact at the FBI. She says Zhirov boarded a private jet just before midnight. The feds think he's headed to Brazil."

"Doesn't matter," Sam said. "If he has the capability to access those networks remotely, he could have done it from anywhere."

"Or someone could have done it for him," Joey said. Nick and Joey exchanged a long look, probably coming to the same conclusion Vero and I had. With the right resources, Cameron could have shut down the power and started the fire himself.

"But who was the target?" Wade asked. "Joey? Or Stu?"

Every eye on the roof turned to Joey. Feliks had broken out of jail for one reason only—to eliminate *EasyClean*. Once Feliks learned *EasyClean* was alive and would be here tonight, he must have realized his mistake and come up with a plan to handle the problem once and for all.

But had the fire been the weapon, or had it been the perfect distraction?

If all the police were at the tower trying to put out the fire, and if the security barriers were cleared for emergency vehicles to enter and leave, it would have been easy for Feliks's men to slip in and out unnoticed.

Roddy frowned. "I should go check on Stu," he said, turning for the stairs.

"Don't bother," Joey said, crushing out his cigarette. "If Feliks had anything to do with that fire, Stuart Kirby is already dead."

CHAPTER 37

Three hours later, after the EMTs had checked us over and Vero and I had given our statements, we stood at the edge of the parking lot in our blankets, our clothes still damp with sweat and soot as we watched the rest of the academy students load their luggage into two waiting charter buses. After the fire, Commander Ortega had ended the lockdown and ordered that everyone be sent home. Feliks had been sighted that morning at an airstrip near São Paulo, Brazil, and when Roddy had returned to the classroom where he had left Stu, all he'd found was an empty pair of handcuffs. Nick and his commander had agreed it would be best to shut the academy down early to let the staff debrief and clean up after the long night.

Roddy and Ty stood beside the charter bus doors, issuing certificates of completion to each student as they boarded. Vero and I looked down at the ones Roddy had presented to us from the top of his pile. The certificates were all generic, the recipients' names left blank. In all the chaos over the last twelve hours, the staff hadn't had time to worry about preparing for the final ceremony. The only things special about Vero's and mine were the two first-place ribbons taped to the corners.

"Too bad we all couldn't stay for graduation," Vero said, tracing the satin ribbon on her certificate with a sigh. "Sure would have been nice to rub it in Joey's face."

"Rub what in my face?" Joey appeared beside her, glaring at her under two sooty eyebrows. It had taken him an hour this morning to convince her to hand over his gun. She'd only relinquished it after he'd threatened to handcuff her and shut her in the back of a patrol car.

"Finlay and I won," Vero gloated. "We had the most points of any team. Bet you regret betting against us now."

"You didn't win," Joey groused. "The tallies closed early. Those numbers don't count."

Nick patted Joey's shoulder with a pitying smile. "As the program director, I certified the tally. We'll settle up later at the bar."

Mrs. Haggerty shambled across the parking lot toward us, waving her certificate. Her grandson gave chase, calling after her. "What's this business with these awards?" she demanded, shaking her paper at Nick. "Why aren't there any names on them? How will we know who won?"

"It's fine, Grandma," her grandson said, trying to coax her back on the bus.

"No, it's not!" she said sharply. "And don't give me any of this 'everyone's a winner' crap. When I was your age, we had real competitions. There were winners and losers, and nobody complained when they didn't get a prize."

Vero gave Joey a pointed look.

"Actually," I said, holding out my certificate. "I think you might have gotten mine by mistake, Mrs. Haggerty." She pushed up the frames of her glasses as she took it, studying the satin ribbon with a satisfied nod. Vero gasped in protest as I handed her certificate to Mrs. Haggerty's grandson, swapping it for his unadorned one.

"I was under the impression we came in second place," he said, politely trying to give it back.

"Extra points were awarded to your grandmother this morning," I insisted.

"For what?" Vero asked. "Answering her damn phone?"

"For answering the call of duty last night." I gave Vero a stern look.

Mrs. Haggerty's grandson touched his chest in a gesture of gratitude. He put his arm around his grandmother, gently steering her back to the bus.

"That woman's never gonna let you hear the end of it," Vero muttered.

"It was the right thing to do," I said, watching as Roddy helped Mrs. Haggerty up the steep bus steps.

Joey's grin was smug around his toothpick. "Guess my team won after all." Vero stared a hole in his back as he sauntered into the building.

"What was that all about?" my sister asked, slinging a bandaged arm around me. Sam stood beside her, their hands hanging close together, their pinky fingers touching.

"Nothing. Just giving a little credit where credit is due. Hey," I said, "have you heard from Mom?"

Georgia nodded. "Dad's fine. They got home from the hospital late last night. I've got to stick around here for a few hours, but I'll run by their house on my way home and check on him."

"Wish I could stay, too," Sam said, "but Nick needs a chaperone for the buses. I told him I'd go." She hooked her pinky finger around Georgia's and whispered, "Call me." Georgia looked a little starstruck as Sam waved good-bye and rolled her luggage across the parking lot.

Max leaned out her window and waved at us from the bus. "Bye, Vero! See you, Finlay! I'll text you about that interview, okay?"

"So glad I never gave her my number," I said to Vero as I smiled and waved back. Vero bit her lip, hiding a guilty grin. I gaped at her. "Tell me you didn't."

"Better to keep your enemies closer, right? And besides," she whispered, "how else will we know what's happening with Ike?"

As soon as the buses pulled away, Georgia took me by the arm and dragged me aside.

"I have a really big problem and I need your help," she said urgently.

"What kind of problem?"

"I invited Sam to dinner."

"That's a problem?"

"I don't know how to cook."

"That's easy. We'll just call Mom—"

"No, Finn! You know how she gets. If you tell her I'm having dinner with someone, she'll buy a bunch of wedding planners and magazines and turn into Mom-of-the-Bridezilla. She'll scare Sam off."

"Okay," I said, gesturing for her to calm down. "Vero and I can probably help."

"Help with what?" Vero asked, waddling up to us in her blanket.

"Georgia asked Sam to dinner, but Georgia doesn't know how to cook."

Vero reached for her phone.

"What are you doing?" I asked.

"This sounds like an emergency. I'm texting your mom."

Georgia lunged for her.

Nick took me by the hand, luring me away as Vero and my sister wrestled over her phone. He opened my blanket, stretching it to fit around his shoulders and closing us in a cocoon. "Is it wrong that I want you to stay?"

"Don't take this the wrong way, but I would really, *really* like to sleep in my own bed tonight."

"That makes two of us," he purred in my ear. He captured my lips and kissed me like he was still smoldering.

Wade snuck up behind me and said, "If you two don't cut that out, we're going to need a damn fire hose to put you out."

Nick's smile was wide as our smoke-blackened faces pulled apart, his bright white teeth shining down at me. He shrugged out of the blanket and wrapped it securely around me, tucking it under my chin.

Vero muttered to herself as she waddled back with her phone. "Javi's not answering. Maybe we can hitch a ride home with your sister later."

"Don't worry about it," Nick said. "Charlie offered to drive you. I want you both to stay inside and lock the doors until I get there."

"Vero and I will be fine," I assured him. "Feliks is in Brazil."

"And I won't feel good leaving you alone until he's here, doing hard time in a maximum-security prison." He tugged me closer by the blanket, his hand soft against my cheek. His slow kiss lingered, becoming another.

"Then I guess we'd better get back to work, Detective," someone growled.

Nick's head snapped up. He turned to the stern-faced man standing behind him, putting a little distance between us. "Commander, I was just saying good-bye to my . . ." I raised a singed eyebrow, curious to hear his next words as he risked a sideways glance at me. "This is Georgia's sister, Finlay. Finlay, this is Commander Ortega."

I extended my hand from the blanket. The captain frowned at my soot-stained fingers as he offered me a tight-lipped nod. Unlike the rest of us, his decorated uniform was freshly pressed, his square jaw was freshly shaven, and his high and tight didn't have a single sterling strand out of place. He frowned at Nick. "Did someone get Ms. Donovan's statement?"

"You could say that," Roddy chuckled as he rolled our luggage to Charlie's car—everything but Vero's suitcase, which she had insisted on carrying herself.

Nick cleared his throat. "Yes, sir. Two statements, actually. Both were very thorough."

Vero snorted into her hand.

"Then say your good-byes and make it quick," the commander said. "I want a full debriefing in the staff room in ten minutes."

"Yes, sir."

When the commander was gone, Nick drew me close again, making sure the blanket was snug around me. "I'll come over as soon as I'm finished here."

"Maybe wait until tomorrow," I said, wrinkling my nose. We both smelled like a house fire and neither one of us had slept more than an hour or two since Wednesday. All I wanted was a hot bath, a clean pair of underwear, a warm pair of pajamas, a snuggle marathon with my children on the couch, and a very long night's rest.

Tomorrow, Vero and I would figure out what to do with the money Javi had made from the sale of the Aston. We had enough cash in Vero's suitcase to pay off her debt to Marco and, if necessary, a little extra to get him off our backs. And as soon as I revised the end of my manuscript, I could collect the rest of my advance. Feliks was halfway around the world, I had an all-you-can-eat buffet of inspiration for my book, and *EasyClean* was . . . well, I didn't really want to think about that.

Everything wasn't entirely resolved. I still worried about Cam even though Joey had promised he would let me know the minute he heard from him. I still had Carl's body to relocate and Steven to contend with—Vero's warrant in Maryland was something we would eventually have to face. And, of course, there was the issue of potty training. But compared to the week Vero and I had just survived, those all seemed like manageable worries.

Charlie appeared, rolling my suitcase behind him, his car keys already in his hand. Nick bit his lip, reluctant to let me go. Charlie clapped him on the shoulder. "Don't worry, partner. I promise to keep a close eye on both of them."

"Text me when you get home," Nick said, walking backward toward the training center, grinning at me like a fool. "How about chili and biscuits at my place tomorrow night?"

"It's a date." I couldn't help stealing a preview of his biscuits as he turned and disappeared into the building.

"Your chariot awaits, ladies." Charlie gestured chivalrously toward a shiny red Cadillac across the parking lot. It looked new, and I already felt bad about the filth we were about to leave in it. Vero grabbed the handle of her suitcase, dragging it behind her. Wrapped in our soot-stained blankets, we followed Charlie to his car.

"Let me help you with that," he offered, popping the trunk and hefting Vero's suitcase into it. He slammed it shut, holding the back door of the car open for Vero. When she was buckled in, he set my suitcase on the empty seat beside her. He stopped me as I reached for the passenger side door. I smiled up at him, expecting another gallant gesture as I waited for him to open it for me.

Instead, he leaned against it, a set of keys dangling from his hand. They didn't belong to the Cadillac. "I think you might have lost these the other night."

My heart stopped as I stared at the keys to the training cruiser. The scar on his mouth made it hard to read his expression. "Where did you find them?" I asked.

"Get in," he said, snapping my door open.

I glanced into the back seat at Vero as I ducked slowly into his car, wondering if she'd seen our exchange. Charlie got in and started the engine, leaving it in park as he let the car warm. He drummed the steering wheel as he stared out the windshield. I braced myself for an interrogation about why we'd stolen the car and what we'd been doing at the Westovers' that night. About how long I'd been lying to Nick and what, if anything, Charlie expected me to do about that.

"We need to talk about that money in your suitcase," he said, adjusting his rearview mirror to look at Vero.

Her eyes leapt to his reflection. "What money?"

"The two hundred and fifty thousand dollars in your suitcase that came from Feliks Zhirov."

I resisted the urge to look at her.

"That money was from Feliks?" I heard myself ask.

Charlie gave a thoughtful nod. "It was delivered to your room after that incident with Joey in the gym the other night. Guess he assumed *EasyClean* was handled, and it was time to pay up."

"But I don't work for Feliks."

Charlie slung his arm over the seat back and pierced us with a stare. "Everyone in this car works for Feliks. Otherwise we wouldn't be having this conversation."

The butt of Charlie's Magnum stuck out of the opening in his coat. My mouth went dry. Wade was right. You could tell a lot about a person by the size of their gun and how they chose to carry it.

"What exactly do you do for Feliks?" I asked.

"I liaise with the department. Keep my eyes open, look for opportunities, eliminate risks . . . I guess you could think of me as a human resources manager."

Vero cleared her throat softly. "These resources you manage . . . are they usually alive or dead?"

"Let's hope you two don't have to find out." I didn't like how grim his answer sounded. As if the task had already been laid out in front of him and he didn't want to acknowledge it yet. "Feliks was under no obligation to pay you that incentive money Kat discussed with you. The payment I left in your room was a token from Feliks, an investment in the future of your working relationship. It was also a gesture of trust, and you broke it. Feliks wasn't pleased to hear that Joey's still alive."

"But Joey wasn't *EasyClean,*" Vero argued.

"Doesn't matter," Charlie said frankly. "Finlay lied to Feliks, and now he wants his money back, so I'm going to take that suitcase off your hands and there isn't going to be any more bickering about it."

"Joey was right about you," I said, angry at myself for not acknowledging the clues that had been there all along: Charlie's moral flexibility, his desire to keep volunteering even after he'd retired, his close personal relationship with Nick. And then there had been that mysterious file in Joey's locked office drawer. Somewhere in the back of my mind, I'd known something was off. *An enemy of my enemy is my friend*, Vero had joked a week ago. But Joey Balafonte hadn't been my enemy. He'd been Feliks's. And that didn't bode well for Vero and me now.

"Doesn't matter what Joey thinks," Charlie said. "Joey Balafonte is a dead man walking. He got lucky last night and so did you." He tapped the steering wheel, thinking. "I'll wait until Feliks has had some time to cool down. When the dust settles, I'll do my best to convince him you're still an asset, but I think it would be wise for the two of you to disappear for a while."

Vero and I locked eyes over the seat back as Charlie put the car in gear. "I'm going to text Nick later and tell him I drove you home. Where do you want me to take you?" he asked.

I looked down at my hands. At my clothes. At Vero. Where could we go? That fire hadn't just been an accident or a distraction. Feliks had intended for us to burn. There was nowhere we could possibly run where Feliks couldn't touch us.

"Not home," Vero said. "Take us to my cousin's garage."

CHAPTER 38

It was a little before seven A.M. when Charlie dropped us off in front of Ramón's garage. We unloaded my suitcase out of Charlie's back seat. He didn't bother to shut off the engine or say good-bye, and we watched as he drove off with Vero's suitcase in his trunk.

"All my hoodies are in that bag." Smears of soot framed her scowl, and her hair was a nest of snarls.

"Not all of them," I reminded her. We'd had to put some of her clothes in my suitcase to make room for the money in hers. She kicked the asphalt as Charlie's Cadillac disappeared from sight.

Her drenched sneakers made squelching sounds as she dumped her fire blanket in a trash can beside the door to the garage. "When Sylvia finally pays you, we're using your advance to buy me shoes."

I glanced down at myself. We both looked like we'd been spit from a volcano.

"Should we be here?" I asked as she unlocked the gate to the salvage yard. I set my suitcase down beside it.

"The garage doesn't open for another two hours," she said, plucking the padlock from the chain. "The money in that duffel bag didn't come from the Aston, which means that car is still here. And, thanks to Stu, your detective boyfriend has a list of all of Feliks's shell companies, and yours is probably on it. If Javi couldn't get rid of the Aston, we'll have to do it ourselves."

The chain rattled as she pushed the gate open. I followed her through the maze of squashed chassis and disembodied auto parts, pausing when we passed a familiar tower of crushed cars. Vero and I stepped around a suspicious patch of motor oil, conveniently spilled where Ike's body had been. "Wonder what they did with him," I said quietly.

Vero shuddered. "For both our sakes, I hope we never find out."

Our feet dragged on our way to the shed. The weight of everything that had happened this week—of everything we had learned during the brief time we'd spent in Charlie's car—was impossible to carry, or even make sense of, on so little sleep.

Vero popped the lock on the shed, drawing the doors open wide. We stood side by side, staring at the dusty blades of sunlight that sliced through the cracks in the ceiling to the tire tracks on the empty floor.

"I'm. Going. To. Kill him!" Vero threw down the padlock, turning back to the parking lot, her gait fast and her eyes wild. "I'm going to run over him with my car and set him on fire!"

"Maybe don't say that out loud," I shushed her. My wet soles chafed my heels as I hurried to keep up.

"He stole our car!"

"You're assuming the worst. We have no reason to believe that."

"*You* have no reason to believe that," she reminded me.

"Maybe you should give him the benefit of the doubt. He probably just moved the car. He probably worked things out with his buyer and he's just running late with the money. Try calling him."

"I *have* called him, Finlay! Seventeen times! And I've been texting him for hours!"

"It's early. He's probably asleep."

"When I find him, I'm going to throw a Molotov cocktail through his window!"

I cringed, slamming into her back as she jolted to a stop in front of the gate. She looked up at the security camera mounted above it. Her fists clenched as she turned on her heels, storming toward the back door of the garage.

She fumbled over her keys as she rushed to unlock it, mumbling to herself in short, irate bites about Javi. How he was a no-good, selfish thief and a liar. How he disappeared whenever it was convenient for him. The door banged into the wall as Vero shoved her way inside. I chased her down the hall as she slapped on the lights and dropped into the chair behind the desk in her cousin's office. She scooted close to the monitor and wiggled the mouse, clicking windows open. Two sets of video footage popped open on the screen: the gate to the salvage yard on the left and the parking lot on the right.

"What are you doing?"

"I'm doing exactly what you said, giving him the benefit of the doubt. And when I see him drive that car off the lot, I'm going to his apartment and I'm going to strangle him with your hair dryer cord."

Vero dragged her cursor over a scroll bar. The grainy black-and-white images on the monitor moved rapidly in reverse. The parking lot was dark, the gate locked. A raccoon's eyes glowed as it waddled backward across the screen. Vero paused the footage as Javi's black Camaro pulled into the lot. Vero pushed the *Play* button. We watched as Javi got out of his car and unlocked the gate. He appeared a moment later in the second window, his image captured by the second camera as he strode into the salvage yard. Vero stiffened, slowing the video as two figures snuck up behind him. There was a burst of motion, and we both gasped as Javi slumped and hit the ground.

The men knelt beside him, rummaging in his pockets before stepping over him and moving deeper into the salvage yard. Vero sped up the footage, ten minutes passing in a handful of seconds. She slowed the recording as a set of headlights approached the gate and the Aston rolled to a stop in front of Javi's motionless body.

The two men got out of the car. Exhaust billowed from the tailpipe, the headlights illuminating them as they bound Javi's wrists and ankles, dragged him to the back of the Aston, and tossed him into the trunk. Vero didn't breathe as the car drove out of the gate.

Neither of us moved. We watched as the Aston appeared on the right side of the screen. The passenger door opened. One of the men got out. He climbed into a familiar Audi with New Jersey license tags. The Audi's headlights came on, and we watched as the driver followed the Aston out of the parking lot.

Vero blinked at the screen. Then she deleted the footage. Every frame.

"Vero? What are you doing?"

"Get your suitcase," she said, swiping a set of keys from her cousin's desk. "We're going to Atlantic City."

ACKNOWLEDGMENTS

As Finlay Donovan's circle of support continues to grow, so does my own. I am immeasurably grateful for the following people, who remind me every day why I love my job.

For my agent, Steph Rostan, words are insufficient to express my gratitude. I was orphaned when I began writing this book, the ink still drying on my contract. I was angry, angsty, and grieving, but mostly I was terrified that I might not find an agent who would welcome the workload Finlay and I carried with us—two yet unwritten books meant two full years of representation that wouldn't yield much of a payoff. But after we spoke, that fear gave way to hope. You have been my tireless champion since, and I am the luckiest author in the world to have you in my corner. Michael Nardullo, Cristela Henriquez, Courtney Paganelli, Miek Coccia, and Melissa Rowland round out my dream team at LGR—what an incredible home I've found with you all!

For my editor, Catherine Richards, who loves Finlay as deeply as I do and continues to come up with the very best titles—working with you has been an honor and a joy. Kelley Ragland, Jennifer Enderlin, Nettie Finn, Sarah Melnyk, and Allison Ziegler, your enthusiasm for Finlay is contagious and your confidence in me is unwavering. I can't tell you how much your support means to me or how grateful I am for each of you. Katy Robitzki, Claire Beyette, Amber Cortes, Asharee

Peters, Amanda Crimarco, Samantha Slavin, David Rotstein, David Lott, Paul Hochman, John Morrone, Janna Dokos, Laura Dragonette, and proofreader Jeremy Pink, thank you for all you do in support of my books. And can we talk about these incredible audiobooks? I am so lucky to have the extraordinary and talented Angela Dawe narrating the voice of Finlay!

For Sanjana Seelam and everyone on Team Finlay at WME, the indomitable Marlene King and Lauren Wagner, and everyone at 20th Television Studios. I'm so lucky for the opportunity to have shared this journey with you.

For my writing besties, Megan and Ashley, thanks for letting me lean on you so hard this last year. For absorbing my tantrums and my tears and for reminding me how to laugh through it all. I'm so damn proud of us and how far we've come. We're definitely going to need a bigger shelf.

For Kara Thomas, Bethany Crandell, and Andrea Contos, thank you for reading the earliest draft of this story. Your notes made me think, made me laugh, and challenged me to write a better book. I'm so lucky to be part of this community of supportive, talented, badass mom-writers.

For Heather Gudenkauf, Gwenda Bond, Sophie Cousens, Liv Constantine, Chantel Guertin, Rachel Lynn Solomon, Kaira Rouda, and Hank Phillippi Ryan, thank you for reading *Finlay Donovan Knocks 'Em Dead* and offering such lovely endorsements about my book. I'm honored by them.

Many thanks to the following experts who offered professional feedback and resources during the drafting of this story. To Amy Impellizzeri, for her courtroom advice. To my husband, Tony, for answering all my IT and networking questions. To Lee Lofland, for creating the Writers' Police Academy, which has provided me with endless resources and years of inspiration. I am a better novelist because of it. And many thanks to instructors Mark and Reese at Colonial Shooting Academy in Richmond, Virginia, for an outstanding beginner handgun class.

Any mistakes I've made in this book are my own and sometimes intentional, in the spirit of creating more engaging fiction.

For my family, thank you for the endless patience and support during the nights when I didn't make dinner and never made it out of my pajamas because I was chasing deadlines. Every word I write is for you.

For Bookstagram, all the buddy readers and book club groups, and for my readers far and wide, thank you for your passion, from the bottom of my heart!

For my friend and bookseller extraordinaire, Flannery Buchanan, thank you and Bluebird Bookstop for lifting me up, sharing coffee, and welcoming me to the neighborhood with so much warmth. I'm inspired by you and all you've accomplished!

And, finally, for the friends who've stayed—the ones who held my hand when I was at my worst and kept cheering for me through my best. Nicole, thanks for always, *always* being there *for all of it*—for celebrating the best parts, supporting me through the worst parts, and even putting up with my ugly parts. Your unconditional friendship means the world to me. I hope fifty years from now we're still laughing, holding on to each other, and sharing stolen umbrellas when it rains.

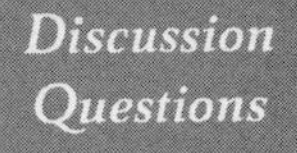

1. *Finlay Donovan Jumps the Gun* opens with the heroine, Finlay, in a standoff—but not in the way you'd expect. How does the author parallel motherhood with negotiations and even crime-solving? Were you surprised by Mo's eventual role in the story?

2. For most of this novel, we stay in one setting: the Citizen's Police Academy. Why do you think the author chose this as her backdrop rather than the more domestic settings of previous books? How did this change of scenery contribute to or change your understanding of Finlay?

3. Finlay's writer's block seems to be worse than ever in this novel. Why do you think she's so reluctant to give her fictional counterpart a happy ending? What do you think the future holds for Finlay and Nick?

4. Once again, we discover in dramatic fashion that Vero has been keeping secrets from Finlay. Why do you think Finlay continues to trust her nanny/accountant? Why do you think Vero keeps holding back?

5. Trust—and lack thereof—plays a large role in the story overall. Discuss Nick's relationship with Joey and Charlie, Joey's with Cam, and even Finlay and Nick's. When do you think our characters take loyalty too far?

6. Mrs. Haggerty, a minor but pivotal supporting character throughout the series, gets her moment to shine in *Finlay Donovan Jumps the Gun*. Why do you think the author gave Mrs. Haggerty this act of heroism?

7. The series' most villainous villain, Feliks Zhirov, remains off-page for the majority of the book, sending threats through underlings. Though we know he is imprisoned, what do these delegation techniques tell us about his character? What about the characters of those he sends messages through—Cam and Ekatarina Rybakov?

8. Fires and heat, both literal and metaphorical, pop up frequently in this story. Why do you think the author has chosen to use flames in both inciting incidents and the climax of the story?

9. In *Finlay Donovan Jumps the Gun*, Finlay and Vero finally discover the identity of *EasyClean*, a paid hit man. Were you surprised by this reveal? What red herrings in particular threw you off the scent?

10. The novel leaves Finlay and Vero driving off into the sunrise on a rescue mission. Earlier, Vero and Finlay (or at least the fictional versions of them in Finlay's novel) are compared to *Thelma and Louise*. Do you see any similarities between our characters and that beloved duo? Where do you think their next mission will take them?

Turn the page for a sneak peek at
Elle Cosimano's new novel

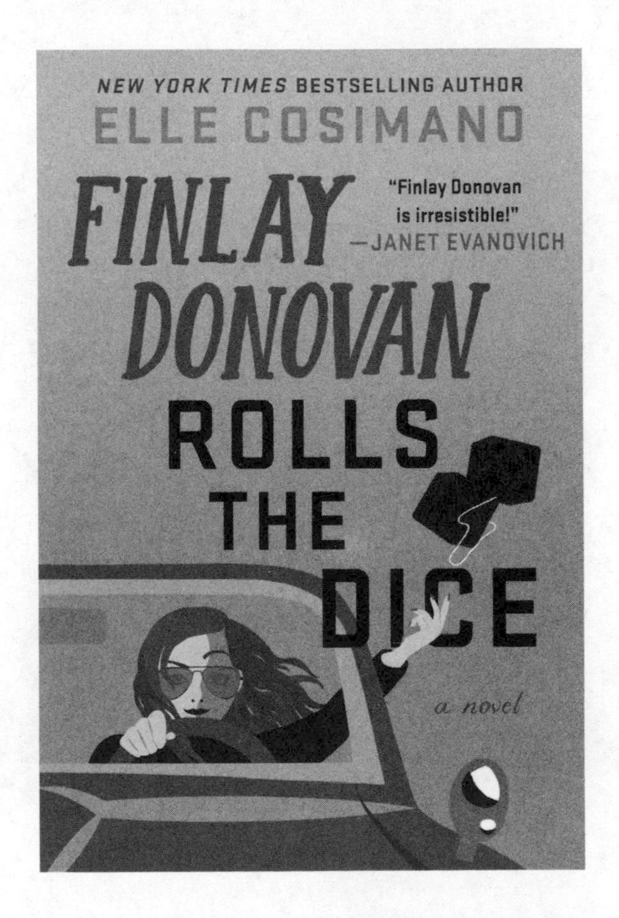

Available Early 2024

PROLOGUE

"I can't look," I said, clapping a hand over my eyes. I had sworn to myself there would be no more dead bodies. Not that any of the other four had been my fault (at least, not entirely), but I already had enough blood on my hands to last a lifetime—or possibly four lifetimes in a state penitentiary—and I didn't think I could stomach one more corpse. Especially not this one.

"Tell me when it's over." I clutched Vero's arm with my other hand as we stood on the shoulder of a six-lane highway. A tractor trailer whipped past us, throwing a thick wave of exhaust at our faces. When my children's nanny didn't answer, I peeked at her sideways between my fingers. Her long, dark ponytail blew across her eyes and she scraped it away, her attention rapt on the traffic in front of us, her neatly plucked eyebrows pinched in concentration.

"What do you think?" my mother leaned toward her and asked, both of them staring intently at my ex-husband's back. He toed the gravel beside the white line at the edge of the highway, knees loose, shoulders hunched, hands shaking out the last of his nerves as he prepared to make what was arguably the most stupid decision of his life. And believe me, that was saying something.

"I give him twenty to one," Vero said.

My mother's eyes went wide. "You think?"

"It's really more like nineteen to one," Vero said over the whine of a crotch rocket, "but I rounded up because I'm an optimist."

My mother nodded, too, as if this all made sense to her.

"You two are betting on Steven's life!" I shouted over the roar of a moving truck.

"We're not *betting,*" Vero said. "We're just calculating his odds of actually making it across—"

"And back," my mother pointed out helpfully.

Vero smirked. "I've got to tell you, Finn. It doesn't look good."

"You two are not helping!"

"You're right," my mother said, touching the cross at her throat.

Vero nodded. "We should probably push him."

"Have you both lost your minds? The children are watching!"

My mother held up a finger. "That's an excellent point. I'll go sit with the children and cover their eyes."

"*Both* of you wait in the car with the children. *I* will handle this." I turned Vero around by the shoulders, back toward my mother's SUV. My daughter's face was pressed against the back window, her little brother wriggling against the straps of his car seat to see where we had gone.

I had tried to convince Steven to keep driving. I'd insisted we could buy our son a new nap blanket at the next shopping mall we passed, but when Zach had pushed his threadbare blanket out the narrow gap in the open window of my mother's Buick, wailing as it flew across oncoming windshields and under speeding tires until it finally came to rest, caught on a piece of rebar in the concrete barrier in the median like a battle-worn white flag, Steven had been behind the wheel and there'd been no stopping him.

Panic had pinged through me when he'd set his jaw and put his foot down on the gas. I'd pleaded with him from the third-row seat not to do it as he'd merged onto the next exit ramp and retraced our path to Zach's blanket, but my arguments had been drowned out by Zach's hiccuping wails as Steven had pulled over onto the shoulder of the highway and put the SUV in park.

I shooed Vero and my mother back to the SUV to sit with the children. Steven hardly noticed when I tapped on his shoulder and repeated his name. His gaze remained fixed on Zach's woobie as he stood beside the white line and hiked up his pants. He leaped back as a mud-spattered pickup on monster tires screamed past him, a pair of steel truck nuts swinging from its hitch. Delia shouted out the window of the van, "You can do it, Daddy!"

Vero called out, "May the odds be ever in your favor."

My mother gave him two thumbs up through the glass, and Zach cheered.

I grabbed Steven by the back of his puffy vest as he rolled up his sleeves. "This is insane! There's a Walmart at the next exit. We can get Zach another blanket. I'll rub some apple juice and car grime on it. He'll never know the difference."

"He doesn't want another blanket. He wants that one," Steven said, pointing across the highway. "And I'm going to get it for him."

"What are you trying to prove?"

He whirled on me, hot breath steaming from his lips. "What am I trying to prove?" He gaped at me as if the answer should have been obvious. "I'll tell you what I'm trying to prove! I'm . . ." Steven's blue eyes grew suddenly wide, focused on something behind me. I turned, my spine going ramrod straight as a state trooper eased onto the shoulder of the highway behind us, rolling to stop a few yards away. I stole a backward glance at my mother's SUV and saw Vero sink lower in her seat.

Steven frowned at the crisp uniform of the buzz-cut police officer who strode toward us.

"Car trouble?" the trooper asked, removing his sunglasses and tucking them into his coat.

Steven crossed his arms over his chest, his lips thinning as he was forced to meet the trooper's gaze. "No trouble."

The officer glanced at the Virginia license plate on the back of my mother's vehicle. "Where are you folks headed?"

"Pennsylvania," I supplied helpfully as Steven grunted, "New Jersey." The officer's brows knitted, and I rushed to add, "We're taking the scenic route through West Virginia. A road trip . . . you know, sort of a family vacation." I took Steven's arm in mine, pinching him through his sleeve before he could utter a word about why we'd circumnavigated the entire state of Maryland to get here. "See, our son accidentally lost his blanket out of the window as we were driving. He's two," I explained, gesturing to the shredded fabric snapping in the wind at the edge of the median.

The trooper planted his hands on his belt, the sides of his jacket spreading around it, revealing his holster and his handcuffs as he squinted across the highway to see Zach's woobie. "I sure hope your husband wasn't planning on trying to retrieve it."

"He's not my husband," I corrected.

Steven turned to me with a look of disgust. "Is it really necessary to point that out?"

"And of course he wouldn't attempt to retrieve it," I added with a stern look at him, "because that would be a completely idiotic thing to do."

"Not to mention illegal," the trooper said.

"Exactly! I was just telling him the same thing, but my ex—"

"Husband," Steven interjected.

"—can be a little bullheaded when it comes to listening to me. I told him we should just buy another blanket."

"You can't just replace something like that!" Steven snapped at me. "Zach doesn't want a new blanket! That one is comfortable. It's familiar. It has history! But apparently, history doesn't mean anything to you."

"The blanket isn't worth saving, Steven. Just let it go," I said through my teeth.

"Our children believe it's worth saving, and so do I!"

The trooper stepped in front of him as Steven pivoted toward the highway. "Put one foot over that line, sir, and we're going to have a problem," he said firmly. "I understand wanting to look like a hero for your kids, but they don't want to see their father splattered all over the highway, and I'd sure hate to have to arrest you in front of them. Your family is better off if you just let it go."

"Would it be such a crime to let him try?" Vero called through the open window. My mother clapped a hand over her mouth.

Steven's jaw clenched. I tugged him toward my mother's SUV before he could give the trooper one more reason to arrest him. "Thank you for stopping to check on us, Officer. It was very kind of you. We'll just be going." We had a woobie to replace. Oh, and a stolen car to find, a boyfriend to rescue, a mob boss to avoid, and a painfully long road to Atlantic City still ahead of us.

Holly Virginia Photography

ELLE COSIMANO is a *New York Times* and *USA Today* bestselling author, an International Thriller Writers Award winner, and an Edgar Award nominee. Elle's debut novel for adults, *Finlay Donovan Is Killing It,* kicked off a witty, fast-paced contemporary mystery series, which was a *People* magazine pick and was named one of the New York Public Library's Best Books of 2021. The third book in the series, *Finlay Donovan Jumps the Gun,* was an instant *New York Times* bestseller. In addition to writing novels for teens and adults, her essays have appeared in *HuffPost* and *Time*. Cosimano lives with her husband and two sons in Virginia.

READ THE ENTIRE FINLAY DONOVAN SERIES BY
NEW YORK TIMES BESTSELLING AUTHOR

ELLE COSIMANO!

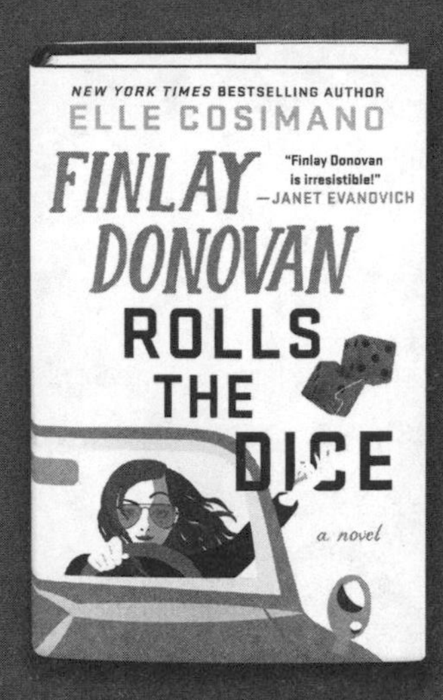

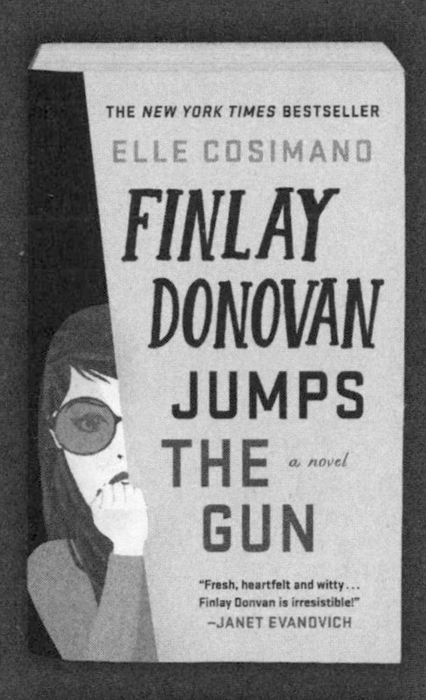

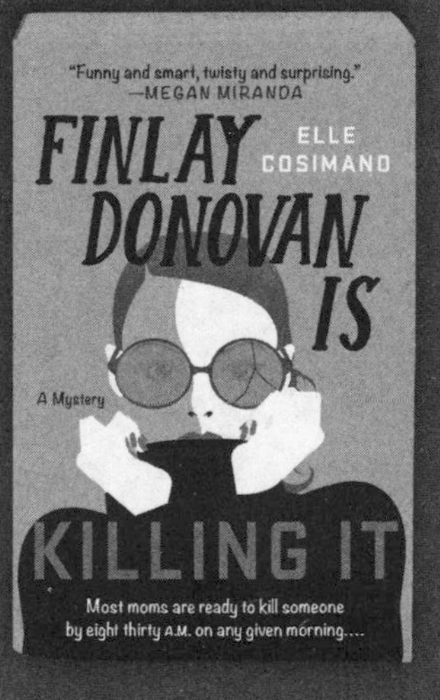

"Finlay Donovan is irresistible."

—JANET EVANOVICH

 MINOTAUR BOOKS